BALL PARK

BALL PARK

John Farrow

This first world edition published 2019
in Great Britain and the USA by
SEVERN HOUSE PUBLISHERS LTD of
Eardley House, 4 Uxbridge Street, London W8 7SY.
Trade paperback edition first published
in Great Britain and the USA 2020 by
SEVERN HOUSE PUBLISHERS LTD.

British Library Cataloguing in Publication Data
A CIP catalogue record for this title is available from the British Library.

ISBN-13: 978-0-7278-8889-1 (cased)
ISBN-13: 978-1-78029-627-2 (trade paper)
ISBN-13: 978-1-4483-0320-5 (e-book)

All Severn House titles are printed on acid-free paper.

Severn House Publishers support the Forest Stewardship Council™ [FSC™],
the leading international forest certification organisation. All our titles that
are printed on FSC certified paper carry the FSC logo.

MIX
Paper from
responsible sources
FSC® C013056

Typeset by Palimpsest Book Production Ltd.,
Falkirk, Stirlingshire, Scotland.
Printed and bound in Great Britain by
TJ International, Padstow, Cornwall.

This novel is dedicated to a certain gentleman
who reads crime fiction voraciously
and collects these books with a grand passion.

Steele Curry, you are a writer's reader.
While you have read thousands of crime novels,
know that this one is dedicated to you
with boundless appreciation.

PART ONE
1975

A Special Joy

(The mysterious dark patch)

Getting inside had been routine. The stress came in getting out.

She had a near-encounter with a nude man who carried a pistol. Hiding from him was like having her nerve endings scraped raw by a hand file.

Nerves were nine-tenths the battle. Hers were shot for the night.

She had to remain dead silent. The woman in the house could return at any second. Quinn crept halfway up the staircase toward the lady's bedroom then slipped out the open side window. The one she'd entered. Propped her bag on the ledge and lowered herself down from the sill. Then she clutched her bag of loot in one hand and held on with the other. Dangled off the side of the house in the moonlight. Fingers slipping. She looked down to locate her landing in the dark before shoving herself outward and dropping from a height above ten feet.

Quinn remembered to flex when she hit the ground. She'd trained herself well. She toppled over – *Nerves!* – yet landed quietly on the grass.

Checked herself out. She wasn't hurt.

Whenever a plan worked, a special joy thrummed inside her.

The young woman spotted her boyfriend's car. Her accomplice. *Excellent.* She walked a little faster than usual despite an effort to keep her pace casual. *God! That guy had a gun! He was starkers!* She had a story to tell. *Deets, you won't believe it!* In a nick, Quinn slid onto the front passenger seat. Slammed the door shut.

'OK, Trucker boy, let's fly!'

Deets failed to start up on her command. She looked at him. Suddenly her nerves, those nerves, flared across her chest and snared her throat in a vise. Deets didn't budge. In the light of a streetlamp a mysterious dark patch across his chest pooled below his belly and fell off his right hip.

That was blood. All over him. Blood.
She caught on. She got this.
Deets was dead.
He was sitting there dead. He was crazy dead.
Deets.
Her getaway driver would not be getting away.
Or getting her away. Not from this.

The Gum Machine

(Fake cargo)

Quinn maintained a weather eye.
   She could operate in the heat of summer. Slip the latch on a frail back door. Cut slits in a screen, detach it, slither inside. In fall, storm windows were screwed on. Winter clothing was too bulky. Spring: mucky, she tracked footprints.
   She'd been raised wild, she loved to boast. In the Park Extension district of Montreal, a congested immigrant neighborhood in a French-English city, she'd hear close to a dozen languages on a few treks to the grocer. Portuguese and Italian. Ukrainian. Polish and Romanian. Japanese. Armenian. Yiddish. In the 1970s, Greeks were pouring in. On their heels, Indians and Pakistanis and the first trickle of Haitians. Each group arrived and moved on as they became established, although, as Quinn was fond of saying, 'Not everybody gets established.' As each fresh wave arrived and departed, a remnant was left behind.
   'We're what's left over from the day before and the day before that. The dregs.'
   She was seventeen. She had time to grow out of the place.
   Her dad? Less likely. He had his job, his union.
   Her mother passed away.
   Some people suggested that that was the problem. She thought otherwise.
   'I'm not a thief because my mom's dead. I'm a thief because I want to be. Because I choose to be. Because I'm *alive*, you moron twit.'

She went to school although she enjoyed stealing more. Smart in school, she believed she was smarter away from the classroom.

Another beautiful thing about summer: no school.

Growing up, she played in the lanes and on the last of the scarce fields before they were supplanted by apartment buildings. A section of small homes did exist, wartime cottages that had been slapped together and since then reconstituted with this repair and that extension. She grew up in one of these and counted it a blessing. Her friends in apartment blocks kept quiet in their homes. They couldn't bounce a ball on the kitchen floor or play music loudly. In her home, she ran rampant with impunity, and that's what she meant by being raised wild.

In winter, if the streets went unplowed, she skidded behind buses, hanging on to a bumper as the stupidest boys did. One lost both his legs above the knees – an event that left a hollow in her gut, although it didn't stop her. Her dad saw it happen. He was shaken by the incident. Bus bumpers were altered then removed entirely to make it more difficult. She found a way to keep skidding to demonstrate that it could still be done. And then, victorious, she stopped. Secretly, that pair of crushed legs bothered her more than she let on. The way her dad had been affected had left an impression.

Boys considered her a daredevil.

She wore it proud.

Quinn did a stint as a tomboy, primarily due to baseball. She didn't throw like other girls who, coming from foreign countries, didn't play the game. She didn't throw like the boys either but developed a semi-rigid overhand toss that was effective. Her good arm allowed her to play the outfield in pickup games and to be a warm-up battery mate for aspiring pitchers.

At fourteen, she coerced the boys' team coach into letting her take batting practice; in exchange, she caught for a pitcher who wanted to work on his curve. She made contact, too. A few Texas leaguers. A pair of line drives. One grounder might have made it through an infield. A good day, until afterwards, outside the girls' washroom as she leaned over the water fountain, the coach casually placed one hand on her bottom and slid the other across her chest. First, she twitched, then jerked up. She cut her lip and nearly chipped a tooth. She knew then why she'd been allowed to take BP. After that, she didn't catch for the boys officially, only when one promised they'd be on their own. No more coaches. Following that incident she let her hair grow long. Being more like a girl, her father said. He noticed. She kept to herself that if grown men were going to treat her like a girl, and badly, she wasn't going to spend time in their company as a half-boy. She'd keep her distance. *Morons.* Irrelevant, it was time. Never her plan to always be a catcher who wasn't allowed to suit up with the boys in a real game.

Around that time, she started stealing.

Pure accident, the first occasion. The last in a line of old-fashioned gum machines. An antique that stood outside a drugstore during the daytime. Quinn dropped in a dime and pressed the lever down. A wee pack of gum slid onto a tray. She was talking to her friends at that moment, laughing hard about something hilarious that was probably stupid. She forgot to take the gum out of the machine. She pressed the lever again and gum dropped down. She noticed *two* packs of gum in the tray. She hit the lever again without putting in more money. Gum slipped out. She said nothing to her friends and covertly stuffed the gum in a pocket.

Soon after that she disentangled from her pals on the walk home. Raced back to the gum machine. Her heart was pounding in her chest. *Pounding.* She pressed the lever down again. Gum came out. She glanced into the drugstore. Then pretended to insert coins repeatedly while pressing the lever. She made room on the tray for more gum by sliding the packs to one side. As the pile built up, she stuffed her pockets. When she had no more room in her pockets, she filled both hands.

That was the best time ever. She felt so freaking alive. She didn't know why.

She walked down half a block to a hairdresser's salon with her fists full of packs of gum and, with the bravado of a soloist in an opera, announced, 'I got gum for sale at a discount! It's for charity. Seven packs for fifty cents.'

'What charity?' some lady with purple-streaked hair under a pair of snapping scissors asked her. *Moron.*

'Like I said,' she told the woman, 'they're at a discount.'

She sold three sets. A buck-and-a-half profit. Then scampered away at reckless speed, propelled so fiercely by her glee.

Falling asleep that night, she knew she'd steal again. She liked the feeling all through her bloodstream. She'd been unhappy lately but no longer felt that way. Why she now felt good wasn't something she could explain. Still, she wasn't going to knock it. She was going to steal again.

Discovering the flaw in his old machine, the druggist scrapped it. Quinn moved on from there.

The first time she got caught she was adamant that her activity had no connection to her mother dying. She could have used that excuse for sympathy and escaped the pickle she was in, as she was being prompted to do. Quinn was having none of it. 'Don't be an idiot moron,' she advised her accuser.

'Don't call me an idiot moron,' the older woman who had nabbed her warned.

'What kind of a moron are you, then?'

'Watch your tongue, young lady.'

'In my mouth? How? You got a mirror?'

'Don't be so damned smart!'

'I should be dumb instead? Give me a mirror. I'll watch my tongue if you think it's so important. Will that be dumb enough for you?'

'I have half a mind to call the police.'

'I agree with you. You have half a mind.'

'The impudence! You're in trouble now.'

'Fine. I'm in trouble now. Just don't blame my mom. My mom dies, and what? I go steal something? Do I look like an imbecile to you?'

A friend of the woman she robbed, who caught Quinn going through her purse, clucked her tongue and spoke up. 'It's in her genes.'

Quinn didn't think she meant her Levi's. 'What genes?' Almost a snarl.

'Her dad,' the woman making the point replied. She turned back to Quinn. 'Isn't that right, honey?' Back to her friend: 'He's a criminal.'

'Was a criminal,' Quinn told the woman, her teeth clenched, her fangs bared. She was quick. '*Was.*' She used her rising adrenalin to burst past the two women and out of the potential arms of the law, if that's what they had in half their minds.

Her father received a call that night. He put the phone down after listening respectfully, saying a few words, thanking the caller. Within earshot, Quinn picked up the gist.

'What's going on?' he asked her. He was always tentative with his daughter, not knowing how he was doing as a single parent; if he could handle this, her.

'She called you a criminal,' she explained. 'Yesterday's news I told her.'

The explanation seemed to settle something. Her father went quiet, more deeply than usual. Two things emerged from the episode. Quinn understood that getting caught was a serious drag, and after that she had no intention of letting it happen again. The second lesson was that stealing from women's purses at the laundromat was now, like stealing gum, ancient history.

She still got a kick out of it, pilfering. She just needed a bigger, better, buzz.

Quinn broke into an unlocked home. The best time ever.

She repeated the crime often, gaining experience.

Then she pulled off a daring heist.

Kids often climbed up in the few trees that grew in patches of backyards next to the lane. Once up in the branches, climbers were all but invisible. They passed the time there. She calculated that if she could climb higher and shimmy onto a certain limb without it breaking, she could drop down to a rooftop. Once up there, she could walk across the flat roofs of dozens of duplexes, from one end of the lane to more than halfway down the block without facing a gap or a higher wall. In the middle of the rooftop, no one below could spot her.

She had a destination in mind.

Though dexterity was required, it would not be difficult to climb down a pole that supported an upper-floor porch. The porch was not accessible from below, only from an upper-level door to the inside. On a hot summer day, only the screen door was used. She noticed residents come and go without lifting a latch or sliding a bolt. She was positive it was never locked. All she had to do was keep an eye on the front door while the man of the house was off at work, wait for the woman of the house to leave – with her shopping bag would be ideal – then run to the lane, climb the tree, race across the rooftops, slide down the porch pole when no one was looking, enter the house, and steal whatever she could fit in her pockets.

She took money. A small wad of fives and tens. She took cheap jewelry and a ladies' wristwatch that potentially had value and a pair of porcelain knickknacks. Fragile items she protected within stolen towels. She snitched a pillowcase off a bed and stuffed it with her loot and a case of genuine silverware. Then she monkey-climbed the porch pole again with the sack in one hand, which she slung up onto the roof, cracking a knickknack, and made her escape.

The robbery became the big event in community lore.

Everybody was talking about it.

Even her father, who wasn't well connected locally and commuted elsewhere to work, heard the story.

Quinn said, 'Probably some neighbor had it in for them.'

Her father disagreed. 'Nope. That thief came from another part of town.'

'How do you know?' He was wrong, but why did he think that way?

'Looks professional to me. A professional thief won't rob in his own neighborhood. Partly for his own protection. If he steals local and someone sees him, he gets recognized. But mostly he won't do it because it's not honorable. Thieves have honor. It's not right to rip off your neighbor. That's true everywhere in the world.'

Her dad's words had an immediate effect. She had planned to take the silverware to a pawnshop on Jean Talon Street. Suddenly, the flaw in her strategy hit home: not far enough away. Her dad stayed out of her room; but if he was ever suspicious of her, or if he was sending subliminal messages, he might decide to have a peek under her bed or in her closet. There, he'd not only find the stolen goods from the infamous balcony robbery, but also from a string of break-ins. She had to get the loot out of her room, and the closest pawnshop was the wrong solution.

She checked the Yellow Pages. And began to explore her city.

Way south on the 'Main' – the common name for Boulevard St Laurent, a thoroughfare that divided Montreal streets into East and West and was notorious for being gangsterland – she found a nesting area for pawnshops.

Quinn didn't think it would be difficult. But a teenager walking in with old-world silverware that to a child was worth a fortune aroused a level of suspicion she had not anticipated. She reckoned pawnbrokers wouldn't care if her goods were stolen. Maybe they'd pay less for hot items, but surely that would be the extent of their concern. An expectation dashed. In three different establishments, they grilled her until she got mad and decamped.

Her presentation improved each time, yet these sad old men behind their counters – gents who so rarely felt a ray of sunlight in their dingy caverns filled with guitars and toasters, gold wedding bands and silverware – seemed to possess an uncanny ability to see right through her. They had X-ray eyes. The third man on whom she tried her *shtick* chuckled aloud.

Chuckled her right out the door.

Live and learn. She tried again.

Number four also looked sad, lonely, and sun-deprived. He was permanently stooped, with wild tufts of grey hair over his ears and none on top. He had untamed eyebrows, and hair on his knuckles that momentarily threw her off her game. She'd never seen anything like that. Hairy fingers. He greeted her as the other man had dismissed her, with laughter, as though a joke had been shared, then prolonged his good humor with a broad grin. When he spoke, his voice was raspy. 'Come here, little girl. Follow me.'

She was not little. Taller than him, although half his weight. He was gesturing with two of those hairy fingers and guiding her behind a curtain into a mysterious back room. She presumed he'd try to molest her there. She believed that he underestimated her ability to fight him off. Pummel him, maybe. She half-wanted to do battle. She'd show him. She'd show all these dusty old pawnbroker men. She'd stick him with knives from her silverware case.

She went behind the curtain.

A pale light shone over a small crowded desk. Dust motes hung in the air. The man sat down in shadow. She remained standing. That helped her feel safer. She looked around and saw an array of stuffed boxes and assorted junk.

The man switched a radio on. Tinny violin music gently wafted between them. He raised a hand momentarily, as if waving a baton in time to the music. 'Show me,' he said, 'whatcha got.' She was pleased that he seemed to mean her goods.

Quinn took out the case of silverware and placed it on top of papers on his desk. He opened it and extracted a spoon to examine under the lamp. Once he had identified the hallmark, he grunted in what seemed a significant way. Then he placed the spoon back in the box, snugging it down into the felt lining.

'Your family this belonged to?' he asked.

'Yes,' she said. 'They died.' Only half a lie. She still had half-a-family.

'If someone you loved passed away, I am sorry,' he said.

'Thank you.'

'Let me ask again. Your family this belonged to?'

'I told you. Yes.'

'The first time I heard you, but in my life I prefer the truth.'

'You think I'm lying?'

'That is not a word to use.'

'Because I'm not.'

He wore a short-sleeved shirt. He held up an arm. As hairy as his fingers. He rotated his forearm in one direction, slowly, then the other.

He put his arm back down on the desk.

When he didn't explain himself, she asked, 'Why'd you do that?'

'I'm sensitive.'

She waited again. 'Aren't we all? Personally, I protect kittens, puppies, and little children. So?'

'Sensitive I am to the truth. What you said about the kittens, that was true.'

She waited for him to tell her to get out. Instead, he turned the music lower.

'We can do business, yes?' A whisper. 'One more time I'm asking you. If this from your family, in the window I can put. If not, then we do this a different way. The last time I'm asking. Your family this belonged to?'

She checked his eyes, how they squinted at her, as though evaluating not what she said but how. She guessed that she also stood in shadow, that he could not see her well. She felt adrift on the music.

'No,' Quinn said.

'You're a thief. Shall I do business with a thief, I'm asking?'

This seemed a crucial moment in her life. She wanted to very slowly pick up the case and very deliberately put it back into the bag, then run.

Instead, she said, 'Why not?' An admission. She felt naked.

'No reason why not. But I must know. What it is I buy. Who from. Yes?'

'I guess so.'

'Good. I saw you down the street walking. To myself I said, that girl has something interesting to sell to me.'

'Oh yeah?' Her wariness was easily detected in her tone.

'I watch as you go in, come out, the other pawnshops. This is what happens to an amateur. Listen to me. What you have here is good. I will take it. I will not pay you what it is worth. Why not, you're asking me? Because I cannot sell these knives and forks, this set, for what it is worth. I cannot put stolen goods in the window. That would be like putting myself in jail for how long? But still I can help you. If you are a good thief, we can do business again sometime. If you are an honest thief.'

She thought about all that. This seemed like an important day. She could feel the whole of her life opening before her, like a great door to a secret vault.

'How much?' she asked, for she also remained wary.

'One-fifty,' he said, and wagged a forefinger. 'For more don't ask. I could give you a lot less and you would accept it, no? But ask for more, that will not be good.'

She didn't argue. He paid her on the spot.

One hundred and fifty dollars. She was that rich. She was thrilled.

'My name is Ezra. Can you pronounce?'

'Ezra.' She had no problem with it. Didn't know why she should. 'I'm Quinn.'

He paused a moment. 'More than I need to know. I hope to forget your name soon, Quinn.'

He knew too much, while she was curious to learn more. 'Knightsbridge. Is that your last name? It's on the sign outside.'

'It's on the sign. Let's put it this way: I came by it rightfully. I go by it.'

'Can I ask you a question?'

'Never hurts to ask. An answer can be painful. Like gout. Gout can be very painful. Answers can hurt like that.'

'You talk funny sometimes.'

'That's your question?'

'No. It's not. If you can't show this stuff in the store, how do you sell it?'

'This is your lucky day, Quinn. You with the name I must soon forget. Other gentlemen on this street are pawnbrokers. Like me. But it is my fate also to be a fence. Do you know what that means?'

She wasn't sure. 'I think so.'

'If you think so, then you know so. Now go. I will give you an empty box. Same size as this one with the knives and forks. Put it in your bag. Here, I give you a can of beans to make it look heavy. The other brokers, they will see that I sent you packing, like they did. As I should do myself. Be careful when you return. Look around. Check cars. Who is in them? Look in windows. Who looks out? Once in a blue moon, someone is watching.' He held up his arm again. 'When you feel a tingling, obey. Do you know what to do then?'

'Go away?' she suggested.

'Do that. Now go. Away. Be good.'

Quinn departed as though walking on air. Blocks from the store she ditched the pillowcase with its fake cargo. She was thrilled. Only later did she realize how thoroughly at ease and how wonderfully safe she had felt in the little room. She wanted to be worthy of being invited back there again.

If she was not going to be a thief in her own neighborhood, she would need to explore other parts of the city. She set out to discover her world.

Her city was on an island, but she only knew that in an abstract way. Its dimensions were unknown to her. Communities could not readily expand outward forever, bound by the circling river, so grew to be congested. She visited Westmount, home to well-heeled English on one side of the mountain, and Outremont, home to affluent French on the other side, and she wandered into the poorest areas of the city below downtown. Poorer than her own district, which was an eye-popper. She was learning that the city was huge. Nobody could walk it. To drive around the island would be an expedition. She'd had no clue.

Quinn became an expert on bus routes.

Stealing in far-flung districts was beset with problems. Was she supposed to carry her loot home on a bus? Or walk with it for miles? A reasonably pretty girl drew unwanted attention to herself; she had to be careful. Taxis cost money, and the cabbie could later be a witness against her. What she needed was a car, except she didn't have a license or know how to drive. That made her think about acquiring an accomplice. Since she was beginning to think that her life would be easier with a boyfriend rather than being on the loose without one, she might be able to kill two birds with a single overhand heater.

Quinn went out with a couple of baseball players who played for Park Ex, one a pitcher, the other a third baseman. Both had been pursuing her. They seemed to deserve her attention due to their own. That's how she felt initially. They both had cars. Both were rambunctious. That she was way more serious about crime than they'd ever be didn't turn out to be the problem. She just wasn't into them. They were cute, and both were physical specimens. Sex in the front seat with the pitcher was laugh-out-loud funny. With the third baseman in the back seat, exciting initially. Her lack of interest in each of them came over her gradually and it wasn't only because their ball club was doing poorly. They were just too *dynamic* in the relationship. She was supposed to be agog, to eagerly spend every passing minute doting on their company. She felt *dangled*. Some girls went in for that sort of thing and were eager to take her place. She broke up with both guys and wondered, 'Now what?' She'd sampled the cream of the crop and found out that the two most desirable boys in the neighborhood didn't appeal. Holy. Now what?

Thoughtful, Quinn conducted a skull session with herself. She also consulted with Ezra Knightsbridge. He agreed that an accomplice with a car was a sound idea. She went out to a ball game and looked around once more. The centerfielder was skinny and pimply. Someday he'd be a catch. Not now. The catcher was vulgar, in both expression and appearance. They were considered the next best choices. Others who were handsome already had girlfriends, and she wasn't looking to make a scene. She scouted further afield. She began to check out the shy boys, the geeks rather than the goons, not only strong silent types but also flimsy silent ones. Some guy who'd never take her for granted, because he was agog. One who'd be at *her* beck and call. The kind of guy who'd be thrilled and even a little shocked to be in her company. All the boy needed to demonstrate was that he was genuinely nice and that he owned a car. If she wanted him for an adventure, he had to be obliging and capable of keeping his mouth shut.

A few might fit the bill. She gave them a whirl.

One, Otto Braup, the fourth candidate she considered, had an excellent chance of becoming a keeper. He was gawky tall. A curved spine gave him away as not being athletic. He didn't look so bad. Sapling skinny. She guessed he'd probably bend before he broke. He spiked his hair to give himself a quirky look. His head looked tiny for his frame, and his neck was stunted. He was the brother of a girl in her orbit – which is how they met, when the sister brought him to the Friday night dance hall Quinn frequented.

Otto was in engineering. That was not so rare in the neighborhood. The guys were either juvenile delinquents or they were doing what their immigrant dads demanded they do – study engineering at university. Most who entered the program dropped out after a year, unable to handle the math, then did what their mothers wanted: studied to become teachers. An exception, Otto stood out. He was flourishing as a student engineer. Sadly, his social skills were a travesty. He knew nothing about girls. She'd have to buck him up in that regard.

Quinn took him to bed. Not that she was an old pro, but experience fell to her side. This was her first time having sex in an actual bed – her own, something of a thrill by itself. He was both overly scared and overly excited, which induced complications, yet sex could be a whole lot of fun in a real bed when the boy let her take charge.

And then, he was so ridiculously grateful. OK, she determined, I can make this one drive a getaway car. He needed a do-over and he was definitely someone she could do over.

As a bonus, not only did he own a car, he had overhauled the engine himself. 'I souped it up,' he told her. That could come in handy.

Poor Otto Braup blew it with her. She didn't have time to work on the socially doltish side to his nature. When she went back to the Friday night dance hall, she discovered that he had informed the universe of their liaison. The bouncer knew. The cashier knew. Her friends wanted to know what it was like. Those who weren't her friends snickered. Otto's sister apologized. 'Sorry. He's such an ass.'

By the time she found him, wanting to dance for the first time in his life, she had only one question. Asked loudly. 'Did you tell everybody how the first time you didn't last four seconds?'

They were done. Back to square one.

Except that Otto's revelation created a furor. Boys who

previously considered Quinn to be out of their league were stepping forward. If she was willing to bed a neophyte loser, maybe the rest of the known universe also stood a chance. Riffraff were easily dispersed. Her penchant for a slick putdown ruined a few lives. Still, one boy emerged from the morass as a candidate. To Quinn's mind he was not a total dimwit when it came to girls. He wasn't a geek. He confessed that he held back from approaching her when she was 'dating the baseball team'.

'Hey!'

'I know when a chick goes in for muscles. Fog between the ears.'

'You're a moron.'

But that was the thing. He wasn't. His name was Dietmar Ferstel, which made her think he was a tractor or a truck, although he was small-boned and on the shorter side. She called him Trucker sometimes. He had lovely blond hair, not so long in the sixties style, although it curled around the edges. Small, he seemed athletic, but preferred books to baseball.

'Do you own a car?'

'Will you sleep with me if I own a car?'

'Buses are inconvenient, I find.'

'I have a big old Pontiac.'

'Did you soup it up?'

'I'm in Social Studies. Do I look like a mechanic to you?'

'I don't know what a mechanic looks like. Different than anyone else?'

'Dirt under the fingernails. Grease on their palms. Look. Me. Nice hands.'

He never imagined she'd do what she did next. Quinn kissed one hand, tenderly, on one side, then the other. He watched. She nibbled his thumb. He nearly fainted. She owned him then, she could tell.

Quinn trained this lad in Social Studies to be her getaway driver.

Whisky Spree

(Close connections)

Detective Émile Cinq-Mars stepped into the room as if he was a member of the Bomb Squad on a mission. With each stride, he urged himself to have courage.

He entered off a dark side street in Old Montreal on the stroke of eleven. By design, the gloomy subterranean restaurant resembled a cavern. Fake flaming lanterns hung on curved stucco walls imprinted with suggestive images. He deplored the kitsch. In days gone by he'd frequented the premises, as the haunt was a favorite with his boss. He respected the man and owed him an immense debt. For that reason he bravely moved forward into the room.

He feared a so-called surprise. A party. If his last hours as a member of the Night Patrol were going to be commemorated, he'd wind up staggering home drunk. He'd take on his new assignment in the morning vastly hungover. Cinq-Mars expected colleagues to put him through his paces, force him to endure pranks and insults for hours. Pure torment.

He checked the other patrons ensconced in the shadows. So far, no cops.

They might be waiting in the kitchen, set to pounce.

His boss had commandeered a booth at the far end of the establishment by the kitchen door, near an illuminated exit sign that reflected a red glow upon his visage.

Just the two of them to start with, and a few drams of whisky.

'Join us,' Touton invited. He was a muscular man, shy of six foot, with wide shoulders and an imposing torso. Even at his age, and while seated, the evident power of his physique was pronounced.

His younger colleague first removed his windbreaker.

'Us?' Here it comes. The gang's arrived. Waiting in the wings.

'Me and my old pal Glenfiddich. I believe you've met.'

Cinq-Mars sat down, adjusted his chair, and took up the single malt waiting for him. The two clinked glasses.

'*Salut,* Émile.'

'*Salut*, Captain.'

They sipped. The drink felt good. He needed it on this night.

'Just you and Dr Fiddich, huh?'

'The others wanted to be invited, Émile. I said no. Cops should earn their salary, no?'

'Of course.'

'You'll see them down the road.'

'Sure.' He was convinced at this point that the place was about to erupt.

'Who knows? After six weeks on the day shift you might beg for your old job back. If you beg properly, you might get it back. You're a big believer in prayer. That might work. Me, I've not seen the evidence.'

'Oh no? I was praying that day with the Cubans. We walked out of there alive. Maybe prayer had something to do with it.'

'Skin of our teeth. I say dumb luck got us out. And balls.'

An old-fashioned standoff. They had stood with their puny pistols against a phalanx of Cuban nationals armed with both automatic weapons and diplomatic immunity, surrounded by explosive. Their fates were dependent upon a negotiation between the leaders of their two countries. Earnest prayer or dumb luck may have played a part. Confronted with near certain death they had also shown what the Cubans called *cojones*.

'With luck like that, I can handle the day shift. Go beyond six weeks.'

'I'll fry if I see the sun again,' Touton remarked. 'It's been so long. Write, kid, tell me how it feels.'

He wasn't a kid anymore. He was thirty. Probably the designation would never change in his mentor's vocabulary, which was fine with him.

'Do you know what's amazing?' Touton asked.

'No. Tell me what's amazing.'

'You're still alive. Usually the naive ones are flushed first.'

'I'm sure we usually are.'

The repartee didn't bother him. He expected to be needled.

'So,' Captain Armand Touton pronounced, 'we part company.'

'It's not that I want to leave the Night Patrol, you know that.'

'You want a variety of experiences on the job. Work under different captains.' He switched to a mock hush. 'Do you know,

I don't have to let you go? I can keep you right where you are. I have that power.'

'I know that.'

Nodding, Touton returned to his normal voice. 'Once or twice men announced to me they were leaving the Night Patrol to see if I'd object. To see if I loved them so much, I'd never let them go. What happened? Hunh. I always let them go. You won't get a reaction out of me, either. A boy should snip his mother's apron strings, begin his life as a man. But also a man should shake the hand of his mentor at a certain point and say, "Enough. Your influence, appreciated, but what else is there?"'

'Your influence has been appreciated, Captain.'

'But?' Touton's toothy grin shone above his solid rock of a chin, picking up the red of the exit sign.

'But . . . what else is there?'

'Good question. You'll find out. That's my answer.'

'I have another question,' the junior detective put forward. He sipped again, and the captain gladly joined in. 'I know you had a say with respect to my next posting.'

'Who said? I know nothing about it.'

'Like I believe you. I'm confused. Why choose Giroux for me?'

'Not saying I did. Since you ask, if I did pick him, why not?'

Cinq-Mars swished his drink in the snifter. He did not usually undertake the ritual or feel the need to be hesitant around the other man, yet he lifted the glass to his nostrils and inhaled. Touton stared him down. The two men were close enough, and had shared experiences together, both defeat and triumph, that their mutual accord remained perpetually present. Even when the captain was on a rant or had a bone to pick with him, both men knew they'd risk their lives for each other if conditions warranted. Both had proven it. Such as the time they confronted the Cubans.

'I've heard things, Armand. He might not be on the up-and-up.'

'The up-and-up? I thought you were gung-ho about your new posting. A day-time cop now. You wanted new experiences.'

Cinq-Mars knew the man was having him on but couldn't figure out why. 'Your BS aside, do you want me to rat out Giroux? I'm not keen on it. Bad cops bore me.'

'Who says he's a bad cop?'

The question seemed serious. Fraught with nuance. And yet illogical.

'Now you're playing with me.'

Touton opened his palms to suggest otherwise. 'Maybe a crooked cop can be a good cop. I know for damn sure that a virtuous police officer can also be one hell of a lousy cop.'

'OK,' Cinq-Mars conceded, although he didn't sound convinced.

'OK what?'

'You're setting me up to fail? Is that it? Either that or you've set me up for reasons only you know. I need to figure it out for myself. Is that it?'

'Isn't it always the way? Hey, Émile. It's nice to talk about the future like this. Guess what? That's not why we're here. I invited you in to chat about the past. At least, to drink to it. Here's to the Cubans!'

'Sure. Here's to the Cubans. Why drink to them in this dungeon?'

'You don't like the atmosphere?'

'Not so much.' Is this when the gang leaps from the shadows?

'You hate the place,' Touton remarked. '*I* like it here. Hey, we've had our days, no? In here and elsewhere?'

The old guy was striking a nostalgic note, not his usual tune.

'A few, Captain.'

Armand Touton turned pensive. He took up his glass and observed the amber fluid in the light of the red exit sign as though mesmerized. Cinq-Mars pegged him to be stalling, and prayed – quite literally, prayed – that their colleagues would not be arriving with showgirls. *Please, God, no dancing girls.*

'Émile, here's some news . . .' Touton leaned his weight forward onto his elbows and powerful forearms. 'A few hours ago I submitted my resignation. I'm retiring. Calling it a career. Game over.'

Cinq-Mars sat there in silence. Stunned.

'Idiot. Say something. Wish me well.'

'Are you serious?' He was obviously dead serious. 'Why?'

Touton shrugged. 'Older. Tired. We've had these fights, you and me. You don't believe I had the right to beat the crap out of some guys. My way of doing things is coming to an end, Cinq-Mars. You know it. This will surprise you – I know it, too. Being a cop is going to be different. You're part of the difference. You're our future man. Me, I can't beat people up anymore. The public wants a stop to it and let's face it, I'm too damn old for that stuff. These days, I have to be careful beating up a bad guy because he might lay me out.'

'Doubt that,' Cinq-Mars assured him, then went mute. He knew that Touton hadn't laid a hand on anyone in at least five years. He wouldn't admit it, but he was adapting to the times. Still, his reputation went before him and the old mythology was permitted to stand. He continued to look the other way when cops under him chose the rough stuff, as long as their purpose was true.

Cinq-Mars acknowledged the irony of the moment. He sensed its importance and gravity. This was a legitimate changing of the guard. He'd still be a green detective, while the one cop who had set the tone, the one guy whom both criminals and the just feared equally, would be absent. Everything would soon be transformed.

Often opposed to the man's methods, he still admired the hell out of him. They were separated by the times, the culture. What bound them together was an uncompromising interest in protecting citizens against criminals.

'My fists aren't up for the battle anymore,' Touton reiterated. 'I'm turning things over to your brains.'

'I've got a long way to go.'

Touton acknowledged that with an expression close to being a grimace. 'Longer than you know, Émile. Who knows if you'll survive? Not everyone does. I wanted to have a drink together to give you a final word of advice.'

A waiter – perhaps in response to a signal from Touton that Cinq-Mars had missed, or earlier instructions – put two more snifters of Glenfiddich on the table, doubles, and absconded with the empties.

'Of course.' Cinq-Mars exhaled. 'I'm still in shock.'

Touton leaned in, spoke barely above a whisper. 'Cops don't get along, within departments, or between forces. You know that.'

'Lay of the land.'

'Unless,' Touton stipulated, 'individual cops within the department and between forces form close personal ties.'

'I should develop relationships with good cops, you're saying?'

'Relationships,' Touton scoffed. 'Sounds like you're sleeping together. Close connections, Cinq-Mars. Use my words. If you're going to be the cop you want to be, you need those connections. I know it's bugged you from time to time that you were connected to me. You think it's given you an unfair advantage. Émile, stick this through your thick, innocent skin. *You need an unfair advantage.* A cop like you, in this world, you won't survive, you won't be *allowed* to survive, unless you develop the close connections I'm talking about.'

'To people in high places.'

'I didn't say that. I won't say that. I'll say this. Find people you can trust and find them in *various* places. High, low, in the middle, everywhere. Cops and crooks, both. Connect with them. You're a loner, we know that, but you cannot go it alone. Otherwise, you won't survive. I don't mean that you won't be promoted or not get the good cases. I mean, Émile, that you will not survive.'

Touton gave him a penetrating gaze, to drill down on the premise that he was not being metaphorical in any way. That he was talking about life and death.

Cinq-Mars clued in to that.

'You could, of course, not bother,' Touton went on. 'Be an ordinary cop. That's safer all around. I'd advise it, except I'm not sure you're capable of doing that.'

Cinq-Mars wanted that deep gaze off him. He understood it too well. 'Captain, here's to your retirement.'

They clinked glasses again.

'Enough with the inconsequential stuff,' the younger cop put forward, 'like your retirement and my death. Why have you stuck me with Giroux?'

That broke the mood. Touton laughed lightly. Yet quickly grew serious again. 'First, yes, I stuck you with him, Émile. You've been on the Night Patrol. Nobody within the department messes with anybody in my group. Starting tomorrow, you no longer have that protection. You'll be tested in different ways. Other cops will be suspicious. Giroux will be. There's no point trying to drop you into a safe environment. You wouldn't learn a thing. Giroux has a reputation. That he's corrupt. Inside the department, he has another reputation. Do you know what it is? Probably not. Did you know, he used to be on the Night Patrol with me? He was once one of my guys.'

Cinq-Mars didn't know that and shook his head.

'Like you, he wanted out. To spread his wings. How did that work for him? Find out for me. How did Giroux get along after he left our group? After he saw the sun rise? What became of him? There, my last command to you.'

No dancing girls. No ribald detectives out to party and humiliate him. A more serious turn had been addressed, and Cinq-Mars grasped the privilege he'd been granted. Other than the necessary superiors, he was the first person to hear about the end of Armand Touton's illustrious career. Touton speaking to him first was meant as a singular act of friendship and respect.

'Who's taking over the Night Patrol?' Émile asked.

'Disappointed you didn't hang around long enough to take command?'

That outcome would never have been in the cards. He was too young, even though Touton was around his age when he formed the patrol. Back then, the captain's war record was worth a hundred years of service.

'No one takes over,' Touton revealed. 'The Night Patrol will be disbanded.'

'What? No way. Why?'

Touton's smile was lined with sadness. 'I had power, Émile. I was only a captain, but what chief would go against me? What politician? You see? That can't be allowed to happen again. All the chairs will be rearranged. So that a cop like me, a good cop with real power, will never be allowed inside the force again. You see? Change. No more cops beating up the bad guys. A small part that becomes a big rationale. At least, no more beating them up without bothering to hide it. Other, more important, changes are coming. The bureaucrats within the department are taking over. Remember this, Émile. My power didn't come from my fists, even though I like to say so and many cops think so. The bad guys thought so, too. Close connections – that's the real power. Crooks and cops, both. Various forces. The bureaucrats can't do anything about that. Keep every connection secret, keep them strong and close, Émile. Only then will you be the cop you're meant to be.'

Cinq-Mars was onside with that. 'All right, I'll drink to close connections.'

'You start tomorrow?'

'At the crack. I hear there's something called a sun that comes up in the morning.'

'Good. First day on the job, show up hungover.'

'Ah, boss. Come on.'

'You come on. I'm retiring. You'll let me drink alone?'

He could not do that, of course. At the 3:00 a.m. closing hour the door was shut to patrons. They stayed behind, drinking on, singing a few tunes, which is why Touton had brought him to this ridiculous cavern. He had a *connection* there, an allowance to drink after hours and sing absurd songs until the cows came home.

Or until Detective Émile Cinq-Mars reported for his new assignment.

The next day awaited him, the next rung in his career as a cop. He'd be lucky if he showed up merely hammered, polluted, and sick, and not rip-roaring drunk.

As the fates and Armand Touton decreed, he wasn't that lucky.

The Getaway Boy

(A significant discovery)

When searching for a district to plunder, Quinn Tanner failed to consider the obvious. Home to thirty thousand souls, Park Extension was a quarter-mile wide by three-quarters of a mile long. The community's poor were hemmed in on every side. The southern border terminated at railway tracks and a protective fence. An underpass served as the sole entry-and-exit point. Tracks and fences demarcated the eastern boundary, penetrated only by a pair of underpasses. A footbridge over the tracks to the Major League baseball field provided access to pedestrians, as did subversive cutouts in the railway fence. A dozen lanes of traffic, submerged and elevated in a labyrinth of veers and circles, made escape north trepidatious by car, suicidal on foot. Boulevard de l'Acadie's six lanes, a chain-link fence, and a stout hedge made the western limit nearly impenetrable. People were permitted to walk through two gates in the western frontier, while cars and trucks had to rumble down to busy Jean Talon to enter or exit the opposing territories. Park-Exers called the fence their Berlin Wall and took note that they lived on its east side.

On a walk, Quinn stopped, stared, and damn near kicked herself in the shin. As a child, she'd accompanied her mother selling tins of cashews for a Christmas charity on both sides of the fence. In Park Ex, the poor bought their nuts. Over the fence, the wealthy shooed them off their stoops as if they were contaminated rabble.

She'd witnessed her mother's humiliation.

Ever since, Quinn ignored everything on the western side of the fence.

But now? She was a thief. She'd been taught to never swipe anything on her own turf. Why not cross an enemy line? A significant discovery.

She scouted the affluent neighborhood. Found various targets. Cased them. Selected one. Executed a dry run. Trained her new boyfriend. And finally the time came to put him to the test.

'Meet me in the park tonight, Deets.'

'What park?' he asked.

Boys. Were they all such morons?

'Ball,' she reminded him.

She could feel him tensing up.

'Show up at ten or so,' Quinn directed.

'I know, park a few blocks away.'

'When we leave—'

'People will think we're going to your place.'

'And remember, Deets—'

'I know, gas up.'

'Good boy.'

Quinn maintained a weather eye. The forecast predicted clear skies and cool air. Perfect. The moon would come up bright, ideal for scrounging around in the dark.

The husband of the lady she targeted worked at night. In the skinny phone book for the Town of Mount Royal, the prefix 'Dr' preceded the name at this address. A hospital guy, maybe. Worked the late shift. Home alone, his wife turned off the air-conditioning before she went to bed when the night air cooled, opening windows on the top floor. Quinn could not enter by the second story; yet with a boost she could slip in through an open window onto a staircase between the floors.

No one played ball at Ball Park. The playground was intended for small fry, with swings and teeter-totters, sandboxes, merry-go-rounds, and monkey bars. A ten-foot iron fence prevented kids from running into traffic. The grounds spanned the short distance between Bloomfield and Avenue de l'Épée, and a third of the greater distance between Jarry and Ball Avenue – hence the park's name.

At night, the park transformed into a hangout for older teens and twenty-somethings. Dietmar and Quinn talked to friends there, then departed at midnight on foot. They bundled into Dietmar's car and headed to the rich man's land.

She could tell that he was nervous.

'Take it easy, Trucker. Drive slow.'

He obeyed.

A drive-by. The woman of the house typically parked her car in the garage, next to a small boat. When he was home, the husband's vehicle remained conspicuous in the driveway, displaced by the boat. The absent spouse at night was Quinn's main reason to choose this house and, as hoped, his car was not in sight.

Deets parked adjacent to the hedge and fence that bordered Boulevard l'Acadie. Folks often parked there to walk through a gate to a hardware store or to the convenience store on the other side. The car blended in.

Deets helped her out. He was to be her ladder.

They walked arm-in-arm. Part of their disguise, Quinn said.

They kissed. 'Is this part of the disguise?' he asked.

'Anybody behind me? You look. On the streets? In a yard?'

She held him in her arms while he studied the lay of the land over her shoulder.

'Nope.'

His instinct was to creep into the yard.

'Are you trying to look like a thief? Look like you live here, you moron.'

'I asked you before. Stop calling me a moron.'

'Then straighten up.'

A slight stoop persisted.

Under the staircase window, Deets stuck his head between Quinn's legs and lifted her onto his shoulders. Balancing herself with her palms against the wall, she eased herself up until she stood on his shoulders. They had practiced the maneuver. From that height, she took a box cutter out of her hip pocket and cut two slits in the screen. One on each side. Low down. She reached in and pulled the latches on each edge of the screen and it plopped out. She passed the screen down to Deets, who, wobbling with her on his shoulders, took it in his right hand and dropped it on the ground. Quinn pulled herself up and, half-in, half-out of the window, kicked her feet like a swimmer as she squirmed inside.

In.

She stuck her head out.

'Get lost,' she whispered to Deets.

He wasn't supposed to get lost, only go back to his car and wait. He obeyed.

Good boy.

Quinn got to work.

Something wasn't right.

She anticipated the hollow silence inside the home. The hum of a fridge like a locomotive barreling through her left ear, the ticking of a desk clock like a carpenter hammering her forehead. A scintillating electricity coursed through her bones. She was never so aware of a home's scent as when she was robbing the place – here, a combination of fresh and stale cigarette smoke – yet she stopped. She strained to interpret auditory clues.

She went back up the stairs, further this time, where danger might reside, where the lady of the house was sleeping. Except, she confirmed, the woman was not sleeping. Nor was she alone. Her husband must be back without the car. Either that, or . . . Quinn stifled an exclamation. *The lady of the house is no lady! Not tonight!* No way of knowing for sure, but Quinn decided that the husband must be elsewhere, looking after heart attacks and stab wounds. The identity of the man in bed with his wife – that was another matter.

A thief uncovers intimacies in the lives of others.

Positive that the woman was not alone, that she overheard the murmurings of a pair entwined, Quinn left them to their fury and crept downstairs.

She needed to exercise greater caution. They were occupied and her soft footfalls should go undetected on the deep plush carpet. So soft, she wished she could take it home. Still, they were awake.

The dining room cutlery was stainless, not silver. No reason to bother. No purse or wallet had been left in plain view. A side drawer offered a few bills, which she pocketed. She turned a doorknob and entered a home office. A masculine atmosphere. Street lamps, none direct, gave her sufficient light to nip a golden pen. There were three watches, which had weight and size, and possessed a luster. Again, that golden allure. She loved men who loved watches. Who would keep three if they were clunkers? Ezra would pay fair black-market value for them or advise her to scrap them.

A photograph showed the lady of the house with her husband in marital bliss. Their hands resting on a knife to cut their wedding cake. Not quite a May–December union, but close. *Well, well.* If other pictures on display were recent, then the woman upstairs was in her late-twenties. Already tarting around. Quinn mentally scolded her, then accidentally knocked a small wooden vase containing pens off the desk. No soft carpet here. The contents clattered on the wood floor.

Quinn snapped up the rolling vase and in three quick moves halted the runaway pens. She gently placed the vase back on the desk then looked for somewhere to hide. Curtains hanging to the floor on either side of the window, and on one side behind a chair, were her best option.

In the aftermath of her racket she could tell that everyone in the house was still, straining to hear whatever might be gleaned from silence.

The bedroom door opened aloft. A woman's voice. 'Is somebody there?' Perhaps waiting to hear if her husband would respond. She became more direct. 'Honey? That you?' Quinn tiptoed to the office door and closed it as before, then tiptoed back and snugged herself in behind the chair and curtain.

She tried not to breathe.

The heaviness of the steps on the staircase indicated that the man in the tryst was coming down. She heard him wander around. He turned on a light, which she detected through the curtain and under the crack of the office door.

The door opened.

The overhead light flicked on.

Quinn shut her eyes, as though that made her invisible.

The man came into the room. Only a few steps.

Quinn opened her eyes.

He was naked, lumpy where it counted, and his silhouette revealed that he carried a pistol. *Christ!*

She prayed that no floorboard under her squeaked. She heard footsteps. They were coming nearer, she thought. But the man flicked off the light and shut the door on his way out.

He, too, wanted everything to be exactly as it had been before.

Quinn tried not to gasp, or gulp for air.

The man opened a door to the outside. *Is he mad? He's not dressed!* Then he went back upstairs. He must have dressed up there because he came down again and the woman returned with him. 'Babes, we got another hour. Two, if you want.'

He didn't want.

She implored him to stay. 'Don't go. I'm crazy about you, babes.'

The man left the house. Quinn believed that she heard his footsteps outside. The window beside her was closed and locked, although she could open it. She could escape that way.

She waited instead.

Lights in the house went off.

The woman returned upstairs. Quinn imagined a slump to her shoulders.

She stirred, stood up, stretched. In discomfort from her lengthy crouch.

She hadn't procured much for her trouble. She did a quick scan of the shelves behind the man's desk chair. Photographs. Not interested. A small case. Inside, a collection of rings. A couple with tiny diamonds, others with semi-precious stones. Ezra had taught her, 'Semi-precious means precious to me and you.' The trip was suddenly worthwhile. She dropped the items into the zippered sack she carried with her. She opened drawers. Brochures. Catalogues. *The man's a clotheshorse.* Files. Assorted junk. A nail clipper. Toothbrushes. *Jesus.* Extra combs. Three calculators. *Moron can't add.* Nothing of interest. In a shallow drawer, although she was being slow and careful, something rolled from the back to the front. A baseball. She held it up. She could always use another baseball. This one appeared to be in good shape. The scrawl of a signature. Might be interesting. Impossible to decipher in the dim light. Quinn slipped the ball into her jacket pocket.

She opened the office door. Listened.

She quelled a momentary panic thinking that the lover might only have pretended to leave. Was he waiting for her to emerge? Pistol in hand? She tiptoed out.

Halfway up the stairs, she slipped out the open window there. She dangled outside with one hand on the sill, the other clutching her loot bag, then shoved herself outward with a knee and let herself drop. She toppled over.

Dusting herself off, she checked herself out, then walked off the property.

She felt a familiar twinge: joy and also the sadness that came with a job being over.

Boulevard l'Acadie was busy. Not a problem. Drivers whizzing by would not notice her through the hedge. She spotted Deets's car. She strode more quickly than usual despite trying to keep her pace casual, and Quinn slid onto the passenger seat.

'OK, Trucker boy, let's fly!'

Cars rushed past them on the other side of the l'Acadie fence. Headlights and taillights shining through the hedge. Other light was scant, although her eyes were accustomed to the dark. Deets didn't budge. She noticed the mysterious dark patch across his chest that pooled below his belly and fell off his right hip.

That was blood. All over him. Blood.

She stared then at his face, as though to insist on an explanation. Deets was dead.

He was sitting there dead.

Deets.

She whispered his name. 'Deets?'

Then forgot herself a moment, yelled, 'Deets!' Shook him by his near shoulder.

He was not moving.

A mass of blood on his chest. He'd been a fountain.

Quinn sat in shock. Staring through the dark. Then leapt out of the car.

She felt wetness on her hands.

She didn't know what to do. How to react.

She slammed her door hard. Then opened it and slammed it again, hard.

The window was open to the summer air and she put her head through. She said, 'Deets.' Very softly. 'Oh, my God, Deets.'

She had an odd, weird, out-of-nowhere sense that she was never going to steal again. Whether that thought was ludicrous or true, another impulse immediately took over. She unzipped her collapsible sack. Stuck it inside the car window, emptied the contents on the passenger seat, and dropped the bag. Then figured she'd better get out of there. Her brain fired conflicting commands and ultimatums. A half-block south, the Jarry Street gate led onto l'Acadie. A thousand people would see her walk through it, maybe a million. But what if ten people watched her cross the street, or just one, who after the news of the murder broke reported her? What then? *A young blond woman was observed crossing the road at the time of the murder.* She was the blond girlfriend, seen with the victim that evening.

Better if she didn't cross the road.

Car lights at a distance shone on her. Immediately, she ducked behind Deets's car, then wedged herself into the prickly hedge. The vehicle was on Selwood Road, the street she was on. She waited for it to pass but instead it turned onto the block where she'd been, then into the driveway of the house she robbed. *The husband!* She'd escaped in the nick of time. Not only her. The lover hadn't left himself much time, either.

She extricated herself from the bushes.

Home cried out to her.

She'd go north, towards Boulevard Métropolitain. A shopping mall abutted the expressway. She'd climb a fence then wait for a chance to cross back into her own community undetected.

Only after she had successfully returned to Park Extension did she notice that she was still carrying the baseball in one pocket, the money she'd stolen in the other. Under a streetlight, she checked out the ball. An heirloom. The ball had not been signed by any of the current Expos, as she hoped, yet it amazed her. Her dad would go nuts over it. A former player for the Montreal Royals – the minor league Triple-A club that had been in town in her dad's day – had inscribed his name.

Jackie Robinson.

She was not throwing it away.

Quinn was tempted to call the cops. She wouldn't identify herself in telling them where to find Deets. But she could do nothing for him and he'd be found come daylight, if not sooner.

Better not to let anyone hear a girl's voice. From that moment forward, she would pretend she knew nothing.

Deets!

She wanted to go straight to bed and weep, and that's what she did.

On the Job

(At odds)

His mentor had secretly bestowed a parting gift upon Émile Cinq-Mars. Neither a plaque nor a wristwatch nor a commendation. Instead, Touton saw to it that his protégé showed up for his first day at his new *poste* sleepless, ragged, stinky, and drunk. Within minutes of his arrival, Cinq-Mars deduced the wisdom of his old boss's plan.

'Heard you were like some kind of priest,' Sergeant-Detective Yves Giroux challenged. 'A squeaky-clean saint.'

Giroux did not pose as a gallant figure. He wore his tie slackened. A protuberance of stomach sagged over his belt buckle, a slap of hairy belly often visible between buttons. He shaved at night, so he could arrive each morning with a five o'clock shadow intact. He had a habit of welling out his ears with his pinky, as if drilling into his brain, nor was he above intrusions into each nostril in plain view. He had a reputation for being loud, vulgar, and argumentative without cause.

Giroux had heard that the new man came from different weather, so on first meeting he was confused. The arrival's sloppy appearance belied his good repute. He'd been forewarned that Émile Cinq-Mars was the moral equivalent of the Pope, that he'd not only think of himself as lead detective, but as judge, jury, and prosecutor rolled into one. He was holier than any thou. Giroux was prepared to receive a new partner who had it in for cops as much as bad guys, someone who might give him a ticket for spitting on a public street. And yet the man before him could barely sit up straight, his tie missing in combat, his shirt partially untucked. Telltale scents of whisky and body odor emitted from his pores. Unshaven, his hair in tangles, bleary-eyed, his general disposition a pathetic wilt, the young detective more closely resembled a derelict dipsomaniac than the keen-bean, tight-assed detective he'd been warned would be a millstone around his neck for the next year. Giroux vastly preferred this revised representation, instead of the Boy Scout he'd anticipated.

A windbreaker, even. Miles outside the bounds of protocol.

As if begging for a reprimand.

Cinq-Mars cottoned onto his advantage. He felt as poorly as he looked, and with the last quart of Glenfiddich merrily swishing through his bloodstream, he remained upright but only marginally functional. Still, Armand Touton had handed him a card to play. 'The lights in here. Why so bright?'

'Usually, it's much brighter,' Giroux attested. 'And in case you're interested, *WE LIKE TO SHOUT!*'

Both hands went to his temples to subdue the clamor. Looking up, he saw Giroux's lips moving although no words above a murmur were coming out. 'Pardon?' he asked.

'ARE YOU DEAF? ARE YOU FUCKING DEAF, DETECTIVE?'

Cops around the room stopped everything to look over.

Cinq-Mars held up his palms in a plea for mercy. He deduced that this was probably the preferred head start, better than arriving as a choirboy. If he was making a favorable impression, he owed it to Touton's treachery.

'Rough night,' he murmured.

'I hope she was good,' Giroux said. He performed a gyration with his tongue that Cinq-Mars could have done without. 'Rubber to the road, Detective. We pulled a case. OK to drive?'

Cinq-Mars nodded, but he wasn't sure.

'Breakfast first. Bacon, sausage, eggs. Tons of ketchup.'

'I'm not hungry.'

'Does someone I know care? We're loading you with coffee. The captain hates drunks. We don't arrest drunkards here. We go straight to punishment. Dish out hardcore abuse. Better we get you out of here fast.'

Sergeant-Detective Yves Giroux had not been kidding about breakfast. He ordered a feast. Cinq-Mars endured the visual unpleasantness and stuck to coffee. He was hoping caffeine might pitch him through his day.

'How's the old man getting on?' Giroux inquired.

'Touton? Fine.' He'd let news of the captain's retirement travel the usual channels.

'He sends you here to screw me? Think you have the dick for that?'

Answer a probing question with one equally intemperate. *Basic.* 'Why would he want me to screw you?'

'He's one mother of a hard-ass prickster. That could be the main reason.'

Cinq-Mars thought as fast as his throbbing brain cells could manage. He could not agree with Giroux without belittling himself. The cop grapevine confirmed him and Touton as protégé and mentor, a connection he would not betray. But if he defended his old boss, things might quickly derail with his new one.

'I agree with you there,' he said, keeping Giroux in the dark. 'He is who he is.'

'I was on the Night Patrol myself,' Giroux revealed. 'Years back.'

'He fired you?' *Ask a probing question.*

'Why think that?' The man posed an equally intemperate question back. Giroux was also familiar with the basics, as though they'd both attended the school of Armand Touton. Both had.

'Before my time. I don't know.'

Giroux pulled the gooey routine with his toast again, dropping a concoction of toast and yolk and ketchup into his maw. Cinq-Mars looked away.

'I quit on him,' Giroux said.

'Heard that. Can't remember where. Something about wanting to extend yourself in the department. Now I remember. Touton told me. Same time I told him almost the same thing.'

'Is that it?'

'Is that what?'

'Why he stuck me with you?'

'Did *he* do that?' Cinq-Mars knew his old boss had done so. Still, he preferred the bliss of ignorance. He swigged his coffee.

'Maybe he wants to pull you back. Sent you to me to change your mind about being a real cop.'

'You think being in the Night Patrol isn't being a real cop?'

'Heard it'll be disbanded, soon as Touton goes. Ever hear that?'

'That would be unconscionable.'

'Un-*what*? Un-*conscionable*? Where are you from, Cinq-Mars, the Ivory Fucking Tower?'

He tried to suppress his elevated vocabulary around cops, without much luck. Like an accent, his language trailed alongside him wherever he went, sometimes to his advantage, often not. Within police culture, which was changing too slowly for his liking, he was frequently caught out.

'You might as well hear it from me,' he told his new boss. 'I attended university. I graduated. Not veterinarian school, although I specialized in the care of farm animals. You don't like it, I don't care. You want to joke about it? Be my guest. All I ask is that you be original because I've heard every bad joke going.'

'I thought it was seminary school you went to.'

So he'd done some research. 'Do I look like a priest to you?'

'Dog shit in hell's kennel is what you look like to me, kid. I can barely stand the sight of you, not to mention the stink. Anybody ever tell you that you have one helluva huge honker? My God. How do you keep your head from tilting forward and getting your nose wedged in the ground? You want to watch it going through a door sideways. Always, straight on. Don't turn your head in a gunfight, either. You'll get that schnoz blown right off. Don't present a target like that. In a gunfight, gently insert your nose up the crack of your ass and *then* shoot. Never show your silhouette. Now, pay up. We've got a case.'

'Pay up? You had breakfast. I had coffee.'

'Do the honors. Incidentally, if you blow that thing, use a towel, not Kleenex.'

Catching up to him outside, Cinq-Mars said, 'Silhouette's a big word.'

'Go fuck a wombat.'

In his thirty years, Cinq-Mars had never registered exactly what a wombat might be. Some sort of Australian animal or bird or something? Intuition told him that Giroux probably didn't know, either.

In the car, the senior cop recited an address in the Town of Mount Royal and sketched the scant details known to him.

'Burglary. Overnight. Discovered this morning. You know what that means.'

'Fill me in.'

'A scam.'

'People don't get robbed?'

'They do. Then the victims, the rich ones, take advantage. In an upscale neighborhood, count on it. Maybe there's a robbery, maybe not. If not, jewels and cash went missing. Jewelry is easy to tuck away until insurance pays, then the bracelets and diamond rings magically reappear. It's a fucking miracle. Not that anybody's checking by then. Extra cash was on hand to pay a contractor under the table, that's what they say, even though there's no evidence that work got done. Of course, the television wasn't taken, because the victim wants to watch his favorite shows.'

'What if there was an actual robbery?'

'Shit happens. That case, electronics probably left the house, plus the jewelry and cash. Again, the cash was at least four grand, in a drawer in the kitchen. They keep that much lying around in case a door-to-door salesman comes by selling encyclopedias. The jewelry, maybe it was worth three grand – suddenly it's eighteen, nineteen, never a round number. Like that's supposed to fool us. They feel they deserve something for their double trouble.'

Cinq-Mars bit. 'What double trouble?'

'The aggravation of being robbed, then cops taking up their precious time. I hate them. They make us their accomplices in crime.'

'I see.'

'You *will* see if you don't.'

Cinq-Mars slowed down to take a corner. They wended through an upper middle-class neighborhood – 'wealthy' to some, although old money would sneer, call the people here *nouveau riche*. Big houses, modest properties. Fat mortgages.

'What do we investigate in a case like that? The robbery or the fraud?'

'A robbery's a reported case. It's on the books. The fraud is make-believe, it doesn't exist in our crime stats at the end of the year. Are you here to break my balls, Cinq-Mars? Did you bring your own hammer or expect me to provide one?'

'Why would I want to do that?'

'Touton sent you. That's a known fact.'

'Touton's retiring.' He might as well reveal it. Pick up a little mileage from the news.

'Get out.'

'He's packing it in. I'm not here on his behalf. He has no interest in you, me, or anybody else. He's handing in his badge.'

Giroux reflected on the news. His eyes shifted rapidly from the road to Cinq-Mars and back again.

'Then why the hell did he ship you to me? That leaves only one option.'

'I'm not seeing it.'

'He expects me to educate you.'

'That I don't see at all.'

'You don't have to. It's not going to happen. Not in any way he might expect.'

Cinq-Mars pulled up against a curb and switched off the ignition. The house where the burglary took place was a two-story brick colonial with a small manicured front yard. Two-car garage. Buick out front.

Giroux stalled Cinq-Mars, tapping his wrist. 'This is how an insurance scam works. Victim files for extra. That gets shared three ways. Adjustor, victim, cop. Foolproof. Tamper-proof. Cop-proof.'

'I'm not taking a share.'

'Did someone offer? Live on Poor Street, no skin off my dick. And I'm not circumcised. I ask one favor. If you wind up in the morgue someday soon, don't think you're the first cop to die under strange circumstances. Don't be that naive.'

Cinq-Mars looked at him. His new partner was gazing down the street and over the fence into the neighboring community known as Park Extension. He had to ask, 'Did you just threaten me, Detective?'

'A killer will kill, that's what I say about that. A serious killer never threatens. Threats are for fools.'

'Then you know where I stand,' Cinq-Mars tells him.

'Where's that?'

'At no time did I threaten you.'

'So we're even. I'm pulling your leg. You know that, right?'

Cinq-Mars had no idea.

'Admit it. You think I'm a dirty cop with his fingers in the pie. The apple, the cherry, the lemon meringue.'

Cinq-Mars offered back a faint shrug.

'The strawberry rhubarb tempts me, that's about it,' Giroux said, leaving Cinq-Mars mystified, his prior suspicions put on hold.

They trundled out of the car. Direct sunlight caused Cinq-Mars to squint. On the crossing street before them, where a fence and a hedge separated the street from traffic on Boulevard l'Acadie, a patrol car whipped by. Then evidently pulled up out of sight, judging by the windy roar of its tires followed by silence. Giroux shrugged, and nodded, granting permission for Cinq-Mars to walk down fifty feet to look around the home that blocked their view. A second patrol car was on the scene. Between them an unidentified vehicle sat parked. When Cinq-Mars hung on for a longer look, Giroux joined him.

'Big fuss for a speeding ticket,' Giroux noted. 'What's your take?'

'They ran the plates, found a prior,' Cinq-Mars said.

'Or the car reeks,' Giroux suggested. 'They checked the trunk. Our officers will be divvying up a kilo. Go. Help yourself to a baggie, Cinq-Mars. I'll wait.'

He had no way to determine what was bluster with this man and what, if anything, was felonious. 'I'll take a pass on that.'

'Good. I'd arrest you otherwise. Come on. Let's check out our scam artists.'

'They might be victims.'

'In whose world?'

They turned their backs on the scene and crossed over to visit the house where a woman had reported being burglarized.

The 80

(Squishing the lid)

Deets was dead. Murdered. He was her boyfriend. A cop would knock on her door.

She hoped Deets never told anyone that he was both her boyfriend *and* her getaway driver.

Her eyes stayed wet through half the night. She couldn't believe what she'd seen. And why? Why would anyone stab a sweet, beautiful boy to death? *Deets!*

She taught him to help her steal. This was her fault.

I got to get stuff out. Cops will be here.

Crying, ranting to herself, changed nothing. Deets promised not to talk about what they were doing, not to anybody, but what if he let something slip? What if he mentioned falling into lust with a thief?

Maybe she *should* go to jail for his murder. His death was her fault.

Still. She had to think up a story. Get last night straight.

She couldn't say she was home alone after Deets dropped her off unless her father was *not* home then, which was something she didn't know. Only that he was in bed when she got back. She'd have to admit to being with Deets earlier, no way around that. They made out, OK? Front seat of his car. She'd be shy about the details, stress that nothing went on below the waist. He seemed distracted. She'd mention it. Real casual-like. He wanted to get going. He let her off somewhere. Oh God, she had to find out where her father had been last night – in or out? – before she could say where she was let off. If her dad was out late, she could say *she* was home. Watching TV. What was on? A baseball game! She could read about it. That made sense. No. No, it didn't. The game would've been over by then. People saw her with Deets after ten, right up to midnight. Maybe, if she was super lucky, her dad went to the game. Or, he had his regular bowling night but sometimes practiced by himself. Maybe he bowled or went to the ball game, then maybe he had a few drinks afterwards. If he wasn't home, she could say *she* was.

She couldn't find out about her dad until he finished work. If it turned out her dad had been home, then she needed a different story. She should think one up. One that didn't depend on either of them being in or out of the house.

In the meantime, she had to get out of the house, and she had to get rid of the stolen loot in her closet and under her bed before any cop arrived.

Think.

She could read about the last inning of the ball game. Maybe her friends wouldn't be sure that she stayed at Ball Park right up to midnight. Gatekeepers at the game didn't care if you entered after the seventh inning. She could've hung out there, after Deets. The park was across the tracks on the east side of Park Ex. Nobody had to know that she was really across the fence on the west side.

She could read about the game riding the bus. Bring it to life in her head.

Quinn packed a suitcase that belonged to her mother. She had to sit on the lid to squish it closed. She hauled it down to the corner bus stop as if embarking on a grand voyage. She hopped on the Number 80. She remembered the boy who'd skidded behind this bus in winter and lost his legs. Her own legs felt queasy. Losable. She headed to Ezra's pawnshop. She wanted to talk to him yet say nothing directly. Maybe indirectly, that way they could chat. They were both smart. He might have advice. She could tell him that she didn't think she should be a thief anymore. Hear what he said to that. Maybe it would mean no more back-room visits. That would be all right as long as he got rid of her stuff. As long as he let her just cry and cry.

The Royals' Ball

(A felony is merited)

Sergeant-Detective Yves Giroux caught on immediately. Hungover, his new partner dialed in soon enough. No doubt about it, the robbery victim was flirting with him.

Detective Cinq-Mars had yet to make it through the door.

The woman's hair was black, straight, long in the sixties style with bangs that touched her eyebrows. Dark eyeliner and heavy mascara. A housedress fell to the tops of her knees which she repeatedly adjusted, wrapping and unwrapping it, cinching the belt, each time exposing a skimpy halter top and modest Bermuda shorts. Perspiration on her brow indicated that she'd been working out. Ignoring Giroux, she had eyes only for the man of her generation who also shared her height equivalency. She was about six-one and looked right over Giroux who pulled in at five-nine and was a few inches lower on the stoop. She took in the rangy Cinq-Mars. Jutted her hip against the front-door jamb and used her right hand to pull down her hair, from ear to breast. She lowered her gaze to the feet of the tall young cop, then slowly brought her eyes up. Thighs, hips, chest, neck, face. And nose.

She gave his nose a more prolonged stare than most people were willing to risk. All the while repeating the stroking motion through her hair.

Giroux smirked. 'Mind if we come inside, ma'am?'

'Be quiet, though. My husband's sleeping.'

'For sure,' Giroux remarked. 'We don't want to wake him right now.'

He worked the graveyard shift at the Royal Victoria Hospital. She explained that he had not been home when the thief broke in. 'I feel violated.' She glanced at Cinq-Mars again.

In the living room, the men settled into plush purple chairs. Cinq-Mars could easily fall asleep in his.

'What's missing?' Giroux asked.

'So far? Cash. Three of my husband's watches. They were keepsakes. A pen. And rings. The man of the house likes rings.'

'How many rings?'

'Four.'

'Diamond rings?'

'Diamond sand on one. Topaz on a couple. One's a ruby. One's steel.'

'Your TV?' Giroux inquired.

'We have several. The thief left them. Too much to carry, I guess.'

'Several, huh? How many exactly?'

'Four. Why? They're still here.'

'So many TVs.'

'He came for cash and jewelry, Detective. Thank God he didn't go upstairs. I keep my valuables there. But he went through my husband's office.'

Giroux conveyed a writing motion, prompting Émile Cinq-Mars to take out a notepad. The woman was fitting the older cop's expectations to a tee. 'Your name, please?'

'Savina.' She looked over at Cinq-Mars. 'Savina Vaccaro.'

'*Mrs* Savina Vaccaro,' Giroux repeated, to remind her of a critical detail. He waited for Cinq-Mars to finish writing. 'Your husband? His name?'

'Dr Howard Shapiro.'

'Jewish,' Giroux tacked on. 'You're what? Italian? That's different.'

'Variety is the spice of life, Detective.'

'I wouldn't know.' Giroux uttered a self-conscious cough.

'How much cash do you estimate?' His eyes slid across to Cinq-Mars, anticipating a healthy tally.

'Small bills. Seventy dollars? Maybe eighty.'

Head down, Cinq-Mars transcribed the amount. Unable to help himself, he asked, 'You didn't have cash in the house to pay a contractor?'

The query confused her. 'Contractor?'

'What value on the watches?' Giroux butted in again.

'The value doesn't concern me. It's the idea of an intruder in my house! I'm alone at night.'

'Of course, ma'am,' Giroux reassured her. 'It's a traumatic experience to be robbed. Truth is, a thief rarely returns. He got what he came for. Also, he'll expect you to take precautions.'

She was looking at Cinq-Mars, waiting for him to show concern, too. The length of her gaze forced a reply. 'You've seen the last of him, Mrs Shapiro.'

'I go by my maiden name. More modern, don't you think?'

Cinq-Mars had no opinion on the subject.

'I take it you never saw the burglar,' Giroux poked in.

'Thank God, no. I thought I heard something. I went downstairs. Maybe he was hiding at the time. He might've jumped out at me.'

'Well, ma'am,' Giroux reminded her, 'we don't need to be concerned about what didn't happen. Now. About the watches. How many and what's the total value?'

'Oh. Three. Howard said they'd run about twelve hundred dollars.' Giroux's gaze remained fixed on her to avoid his partner's amusement. 'I don't know if that's the value when new or now.'

Again, Cinq-Mars could not resist. 'Twelve hundred dollars. Not twelve thousand?'

'Hundred. It's not the value. What's your name again? Cinq-Mars. That's a new one on me. What ever happened on the fifth of March?'

She was translating his name. He wasn't willing to get into it. He did not have a definitive answer, regardless.

'The rings,' Giroux stipulated. 'Their value?'

'Three hundred, approx. In a garage sale, I doubt I'd get fifty.'

'Fifty dollars,' Cinq-Mars announced, triumphant.

'It's the principle! Robbed! While I'm sleeping!'

'Are you insured, ma'am?' Giroux inquired.

'I checked. A thousand-dollar deductible. Not worth the trouble.'

'You could increase the cash amount of what's missing. The value of the jewels,' Giroux suggested. He spoke as a waiter offering ice cream with the pie.

She stared at him, a prolonged silence that caused both officers to check on her.

'I wouldn't do that,' she stated, her tone flat, brittle.

'A little trick to see how the victim responds,' Giroux explained. 'Now I know. You're on the up and up.'

'*I'm* on the up and up? Good to hear. I am not a thief. A thief, however, came into my house. That's why I called you, Detective, in case you're interested.'

'Ma'am, I didn't mean to offend you.'

'Does this mean you won't investigate? Too little value to waste your time? We want the watches returned. The rings, who cares? The watches we'd like to have back. They are my husband's keepsakes.'

The husband, having heard voices, appeared at that moment in the wide doorway. Jeans and sweatshirt. He had greying temples. He looked to be a dozen years older than his wife, and about three inches shorter. In presenting himself, he displayed an athlete's easy physical confidence. He extrapolated on her point of view. 'They mean a lot to me. Luckily, the most valuable one was on my wrist.'

'What value do you place on the others?' Giroux put to him. Time to test his theories on the husband. He subtly raised an eyebrow to warn Cinq-Mars that the worm may yet turn.

'Three-fifty for one. One seventy-five for another. The best one, my dad paid about six hundred. A present for graduating med school. What's that? Eleven hundred?'

'Sorry. I said twelve,' Savina Vaccaro apologized. 'Will you arrest me?'

'Savina,' her husband said curtly, silencing her. He added, 'Those are prices when new. They're worth less now. It's not the money. It's the idea that some bastard breaks into my house while my wife is home alone. That can't be tolerated.'

'Could you show us how the thief broke in?' Cinq-Mars requested. He'd won the round and was trying not to gloat.

The husband had returned earlier than usual and gone straight to bed. Hours later, his wife took her morning coffee onto the back porch. She was strolling around the property, enjoying the gardens, when she discovered a curious rash of footprints. Then found a bug screen on the ground. She rushed back inside and noticed dirt on the floor under the window by the stairway landing. Woke her husband. They canvassed the house together to find what might be missing.

'The seventy or eighty bucks,' Giroux said.

'I thought it was more,' the husband replied. 'Whatever.'

Outside, Giroux and Cinq-Mars studied the footprints, each arriving at the same conclusion. Two sets. One foot slightly larger than the other. One man perhaps had elevated a smaller one high enough to make it through the open window. They agreed that the heels of a ladder would have left marks in the soft earth. There were none.

'Kids,' Giroux surmised. On their own, they switched back to speaking French.

Cinq-Mars didn't like to automatically blame youth. 'Why kids?'

'Bigger kid. Smaller kid.'

They were distracted by sirens. 'That's some speeder,' Giroux remarked.

The two detectives returned to visualizing how the entry was accomplished. Fingerprints could very well go up the outside wall. 'Call for a dusting,' Giroux directed.

Cinq-Mars went back inside to use the phone. While there, Dr Shapiro came out of his office and spoke to Giroux. He seemed exercised. Cinq-Mars couldn't make out his complaint but noticed the light in his new partner's eye. Off the phone, Cinq-Mars went over.

'Dr Shapiro owned a special baseball,' Giroux explained.

'Signed by Jackie Robinson,' the physician made known.

'Signed by Jackie Robinson and appraised for how much again?'

'It was an heirloom of my father's.'

'You know who Jackie Robinson is, Detective?' Giroux asked Cinq-Mars.

Robinson's career in the majors, breaking the color barrier, was legendary. Montrealers had a special place in their hearts for him due to his time on their Triple-A club, the Royals. Baseball fan or not, everyone in the city knew about Jackie Robinson.

'How much again?' Giroux, unable to conceal a smug attitude, inquired.

'We had it appraised at twelve grand. Time's gone by. It's probably worth seventeen, eighteen grand now. Hard to say.'

'But not twenty. Not a round number like that.'

The doctor seemed taken aback. 'I'm calculating ten percent a year over four or five years. So, seventeen, eighteen grand.'

'Good deduction. The value's important. Sir, the crime now merits being called a felony, rather than a misdemeanor. That's important. This way, we might be allocated more time to investigate.' Giroux raised an eyebrow in his partner's direction, convinced that they were now included in a scam. He didn't believe anything about the ball. If it ever existed, the doctor probably had it tucked away in a drawer. An insurance claim would now be submitted for the loss of the ball and the nuisance of being burglarized.

'Finally, we're getting somewhere,' Savina Vaccaro said.

Before heading out, the detectives advised the couple to wait for the crime-scene unit to take fingerprints before cleaning up. The instruction pleased them. Satisfied, the doctor headed back to bed while his wife showed the policemen to the door. Her ardor for the handsome, tall Cinq-Mars had apparently chilled.

Giroux expressed an opinion on that. 'Your nose. For a while there, she was intrigued. Then she decided she doesn't like it. She thinks it'll get in the way. For kissing, and like that.'

'Folks can be shallow,' Cinq-Mars concurred. He could not show vulnerability when moving to a different department on the force.

'Let's check out the fuss down the block,' Giroux suggested.

An initiative Cinq-Mars welcomed.

His Last Tiny Marble

(The stench of him)

'Both wrong,' Giroux grumbled, probing a cavity with his tongue. A police cordon diverted traffic away from Selwood Road, which bordered the hedge and fence. Six cruisers and unmarked cars were present. 'Not a speeder. Not a drug bust.'

'That a fact?' Sometimes cops came out in force over nothing.

With his chin, the senior cop indicated two detectives standing next to a black Pontiac. 'The short one, who looks like he's wearing diapers? Paul Frigault. The tall one who thinks he's Einstein with the frizzy hair is Marcel Caron. You know what they say about stupid people.'

Cinq-Mars waited to hear.

'They think they're smart because they're too dumb to know better. Smart people know they're not. You, Cinq-Mars, think you're a smart guy?'

Either way, the answer would defeat him. 'Who are they?'

'Homicide. Our station.'

Cinq-Mars and Giroux ducked under the yellow barricade ribbon, flashed their badges at a patrol officer.

'Speaking of people who look like shit,' Giroux stated, and rummaged around an inside pocket of his sports coat. He pulled out a pair of sunglasses. 'Hide the redeye. And keep yourself downwind.'

'I'm not that bad,' Cinq-Mars argued, but he accepted the glasses.

'The man who thinks he smells like a daisy is usually the one who stinks to high heaven. He's the only one immune to the stench.'

Beyond the man's gruff guard-dog demeanor and hangdog look, Cinq-Mars was appreciating that Giroux could deliver a salient remark. They moved toward the detectives, who greeted them with attitude.

'Why you here, Giroux?' Detective Frigault wanted to know. The man's trousers were frumpy, which gave merit to the crack about diapers. 'No pizza parlor in sight. No strip joint, neither.'

Caron added his two cents. 'Children live in this neighborhood.' The remark hung in the air without explanation.

'Visiting lonely housewives. They have urges. A few of us benefit. Others don't, as you well know. What's going on?'

'Help yourself. Just don't upchuck on my shoes.'

What Giroux could not see through the windshield of the Pontiac, due to the glare of sunlight, became apparent through the open side window. He had a long look. Rather than step away, he pulled his jacket tight to his belly, then stuck his head deeper into the car. When he resurfaced, he indicated to Cinq-Mars to check it out for himself.

Under the circumstances, Cinq-Mars was not shocked to find a dead man behind the wheel. He removed the sunglasses. He'd seen the dead who'd been victims of violence before although he was not accustomed to the view. The victim's youth and the bloodiness were disconcerting. He repeated Giroux's movement, not coming into contact with the car but poking his head further inside. On the seat he counted three watches, four rings, and a gold pen.

The guy with the Einstein cut – his hair only half as extravagant as the physicist's – suddenly stood next to him. 'I'll show you,' he said.

Wearing nitrile gloves, he opened the passenger-side door. Along the sill below the window, blood had been smeared in a way that stood out from the pooling and splatter elsewhere. 'The killer left prints in blood. He had nothing to wipe them clean, so he smeared them. Equally effective.'

'Hmm,' Cinq-Mars murmured, neither in agreement nor in dispute. He went around to the driver's side. He crouched to gaze inside. Detective Marcel Caron followed him around. 'Mind if I look in?'

Caron checked with his boss, who shrugged, then opened the driver's door.

'Don't touch,' Caron warned.

'Not my first,' Cinq-Mars revealed.

He seemed to be concentrating on the fatal wound.

'Puncture wounds,' Caron declared, in case the new guy hadn't figured that out. 'Choose your weapon. Knife. Ice pick. Screwdriver.'

'Hmm,' Cinq-Mars said again. He put the sunglasses back on.

The repetition of his murmur seemed to irritate the homicide detective.

'What's that supposed to mean? You think it's an axe wound? It's not a bullet.'

'Small. Sharp,' Cinq-Mars agreed. 'I'm not convinced by what you said before. The killer didn't smear his prints.'

'You think the dead guy did it.' He enjoyed a chuckle.

Cinq-Mars waited for the laughter to simmer down. 'The clothing was pushed into the wound by the knife, then came back out in this direction when withdrawn. He was killed through this window. Driver's side. Not from the passenger seat. Which means the smearing was done by somebody else. Maybe somebody who was in the car. Not by the killer. If by the killer, why didn't he smear his other prints, which are obvious on the dash, and on the inside and outside of the passenger door?'

The other three detectives stood still. Giroux broke the stalemate. 'Bad enough we got Einstein, now we got Sherlock Holmes. We'll bust this case wide open by noon.'

'What do you mean, *we*?' Frigault interjected, chuckling away. 'You're not on the case, Giroux. Time to run along and play.'

Giroux stewed, and waited for his new partner to come around to his side of the car before he announced, 'This is my case now.'

Frigault's head drooped with exaggerated incredulity. Detective Caron finished lighting a smoke, shook out the match and tossed it. He spoke in a voice so dry that Cinq-Mars thought he sandpapered his larynx at night. 'The man has lost his last tiny marble, boys. Had to happen. You're brain-dead, Giroux. That it took so long, the only surprise.'

'My case,' Giroux insisted. 'You boys can head home now. Wait for some lover to shoot a rival. That's as close as you'll get to sex.'

Caron inhaled down to his toes before he enumerated the obvious. 'We've been assigned. Not you. You're B&E. *Petty* crime. We're homicide. You're tiddlywinks.'

'Who's the new playmate?' Frigault inquired.

Cinq-Mars identified himself when his new partner showed no interest in doing so. Perhaps he'd forgotten his name.

'From the Night Patrol,' Giroux added. Cinq-Mars wished he hadn't done that.

The raw-throated warbler, Caron, responded. 'Heard of you. Touton's boy. You must've had a miserable falling out to land with this joker.'

'I committed a cardinal sin,' Cinq-Mars deadpanned. 'Requested a transfer.'

'Whew. Live and learn,' Detective Frigault advised him.

'You have my sympathies,' Caron remarked.

'He wears sunglasses,' Giroux chimed in, betraying him. 'Thinks he's so cool.' Giroux had extended a plank, helped him to step up on it, and now forced him to walk it. Cinq-Mars was on his own amid these pirates.

'A windbreaker on the job,' Frigault pointed out. 'No dress

code for you, huh? Cinq-Mars, do you get a free pass because
you were on the goddamn Night Patrol?'

'Easy, Paul. He'll pull out his Night Patrol wand. Zap you into
a frog.'

'I'm already a Frog.'

'I don't mean he'll make you French. He'll send you back to
the swamp to croak in the sun.'

'Beats the life I have now.'

'All right,' Cinq-Mars said. He could not show irritation. Easy
to remind himself of that, more difficult to pull it off.

'He thinks he's had enough,' Caron said. 'Detective! I don't
believe that part about asking for a transfer. You got shoved down
here for a reason. We'll find out why. Might as well tell us. How
bad did you screw up?'

Cinq-Mars ignored the question. 'You have a dead boy in a
car. Isn't that more important here?'

'Not your concern. Not your partner's either.'

Finally, Giroux pitched in. 'Stolen property on the car seat.'

'The watches?' Frigault inquired. 'The rings? Could be stolen.
Who's to know?'

'The stolen goods come from a house around the corner, right
over there.' He pointed to it, an edge of the house visible. 'My
B&E. It's my case now.'

'Seriously? You pulled a B&E connected to our homicide? I
guess that makes your break-in mine.'

'Frigault, get over that idea in a hurry. Too much time in. I'll
take the homicide.'

'Murder is out of your league, Giroux,' Frigault said.

'Thanks for the input,' the gravelly Caron added. 'Maybe you
solved our case, maybe we solved yours. If you don't mind too
much, we'll take credit for both.'

Initially surprised by his partner's argument, Cinq-Mars cottoned
on. They were not usurping a homicide investigation. That idea
was ludicrous from the get-go. Giroux was putting up a fight not
to take on that case, but to keep from losing the one he had. That
a murder was part of it made it exponentially more interesting. If
he fought well, he might win the right to continue investigating
his minor B&E. The best he could hope for.

The men goaded one another on. Another sour internecine
skirmish between departments. They did not acquit themselves

well. Had they been members of the Night Patrol, Cinq-Mars mulled, Captain Touton would have taken a sledgehammer to their kneecaps. Not governed by that example, the men sounded as though they'd soon insult one another's lineage.

Miffed, somewhat embarrassed, Cinq-Mars walked away. He took the opportunity to sidle up to a uniformed officer guarding the perimeter. A man about his own age. As it turned out, he'd been the first officer on the scene.

'Rough start to your day,' Cinq-Mars commiserated.

'A lousy way to end it, actually. I'm coming off an overnight.' Average height and solid build, in uniform he looked fit.

'We're keeping you up.'

'That's the job.'

Émile Cinq-Mars put his finger on what was different. The constable was English. Within the Police Service, French was the language of discourse. He conversed in English when it was the first or preferred language of a witness or suspect, or of anyone from the public, but typically he spoke French to colleagues, including those who were English. Other than with the couple that morning, he hadn't spoken English in weeks, so seized the opportunity to switch from French for the practice.

'You were driving by. What made you stop?'

The man hesitated, as it was not the usual form, then also continued in English. 'Two girls. We took down their names and addresses, let them carry on to high school. Before class they had ballet, why they were up so early. They thought the guy was asleep. They yelled at him. They wanted to startle him, run away laughing. Schoolgirl stuff. Instead, they got the shock of their lives.'

'Then you came along.'

'They rang a doorbell. That one,' the officer said, and indicated the nearest house. 'Nobody was willing to answer. They were running back to one of the girls' homes when they spotted my cruiser.'

Cinq-Mars changed his angle to the officer, obeying Giroux's edict to stay downwind of folks. He noticed scarring on the man's right cheek. He suspected that the cop had endeavored to make it as a pro hockey player; when that didn't work out, unprepared for the real world, he became a cop.

Recruiting off the rinks provided the force with both good cops and bitter ones.

'I know who you are,' the uniform said. 'Seen you around. You're Night Patrol.'

'I guess because you work nights, you've seen me.'

'That's why I do.'

'Sorry?' He felt he missed something.

'Hoping to be noticed for the Patrol. Up to now, that hasn't worked.'

'I have a feeling you'd do well.'

'Put in a word?'

'Sorry to say, they're disbanding.'

The cop was instantly demoralized, as though his hope for the future was dashed.

'Good cops have an option,' Cinq-Mars mentioned.

'What's that, sir?'

'Form our own.'

The uniform looked to be both skeptical and interested.

'Not our own Night Patrol, obviously. Our own alliances. Good cops will be dispersed. That makes them less effective, less of an influence. Doesn't have to be that way. If good cops stay in contact, they can help each other out. Especially when the bureaucrats stub their toes getting in our way. Nothing illegal, nothing vigilante. A willingness to collaborate.'

He caught the man nodding with genuine interest.

'What's your name?'

'Wyatt, sir. Brandon.'

'When it's just us, go easy on the "sir" bit.'

'Sure.'

'Now help me out. Maybe my English is coming along, but English names kill me. Which is your first name, which your last?'

The officer released a laugh, perhaps finally feeling at ease. 'It's Brandon, sir. Sorry – not sir. Brandon comes first. Brandon Wyatt.'

'I'm Émile. Most of the time. I'd shake but the old guys would ask what's going on. Listen, did you find a baseball in the car?'

He believed the man's shrug to be an honest expression of incomprehension.

'Cash?'

'Nope.' The mention of cash got his back up.

'What about the girls? Any chance they snooped around?'

'Hard to believe. They're kids, Émile. Maybe they're not seriously traumatized, but they went through the shock of their lives. They wouldn't root around for something to steal.'

'I hear you. I want to check your car. I believe you, Brandon, but the brass might not unless I do a check. Any objection?'

'Knock yourself out.'

'By the way, the dead guy's car? Motor running or off?'

'Off.'

'And the young guy? Has he been identified, do you know?'

'His name is Dietmar Ferstel. His car. He lives on the other side of the fence.'

'In Park Ex.'

'On Champagneur.'

'Thanks.'

Checking the patrol car for stolen property, Cinq-Mars was happy to come up empty.

Giroux was wondering what his new sidekick was doing.

'What the hell was that about?' he pressed him.

'Let's wake up the doctor. Have a chat,' Cinq-Mars suggested.

'Do we have a purpose, or do we genuinely dislike the guy?'

'Where's the baseball?'

'Proves my point, right? He's a scammer. You want to nail him. Are you learning the ropes, Cinq-Mars? We'll get him to understand we're fine with him ripping off the insurance company . . . if we get our cut. Is that your angle?'

'You're full of shit, Giroux.'

'Is that significant? Helps you with absolutely nothing in your life.'

'I'm thinking, if there is a baseball, we have a clue to hunt down our B&E guy. Find the baseball, find the killer. Or, let's say our doctor coming home interrupted the robbery and wanted his baseball back. The other stuff, not so much. I mean, maybe he doesn't want to tell his wife he killed a man, right?'

'Whoa, whoa. Way ahead of yourself, Cinq-Mars.'

'Miles and miles. Still, we need to talk to the doctor before homicide does. Let's see if he can prove the baseball exists. If it's real, not an insurance scam, then either homicide stole it –

unlikely in my books, though you'll call me naive – or the doctor still has it, for scam purposes. Or the killer does. In that case, we have a clue to hunt the killer down. If the doctor cannot prove it exists in the first place, then sign up for his scam. Keep me out of it. At least we won't waste time looking for something that doesn't exist.'

Giroux put a hand on his partner's sleeve to stall their progress.

'Is it the woman?' he asked. 'You want to see her twice? Maybe she'll overlook your schnoz, get the hots for you again? Cinq-Mars, her husband is in the house. Cool your jets.'

'Why work so hard to piss people off, Sergeant-Detective?'

'People are slime. Every stinking soul. Let's go talk to your doctor and his sultry wife. How's that for a word? Sultry. She's something. Salty, too. One thing I like about what you said – "Talk to our doctor before homicide does." Keep the attitude. In B&E, we don't bend over for nobody. Never.'

On the stoop, Giroux asked, 'What were you looking for in the cruiser?'

'The baseball.'

'Ballsy.'

'Is that a pun?'

'Every drunk has the impression he's funny. That's the problem with drunks.'

Cinq-Mars took off the sunglasses and handed them back to his partner. 'I made friends with him first. Then I searched his car.'

'I got to watch it around you, Sherlock. I'll keep an eye peeled.'

'Here she is.' Savina Vaccaro was undoing the locks on her door.

'You know why she went off you? Not the nose. I said that to be nice.'

'You don't say anything to be nice.'

Giroux made a motion of squeezing his nostrils to diminish the stench of him. Although annoyed, Cinq-Mars conceded that the man might be right. His stink turned her off.

Forty, On a Scale of Ten

(Provenance)

Going in, Quinn felt shaky.

She had no idea that Ezra Knightsbridge was expecting her.

She rode on two buses. Images of Deets vibrated behind her eyes. She imagined telling Ezra everything, even though she intended to be circumspect. She wished she could tell him about Deets and the nude lover who carried a pistol. On the bus she was tearing up. Passengers noticed. They tried to be sensitive and look away, then kept glancing over. Quinn wanted to tell them everything, too.

'How you do today?' Ezra asked her, that simply.

Her eyes had reddened. Her left hand clutched her right wrist to keep it from trembling.

'Lock the door,' he instructed her.

She was learning to trust him and needed to do so now. Quinn turned the lock and flipped the *Ouvert* sign to read *Fermé*. 'How much time should I put?'

She was referring to a cardboard clock, the hands denoting when the proprietor might return.

'You decide.'

Quinn chose half an hour. She hung the clock in place under the *Fermé* sign, then joined Ezra behind the curtain in the dingy back room.

He put the kettle on, then shook out butter biscuits from a box, placing two on a saucer beside her cup and one next to his. He requested that she fetch a chair from the far corner of the storage space, which she positioned at a forty-five-degree angle to his, their knees almost touching. They shared a side table recently in for resale. The oval surface was sufficient for their two cups, a wee bowl of sugar, and a miniature jug of milk. Quinn experienced the fleeting sensation of being a child in a dollhouse.

'Something interesting to show me?' the pawnbroker asked.

She put a fist to her mouth. Then said, 'I want to learn stuff.'

'What is it my little thief wants to learn today?'

'Lots of things.'

'Like what?'

'Like why are you so nice to me?'

'That is a mystery. Next question.'

'What kind of a mystery?'

'The mysterious kind. Any practical questions have you that make sense?'

'You're stubborn.' She worked an object out of her jacket pocket. 'If you were selling this, how would you do it?'

'A baseball,' Ezra noted as she held it up. Taking it in hand, turning it around under his lamp, provoked a heightened level of approval. 'The provenance counts,' he told her. 'This signature, also.'

'What does that mean – provenance?'

'A French word in English,' he explained. 'It means "Where is this ball from?" That's provenance. Significant, the home run? Provenance. How did this player come to inscribe his signature? Provenance. It means to tell to me the story. Applies to antiques, a history, celebrities. A stolen baseball signed by Jackie Robinson is worth X amount. Who owned the ball, how that person gained the signature, the value can change. Up. Down. It's inscribed to Mr Sal. Who's he? That will count.'

'I'm supposed to make up stories now?'

He gently corrected her. 'Provenance refers to the *true* story. With old items, through the wars, a story can be hard to know. This baseball,' he said, as he handed it back to her and she forced it into her jacket pocket, 'maybe not so difficult.'

'For the hell of it, let's say it's stolen.'

'We are only talking.'

The kettle whistled.

Ezra poured the water into the teapot, let the bags dangle, and adjusted a cozy over the pot. His hand shook. He noticed; she did not.

'Honey in your tea? Sugar? Lemon? Milk? Or nothing at all?'

She smiled in a demure way, rare for her, and scrunched her shoulders. 'I've never had tea. My dad drinks coffee.'

'Tea you shall drink. Prepare to be corrupted.'

'I think that's been taken care of already.'

'Not by me. Now, your request for knowledge. To handle a unique item, since a silly girl stole it—'

'I'm not silly,' Quinn pointed out.

'Were you mentioned in our talk? Not by me.'

'Gotcha.'

'One solution is to approach the original proprietor. A special skill I have for that. I phone the one who bemoans the loss of a precious possession he no longer possesses.'

'Won't he pitch a fit?' She recognized the phrase as an old one of her mother's.

'I expect abuse. I make clear I am the intermediary, not the thug who invaded his home. I want to help out.'

'Oh yeah. That's believable.'

Ezra flicked his own nose with a forefinger, dismissing her sarcasm. 'I suggest to the man who's been robbed, who gouges me with his bad words, to go ahead and collect the insurance. Why not? He was doing that anyway. He won't get his property back, but he will have cash. Then I say to him, "Kind sir, you can have both."'

'Both what?'

'That's what he says. Both what? If it is a baseball we are talking, I say to him he can have it back. I say, take the insurance at X amount of dollars. I will see the baseball returned to you at half that price.'

Time to pour the tea. Ezra added a touch of sugar and a smidgeon of milk. Quinn followed suit. She tasted it tentatively. Without offering any definitive opinion, she gestured to indicate that she'd persevere. She found it oddly familiar, as though she did drink tea previously, years ago.

'Now,' Ezra continued, 'a guy robbed of a baseball hears on his telephone that he can keep half the insurance for his baseball, and also keep the baseball. A good deal, no? A stuffed shirt might get his back up, say it's the principle. Somebody might want to see if he can't catch the crook who broke into his house. Get the ball back that way. Somebody might call the cops. Most of the time, the injured party sees how he can be better off. He takes half the money, plus the baseball. To pull that off is a skill of mine.'

Quinn mulled it over. Sampled her tea again. 'Doesn't that mean the crook gets half the value? Even less, if the profit is split with an intermediary.'

'Sometimes. Other times, fifty percent of an insured value can be more than market value, much more than black market. With paintings, it works that way. Honest I'm being with you today. I have no experience with baseballs.'

A quiet time ensued as the tea was consumed. Then Ezra altered the mood again, asking, 'How is it that trouble finds you, my Quinn?'

The gentleness in his voice, the evident care: she might have broken down at that moment. Quinn took a sharp breath and clenched her hands into a single fist. For two minutes, she did not speak, nor look at him. While it had not yet come fully down around her ears, she could not escape the trouble she was in. The matter could go very badly. The police would want to talk to the dead boy's girlfriend, to the last person known to see Deets alive. What then?

Gauging that she was not in a talkative mood, Ezra said, 'Take your time.'

'Why are you good to me?' she whispered. She needed to understand.

'Am I? We do business. Who is good to who?'

'You know what I mean. I'm a girl. Halfway pretty. You're not gross with me.'

'Very much more than halfway. You are saying that if I touch you, that is gross. Such a compliment.'

'I think you know what I mean.'

'I prefer not to be that way. I work outside the law, but am I wicked? I say not.'

She thought it over. Then said, 'You're a strange old man, Ezra.'

'You prefer I do what you expect? To push my hand inside your shirt?'

'I'd get that, if you did. I'd kill you, but I'd get it. You, as you are, I don't get.'

'Maybe you don't know so much. What you mean to say, you are not saying. You still expect a hand down your jeans someday.'

Another of her shrugs implied that he might not be wrong in that assumption.

Ezra poured more tea, speaking as the liquid filled each cup.

'I had my share of trouble as a young man, Quinn. Trouble is not unusual. Kids step off the rails, or get lured away, or they're snagged. I stepped off the rails on my own accord. The wrong crowd for me. I was attracted. One day I would change my life, except I got caught. Then I could not change it. I was sent to juvie. In juvie, I went with a crowd worse than my first. Something to learn. Go the wrong way, people will help you continue. You are recruited and you will be fooled. You are down the wrong path with worse people. I took my training after that to steal cars – yes, me, cars – then a jewelry thief I became and a fur coat thief. Thank God, no banks. I was not an enjoyment to myself. Women did not favor me. Not hard to guess why not. A shame, when I had so much to offer.'

He winked, and Quinn smiled back.

'Hooligans, my friends. A few I loved. Some were mean, all of them unreliable. Apply pressure to any old friend of mine from those days and listen to him sing. An aria! I had no enemies, I made sure. Also, not too successful. A little success came by, I did not brag. When your life is among thieves, success breeds incarceration.'

The tea ceremony continued. He sipped delicately, then took a small bite of his biscuit. Quinn did likewise initially, but once she had a taste she devoured the biscuit in a trice.

'You eat like a chipmunk,' Ezra said.

'You look like a goat.'

'Long story short, I wanted out. How? Take yourself out of the picture, old pals give up your name faster than a comet. To protect the band they run with, they betray who they used to run with. An old code. To leave is big danger. What happened, off the grid, I stole from a warehouse.'

She cocked her chin, curious. 'What does that mean, "off the grid"?'

'Not sanctioned. No boss involved. Petty crime, we run our own deals on the side, nobody is to care. Bosses let us have our fun. To them, we honed skills later they could use. I fenced what I stole. One transaction, boxes of transistor radios. I knew what I should get for them. Not that much, but I did not get close. Ripped off by a fence. That aggravation in me led to this: I would be a fence myself. Offer honest prices for dishonest goods. I learned. Using your word, I learned "stuff". You need for this business a stake. To borrow from sharks you must be three-quarters mad. How do I get the big paydays to establish myself in business?'

He allowed the question to hang in the air while they both sipped tea.

'How did you?' Quinn asked.

'I go to a boss. Tell to him my plan. He understands my heart. I was not leaving the life. Only a new path to walk on. I was not putting myself outside the influence. To help me build my stake, the boss hired me.'

'To do what?'

'To set fires.'

'Wait. What?'

'Restaurants I burned. Factories almost out of business, apartments under construction, bars that lost their license. Insurance scam. Also, intimidation or retaliation. The gamut, Quinn. I burned my way to success. Nobody was hurt. Sheer luck. I might have killed somebody. Killed children, the wee tots. I thank the Man Upstairs I did not.' Ezra pointed up. 'Blind and stupid I was. Young, like you, but more foolish. I made my money then walked away. Established my business.'

'You became a fence,' Quinn summed up.

'A surprise to you the people I meet in my profession.'

She didn't understand why he said that or why he was drilling her with a look.

'Like me?' she asked.

'You are one. Also, your father.'

'My father?'

'Your mother, too.'

'My mother!'

'In olden days. Do you know when your father left the rackets?'

'I do, yeah.'

'The day you were born.'

'I know. How come you do?'

'Before you, not even his most wonderful wife could stop him. Suddenly,' Ezra snapped his fingers, 'like that.'

'How do you know my father's my father?'

'When you walked in here, I did not. Then you told me more than I needed to know.' He looked at her slyly.

'My name.'

'How many Quinns and at your age? Your mom was an O'Quinn.'

'I was named after her.'

'Rachel Quinn Tanner. I heard about you three days after you were born. Your father, he gave to me a cigar to celebrate. Disgusting thing, a cigar. But I smoked. I shared in the good news of your arrival.'

'Wow.'

'Yes, wow. The cigar made me sick. The same day, he told me he was done. Easy, for him. He was a tough guy. He had a baby girl. I hope I have not betrayed him with you. In his old life he was a thief. You know this, right? A safecracker.'

'My mom told me when she was dying. She wanted me to look after him.'

'He didn't send you to me?'

'No! Have you told my father—?'

'Quinn. Look at me. Am I looking like an idiot?'

'I don't think you're an idiot.'

'Why would I betray you? Or break your father's heart? He quit the business to work in a factory, and that is how hard? He did this to be a good father to you. Am I supposed to tell him his daughter now follows in his original footsteps? I prefer that my bones not be broken.'

'OK, OK. Don't have a bird.'

'A fence, I became. Figured out how to move merchandise the safest way. At reasonable prices. I prospered. Years go by. I have no record as an adult. Clean as a whistle. Under my new name, that is the truth. I have a legitimate license to be a pawnbroker. An objection gets raised, an allowance is paid. Besides, friends I have.'

She scoffed at the word he used and repeated it. 'An allowance . . .'

'Say what you want. I am a legitimate pawnbroker. Some will become fences, tempted by stolen property. Their morals split at the seams like old pants. With me, I am a fence first, with a legitimate facade for my work. Everything is small time. No attention to me. I live a good life, better than deserved. Along the way, if I help a young person who is on the hard path, that gives my life something extra. I protected you, Quinn, *before* I heard your name. For sure, after.'

'I'm not arguing with you. Only trying to understand.'

He went on as if he was explaining it to himself. 'Maybe you had extra attention because your parents I admire. But I treated you with kindness from the start. Tell me no different.'

'Don't have a bird.'

'I work, I live, outside the law. That does not mean I have no heart. It does not mean I have no conscience a man can depend on for his life.'

'I never said you didn't!'

He was momentarily startled by her outburst. 'No, but still you wonder when I will grab you in the dark. Forget it. Instead, if you have business to do, Quinn, bring it to me. If you are smart.'

He tried to elicit a smile with his last remark, and she gave back a tepid one.

'One thing more, my young Quinn. I did not tell your father I know you. Believe me, he does not want to find that out. Do the same. Don't tell him you know me. I say this for your sake, and maybe for mine. Your father is a calm man. But a man no one wants to cross. You are my secret. I must be yours. We agree?'

'Agreed. Ezra, how come, if you're looking out for me, you never try to stop me stealing?'

He gave his chin a melancholy rub. 'To a man in a wheelchair, I'd like to say, "Pick up your chair and walk, don't run." When I do that, nothing happens. He keeps wheeling around. To the blind man, I say, "Here is mud in your eye. When I wipe it clean, you will see again." They never do. They stay blind. They do not appreciate me making their faces muddy, either.'

Through all her woes, he was causing her to giggle.

'Oh, they get so irritated. If I said to you "Stop, thief! Steal no more!", what would you do?'

She admitted, 'Tell you to eff off.'

'Why then I bother? If you want to quit the business, Quinn, quit. Quit. Quit. Quit. If you don't want to, no point for me to say "Quinn, it's time." Say nothing if you want, but if you want to tell me how big the trouble it is you are in today, say it. On a scale of one to ten, how big your trouble?'

She suppressed a quaver in her throat. 'Out of ten? A twelve. About. Fourteen?'

He inhaled sharply. 'That's a lot of trouble. What can you share?'

She decided that she liked tea. Perhaps in the old days her mother had her sample some. She sipped. She said, 'I had a boyfriend. He had a car. That was key because I needed him to be my getaway driver.'

'About this we talked. You progressed with that idea.'

'What doesn't make sense is, last night—'

'Not to tell me this.'

'Why? Is it on the radio?'

'A boy is found dead behind the wheel of his car.'

'That was Dietmar.'

'Oh no!' The old man's face had a look of sudden dismay. Then he seemed to pull himself together. 'On the radio, they did not say his name. He was murdered?'

'Killed when I was inside a house.'

'You didn't do it?'

'Hell no!'

'Sorry. I had to ask.'

'No, you didn't.'

'My sorry apologies. I am in shock. This is more than a twelve, Quinn.'

'I know.'

'It's like a twenty-six!'

'I know. Maybe a fucking forty!'

'Don't swear. You can steal, but don't swear. The police will learn about you, Quinn. They will talk to you. They will ask what you did today.'

'I went for a long bus ride.'

'Good. Good. They will want to know what you did last night.'

'I can't tell them that.'

'Stealing the baseball, you can't tell. This is a twenty-six. Or a forty.'

They sat in silence, the gravity of Quinn's predicament binding them together. Ezra leaned in closer and whispered. 'The baseball,' he said, 'must stay here. I will hide it for you. The ball, it can implicate you.'

'I can throw it down a sewer.'

The man considered the option. 'You never know when something that can be used against you, can be used for you.'

'That's what I need to learn,' Quinn whispered back. 'Stuff like that.'

Ezra solemnly nodded. 'Sorry to say you will find out. Quicker than you want.'

'I know.'

'No. What you think you know is what you don't know.'

As though to commence her education, he opened a drawer of the desk on his right. Removed a slim box, and from it a pair of nitrile gloves. He put them on. He asked, 'Gloves you were wearing when you entered the house last night?' She shook her head. 'Why not?'

Quinn shrugged. 'My prints aren't on file anywhere. I can't be traced.'

'They *are* on file, and you can be. The police have no name attached to your prints, not yet. Cops don't arrest thieves for one burglary. They wait to nail a crook for ten or twenty. Courts are not lenient on a crook who is active in his line of work. When they attach your name to your prints, they will have you for how many crimes, Quinn? One dozen? Two? Don't answer.'

He rubbed the baseball with his gloved hands and against his shirt.

'Do you see the name on the ball?'

'Jackie Robinson.'

'The other one. Mr Sal.'

'I saw it, yeah.'

'He's the man who gave me my first chance. The one I lit fires for.'

'No!'

'Trust me. This is not good news.'

'Why?'

'Never mind for now. Your prints are off this baseball. As are mine. Tell me, are your prints inside the dead boy's car?'

'I was in the car a lot.'

'After he was dead or only before? None of your prints with his blood?'

Quinn stared back at him. Her eyes widened.

'Quinn?'

After his visitor departed, Ezra flipped the sign on his window to *Ouvert*. Once a day he dusted, to keep ahead of the game, and that day he decided to do the guitars. First, he checked his watch. He allocated exactly twelve minutes to the task. After twelve minutes to the second, he quit.

Time enough to deflect suspicion if anybody had bugged his phone. He didn't want the visit and the phone call to be connected in anyone's head. None of this putting two-and-two together crap.

He doubted his phone was bugged, yet long ago he learned the virtue of assuming the worst. In his world, the criminal had a choice between two poisons: paranoia and prison. In his mind, one existed as the antidote to the other.

He went behind his counter and pulled his rotary-dial phone towards him. He dialed, patiently waiting for the rotor to tick back after each number. A male voice responded.

'Drop by for a tête-à-tête,' Ezra said. 'Something beneficial to the situation.'

'Tied up right now,' the man said.

'Hope you don't mean literal.'

'Not me. Can't speak for the poor sap who sits across. Open late?'

'As usual.'

'I'll come over after dinner.'

Neither said goodbye. Ezra returned the receiver to its cradle.

His gambit required skills at the height of his powers. His own life, not to mention Quinn's, could hang in the balance. He shouldn't be sticking his neck out, yet he planned to do just that. Not a matter of conscience. Only partly self-preservation. Sometimes a man arrived at a place in his life when he required a purpose, and Ezra's purpose from that moment forward – within reason – was to save Rachel Quinn Tanner from the mob. He had smoked a cigar to celebrate her birth. He'd be damned if he was going to stand by and watch her die. She didn't know it, but nasty men soon would gun for her.

If he could save her, good. He was no saint; if he also took a cut from his good deed, so much the better. Quinn had no clue what trouble followed her now. Only Ezra knew that. He alone could save her. Best if he preserved his own neck, too, as she had exposed it.

She was worried sick about the police. Yet her problems only started there.

At the opposite end of the spectrum, mobsters would be closing in.

Quickly.

Ezra knew exactly why Quinn's life lay in mortal peril. That made him twitchy and instilled within him a sense of urgency.

Clunker Free

(Meatballs)

Years had passed since Jim Tanner relinquished his clunker, selling it for the cost of the tow. Repair bills had been eating him alive, and parking on the streets of Park Ex in winter had become too damn frustrating. The snowbanks were mountainous. As a single dad, he accepted that he was dirt poor. No more wheels for him.

For a time, he bussed to work, until the day a coworker gave him a lift to the plant. A significant portion of employees at Continental Can lived in Park Extension. Ukrainians, Romanians, Hungarians. After that he chipped in a few bucks every week for gas and discovered that he'd landed a new pal. He had wanted a non-criminal friend. Gabor Szabo was unaware of Tanner's background and might not have cared. He knew him as a single dad who did his job at the plant, what else mattered?

Arriving home, Tanner wanted to say, 'Gabs, don't stop. Keep driving.' He couldn't say that. He could not admit that the two men clambering out of an unmarked car up ahead struck him as being detectives. They ignited in him an urge to flee as they walked toward his front door.

When he emerged from his friend's car, he reached back to pick up his lunch pail from the floor and looped his denim jacket over his forearm. Whatever was going on couldn't be about him. The other option was scarier. If cops were knocking on his door, his daughter might be in trouble.

At first, he hadn't thought of that. Suddenly, he did.

Jim Tanner strode quickly to his home. The detectives were giving up at that moment and coming away. He could let them leave without identifying himself, except that if this was about Quinn, he needed to know.

'My house,' he said. 'What's up?'

'Sir. Hello. I'm Sergeant-Detective Paul Frigault. This is Detective Marcel Caron.'

Caron, who had wild frizzy hair, extended his hand. Tanner shook it. Less willingly, Frigault did the same. Tanner introduced himself. He started in English, and both officers continued in that language.

'What's this about? My daughter? Is Quinn all right?'

'Is she home, sir?' Frigault asked him.

'You know better than me. I just got here.'

'She didn't answer. Mind checking? We can talk inside.'

If they were looking for her at home, that meant they weren't about to tell him she was in hospital or a jail cell. Tanner unlocked the door and from the narrow foyer shouted through the house. 'Quinn! You here? Quinnie!'

The three men listened to the ensuing silence. Tanner said, 'She's usually out when the weather's good. What's this about?'

The sitting room provided cramped quarters. Each detective took a seat and Tanner chose the sofa, perched forward, wary of their news.

'Do you know a young man named Dietmar Ferstel?' Frigault asked him.

'No. Who's he?'

'You don't know the name?'

'I'd remember a name like that. What does he have to do with Quinn?'

'They were boyfriend and girlfriend, some say.'

'Who says?'

'His family, his friends,' Caron told him.

'When was this?'

'Sir?'

'When they were ten? Last month? When?'

'Recently, sir. Current.'

'She hasn't mentioned him. Maybe she was trying him out. Why does it matter?'

'The boy was killed last night, sir.'

'Oh God.' Jim Tanner's hands had been raised. They dropped to his lap.

'To our knowledge, Quinn was the last to see him alive. We'd like to talk to her.'

Tanner couldn't immediately process the news. He'd been running ahead of himself, guessing at possible scenarios that might have precipitated this visit. This one never crossed his mind.

'Sorry, wha—? What happened? How was . . .? How did he die? Car crash?'

'He was murdered.'

'My God. Wait. Quinn wasn't involved. She was home last night.'

'When did she get home?'

Experience warned him to be careful. 'I'm not sure. I hit the sack early.'

'We want to talk to her. About the boy, about last night. Routine questions.'

'This isn't routine. But sure. She's usually home for dinner. Sevenish. Oh God, that's . . . bad news. I can give you a call.'

Caron was extending a card, which Tanner accepted.

'You never heard the name, Dietmar Ferstel?' Frigault probed again. 'Sir, is your wife home soon?'

'She passed. Cancer.'

'I'm sorry to hear that, sir.'

'I'll give you a call when Quinn shows up.'

Caron and Frigault were exchanging glances, as if trying to figure something out between them without resorting to direct communication.

'Something wrong?' Tanner asked.

Frigault made the executive decision for his cohort. 'My partner and me, we're already off-shift. If Quinn could call us tomorrow, we could set up a time to visit.'

'No problem.' He was already feeling a hundred percent better. They weren't gung-ho to interrogate his daughter. 'She'll call in the morning. I'll make sure.'

They shook hands on the stoop. Jim Tanner went back inside. He was starving and needed to think about dinner. Quinn enjoyed spaghetti. With meatballs. He had the fixings. He hoped she'd be home soon. God knows, they needed to talk.

He hoped she knew nothing about the murder. That he'd be breaking the news to her. That would be tough on her, but he hoped she knew nothing.

Jim Tanner changed from his work clothes and went into the kitchen. He put both hands on the sink to keep them from shaking. Two detectives had been seated in his house. The memories provoked were times he did not care to revisit.

Quinnie, he was thinking. *Quinn.*

He had to do something. He got busy on the meatballs.

Paying for the Mercy

(Touton's punk)

Sergeant-Detective Yves Giroux thought it a hoot when Cinq-Mars explained that his exit from the Night Patrol accounted for his inebriation and rank scent. Kept busy and feeling miserable through the morning and into the afternoon, Cinq-Mars was relieved when his new boss cut him some slack and sent him home early.

A small mercy, for which the younger detective was grateful, although Giroux made things clear as he went out the door. 'You owe me now.' A mercy, then, that would cost him.

He was suffering in the throes of a recent romantic breakup. Not utterly brokenhearted, yet his hopes for a better outcome had been dashed. He never told Armand Touton about being dumped, not wanting him to know that it played a part in his transfer. The Night Patrol had been a tremendous springboard to his career. The guys were tough, often ruthless, yet they defended the moral high ground with their lives. In a city of corrupt cops, no one on the Night Patrol accepted an illicit dime, not if he valued the existing contours of his bone structure. A farm boy, Cinq-Mars was tall and physically powerful – no martial arts training, only strength to burn and an inherent calmness amid chaos. Yet he wouldn't have wanted to take on Touton, certainly not when the man was younger and, out of respect, not at his retirement age, either. A tabloid's front cover, framed and signed, hung in the old man's office: a photograph of two fists side-by-side, Touton's and Rocky Marciano's. Ring rats agreed that the heavyweight champ's undefeated record might have been in jeopardy if he'd been up against the captain in a dark alley. A debate never to be resolved. Had they fought, one man or the other might have lost a legendary reputation.

Although Cinq-Mars thrived as Touton's protégé on the Night Patrol, a truth sailed home: working nights and sleeping days gave him little opportunity to meet the women he'd like to meet, as opposed to the ones he'd rather not. He needed to work the day shift to give his non-existent love life a chance. To Touton, he called it a career move. If the Old Man saw through the fib, he didn't mention it.

He moved into new digs in Park Extension, an area known to him when he first arrived in the city. The bedroom was cramped, the living room constricted his limbs. The kitchen was fitted out in miniature, and the bathroom had been constructed for elves. Technically, he had a tub. If he stooped, it could be used as a shower. Something he did not want to admit: the monkishness of the space appealed, as if, having failed lately at romantic love, he'd been thrown back into the cloister.

Cinq-Mars showered when he arrived home. Refreshed, he lay down nude upon his bed. The window behind the blind was open, but not a whiff of breeze stirred. Much later, half-dead to the world, he struggled to pull a sheet over himself.

The time of day conspired to deprive him of a lengthy snooze. Light shone around the edges of the blind, kids were noisily at play, and cars were on the move. Three hours after lying down, he sprung up again.

Partly, he was hungry. He also wanted a smoke. Quitting did not come without challenges.

Cinq-Mars alleviated his hunger pangs by reheating meat loaf. The sort of meal that was easy when coming off a 6:00 a.m. shift. He was counting on the essential aspects of his life – sleeping, eating, dating – to take on a measure of normalcy once he was ensconced on the day shift. Day One, he was chowing down leftovers and sleeping at a ridiculous hour, fitfully at best. Like always.

He went down the block to buy smokes.

He planned to stay in for the night. The evening air and the toxic energy that zapped through him when he bore away from buying cigarettes conspired to undermine the notion. His brain stirred. Thoughts buzzed like the itch in his bloodstream and started coming together. He focused on the robbery, the murder. Outside his flat, he shoehorned himself into his Volkswagen Beetle and drove to his new *poste* in the Town of Mount Royal.

The affluent suburb was situated within the confines of the larger city, a short hop from downtown and surrounded by poorer,

congested districts. His new station reflected its location. A fire
hall took up most of the building, next door to hockey and curling
rinks. At its back shone a baseball diamond, and beyond that the
high school's football and track field. The school itself stood
south of these playgrounds, with City Hall to the north. Open
air, open sky. The interior augmented the theme: more office
space than he'd ever known as a cop, the desks sitting wide apart.
The privileged few with offices of their own enjoyed spacious
rooms. In the shank of the evening, his impression was of a
clubhouse exhibiting the serenity of a library.

Murder within the Town of Mount Royal was colossal news.
The homicide contingent stationed there would idly twiddle their
thumbs most days were it not that they served a significantly
broader territory. Usually, the Town's troubles pertained to a
socially advantaged class rather than a criminal element. The
kids had access to drugs, cars, money and alcohol, in that order,
with a penchant for raising Cain. Cinq-Mars expected that he
might have to be a glorified babysitter. Compared to what he'd
been through on the Night Patrol, when the whole of the city
had been his turf between dusk and dawn, this new posting struck
him as being a walk through a nicely shaded park.

To begin with a robbery and a murder put the kibosh on that
expectation.

Which pleased him.

The night-shift captain was chewing an unlit cigar in the
common room.

'Captain Honoré, sir, I'm Émile Cinq-Mars, the new guy, days.'

'Touton's punk.'

His reputation could be a problem.

'Not anymore,' Cinq-Mars replied.

'Are you confused, Cinq-Mars? Can't break the habit?'

'Sir?'

'It's night. You work days now.'

'Just came in to access information.'

'Like what?'

'Fingerprint analysis for the robbery I'm working on with
Sergeant-Detective Giroux. It might've come in by now. I'd like
to check.'

'Planning to book overtime? Don't.'

'I wasn't thinking that way, sir. I booked off early. I owe hours.'

'No sweat up my crack. Do you know where to look?'

'Giroux's desk. I didn't want you to come across a stranger shuffling through his papers.'

'Usually I shoot those people. No, wait. I ignore them. No, wait, nobody's done that before. I don't know what I'd do. Good plan, talking to me first.'

Maybe he was trying to be funny, or maybe he thought he was being savvy. Cinq-Mars felt stymied in the man's company and waited to be dismissed.

'What?' The captain barked with the unlit stogie still wedged in his mouth. 'Do you require a guide to get lost?'

'I'm good,' Cinq-Mars said.

'Will miracles never cease?' He seemed to demand an answer to his question, then waved at Cinq-Mars with the back of his hand. 'Shoo,' he said. 'I'm thinking.'

Something he did not encounter at his previous station: a cop publicly admitting to being thoughtful. Cinq-Mars doubted that the rumination related to police work.

In the detectives' main room, he scouted around. No one present. The contingent pulling the night shift was small and, save for the captain, out on the job. The uniforms who briefly appeared were pushing paper. No one interviewed a witness or hauled in a suspect. Cinq-Mars identified Giroux's desk but did not head there. Finding out about the fingerprints at the scene of the robbery could have waited until morning, and there was nothing he could do with the information that night. In the morning, however, he would not have access to the vacant desk of homicide Sergeant-Detective Frigault. At night, he did.

In this suburban precinct, senior sergeant-detectives merited an office that had large windows to the interior, none looking outside, which made Cinq-Mars conspicuous going where he did not belong. He elected to brave it. As a newcomer, he could plead ignorance or error. The fingerprint evidence with respect to the murder interested him, and the file would have landed on Frigault's desk. If it arrived late in the day, he might be the first to have a peek. He easily found the document. Different sets of prints from the dead boy's car had been examined: None provided a positive ID beyond that of the victim.

Hearing footsteps, Cinq-Mars dashed through his reading. The cigar-chomping captain rambled down the hall. Unable to flee the office elegantly, Cinq-Mars stayed put. The captain remarked on his trespass. 'Touton's punk boy. Touton's boy,' he said, half under his breath, as if that held dire meaning. What he was seeing finally registered, and he turned on his heels. 'What're you doing in there?'

Nabbed, he chose to broach the truth.

'I'm comparing the fingerprints from the robbery with those from the murder. See if there's a connection.'

'Is there?' the cigar chomper demanded.

'Not here. Let me check Giroux's files.'

The captain kept a keen eye on him as Cinq-Mars hustled across the room, found the file he wanted on top of Giroux's IN tray, and gave it a quick study.

'Well?' Honoré asked when the new guy returned.

'No connection's been made,' Cinq-Mars informed the man.

'All right then,' the captain said.

'All right then, what?' Cinq-Mars asked.

'Get out of here. You're bothering me. Touton's punk is pissing me off.'

Cinq-Mars gave the captain an offhand, secretly discourteous, salute and decamped. He knew now that any plans for the evening were shot, for he had picked up an interesting tidbit. No connection had been made between the two crime scenes because none had been ordered. The files had been processed separately, not jointly. If a fingerprint in the murder case matched one from the robbery, that was unknown to all investigators. As well, an anomaly snagged his attention. He needed to run that down before returning to his flat and bed.

He was coping on adrenalin.

He planned to add a heavy dose of caffeine to the mix soon.

Cinq-Mars drove downtown to visit his old stomping ground.

Ezra's Visitor

(A bloody hand)

The bell above the pawnshop door welcomed a visitor. A man in a black suit entered. The bell jingled again as the door closed.

'Want I should lock up?' he inquired.

'How do I earn my living closed?'

'A yak in private, you wanted, Ezra.'

'I can stand the interruption if somebody wants to buy.'

'Your tone. I thought our talk was serious.'

'Only a serious man can have a serious talk, Arturo. Go in back.'

'I never told you I hate your back room?'

'Is it for you to like? Go in.'

The man at the door was Arturo Maletti, a soft-core punk in the local Ciampini syndicate. He possessed cachet by virtue of being a friend to a cousin of a cousin to a gang boss. On occasion, he participated in marginal rough stuff, earned a stripe that way, enough to strut down the street with his chin stuck out. His main claim to fame was legitimate: He did time for a crime he did not commit. He pulled twenty-nine months without naming the name that would have gotten him killed if he was foolish enough to repeat it. For the inconvenience of losing time off his life, he was handed a soft-dope territory to manage. That gave him the status he craved. Never to be a made-man, in the parlance of the trade, yet acknowledged as a trusted punk.

Swarthy, Arturo Maletti at thirty-one exhibited Italian machismo, in his mind. He preferred black suits and white shirts with broad stiff collars. The top buttons perpetually undone to show a tuft of chest hair. He was heavily gelled. A detriment: he trimmed his unibrow. Solid through the chest and shoulders, Maletti worked out, and augmented his look with bling: a silver-chain necklace, a gold nugget in one earlobe, a diamond stud in the other. Rings large enough to serve in lieu of brass knuckles if a situation warranted. His one liability contributed to his general insecurity: his eyes were remarkably close together. That gave him a bird-like appearance, damaging the overall impression he was gunning for.

Easily, he could snap the aging Ezra Knightsbridge like a barstool over a drunkard's noggin, as in a Wild West movie, yet he dutifully ventured into the back room and grabbed a seat. Ezra followed and plugged in the kettle. Waiting for the boil, he said 'Arturo.' Then slapped the young man hard across the face. Once. Violently. An imprint of fingers reddened on the visitor's left cheek.

Maletti jumped in his chair. 'What the—!'

Ezra slapped his other cheek – less hard, as he used his weaker left hand.

'Stop! What's the matter with you?'

Ezra lifted his right hand as though to strike a third blow. Maletti had learned, he kept his hands up for protection.

'What's wrong with *me*? What's wrong with *you*, Arturo? Why did you do that?'

'What'd I do?'

The younger man could deck the pawnbroker with his closed fist, and any argument between them would conclude. But rather than strike back, he guarded his face against more slaps.

Ezra attended to the tea. His guest was undeserving, so he poured a single cup. He sat, sipped his tea, and shook his head.

'What?' Maletti wanted to know.

'One question. You are out of your mind since when?'

'Why say that?'

'You sleep with Savina.'

The visitor remained silent a moment. 'You know that how?'

'How I know? Who else knows is your problem.'

Maletti figured the face-slapping had concluded and put his hands down. 'Who besides you?'

'Who came home early last night?'

'You know that?'

'Surprised? Tell me who.'

'The husband,' Maletti whispered.

'How did you get out in time?'

He shrugged. 'I left early. Luck, I guess.'

'If the husband found you in his bed, you would not be in

luck. Maybe he shoots you. Maybe you shoot him. Maybe nobody shoots nobody. No matter what, the world finds out that Arturo Maletti sleeps in Savina Vaccaro's bed. Then what?'

Embattled, the hood lifted and dropped his shoulders again. The gesture conveyed that he knew the answer but didn't want to say it out loud.

'You're dead, that is what. What's wrong with you, Arturo?'

He dipped his chin. 'I'm a man. She's a woman. It's not like this has not happened before in human history.'

Ezra put his tea down. He had to either do that or throw it at his guest. 'You are a punk. Did you forget? She is a married woman.'

'It's not like it never happened—'

'I don't want to hear your stupidity about history! Don't come to me like you're a philosopher now. Plato, you are? Her father is your *boss*. You, his *punk*. And *she* is married to a surgeon yet. Now, does the father – does he let the daughter – sleep with his *punk* when she is already married in her life to a surgeon?'

'She's not that happy with him.'

Ezra slapped the top of Maletti's head, the blow glancing off his scalp as he ducked.

'That means to me what? Nothing! The answer is, the father does not let this happen. Who does he prevent? His daughter? Savina? Or the punk from taking his next breath? Who?'

Maletti was reluctant to reply. 'I guess me,' he finally conceded.

'At least, you figured that out without it took ten years.'

He was still unable to fathom a large part of the discussion. 'How do you know?'

'Arturo, you're not here to ask questions. You're here to answer.'

'What am I supposed to answer?'

'Whatever I ask you, answer it,' Ezra advised him. He was rising to see who else had arrived. The bell above his front door was jingling. 'With the truth, Arturo. Nothing but.'

Out front, a young woman wanted to repurchase her violin. Ezra took her receipt, returned to the back room, located the instrument on a shelf, and concluded the transaction at the front counter. Then he returned to his other duty. Which he felt was going well, overall.

'Tell me everything from last night,' Ezra instructed his guest.

'What do you know already?'

'Don't ask stupid questions.'

Maletti sighed heavily, falling into troubled resignation.

'Like you said. Me and Savina, for old time's sake.'

'In old times, she was a single woman. You were a punk bum. Go on.'

'I left. I parked my car in Park Ex. Other side of the fence from where she lives.'

'I know where she lives.'

'I went to my car and saw the husband come home. That's it. That's all.'

No sooner had Ezra made himself comfortable in his chair than he stood again to root around in a tall box that had the lid cut off.

'What you looking?' Maletti asked him. 'I'm sorry if that's a question.'

'A stupid one.'

'What you looking?'

'A baseball bat,' Ezra informed him.

'For what, a bat?'

'Nothing but. That's what I told to you. That means, nothing but the truth. What do I get? Bull crap I get.'

Ezra retrieved a bat from the cardboard bin and wielded it. Not as though he was swinging at a pitch, more like a golfer lining up a tee-shot.

'I will crack your kneecaps,' he told his victim.

'Ezra, put the bat down.'

'Then your head. Crack it.'

'Put it down. What can I say if I don't know what you know yet?'

'Another stupid question. Answer me this. Which knee first?'

'Put it down, Ezra. I'm serious. I'll talk to you, no problem.'

The pawnbroker returned the bat to its place, then returned to his seat.

'Let me explain to you,' he said, 'why it is good to hold back nothing. Hold back, I will know you are a liar. Can you count to two? Number one. You cause me trouble. If I don't find a way out of my trouble, I have no choice. To save my skin, I will speak to Mr Ciampini. When I do that, you are deader than a man already in his grave one year. What choice I have? Number two—'

'Ezra. Please.'

'You cannot lie to me when you try. Last night, you were with Savina, like I told you. Am I right or not wrong? Tell to me.'

'We covered that already.'

'Right or not wrong, Arturo?'

'You were right. You weren't wrong.'

'You heard a noise. When you bounce-bounce with Savina. You go downstairs naked. In one hand, your dick. Other hand, your gun. Right or wrong?'

Maletti was disturbed now by the way their talk was progressing. He complained, 'I wasn't holding my dick.' He denied no other aspect, shocked by Ezra's knowledge.

'So scared, your dick shrunk. Too small for you to find. So, you walked with a gun. In Savina's house. If it was the husband, if he came home and made noise, would he be dead today?'

Maletti had a glimmer. 'Was it the husband?'

'Was he the one hiding? In his own house? What you think?'

'I don't know. Was it the husband?'

'Lucky for you, you had a gun. Maybe he was there. Maybe he saw the gun. Maybe he left. Then you left. Then he comes back, not for the first time early. A coincidence, the timing?'

'Ezra. What are you saying? Was it him?'

'Did you talk to Savina today? Were you a good boy, you called?'

'She called me. When she was free.'

'She was still alive? Good. Then it was not the husband. You know that much.'

No doubt Maletti would have preferred to conceal his sigh of relief, but he failed. He tried to breathe normally, failing again. A new thought slipped into his head, which he presumed to be correct, a knowledge that did not set him free. Sheepishly, he said, 'Somebody was in the house. That's what you're saying. One of yours? From your gang of kiddie thieves? One of your juvenile delinquents?'

'You were one of mine yourself.'

'I grew out of it. I do better things now.'

'A matter of opinion.'

'I'm doing good. You don't think so?'

'Sleeping with the boss's daughter, that's good? You could lose your life. Screw this up, you could cost me mine, too.'

'Yours? How come?'

'Because I haven't turned you in and I don't plan to. I'm protecting you. That's the only way I can protect who you call my kiddie thieves. My skin I'm risking, Arturo, to save yours. Indicate to me you know what I'm talking about.'

Outwardly, Maletti took the news in stride. Inwardly, he was baffled. He was trying to determine exactly how the events of the previous night affected him.

'Tell me again, Arturo, about last night. This time the whole truth, nothing but, or I will use my bat to teach you a lesson you won't forget before midnight. After that, you're so mental, I don't know.'

Both men held the threat to be idle. Maletti might submit to a face-slapping by the man who had introduced him to a life of crime, but not to a serious drubbing. If Ezra swung a bat in the younger man's vicinity, he'd be thrown through a wall. The overture to violence merely underscored the imperative that truth be spoken.

The story that Maletti related confirmed Quinn's recollection of what had happened. He had departed the premises early, unnerved by the noises he and Savina heard, which they were thinking came from downstairs, although they eventually convinced themselves it was the street. Leaving, he noticed a car parked along the hedge with a driver inside. Peculiar at that hour because businesses in the area were closed. Maletti had been trespassing in another man's house, he'd heard an unexplained noise, and he was a small-time hood sleeping with the married daughter of a gang boss. He was concerned. He waited in his car to see what the other driver might do. He saw someone come along the fence, on the far side which made identification impossible through the hedge. That person stopped at the car. Then quickly went on. A second person – he used the word 'boy' to describe him – whom he noticed under the street lamps was blond, also stopped at the car. This one got in. Then jumped out again. Arturo Maletti found that weird. Weirder, the second person snuck in behind the car when another vehicle came down the street. That turned out to be the husband's car, and the husband drove it onto his driveway. A close call, normally he'd still be in Savina's bed. After the husband had parked and gone inside, the person hiding near the car looked in the car again, maybe spoke to the driver, then departed. Maletti was overwhelmingly curious. Was this a pusher, the guy in the car? Someone horning in on his turf? Or someone spying on Savina, to find out who was sleeping in her bed? That possibility made him nervous. Should he run? Should he shoot himself in the head? If the husband had hired a spy, he could take care of that. But what if her crime boss dad had done the hiring? A very different outcome, depending. Maletti was too curious. He had to go see.

He found that the driver behind the wheel of the car was a dead boy. He got out of there fast.

'Except I got my hand bloody.'

'What?'

'How was I supposed to know the car was covered in blood? My hand went inside.'

'By itself? You idiot.'

'So I smeared my prints. Over the inside of the door . . .'

'Less of an idiot. All this because you could not stay out of Savina's bed.'

'You have no idea, an old man like you. We're special, me and her. Honest to God, Ezra, she's not happy in her life.'

'Get that out of your head, Arturo. You are not being in her life.'

He seemed sullen, saddened.

'I'll break it off,' he said.

'Not yet you won't.'

'Why not?'

'The timing. You want her to think nothing. You want her to think the dead boy outside her house and her husband home early had nothing to do with you. Quit her right now, she might wonder something different. Put time between last night and when you break up. Don't fit those two things together. Just be careful. Remember who you are dealing with. Savina is not Snow White, even in a blizzard. The husband, what about? Does he suspect?'

'How would I know?'

'You live in his house at night.'

'I have a question. How many of them were yours?'

'Them? Mine? Make sense to me.'

'How many were your thieves? The dead boy in the car? The first guy who went by? The second? If the driver was not dead already, one of those two did it. How many were your kiddie thieves?'

'Don't ask stupid questions. Especially, don't ask that. Are you hearing me when I talk? We're done here for now. Go. I'll do my best to keep you alive. I'm keeping my mouth shut. Do the same.'

'Twenty-nine months I did inside. Never said boo.'

'Under threat of death, not so hard. A medal you want? Do it again. This time, not for twenty-nine months. This time it is forever, and a lot longer time after that.'

'Ezra. Please. How did you know it was me?'

'Who else can be so stupid? Besides, always she was crazy about you. Something that life cannot explain.'

Ezra felt pleased as Arturo Maletti departed his premises. With luck and a soupçon of ingenuity, he could pin the murder on him. Whether such a gambit would prove necessary remained to be determined. Good to have the option.

He refreshed his cup.

Smashing Bones

(The total absence)

D r Eudo Lachapelle had landed in Canada from Belgium in lamentable disgrace. A scandal festered in his wake that in his new land would never be divulged.

He stepped onto a pier in Montreal seeking to remake his life, although surely not from scratch. To his dismay, he learned that he was not to be a licensed physician in his adopted country without returning to the study of medicine. The difficulty with that proposition, apart from the insult attached to his credentials, was poverty. He'd been permitted to exit Europe with his skin intact only after his properties had been sold and his accounts emptied. To enroll at a university in his new country seemed inconceivable when he had access to neither food nor shelter. His energies were invested in dashing from pillar to post for a snack and temporary lodging, and in railing against the system.

With a flair for bluster, he complained to anyone in authority that his adopted land was passing up a singular opportunity for enrichment.

To many, Eudo came across as a bore; others responded with sympathy to his plight. He managed to endear himself to the men arbitrating his grievance at the Collège des Médecins du Québec. Still, rules were rules, and Dr Lachapelle floundered under the weightiness of the law.

Prematurely white-haired, with an impressive handlebar mustache, overly large brightly-rimmed eyeglasses, and an angular visage with outsized ears, he augmented the eccentricity of his appearance with a penchant for histrionics. The lack of care afforded him by his new compatriots, he stated without embarrassment, was reminiscent of Napoleon's banishment to Elba. The assault on his intellectual integrity was depriving the Province of Quebec of its most learned and illustrious physician. He was willing to transform the study of medicine on this side of the Atlantic. A student again? He should be handed a professorship! He was not requesting that a jury of his peers bend rules to favor him: He insisted that the rules be incinerated in a public blaze.

In the meantime, he found shelter in a storeroom in the rear of a bar where he successfully cadged drinks. Still, no license.

Eventually, Eudo's daily agitations elicited an offer of employment. While he would not be permitted to examine patients without taking the prerequisite study, he would be allowed to participate in the police laboratory and assist in their morgue. No living person would be entrusted to his care, but stewards determined that he was unlikely to do significant harm to the dead.

They were right.

Dr Lachapelle took to the cadavers with such relief that he never stepped into a classroom in order to be licensed by the Collège.

His eccentricities caused a few officers on the Night Patrol to pull their hair out – one attacked him with a femur – but Cinq-Mars enjoyed both him and his capable assistant, the skittish Huguette Foss. Hu had mousy hair pulled back along the side of her scalp and drawn forward over the shoulders and around her throat. Under her bangs, her face appeared encircled by an oval picture-frame of hair. On the street, her manner suggested the personality of a timid waif. In the lab, she was a crackerjack: quick, incisive, witty if anyone caught what she murmured under her breath; and with Cinq-Mars and others, flirty. In Émile's and Huguette's running repartee, they celebrated the mythic day when they'd be free to run away to Spain – Hu's choice of country. Cinq-Mars was one of the few people aware that Eudo and Huguette were mutually exclusive, having once interrupted their congress in the lab. Perhaps the age difference of twenty-three years embarrassed them, or perhaps being friends only in public suited them, or it was a professional choice. Cinq-Mars played along with the charade.

As Émile entered the lab that night, Eudo shouted a joyous greeting. He was often boisterous in the eerie silence of the basement enclave. Oddly, Huguette had nothing to say, no quips, and bore out of the room as if Cinq-Mars had admitted a virus.

'What hauls you down to our murky gloom?' Eudo called out. 'You've departed our company for the sunny side of the street. Abandoned your witches and ghouls, not to mention our preening prostitutes and midnight muggers, and our sweet drunken derelicts with their kitsch tunes. You have distanced yourself from the company of our manic murderers, Émile. For what? To investigate the theft of car radios? *Hurry!* A bracelet has gone missing from the tennis court! I had always assumed you were a vampire who sleeps in a coffin by day. Yet now, you stumble among the living wearing suntan oil.'

'A vampire, Eudo? Nice.'

'The nose, Émile. You have considerable Bela Lugosi in your face.'

'Thanks again. What the heck happened to Huguette?'

'She's on a mission, Émile. What brings you down here, you betrayer of your nocturnal cohorts?'

'Fingerprints,' Cinq-Mars stated.

'Whose?'

'A murder took place last night. Town of Mount Royal.'

'Night murders no longer concern you, Émile.'

'When the sun came up, I was called to a home robbery.'

'And the murder?'

'Discovered by the light of day. Fingerprints were taken from both crime scenes.'

'By the day squad, Émile, from the Mount Royal *poste*. Not by me.'

'I know that. Eudo, the two crimes were not compared, one to the other. Could you do that for me? For old time's sake?'

'They should have been compared,' Eudo grumbled.

'Two investigations, two sets of detectives. That's how it goes on the day shift.'

Eudo removed a hammer from a drawer and took it to a table where a lone bone fragment awaited inspection. He covered it in cloth, then smashed it.

'What did you do that for?'

'The exercise.'

'Eudo?'

'I can do the fingerprint comparison. Are they here, at this station?'

'You'll have to make a call. I memorized the file numbers.'

'Did you?' Eudo held up a bone fragment to a light. He nodded. Then looked over at his younger colleague. 'You memorize file numbers. Which means what?' He smiled. 'You don't have access to the files yourself.'

'All in the pursuit of justice, Eudo.'

'I'm up for that, some days.' Putting the bone fragment down, he crossed his arms and tucked his fists under his armpits. 'You didn't need to make the trip, Émile. Any technician can help you. Tell your Uncle Eudo. What are you up to? Are you lonely for the nightlife? Do you miss us?'

First, Cinq-Mars asked, 'Why did you smash that bone?'

'I didn't.'

'I saw you.'

'Oh that. Why are you investigating a homicide and not bicycle theft? What does that get you?'

'I said. The homicide might be related to my burglary.'

'Let the big shots from homicide investigate your robbery. Any other way around is backwards.'

'I'm not stopping them. Why bash the skull? What does that get you?'

'I was testing the hammer.'

'Of course you were.'

'This,' he motioned with his chin to indicate the hammer, 'is a ball peen. Over here,' he returned to his drawer and lifted out different hammers for his show-and-tell, 'I have a claw, a cross and straight peen, a cross-peen pin and, for the brute within us all, a club hammer. What are their various effects upon a skull, Émile? Now that I have met your criteria, tell Uncle Eudo what you're up to.'

Cinq-Mars had a vague sense that Eudo Lachapelle was stalling. What was going on with him? Talking gibberish? Smashing skull fragments? Émile brought his own question forward again. 'Last night, the dead man was sitting behind the wheel of a parked car.'

'How was he killed?'

'Knife to the chest.'

'Knives do kill. They are dangerous that way.'

'The thing is, on the passenger side door – on the interior panel – is a blood smear. Someone deliberately smeared the blood, most likely to obscure the fingerprints. In the opinion of the daytime tech, the smearing obliterated any chance of getting a print.'

'But Mr Oh-So-Smart Guy, you think otherwise?'

'Anyone who took the trouble to smear the prints had a reason. Such as, his prints are on file. I was wondering, even if there's only a bit of fingertip showing and maybe a different side of the same finger somewhere else, perhaps a whole print can be stitched together? What do you think? If there are bits of several fingers, you could make a match that way, no?'

Eudo raised an eyebrow and prolonged the gesture.

'What?' Cinq-Mars questioned him. 'A longshot, but doesn't it make sense?'

'Hate to tell you this, Émile.' He picked up the cross-peen pin hammer and returned to his smashing table. Another skull fragment cracked under a blow. 'The Mounties had a case where fingerprints were deliberately smudged. Their lab lifted a corner from this finger, a snippet from the hand, a tiny bit of the tip off the pinkie. Nothing definitive, but enough for the Mounties to make an arrest.'

'That's what I'm looking for.'

'Is it? The match did not stand up in court. The technicians explained how the whorl off the side of the thumb, the tented arch off the tip of the forefinger, and the partial double swirl on the ring finger all pointed to the killer. How did the judge rule? Too great a chance for error. Threw it out.'

'Eudo, that's down the road. I want to know who to arrest.'

'True. Fine. I'll requisition the prints. Is the car, or the door panel, in our possession? Or only photographs?'

'Both, I presume.'

He brushed his flowing mustache with the fingertips of both hands while deciding. 'I'll look. Render an opinion. Fair warning, I can only check fragments against local felons. Burglars. Murderers. A short list. With fragments, an extended check takes eons. Literally. Someday, I'm told, a machine to do the search will exist. Hard to imagine. The size of a bank. A computer, it will be called. By then I'll be gone to my just reward.'

Suddenly, the lights went out.

'What's going on?' Cinq-Mars asked.

'Power outage. Happens often.'

He'd been downstairs in a power failure before. Why weren't the emergency lights on? He heard a door opening. He turned. Lights were on in the hall. Shadows moved. A figure, then several, scooted through the door, bent over. Marauders in the morgue.

Lights snapped back on again and the roar that ensued practically lifted Émile Cinq-Mars out of his skin. There stood Huguette, an impish, devilish grin on her face, surrounded by about twenty elite detectives from the Night Patrol. They were roaring at him. No other word for it. Roaring. Cinq-Mars saw the beer, wine and whisky hauled in and ready to be poured.

Touton had given him a private send-off. These guys had missed out. Cinq-Mars could only pray he'd survive their turn.

One small mercy. The total absence of showgirls.

Confetti Money

(Red wine)

When Quinn arrived home, her dad was sitting up past his usual bedtime.

'Where've you been?' He tried to moderate his dread.

'Who's asking?'

'I'm your father, for crying out loud.'

'Not what I meant.'

'What did you mean?'

'You never ask me where I've been. I mean like you're somebody different. It's a joke.'

'Used to be I could count on you being at a game.'

'Used to be,' Quinn said. She went to the pantry, hauled out a box of cereal.

That seemed to awaken her dad from his coma. 'I made spaghetti and meatballs. You want, I can warm them up.'

'No thanks. I'm kind of hungry, but not. Maybe later.'

'Sure. Like in the middle of the night. Quinn, the police were here today.'

She stood frozen a moment. Then continued to shake out her Cheerios. 'I know why,' she said.

'You have a boyfriend?'

She sat down opposite him. 'We went out a few times. His name was Dietmar. Somebody killed him, Dad.'

'Quinn.' Jim Tanner scratched a side of his forehead. They didn't have formal father-daughter talks. Instead, they communicated in brief asides, snippets of news, sudden bursts of chatter unrelated to anything pertinent in their lives. They got along but had found a way to communicate without saying much. 'Were you there?'

She shrugged a shoulder. 'If I was, I'd be dead, too, I guess. Or maybe Deets would be alive.' She poked around in her Cheerios with a spoon. Quinn recognized that flip didn't strike the right tone. If she was to stay on top of this exchange, she needed to ease off her usual sass. 'I wasn't there. OK? He was a really sweet boy. He didn't deserve that.'

Her voice broke then. Tears surprised her by springing up so quickly and forcefully. She came out of her seat. Jim Tanner adjusted his own chair and she fell onto his lap like she used to as a child. He held her. Only after a minute had passed did she grasp that she was way too big for him now, and for the kitchen chair, and she struggled back up. She wiped her eyes and sat back down in her seat.

Jim Tanner was too stunned to speak.

Quinn could tell that her dad was fighting to find a way back into the conversation. Questions, worries, doubts swarmed through him.

'The police want to speak to you,' he managed to say finally.

'I promised you'd call in the morning. I got a card. Name and number.'

Throughout the day, she had feared a tap on the shoulder. A badge in her face. Handcuffs. A squad car. Making bail. Who knew how to do that? She imagined calling her dad from jail. That the cops were willing to wait for her to call lightened her burden. She might pull this off, get away scot-free. Fingers crossed and hope to die.

'You have to call them, Quinn.'

'I will.'

'You were the last to see him alive, they said.'

'The killer had to be the last person, Dad. The last time I saw him, Deets was fine.'

'Yeah. Were you going out a long time?'

'Not long. He was in . . .' She stopped herself, partially overcome, partially aware of a sleight of hand inside her head. 'He was in Social Studies.'

'College kid.'

She wanted to tell her dad that she had a boyfriend who was a university student, that she'd come up in the world. He'd be proud of her that way, perhaps be more receptive to her guy. Yet the notion was seriously out of whack – Dietmar was dead. He lost his life working for her. Not something she could talk about to her father.

'Yeah,' Quinn acknowledged.

Jim Tanner decided to warm up the spaghetti and meatballs for his daughter whether she wanted the meal or not. He knew something about a young person's appetite. If he put good food in front of her, she'd devour it. She thought she wasn't hungry because she was sad and upset, but she might find out differently.

'You used to watch baseball a lot,' her father said.

'The Expos, yeah.'

'The local boys, too. The juniors.'

'Not so much anymore.'

'We used to play catch a lot, you and me.'

'Fun. Good times.'

'I played baseball in the old days.'

'You played third. Catcher, a bit.'

'Second-string. First string at third. I enjoyed watching the old Royals.'

'We have the Expos now, Dad. The majors. Not Triple-A anymore.'

'You think I don't know? That Rusty Staub, he's a good one. Like the man said, "What's a *staub*? And why do we need a rusty one?" I like that joke. Mack Jones, he's gone. I liked him. I like this new kid, Parrish.'

'He's a hunk. He's so gorgeous. My god.'

'That I don't know. And Barry Foote. He'll be good.'

'You like third basemen and catchers.'

She didn't know why he was going on about this. Probably he just needed to talk. Or, he was working his way around to something, which might have to do with her and her dead boyfriend and the police.

'The Royals had Drysdale one year. Dick Williams, he's a manager in the bigs. I remember when they brought him in to play short for the Royals. He joined the team in Havana. Had a good first game. Two hits. One a double. A spark plug, Sparky Anderson, he played second. He's a manager now, too. That guy with the TV show, Chuck Connors, he played first.'

She was beginning to wonder if he wasn't having a breakdown.

'Are you all right, Dad?'

'Jim Dandy. You?'

'I'm fine,' Quinn said. 'Maybe a few guys on the Expos today will be managers tomorrow.'

'You never know. Tommy Lasorda. He's a manager now. He pitched for the Royals. A lefty. He took Drysdale under his wing when he was here. I could coach third base for the juniors, Quinn. I got asked.'

'What?' So that was it. 'How did this come up?'

'I been asked before. I said no. I got asked again.'

'When?'

'Tonight.'

'Who by?'

'The field manager called me. Gus Jornet. You know him?'

'I know him. He's a . . .' She stopped herself. He looked at her. 'Dad, I'm not allowed to swear in the house, right?'

'I promised your mother.'

'So I don't. Neither do you. Maybe on the shop floor you swear. I bet you do. Maybe in the lane a word comes out of my mouth. It'll happen. But I'm going to swear this one time in the house—'

'No, you're not,' he corrected her, forgetting how stubborn she could be, and what little authority he'd exercised through the years.

'Jornet, Dad, the manager, he's a . . .' Once again, she stopped herself. She would have thought otherwise, yet when push came to shove, she did not have the audacity. 'The c-word, Dad. Not the one for a man.'

'Quinn! Don't you dare say that word!'

'I didn't!'

'Get it out of your head!' He shook the spoon at her, the one he was using to stir the meatballs. Red sauce splattered across the floor.

'Dad! Watch what you're doing!'

'Get it out of your head!'

'All right! I didn't say it. But that's what he is. Coach Jornet is a c-word. The word for women.'

'Oh, will you please—?'

'Ask yourself, why am I saying that? Think. He used to coach the juvenile team. Before that, the midgets. How old are they, Dad? How old? Think. I hung around those teams. Your daughter. Around that age, I had a clue. Since then, I had it confirmed. Confirmed, Dad! Coach Jornet is a c-word for women.'

He stared at her, then went back to stirring the meatballs in their sauce. He turned on the burner under a second pot to boil water for the noodles. 'I'll kill him,' he said.

'I took care of it,' she told him, the words out before she could stop herself.

He looked over his shoulder at her. 'What's that supposed to mean?'

'Nothing.'

He turned. For once in his life, he stared her down. 'What does that mean, Quinn?'

'Nothing! I broke into his car. He left his wallet in the glove box during games. Safer than the clubhouse, which is like an open invitation to thieves. Money, credit cards, driver's license, the whole nine yards. I took his wallet and went down to the expressway. I ripped his stuff into bits and dropped them off the overpass, like confetti. The money, too. I wasn't taking nothing that belonged to that c-word for women.'

He gazed at her and pictured her doing all that and wondered who this woman could be. Not his little girl. 'When he asked me, years ago, to coach, I didn't want to interfere in your life. You were at the ballpark a lot back then. I didn't want to be in your way. I thought I should be home for you, when you came home. You're older now. I thought, maybe it would be all right now. Me, coaching third.'

'Dad.'

'Don't worry. I won't. I might kill him instead.'

'Don't do that, either. Like I said. I took care of it. I left his wallet on a railway track. Oh, and maybe I keyed his car a little.'

'You keyed his car? Who are you?'

That made them both laugh, through tears flooding their eyes.

'Don't do anything, OK? I don't want you in jail. I need you around. For your spaghetti.'

'You're growing up. Spaghetti goes good with red wine.'

'I'm underage, still.'

'Right. If you're underage, I'm the middleweight champion of the world.'

'Really? You think you can take Monzón?'

'You know Monzón? He's a great champ.'

'You can take him.'

'Not in this lifetime. But saying that makes you not underage.'

'That makes no sense.'

'Cops on my doorstep looking for my daughter makes no sense.'

'Dad, come on, I'll call them. But there's nothing I can tell them.'

'Red wine. In the pantry. Pour.'

She went looking. 'Is this that homemade stuff from the Italians down the lane? It's terrible!'

'How do you know it's terrible? It is, but how do you know?'

'They let us kids drink it. They don't think it's wrong. It's a different culture.'

'Top shelf. A real bottle with a real label. Not the rotgut from down the block.'

'Thank God.' She found it.

'Tonight, we'll be a different culture. Your mom enjoyed red wine.'

'Did she?'

They so rarely mentioned her. They both thought of her constantly and yet kept those reminiscences private.

They had a good time. When they both headed off to their bedrooms, they were rosy and laughing. Quinn had to promise to call the police in the morning, which put a damper on her mood as the dizziness in her head hit the pillow.

Homicide Won't Know

(The fireball)

His skull felt like the clapper inside the Liberty Bell. Once again hungover, a morose Émile Cinq-Mars met his station commander for the first time. He wore sunglasses, which he declined to take off. Captain Pierre Delacroix tore a strip off his hide and demanded for a third time that he remove the sunglasses 'in-fucking-doors!' He brayed an assessment to the entire *poste*: 'Now we know why he got his soggy ass kicked off the Night Patrol.'

He objected to the description 'soggy', but feebly. And thought, 'Saggy, not soggy.' Though he didn't approve of that description, either.

Second day on his new job and he was being sent home. Sergeant-Detective Yves Giroux watched him go out the door. Back-to-back epic hangovers provoked suspicion.

Home, Cinq-Mars slept it off in a comatose stupor.

The telephone woke him. A buzz-saw slicing through his scalp.

'Yeah, what?' he answered. He slurred both words.

'Get washed, shaved, feed yourself. Picking you up in forty minutes.'

The commands struck him as reasonable, yet he had to ask, 'Who's this?'

'Shit-bucket, it's Giroux.' His partner hung up before Cinq-Mars acquiesced to the edict. He sat up to verify that he remained ambulatory.

In the shower, the water assailed his chest. Twenty minutes passed before he stooped to wet his head. He was daydreaming of a tommy-gun from an old Al Capone movie. Rat-a-tat sound effects. In his fantasy, he lined up ex-cohorts from the Night Patrol and replicated the St Valentine's Day Massacre.

He passed an electric razor over his jaw and chin. Dressed. Slapped peanut butter onto bread and wolfed it down.

He was standing by the curb when Giroux pulled up.

Checked his watch. He realized he'd slept with it on and worn it in the shower. Five forty-one. Late afternoon. An entire day lost.

He burrowed into the car.

They drove as far as the corner before anyone spoke.

'How'd you know where I live?' he asked Giroux.

'I'm one helluva detective, Cinq-Mars.'

'I'm not in the book.'

'You're in mine.'

'Where're we going?'

'That's your fault, too.'

'Ah. Excuse me? What is? I was in bed all day.'

'About that. You work *days* now, Cinq-Mars. *Nights* you sleep. Figure that one out in a hurry.'

'Last night, it was the whole damn Night Patrol.'

'I called. I got the story. Relayed it to the cap. Your ass survives for one more day, max.'

Cinq-Mars didn't believe him. Then he did and thanked him. He asked, 'Where we going?'

'You asked that already.'

'You didn't answer.'

'The fingerprints match, Cinq-Mars.'

'Who matches?'

'Not who. What. The robbery to the murder. Homicide doesn't know yet. They may never.'

'Why don't they? You're saying there's no name?'

'Still drunk? Catch up. Fingerprints are all over the passenger side of the car. Including in the blood. Those prints are a match for whoever went up the wall and into the house. What does that tell you?'

Cinq-Mars wasn't turning over information in his head with his customary élan. 'A buddy. A pair of thieves.'

'Could be. Who'd be in the car a lot? Frigault and Caron asked around for us. About the dead boy. Visited his family. Talked to friends. Did their job.'

'They weren't asking around for *us*.'

'A detail. The dead boy had a girlfriend. Who rides in a car if not the girlfriend? If those are her prints in the car, why are they also up the side of the house? If they're not hers, she can probably tell us who drives around in her boyfriend's car at night.'

Giroux was circling to navigate the one-way streets. They stopped outside a tiny detached house on Bloomfield Street.

'You talked to Frigault and Caron,' Cinq-Mars pointed out. 'They're cooperating with you. Not you with them. How does that work?' When Giroux didn't volunteer a reply, he tried a different tack. 'The girl. Anything of interest?'

'A phone call between her and Frigault.'

Cinq-Mars looked over and his partner fluttered his lips.

'Lazy, huh?' Giroux confirmed. 'They got what they wanted to hear. Dietmar Ferstel was a sweet boy. She saw him late that night but not for long. He had somewhere to go. Didn't say where. If she's broken up about it, they couldn't tell because they weren't in the same room. They were on the goddamned phone.'

The two men emerged from the car. 'They told you all that,' Cinq-Mars pointed out. 'They're cooperating, Yves. You don't reciprocate?'

'They told me squat. My eyes happened to wander across a file left lying around. Maybe on Frigault's desk. Maybe the breeze blew it open and I caught a glimpse. You owe me big time now, Cinq-Mars, did I mention?'

'For what?'

'I called a buddy on the Night Patrol. Pay attention. I heard what they did to you. Otherwise, Delacroix would've stuck your shield where you don't dare pull it back out. You think I mean someplace nasty? I mean like in your right eye. When it comes to drunks, he's a total psychopath. I explained about the Night Patrol giving you no choice. I was convincing. Delacroix said you can stick around, hanging by a thread. I'm supposed to put it to you that way, he said. The thread part. The hanging part, too.'

Cinq-Mars conceded. 'I owe you a favor or two.'

They were at the front door. 'Ring the bell, Cinq-Mars. Conduct the interview. Show me what you got.'

'You didn't answer my question.' Cinq-Mars pressed the buzzer.

'Which one?'

'What's my fault?'

'It was you who asked the lab to match the fingerprints. The night boss told me you came in. I'm blaming you for that. Between you and me, I'm not complaining. Just like you're not complaining about me reading a wide-open file on a desk.'

'Frigault's desk is not exactly out in the open.'

'Split hairs. I heard you were in his office, too,' Giroux carried on.

'The file was not accessible.'

'Are you going to shut up about that in this decade?'

The door was opening. Before them stood a tall willowy blond, quite young, her eyes darting between them. 'Yes?' she asked. Then she grew more challenging. 'Who're you?'

'Nice house, sweetie,' Giroux replied. He made up his mind about her on the spot. 'Really? You prefer prison to this pretty place?'

Cinq-Mars displayed his badge before his partner gummed up his interview. 'Police, miss. I'm Detective Cinq-Mars. This is Sergeant-Detective Giroux. May I ask your name?' He didn't know. His partner hadn't told him even that much.

'Quinn Tanner. I talked to the police already.'

'Only on the phone,' Giroux interjected.

'You were a friend of . . .' Cinq-Mars had a hard time keeping non-French names in his head. He turned to his partner for assistance.

Quinn answered for him. 'Dietmar Ferstel.'

'She should know,' Giroux chipped in. 'The girlfriend. Even money says we'll find her footprints on the ceiling of the boy's car.'

Cinq-Mars moved over to stand in front of his partner. 'May we have a word?'

'That man can stay outside.'

'He wants to sound tough. That way I'll seem nice to you and you might be willing to talk to me. We don't need to play those games, though, right?'

Gut instinct, the girl was clever and savvy. Meeting her on her own terms might have merit. Her blood was boiling. He couldn't blame her. She stared at him with a judgmental gaze and tried to look over his shoulder at the one she already despised, except that Cinq-Mars was too large to permit a view. She finally gave a shrug, opened the door wider, and let them in.

'That's it from you,' Cinq-Mars said.

The girl said, 'Sorry?'

'Nothing,' he said. 'Having a word with my partner.'

Giroux was all smiles, Cheshire-cat like.

'That *better* be it from him,' Quinn Tanner tacked on. She led them into the living room, a small, tidy space with scant light. She turned on her heels to face them. She clutched her left elbow with her right hand. 'I spoke to the police this morning.'

'On the phone,' Giroux cut in. 'Like that counts.'

'Yves,' Cinq-Mars censored him, 'I'll conduct the interview. As we agreed.'

'Conduct. Pretend I'm not here.'

'I wish,' the girl said.

'First,' Cinq-Mars said, 'you have my condolences on your loss. Was, ah . . .'

'Dietmar.'

'Was he your boyfriend for a long time?'

'Part of the summer. He was super sweet.'

'Tell her, Cinq-Mars,' Giroux insisted.

This time he censored his partner with a look, and Giroux backed off.

'Do you have identification, Miss Tanner?'

She shrugged. 'Sure.'

'She told us who she is,' Giroux pointed out.

Her wallet was handy, on the arm of the rust-colored sofa. What she chose to hand over indicated that she went to school.

'Do you have a birth certificate?'

'Cinq-Mars,' an impatient Giroux complained.

'Born in Quebec,' Quinn Tanner told him. 'We don't have birth certificates. Not from back then.'

'Your baptismal certificate, then.'

'Yeah.' The document was a full sheet of paper kept safely in a corner desk drawer. Giroux raised his hands to question the infuriating strategy. She returned with the document.

Cinq-Mars asked, 'How old are you?' He had checked her birth date and done the math. Still, he wanted her to confirm it out loud, and for Giroux to hear.

'Seventeen.'

Giroux's shoulders visibly slumped. He had figured her for

nineteen, twenty, like the dead boy. Being only seventeen changed everything.

'Thanks,' Cinq-Mars said, and handed the document back. She returned it to the drawer, then resumed her protective pose. 'Here's the thing, Miss Tanner.'

'Quinn,' she said.

'Quinn. You're seventeen. That gives me a bit of leeway. I have some discretion when a person is underage. If I think you committed murder—'

'I didn't commit murder! Come on! That's ridiculous!'

'I'm not accusing you. I'm only explaining that I'm permitted to bring you in if you're only seventeen. The law does not allow me, however, to hold you in custody without permission from the DPJ, in which case they would take over your case. Do you know who that is?'

Her shrug suggested that she didn't.

'The director of youth protection. In French, "Directeur de la protection de la jeunesse." Hence DPJ. That takes time and evidence. Legally, Quinn, I must inform you that I cannot hold you overnight in custody.'

'Give her the "But . . .",' Giroux instructed Cinq-Mars.

'But,' he warned her, 'I can bring you in, fingerprint you, take your photo to be placed on file. I can question you. I must notify your parents that I'm doing so. Now, you say that you did not commit murder.'

'That's ridiculous.'

'Is it equally ridiculous that you broke into a home on the night of the murder and committed a robbery?'

Quinn said, 'What?' Her response a heartbeat too slow.

'Is it ridiculous that the fingerprints in your boyfriend's car – which match the fingerprints of the person who broke into a house close to where he was killed – belong to you? Remember, before you reply, that we will have the answer to that question very soon. The fingerprints in the car and the house, do they both belong to you?'

In a search to remedy her plight, Quinn glanced at Giroux, as if help might arrive from that quarter. Cinq-Mars knew then, and Quinn Tanner caught on, that she was trapped.

'It's not ridiculous,' she admitted.

'You told the police in your phone call today that you were

nowhere near the crime scene. I can understand why you lied. Would you like to change your testimony now? Better if you do.'

On meeting her, Giroux had assumed the girl to be an adult. Had he met her in her current state, he'd have guessed the truth. Her face contorted into that of an upset child. She was seeing something through the front window behind the detectives. 'Oh no! My dad. He's home.'

'You lied to him, too,' Cinq-Mars stated. In seconds, her father would march in.

She nodded to confirm the jam she was in now.

'Who the hell are you?' Jim Tanner demanded to know. He slammed the door shut. Two men were alone with his daughter, who appeared under duress.

'Police,' Giroux informed him. Civil, at last. He was taking point as the senior officer and showed his badge. 'Sergeant-Detective Giroux, sir. This is Detective Cinq-Mars. We're here to speak with Quinn.'

'You're not the cops from yesterday.'

Giroux had believed that the only communication with the family had been over the phone. That the father had had direct contact with Frigault and Caron undermined his jurisdiction. 'We're here to discuss a different crime.'

Jim Tanner held his gaze for an extended period, then looked at Quinn. She was crumbling. 'Quinn?'

In their talk the night before, she'd told a few fibs to cover her tracks. Cinq-Mars noticed her deer-in-the-headlights look. A kid frightened to be in trouble held more promise than a kid digging a deeper hole. In his quick judgment, she was falling apart because she respected her dad. Her greatest fear was in disappointing him.

'Do I know you?' Giroux asked Tanner.

The query surprised Cinq-Mars, while Tanner ignored it.

A policeman on duty suggesting that he had 'met' someone did not typically suggest that they had bumped into each other or frequented the same deli. A meeting on the job implied a negative connotation. Oddly, Giroux appeared to be looking around Jim Tanner at that moment, out the front window.

'A visitor.' Giroux announced. Suddenly, his whole face seemed to expand. 'Down! Everybody get down!'

Giroux jumped toward the front window. His command came

too suddenly for the others to react. No one got down. Cinq-Mars instinctively moved the girl to his back while Jim Tanner spun around to follow the detective who'd yelled. Giroux pulled the heavy front curtain partially closed when the sound of shattering glass assailed their senses. Flames from a Molotov cocktail leaped up the fabric.

'Quinn! Water!' Tanner shouted and seized a large cushion from the sofa to beat the flames. Giroux was trying to yank the curtain right off its moorings to smother the flames that way. He was a strong man, but the mechanism resisted. Cinq-Mars was out the front door in pursuit of the attacker.

The incendiary-thrower dove into a black American sedan, which burned rubber and raced off. Then it braked hard. A city bus had passed by and then, perhaps because the driver had spotted the sudden burst of flames, stopped. The sedan's driver spun out and ripped down a side lane on the left. Cinq-Mars ran hard. Lanes were sometimes obstructed, often by children on bikes or in the middle of a game.

He found the lane clear. The fleeing car careened onto the next street, bound north. Cinq-Mars had no radio. He wasn't even carrying a revolver. The only official item brought with him was his badge as, off-work, he'd left his house in a mental daze, unprepared for anything like this.

The chase was over before it began.

Giroux jogged up. 'Anything?'

'Plymouth. Gran Fury. Black.'

'Plate?'

'Sorry. First letter G, nothing more.'

'I'll call it in. Guesses on the year?'

'Like I said. A Gran Fury. This is their first year. So a '75.'

Giroux called the details in from his car, then returned to the house where Jim Tanner and his daughter were waiting on the front stoop. Cinq-Mars was trying to shoo onlookers away, but failing. The policemen went inside with Quinn and her father and surveyed the damage. The curtain, soaked and charred. A scar of burn marks on the floor. A pair of cushions, blackened. An empty bucket lay tipped on its side, devoid of water. Bits of glass across the hardwood and carpet.

An unpleasant smell. Something plastic may have melted.

'Here's an interesting question,' Giroux started in. 'There's four of us here. As it happens, no one knows much about anyone else, except for you two, father and daughter, although I'm not so sure about that, either.'

'What's the question?' Jim Tanner inquired. He had a right to sound irritated.

'Who was it for, the firebomb? You? Your daughter? Me? Or him?' With his thumb, he gestured toward the junior detective. 'I'm guessing one of you two, since it's your house, but you never know. Pissed anybody off lately?'

Although they had not coordinated a response, the men in the room looked at Quinn.

She resented the implied rebuke. 'Nobody,' she said. Then, when no one appeared to believe her, she repeated it more emphatically. 'Nobody!'

'We'll talk,' Sergeant-Detective Giroux told her, and advised her father, 'down at our *poste.*'

The Synchronicity of Events

(What sunshine looks like)

Cinq-Mars did not get much sleep. Awakened by the telephone, his alarm clock read 3:54 a.m. The crotchety voice of Armand Touton bore through him when he lifted the receiver.

'Middle of the night, Armand. I sleep now.'

'Your name came up, kid. Also, I been hearing things. Drunken orgies in the morgue.'

'In the lab.'

'Such a big difference.'

'Don't believe everything that comes across your radar screen.'

'You mean you weren't screwing the dead?'

'Or the living.'

'Don't tell me your problems. Two days on your new job, Émile, and people want me to take you back before they fire you. I'm not taking you back.'

'My name came up, you said. About what?' He'd rather sleep
than carry on the repartee.

'Burglary. Town of Mount Royal. Your name is on the sheet.'

'How does that affect you?'

'Go to the same house. Now. Lickety-split, Émile.'

'Another break-in?'

'Would I rush you out for a bent doorknob? Homicide, kid.
Not your line, but you know what they say about the early bird.
Want to catch that worm or not?'

'Who's dead?'

'Show up and find out. Or sleep it off. Up to you.'

'Wait, are you there yourself?'

'Good. You're alert. It'll be nice to see you again. It's been
so long.'

They signed off, and Émile Cinq-Mars got on his horse.

He clawed his way out of his Volkswagen Bug. In the dark, the
crime scene was festive with lights. Ambulances, squad cars,
forensic trucks. Revolving cherries, blue and red; headlights
blinking. The morgue van stood out as demure. The cops on duty
knew him, the old gang together again, and he entered the house.
Facedown on the floor of the foyer – either arriving or leaving
– lay Dr Howard Shapiro. Blood seeped from under his torso.
Émile Cinq-Mars stepped gingerly around the corpse.

Inside, Savina Vaccaro Shapiro sat in a purple armchair.
Although her posture seemed self-comforting, she appeared less
distraught than might have been expected. Touton stood beside
her. He slipped away, indicating to Cinq-Mars to follow.

They met up in the dining room.

'Hoo, boy. What's the tall tale here?' Cinq-Mars asked.

Touton spoke in a hushed tone. 'The lady of the house pleads
blessed ignorance. If you haven't heard, it's a form of innocence.
Her husband was at work. You know he's a hacksaw surgeon,
right? Home by sunup, if he's lucky. Less lucky tonight. The
killer was waiting inside. Two rounds: one to the heart, or close,
one to the abdomen. The shooter took off before she got downstairs. No one, or gun, in sight. The wife can't recall hearing a
car. Maybe she was in shock. I can give her that. Maybe he left
on foot, the killer. Maybe she did it and planted the pistol in her
flowerbeds. It's not shown up. I've checked her hands. No GSR.

Forensics checked her out. She's clean unless she had time for a bath and a change of clothes, which she didn't. Neighbors woke up to the shots, but you know how it goes. By the time they talked it over and got to their windows there was nothing to see. Does your robbery here give us anything, Émile?'

In the past, Cinq-Mars would have arrived ahead of Touton and reported to him on what had occurred. This felt backwards.

'The murder around the corner might help more than the robbery. They're lining up. The victim was the getaway driver. That doesn't tell me what this is about.'

'I'm not buying coincidence.'

'Here's one that's not for sale. Both nights, the husband came home early.'

'That so? Curious. Why?'

'Ask her. You can't ask him.'

'You ask her. She was looking forward to seeing you again.'

'Seriously?'

'Be careful. You know who she is, right?'

He shrugged without comprehension. 'The doctor's wife.'

'She's Savina Vaccaro. She uses her mother's maiden name. Her father is Giuseppe Ciampini.'

'Joe Ciampini, the Mafia honcho?'

'Kind of changes the perspective, doesn't it?'

'An understatement.'

'Heads-up, Émile. Get on the ball with your case. Anything we should know from the robbery, now that you know how this can play?'

Being pushed back to square one happened from time to time. This was more like being on a trip where the itinerary and the destination were suddenly altered. A suburban burglary by a couple of kids that yielded a tragic homicide now had a whole other dimension tacked on.

'A couple of things. The thief didn't do this.'

'You think that way, why?'

'I know who committed the robbery.'

'You solved your case?'

'A kid. She wouldn't know the Mafia connection.'

'A *she*? A girl robber?'

'The dead boy was both her getaway driver and her boyfriend. This is not her playing field, Armand. Anyhow, what are you doing here? Didn't you retire? We drank to the good old days, remember?'

'Turns out I have twenty-eight more of them left to twiddle my thumbs. Maybe enough time for a major bust. Can I take down the Mafia in four weeks?'

'How long have you been at it so far?'

'Thirty years, about.'

'Then good luck. Do you mind if I talk to the grieving widow?'

'Knock yourself out. Here's your mystery question: Is she happy or sad, our lady, deep down in her heart of hearts, now that her man's been whacked?'

Savina Vaccaro Shapiro gazed up at the tall detective from her armchair. She was wearing mascara, which had run.

'You were wrong,' she told him.

'How's that?'

'My intruder would not come back. You promised. Looks like he did.'

'Could be. Of course, if I knew then what I know now . . .'

Cinq-Mars sat in the matching chair.

'What do you know now?'

'Who your father is.'

'Oh, don't tell me. You think because he's Italian, he must be a mob boss.'

'No, I think he's a mob boss because that's what he is. Or do you think he went to prison for parking tickets?'

She straightened herself in the chair, and seemingly rearranged how she intended to comport herself. 'Something you wanted, Detective? If not, run along.'

Her animus was well practiced.

'You don't seem terribly upset,' Cinq-Mars remarked.

She raised an eyebrow to acknowledge as much. 'I'm not into drama-queen theatrics, Detective. If I choose to keep my grief to myself, that's my prerogative. It's not cause for my arrest.'

'Why would I arrest you?'

'I'm home. My husband is dead. Do the math. One person on the scene, one person dead. Either you arrest the corpse or the person who's still breathing, who happens to be the local godfather's daughter. Murder runs in her veins.'

'You seemed more upset about the robbery than you are over the death of your husband.'

She evaluated his take on things, how her demeanor might look from an investigator's vantage point. Agitated by a break-in, yet cucumber-cool in the face of real calamity, her reactions sent out conflicting signals. She hadn't done herself any favors.

'I'm in shock,' she said.

'Perhaps you are.'

'I hope you will investigate the robbery still. I'd like that baseball back.'

'I thought it was your husband who wanted it back.'

'My husband,' she reminded him, 'is lying face down on tile especially imported from Italy. He no longer cares about the baseball. I do.'

Cinq-Mars was confused. 'I'll keep on it,' he vowed. 'With respect to tonight, it's not my investigation, but may I ask a question?' He gave her no more than a moment before proceeding. 'In recent days or weeks, has your husband expressed concerns about your marriage? Has he been agitated?'

He realized, as he spoke, that he was declaring himself to be an adversary. She welcomed the news.

'What're you accusing me of, Detective? Am I a fallen woman in your eyes? Or is it because I married a Jew? Are you one of those? Maybe it's my Mafioso papa, huh? You do know I can have you shot if I feel like it? I came out of the womb with my finger on the trigger. Life and death mean nothing to a girl like me. Why, I probably had my husband shot in my own home on a whim. Except, I can pretty much guarantee that I'm innocent of the charge. Know why? His blood, Detective, is all over my Italian marble. The mess can be cleaned up, but I'll never look at the tiles with the same pleasure again. If I wanted to shoot my husband, Detective No-Brain, I'd do it in the basement. Or the garage.' Finally, she lost her cool, her calm, her exasperating control. 'He would not bleed out on my Italian tile!'

Armand Touton came over then.

She lashed out once more, demanding they get him the expletive out of her face.

Cinq-Mars did so on his own.

'That went well,' Cinq-Mars noted.

'Your bedside manner, Émile, where'd it go?'

'I'm curious, why has her husband been coming home early?'

'Why do you think?'

'The thief told me a man was in the house the night she broke in. Sounds gave him away. Yeah, she had a lover. One who carried a pistol.'

'Émile, aren't you the helpful detective?'

'Ask her who the lover was. She doesn't need to conceal him from her husband anymore. He may have found out, of course. Maybe that helped engineer tonight.'

They smiled. The synchronicity of events was coming together quite neatly.

'I should get a medal for calling you in. Or a beer.'

'Don't make it a habit. I sleep nights. Which reminds me: I'm going back to bed. One more thing. Rings and watches were stolen, then deliberately dropped in the getaway car by the thief when the driver was found dead. Our now-dead surgeon reported a baseball missing, signed by Jackie Robinson. It's still missing.'

Touton whistled in admiration. Then he stopped, as though a thought abruptly occurred.

Cinq-Mars breezed along. 'The wife didn't give a damn about the baseball or the insurance money. Suddenly, her husband is dead and what does she go on about?'

'The baseball.'

'Right now, given a choice, she'd take the ball over the husband. Keep it at the back of your mind, Armand.'

'I might keep it up front. Any other thought?' Touton asked.

'It's off the wall.'

'I have ears.'

'In the beginning, before anything broke, I thought the baseball could give us the killer, and/or the thief.'

'Now?'

'Same thing. Except that now our grieving widow might know it, too. The baseball might give us the killer. The difference now is, I don't know why.'

'You think that way, anyhow.'

'I have the feeling that's how *she* thinks.'

Touton gazed over at the woman. She mystified him in various ways. Cinq-Mars had given him an understanding that, for now, he was keeping to himself. 'All right. Back to bed. I got this.' They gave each other a pat on the shoulder, and when Cinq-Mars was halfway to the door, Touton called out for others to hear. 'Cinq-Mars!'

The younger detective stopped and turned.

'What does sunshine look like? How does it feel?'

Every cop and technician in the room awaited his reply.

'Brighter than the moon,' he advised them. 'Outside, you actually see where you're going. You get used to it.'

Home, he tumbled into bed. He wasn't asleep for long before his phone rang once more. This time it was Dr Eudo Lachapelle at the crime lab. He'd come up with an ID from the blood smears in the dead boy's car. Cinq-Mars was delighted. At this rate, it looked good to have two murders and a robbery solved before the sun set on his first week of daytime policework. The possibility arose that the man who smeared his fingerprints on the car's door panel had not only killed the boy but had gone back to shoot a jealous husband in cold blood. He'd hedge his bets, but that was how the young detective placed them on the table.

PART TWO
THE BALL

Red Ants and a Silver Bullet

(The deal)

Sergeant-Detective Yves Giroux fiddled with a shirt button that, undone, exposed a disagreeable montage of protuberant belly. Cinq-Mars bumped his way past him and selected a booth in the restaurant's far corner. Giroux slid in next to him, leaving the opposite banquette free, only to have the button disassemble again.

'They won't show,' Cinq-Mars stated flatly. He felt pinned in place. 'Sit across.'

'Smart money took the bet, kid. I dropped a silver bullet in Frigault's tray.'

'I'm not that gullible.'

'Did I mention my note? *Show up or red ants will hike across your arse.*'

'Right. That'll make them jump to it.'

'Suit yourself, if you don't believe. Your funeral.'

Sergeant-Detective Paul Frigault and Detective Marcel Caron did arrive. Not far off schedule, either.

'Heard you're buying,' Caron remarked in his gravelly voice. Perhaps the morning hour exaggerated its tone.

'Worth it to see your faces,' Giroux implied.

Cinq-Mars got over his initial surprise that they showed up. He was no longer impressed. To ensure that their fellow detectives arrived for a meeting, his partner had bribed them with a free breakfast.

'What about our faces?' Frigault demanded. Itching for a scrap. The waitress came by and took their orders. She remarked that she was glad the new guy ate solid food.

Coffee was a foregone conclusion. She put mugs down and a second server poured.

'Like I said,' Giroux advised them, 'my new partner will open your eyes.'

Cinq-Mars knew the comments impeded his proposal.

'Anytime you're ready, kid,' Frigault invited.

If he asked these men to never call him 'kid', they'd never call him anything else. Cinq-Mars was at the table to make a deal, which meant devising a trade. On the spot, he adjusted his list of what he required in return for his offer.

First, he posed a question. 'You heard about the homicide last night?'

'Confessing?' Frigault put to him. 'Why'd you do it? Was it the wife?'

Caron picked up the thread, his voice as gnarly as tree bark. 'I get it. She said no. You were down on your knees. Full beg. Weeping, gnashing your teeth. The husband comes home and curses you out for not being a man. At that point, I don't blame you, you shoot him in cold blood. Tell me I'm wrong.'

'Twenty to life,' Frigault summed up. 'All because the gal said no.'

'Why do homicide cops fantasize about murder so much?' Cinq-Mars asked.

'Oh goodie. A riddle.'

'Give the kid a break,' Giroux butted in, bailing him out for once. 'What's coming, I'm telling you, is the look on your faces. The first time a woman says yes to you, if it ever happens, that's the look. I can't put a dollar sign on it. Why I'm paying for breakfast.'

The pair of homicide detectives couldn't fathom this – for some incomprehensible reason, Giroux was buying breakfast. Wary, they kept their guards up.

'Armand Touton and the Night Patrol,' Cinq-Mars started up again, 'caught the case last night. Touton himself, in person. He's not doling it out. Next step, he'll tie that murder to our robbery. Not hard. The same house. After that, he'll tie our robbery to *your* murder. Fingerprints the link. Also, the loot from the robbery was left in the dead guy's car. Bottom line: Touton and the Night Patrol walk away with the whole shebang for themselves. Our *poste* gets nothing. They take their murder, your murder, and the burglary. Yves and me go back to bicycle theft, where you think we belong, but you go back to praying that a wife will slice-and-dice her husband so you can root around for body parts. Except it's a fantasy. Instead, you read the headline news. You're not in the story. Guys, you know this dance. You know the tune.'

'Touton has you by the short hairs,' Giroux piled on. 'You don't have the weight to stop him.'

'Nobody does,' Cinq-Mars confirmed.

Frigault and Caron glanced at one another, then stared back at Cinq-Mars.

'Grim news, hey boys?' Giroux egged them on in their misery. 'Wait for what's coming. That's not the half. Your faces. I wish I had a camera to take the picture.'

'I'm going to eat the eggs you're paying for,' Frigault told him, his tone mildly threatening. 'The bacon. But enough about our faces.'

Giroux held his hands up in an attitude of mock surrender.

Food was arriving, and they broke off their talk as the plates were put down. Cinq-Mars bit into his bagel and cream cheese while chewing on an afterthought. He had noticed Caron – the tall one with the fifth-rate Einstein hairdo and gravelly voice – taking a moment prior to commencing his meal. The tough talker, of all people, secretly said grace!

Religious in his own unique way, saying grace was something Cinq-Mars had let drop. The real surprise to him was his reaction to Caron. He had something on him now that one day, in some bizarre fashion, he could use against him. In the meantime, he chewed on the city's great claim to fame, the Montreal bagel.

'Go on,' Frigault encouraged him. 'What do you want to say?'

'We brought the girl in for the robbery,' Cinq-Mars reminded them, 'but we can't hold her, she's underage. I've started a dialogue. She's my responsibility until she's turned over to youth protection.'

'Turn her over,' Caron stipulated. 'Why not?'

The one who said grace before eating was the one who delivered the tough-guy remarks. Cinq-Mars found he was already using the man's religious bent against him. He was taking Caron's antagonism less seriously now.

'More useful to keep a line of communication ajar.'

'Are you a bleeding heart, Cinq-Mars? Are you sensitive? Out to save the world, one bad girl at a time?'

'Given the two murders, the robbery, the attack on the girl's house, keeping her under our jurisdiction is the better option. More to learn that way.'

'Like you said,' Frigault reminded him, 'Touton's in the driver's seat. Winner takes all. The murder in the house puts him out front. Who he is – his weight – that does, too. Grapevine says the old boy's retiring. I say we kill time until he leaves and get the case back then.'

'That's your plan?'

'What else you got?'

Cinq-Mars and Giroux exchanged a glance. Time for their critical move.

'Touton's not giving up the case anytime soon. Let me tell you why.' Cinq-Mars extracted a scrap of paper from a jacket pocket and read it aloud. 'Savina Vaccaro Shapiro,' he said. 'I can't keep track of names that aren't French. The grieving widow. Her father is Giuseppe "Joe" Ciampini.'

The detectives on the opposite side of the table stopped masticating. They stared back at him with their mouths ajar. Not a civilized sight. Moments passed before they recovered sufficiently to chew and swallow.

'Not the look I was waiting for, but I'll take it,' Giroux pronounced. He waved his fork. 'The case is out of your league, guys. You don't do Mafia. The kid here, that's different. He does Mafia when he's in the mood.'

Once again, Giroux's interference was neither warranted nor welcome. Cinq-Mars's body language demonstrated as much. Giroux shrugged and shut up.

'What Touton does not know,' the younger detective revealed, 'is that I ran the fingerprints from the passenger-side door in your murder case.'

The breakfast guests looked puzzled.

Frigault spoke up. 'We ran those prints. That gave us a connection to the house break-in.'

'He's talking about the smeared prints,' Giroux interjected.

'Those prints,' Cinq-Mars confirmed. 'Your lab said they were useless because they were smeared. My lab worked the edges of the smear and scored a positive ID.'

The two detectives opposite him had their mouths open again.

Finally, with a sliver of sarcasm, and perhaps one of admiration, Frigault said, 'Your lab?'

'Private access – let's put it that way.'

'And?' Caron asked. In his mind, results outweighed method.

'An ID. Local thug. If we look at the house again – dust for prints, this time in the bedroom – and if the guy's thumbs and his little pinkie show up, that will make him first on the payroll for the house murder *and* the car murder. If you arrest, what does that do for your position on the case?'

'You will request the comparison,' Frigault told him. 'Your lab and whoever's. You're a cop. It's something called your duty.' He could be a stickler for the rules when it suited him.

'Duty, duty, but is it *my* case? Do I want to interfere with another cop's case? Especially when that cop is Armand Touton?'

Frigault and Caron were beginning to grasp the train they were riding on.

'He just joined us,' Giroux put in. He flexed only one cheek while grinning. 'He doesn't want to step on anybody's toes. Or on your knees. Or on your fingers while you're clinging off a cliff.'

'He has his own lab,' Frigault reiterated. Then posed the obvious question, 'What do you want, kid? What are you looking to get out of this?'

Cinq-Mars was direct. 'We processed the dead driver's girlfriend. She's our thief.'

'We talked to her first. Before you. You were horning in where you don't belong. Maybe it got her house firebombed. How about we give that one a dry-run through the rumor mill?'

'We talked to her in person,' Giroux reminded them. 'Face to face. Not on a bloody telephone.'

'Hey! Nobody said it was our last conversation. Only our first. You went there off-duty – off-the-case. I see nothing here we need give up to you.'

Frigault and Giroux went at it. Cinq-Mars made eye contact with Caron, directly across from him. The man was waiting for the other shoe, or a fork, to clatter onto the floor. Cinq-Mars could tell that he knew it would.

As the two bickering detectives went silent, Cinq-Mars declared, 'I want to keep the robbery case for Yves and me. Full charge. I also don't want the thief turned over to youth protection. I'll run her myself. The DPJ will wreck any chance she can help us. I will be the only officer responsible for her case. I'll turn her over to DPJ if things go south, but that's my call and mine alone.'

'Sounds like you're in love, Cinq-Mars,' Caron said. Contrary to his words, his inflection indicated that he wasn't being combative. 'A horn-dog on? Woof, woof.'

Cinq-Mars restrained himself from telling Caron to say a Hail Mary for that.

'In exchange?' Frigault asked. He already knew what response was coming.

'You get the hood's name and a clear shot. If you make the collar, the car murder is yours. Play it right, you'll be the daytime slugs on the house murder as well. A win-win. To top it off, like the cherry on a sundae, Giroux buys breakfast.'

The cops opposite him shared a nod and arrived at the right conclusion. They accepted the deal. But Cinq-Mars hadn't finished enumerating his terms.

'Another thing.'

'Don't push it,' Frigault warned him.

How he approached the matter was critical. He had to accomplish an end-around before they knew what direction he was coming from. 'The captain of the Night Patrol and me, we trace back in time. That's also what makes this work. My helping him keeps you on the case. Out of our long history, Touton gets to call me "kid". There's stuff behind that. Life stuff. Death stuff. Cop stuff. I'm fine with it, and that's all I'll say.'

'What's he going on about?' Caron was legitimately confused.

Frigault knew. 'I'll explain later,' he told his partner. 'We have a deal, Cinq-Mars. Not bad work, even if you do have a private lab.'

Giroux was the only one at the table beaming. 'Your faces,' he burst out. 'Worth buying breakfast for.'

'The name,' Frigault demanded. The last detail to seal their deal.

'Arturo Maletti,' Cinq-Mars told him.

Highly credible. The two homicide cops knew him.

A Painted Big Toe

(Hands in tills)

As his partner was putting in time on a case two months old – the theft of a painting from an octogenarian's parlor – Cinq-Mars took the opportunity to visit his young thief, now that she was officially under his supervision.

Home alone, she admitted him.

'I'm surprised to find you in,' he mentioned.

'You rang my doorbell. How surprised can you be?'

'Nice day out. Why be cooped up indoors?'

'Why ring my bell if you think I'm not here?'

'A starting point. Did you think of that? If you weren't home, I'd hunt you down.' He wanted to keep things light before getting serious. 'Why not be outside?'

'Maybe I'm grounded,' Quinn said, then repeated his phrase back to him. 'Did you think of that?'

'Are you?'

He caught a quick smile. 'According to my dad, yeah.'

'Meaning?'

'He didn't think it through. I told him, "You're at work. How do you know if I'm in or out?" He's never tried this before. He has no clue how.'

Cinq-Mars weighed in with another concern. 'Is it wise to be here alone? What if there's another Molotov cocktail?'

Quinn tried a dismissive shrug. Cinq-Mars mimicked her motion, mocking the attitude. She ceded ground. 'My dad was worried, OK, but where do I go? If somebody's looking for me, who? If I don't know, I could walk right into him. Besides, my dad might be thinking it's not about me.'

About him, then. Cinq-Mars had wondered that himself.

'You take care of yourself, is that the deal?'

'Pretty much. We made an arrangement. When I go out, I write down where.' With a painted big toe, she indicated a blank sheet of paper on the coffee table between them. 'Coming home, I write down where I've been. Our version of me being grounded.'

They shared a laugh. 'I guess that works. Otherwise, you're a free bird. The only constraint is to be honest.'

'Not exactly a restriction. My dad tries. He means well.'

'If you ask me,' Cinq-Mars suggested, 'it's more effective than you admit.'

'Was I asking?' Quinn challenged. Her underlying distrust leaked out. 'Why think that way?'

'Yesterday,' Cinq-Mars reminded her.

The day before, he and Sergeant-Detective Yves Giroux had brought her in for questioning, her dad in tow. The father waited in the detectives' room while Quinn sat in the interrogation chamber which normally received tough punks or rowdy youths. Not many women had entered, and when they did, it was usually for hit-and-runs or shoplifting. The neighborhood notched upscale white-collar crimes, rarely anything down-and-dirty where the prime suspect was female.

Cinq-Mars fingerprinted Quinn himself, rolling each digit to make a clear impression.

'Cool,' she said, when they were done. 'I hope it was good for you.'

He handed her a wet cloth to clean off the ink.

In the interrogation room, Giroux started in on her. 'About the break-and-entry.'

'I don't break,' she insisted. Then more quietly, with pride: 'I only enter.'

'Not true. You cut the screens. Do you want to play smart with me?'

'I can play dumb. Should I?'

'Really? Are you too stupid to know the trouble you're in?'

'Are you too stupid to know that I don't give a flying fuck?'

Giroux's temperature was rising. When a juvenile came into custody, the captive was usually a boy and on the verge of wetting himself. His hands would shake, his voice quaver. The kid was wary about what came next, such as the arrival of parents, or being roughed up, or spending a night in jail with degenerates.

'Shall I pick up the phone, Miss Tanner?' Giroux taunted. 'Turn your ass over to youth protection? The neighborhood you live in, you've talked to kids. You know what it means.'

'I talked to boys about it. Girls? The only trouble they know is getting knocked up. The Boys' Farm, yeah, I heard about it. Is there a Girls' Farm? Oh, never mind. I'll go to the Boys' Farm. I don't have to worry about the counsellors there. They prefer dicks to chicks, I hear.'

'What do you mean by that?'

'If you don't know, I'm not telling. You're probably one of them.'

'If you're saying what I think you're saying . . .'

'No biggie if you're queer. My best friends are. Helps me out in a way.'

'Cinq-Mars,' Giroux stated, 'should we haul her downtown? Lose track of her for a couple of nights? We can slip her in with the drunks and lunatics. I'll send you to pick up whatever bones are left.'

Quinn responded with a smirk.

'What?' Giroux pressed her. 'You don't think I'm serious?'

'With my dad outside? I know you're not. I think you're so full of shit there's probably nothing left of you after a dump. Be careful when you sit down on the can, Mr Detective. You might flush yourself away.'

'Girl, you need to smarten up in a hurry.'

'I like to take things slow in life. My motto.'

'I'm making that call.'

'Hang on,' Cinq-Mars advised him.

He got up and left the room. He returned with Quinn's father. Jim Tanner sat quietly in a corner. Quinn now had to speak her sass in his presence or mind her manners.

'Let me talk to her,' Cinq-Mars offered.

'Be my guest. I've got a sour taste.'

He sat opposite Quinn. He let her stew under his gaze down the lengthy line of his hawk-like beak. She began to squirm.

'What?' she said. She could not protest more than that, or hurl insults, not with her father ensconced in the corner.

'I was wondering,' Cinq-Mars said, 'if Dietmar Ferstel had girlfriends before you? What about you, did you have boyfriends before Dietmar? Were any of them, the girls or the boys, upset when you two got together?'

Quinn was twice defeated. In the first instance, her dad was in the room. She could not misbehave in his presence. Then the question took the focus off her onto the curious matter of the dead boy. The query motivated her to participate in the discovery of what happened to Dietmar. She was up for that, and Cinq-Mars hoped to ease her into helping him and helping herself. Her culpability could still be drawn out, perhaps without her noticing.

Giroux remained quiet, observing the new guy's progress. He kept an eye on the clock, though, and after fifty minutes wrapped up the discussion to send everyone home. He and Cinq-Mars were working voluntary hours and he'd predetermined a limit.

In her home the next day, Cinq-Mars again caught her off-guard. 'Yesterday,' he reminded her. Her father, in concocting a scheme where she filled out a sheet of paper to record her whereabouts, had created a restraint as effective as any. Quinn would avoid abusing his trust if she could help it. Jim Tanner knew that, and Cinq-Mars had learned that that was true. Quinn couldn't step around it.

'What do you want to talk about?' she asked. The question lacked her customary impertinence. 'I thought we covered the whole gamut yesterday.'

'We barely got started. Your life as a thief, Quinn. We'll begin there.'

'You're not serious.'

'Dead serious. I'll give you immunity so long as nobody died. Spill the beans.'

He could tell, as she spoke, that despite her outward reluctance, she was proud to do so. Her rundown was brief and to the point, although he noticed that she was careful to blur incriminating details.

'Any idea why somebody tried to burn your house down?'

That kept her onside as well, as she'd wrestled with the question on her own.

'Maybe my dad's in trouble. I don't know.'

'What kind of trouble?'

'With his union, maybe.'

'I see. Quinn, here's the deal. I'm officially overseeing your situation. I am now the only person who can send you into youth protection, and the only one who can keep you out. Obviously, your cooperation is necessary for me to keep you out. You want that, whether you know it or not. Why do you think that is?'

She wasn't sure. She broached a different issue, her defiance rising to the fore again. 'If you want to do something bad to me, you can't scare me with youth protection. I'll go to youth protection if you try anything.'

He was pleased. She'd need that layer of armor in this world, especially with how she contended with society. 'Fair point. If anyone tries something with you, tell your dad. He'll defend you like a mother bear defends a cub. I've seen it in him.'

She conceded that that was true.

Which left an open question. 'What am I supposed to cooperate about?'

He laid out the simplest plan. 'Yesterday, I brought up the matter of your previous boyfriends and Dietmar's former girl-friends. You know nothing about the latter, you said. I want you to find out. Talk to his old friends. Draw out that kind of infor-mation. As well, check what your ex-boyfriends have been up to. Make sure they're acting normally, not covering up any big grievance. While you're at it, keep your ears to the ground. You and Dietmar weren't together long. He agreed to be your getaway driver a little too easily, I think. I'm sure you possess powers of persuasion, but still. We might find out he wasn't squeaky clean. Or not. Nothing's certain yet. Also, he may have had friends who are less than law-abiding. He may have had a few nefarious contacts. Follow me so far?'

'I'm supposed to, like, what? Do your job for you?'

'Yes. Help out. Police work. Can you dig it?'

Put that way, she seemed both reluctant and pleased. 'I'm cool with it.'

'Keep your head up and your eyes open. Why were you fire-bombed? Anything you learn about that, even a suspicion, tell me. Your dad has enough on his plate. He doesn't need to see his house burned down.'

She agreed.

'I'm going to give you a name. Tell me if you know it, or if you've heard it before. Doesn't matter what context. OK?'

Secretly, she was curious. She nodded.

'Arturo Maletti.'

Judging by her reaction, she didn't know the man.

'Probably, he was in the house the night of the robbery.'

'My naked guy?' She was excited. 'You figured that out already?'

'He has his hands in a few tills. When you're asking around about Dietmar, let me know if his name surfaces. Keep your distance. He may have a score to settle with you. You saw him where he was not supposed to be.'

'I didn't see him. Only his – you know – privates, and his pistol.'

'I'm not saying it definitely was him, either. But likely. If him, he doesn't know what you saw or didn't see. He's not going to take your word if you try to explain. So don't. Are you hearing this? Stay clear if he ever comes around. Anything you hear, pass it onto me. That helps me, it helps us find justice for Dietmar, and it helps you stay out of more trouble than you can handle.'

Cinq-Mars counted on the assumption that to build trust meant keeping her involved. She was the type to break chains, bound over walls if confined, and dismiss anyone trying to help her if she felt belittled.

His pager went off. He gave it a glance.

'Where do you hang out?' he asked.

'Hang out?' She'd heard the question. He didn't repeat it and waited patiently. 'I don't know. Hill's. That's a snack-bar-type place.'

'I know it.'

'Friday and Saturday nights, sometimes I go to a dance hall on Jean Talon.'

'Where else? I won't follow you around. I just want to know.'

'Why?'

He stood and moved toward the telephone sitting on a small cabinet.

'Where you hang out tells me who you're hanging out with. A boy is dead, Quinn. If you didn't kill him, who did? We have a lead, but no stone can go unturned. You agree with that, right?'

'Yeah, but I don't want you hassling my friends.'

'What I do is my business. If it's police business, it's warranted. A boy is dead, Quinn. Where do you hang out in the daytime? In the evenings?'

A defensive shrug preceded her reply. 'In the summer, Ball Park. Know it?'

'Very close to where I live.'

'Really? You live in Park Ex?'

'Everybody has to live somewhere. Why not Park Ex?'

'Mostly its immigrants here.'

'You're not an immigrant.'

'True.' When in trouble in a talk, he noticed, she quickly dove into a different topic. 'Do you have a girlfriend? A wife? I see no ring.'

'Nope. Recent breakup.'

'Sorry about that.'

'Me, too. Do you mind if I make a phone call? I was paged.'

'Go for it.'

He said very little during the call. When he turned back to face her, he maintained a nonchalant voice. 'I'll be in touch. Call the station if you need me. They can page me if it's urgent. Do you have the number?'

She'd kept it, and his partner's card. A good sign.

Cinq-Mars fell into thought. He had more questions yet wanted to avoid an overload. His approach was two-pronged – put her on the spot while giving her sufficient room to come around on her own. A variation of the carrot-and-stick. He'd just learned, during his call, that Giroux's suspicion about having previously encountered the father held merit. Jim Tanner had a record. Cinq-Mars needed to check the man's background himself, to see what that divulged.

Quinn was the first to turn restless. 'Don't let me keep you,' she said.

'Just waiting.'

'For what?'

'Are you worried?'

'I'm good. Checking that you weren't having a stroke or nothing.'

'I'm waiting on my team, Quinn. Uniforms. They'll be piling in here shortly.'

She went as still as stone.

'Don't be alarmed. Everything will be put back in place. They're only looking for stolen property. Is there anything you want to show me before they arrive? Save us the trouble?'

He could tell that she was thinking. 'What,' she asked, 'would I show you?'

'You tell me.' He hoped she might suggest a baseball. She didn't, and when his officers arrived, they did not find one that was signed. She was more professional than he gave her credit for, and Cinq-Mars realized that she might be a more difficult nut to crack than expected. As he departed her home, it occurred to him that she might have help, someone to teach her how to deal with loot, and to guide her. Such as how to deal with the police. The father? He had experience. If not the father – and based on his observations, he doubted it was him – then who?

Jars of Honey and the Lurid Carcasses

(Trunk boy)

P artially open-air and considered the largest farmers' market on the continent, the Jean Talon Market stood brash with summer bounty – cut flowers and potted plants, jars of honey and jam, the lurid carcasses of lambs and pigs, slabs of beef, sausages, and swarming fragrances of spices on the wing that intoxicated the two cops. Detective Marcel Caron's eye fell upon the fruit. The berries, especially. He wanted to plant his face in every basket at once, and not resurface. His partner was enchanted by an idiosyncratic choice – root vegetables.

They'd nearly forgotten their purpose in being there when the legitimate object of their desire crossed their field of vision. Arturo Maletti, known to frequent the market daily to contact a crew of riffraff drug dealers there, tossed an orange in the air. His carefree insouciance vanished the instant Caron nudged Frigault and nodded towards him. Maletti knew the look if not the men. Understood that he was their prey. The orange landed magically back into his palm, like a high pop-up to short. He looked around – a pitcher checking baserunners. The contraband in his pockets vexed him. He figured he might walk away, then quickened the pace and, since they followed, ran.

They charged, and the chase was on.

The market was perpetually populated by the aged and the young, the married, the gay, housewives, bachelors, and an astonishing array of ethnicities. Arturo Maletti ran in his patent-leather shoes ahead of the two older men, one spry and tall with an

Einstein-like hairdo, the other less fit for the chase than a hippo lumbering behind a gazelle. The man with the Mediterranean complexion was identified by his attire and the bling around his neck as a Mafioso, escaping police. Some cheered him on, others scolded the cops, while others begged both sides to take care. A merchant put forward a request that a rule be considered sacrosanct: 'Don't nobody shoot!' He spoke under his breath. Nevertheless, several patrons ducked.

The general bedlam of the place, the congestion, the welcome hordes, blessed Maletti's flight to safety, as did his youth and the cops' poor athleticism. He felt impeded by his pointy shoes, which had slippery soles, yet exhibited power in his stride. He ran beyond the customary limits of his endurance, limits that greatly exceeded those of Caron and Frigault. After four minutes, Sergeant-Detective Frigault had been left a block behind, bent over, hands on knees. Caron returned to make sure he wasn't having a heart attack.

'Did you get him?' Frigault asked, sucking air.

'No. You?'

Both questions were ridiculous. They shared a laugh even as they heaved.

'Do you want to sit down, or should I call an ambulance?'

'Either,' Frigault said. 'Neither.' He was beyond caring.

Caron waited beside him while his partner caught his breath. He didn't want to admit that he felt like Jell-O. If an ambulance did show up, he might ask to borrow the defibrillator for his personal use.

Having exerted himself less, Frigault recovered sooner. 'The gym membership? Not worth it. I want my money back.'

'You have to actually *go* to the gym, Paul. You can't just carry the card in your wallet.'

'Never thought of that. Look, this one we keep to ourselves. We did not encounter Maletti today.'

'That's right. He never saw us, either.'

'If we ever do see him again—'

'Not *again*. We never saw him in the first place.'

'Correct. If we come across him in the future—'

'Shoot the bastard before he hurts himself running away like that,' Caron stipulated with a straight face.

'A mercy killing. What court would not uphold?'

'Agreed. But, Paul, seriously, did you see him? He ran like hell.'

'My thought. The guy's afraid. We have to find him. Next time, we stay in the car. Speaking of the car, I wouldn't mind sitting inside with the air on.'

They stumbled back the way they came, amused by their own ineptitude.

'Next time, we set a trap.'

'As long as we don't have to run.'

'He better not tell nobody, that guy. I'll arrest him for it.'

Arturo Maletti could not afford new automobiles, nor could he turn down the right look for himself. Consequently, he owned a third-hand Cadillac. As big as a barge and as black as midnight. Returning for it, he caught sight of the two cops who had pursued him clambering into their lowly squad car, a junk Ford. He watched them leave. He started up his Caddy and followed behind at a safe distance until he could break away in a different direction. Pathetic, those guys. They'd chased him as if they were in a sack race. He took only limited solace in that. Cops were looking for him. Not welcome news. He would work his sources to find out what itch they were scratching, and what it might take for them to bug off.

Cops today. Some did not understand who ruled the roost. He should be able to figure their angle. If not, another strategy needed to be devised.

Good advice was warranted on various matters. Going to his boss could invite the wrong sort of attention from the wrong quarter, advice that might prove detrimental to his enjoyment of life. He headed instead to the Knightsbridge pawnshop for a chat with Ezra. His mentor from years ago usually gave him the straight dope. Along the way, he stopped to punch a guy in the gut, partly because the bum still owed him one large, but mostly because he felt like hitting somebody. To restore his energy after all that exertion and the run from the cops, he stopped for a beer. What happened while quenching his thirst evolved from pure accident. Never his intention for the day.

Arturo Maletti was on a barstool when he noticed a guy in the mirror behind a shelf of liquor bottles. Even before he recognized him, he detected what the guy was doing. The squirmy sap was edging toward an exit sign. Toilets were down that hallway, and beyond them a back-alley door. The sap might be going for a leak; from the look on his face, Maletti knew better. Shit-for-brains was trying to elude him.

Maletti spun on his barstool and crooked his middle finger at the lad. The young man had a choice: make a run for it or come over. He crossed the floor to chat with his handler.

'No kidding, I was gonna come see you,' the young fellow said. Long-haired, with a scruffy beard. Black T-shirt. Patches on his pants. Trotsky glasses that he habitually adjusted higher on his nose. Short, bony, sickly pale, despite his youth he resembled a patient escaped from a palliative care ward, as though he trailed an IV in his wake. He hung out with students but was not enrolled. His street-urchin status gave him cachet with the higher-IQ boys and girls, which he used to handle a piece of Maletti's marijuana action. Both men were aware of a problem. A story had made the rounds. The young pusher was reportedly selling hashish from a foreign supplier. 'Foreign' included any person who was not Arturo Maletti, an entrepreneurial independence that required discouragement.

'Your lies – try them out on some chick,' Maletti replied. A bartender set his beer down before him. He took an extended, thirsty gulp, then wiped his mouth on the back of his hand. 'Selling hash? After what I do for you?'

The young man had brought over his own beer and raised it to his lips.

'You don't want to do that, Lenny.'

'Leonard,' the boy corrected him. He adjusted his wire-rim frames again.

'Yeah, right, like that singer with the croaky voice. You think it gets you some. You're Piss-Puke to me, Lenny-boy, from now on. You're not no fucking Leonard.'

The boy shrugged.

'Piss-Puke, like I said, you don't want to drink that.'

'Why not?'

'You'll need to take a leak. Riding in the trunk of my car, you don't want to take a leak. The less you're holding in, the more you will appreciate my advice.'

Leonard turned paler than his usual alabaster glow.

'Arturo—'

'You don't call me that,' Maletti warned him.

'What do I call you?'

'Mr Maletti from now on. Try it. You'll like it.'

'Mr Maletti—'

'This is what happens when you fall in the world. You get to call me Mr Maletti. I call you Piss-Puke. You get to pay for my beer. I drive you in the trunk of my car. Around and around we go. Where I let you out, nobody knows.'

'I can explain,' Leonard said.

'If you think it's me who's interested, you're wrong. An explanation, that's not something I want to hear in my life. College boys, you think you're so smart.'

'I'm not a college boy.'

'Shut up. I'm talking now. You're not a college boy but you read books. Admit it to me, you're that way. It's the same thing because there's no difference. You think you learn so much? You're smart? You don't know squat. College boy. Bookworm. For that, you get to ride around town in the trunk of my car.'

'Look, I'm sorry, all right?'

'That's good, Piss-Pot. At least you're not denying it. That's worse. But I don't want explanations. And here's what else, no apologies. You don't want to cross me.'

'I wasn't crossing you—'

Maletti silenced him by holding up his right hand.

'Explanations. Apologies. Excuses. These things. Promises. These things that I'm hearing, I don't want to hear. Not me. Let me drink my beer in peace. And hey, pay the man, Puke-Face. Why should I pay for my beer in a dive like this?'

Leonard agreed, though he couldn't hide his reluctance. He wished he could chug his beer while waiting for Maletti to finish his. He wanted to ask if it would be all right if he had a leak before he climbed into the car, so he'd be less likely to soil the trunk. He figured that, like promises, explanations, excuses and apologies, Maletti didn't want to field any requests, either.

He paid for the man's beer and settled his own tab. When Maletti was ready, he went out to Park Avenue, then around the corner to Milton. The area known as the McGill Student Ghetto remained chockful of young people in their summer lives. Maletti opened the lid of his trunk and invited Leonard to climb in. Then stopped him. 'Piss-Puke, wait. So nobody's looking.' They waited.

When the coast was clear, the young man climbed in. Maletti slammed the hood down, tidied his hair in the reflection of the side window, shot his cuffs, and slid in behind the wheel. The Caddy drove off with the young dealer curled up in the expansive trunk. The fetal position, he found, provided the most protection as they swayed and bumped along for what seemed like a weekend.

He guessed that Maletti was taking roads that were under construction and those still stubborn with potholes.

Russian Rabbit

(Speaking Swahili)

Quinn did as Ezra Knightsbridge had instructed her to do when paying a visit. She observed the street before entering his store.

She checked the down on her forearms. She was uncertain what windows she should peer into, what vehicles required her attention. She had no clue what face might be suspicious. The light hair on her forearms was not standing on end. Still, she felt uneasy. Hard to determine whether a foreboding had insinuated itself into her bloodstream and she was now perpetually on edge, or if someone had staked out Ezra's place and covertly observed her.

Something was off. She felt eyes on her back. Which meant she was supposed to take a hike. Was she only being paranoid? She desperately wanted to talk to Ezra. Twice she walked the length of his block to work the gel out of her kneecaps. On her third pass, he invited her inside.

'Swing by,' he declared, holding the door open. 'Nobody here to arrest you.'

She wondered how he knew that, and if he was right.

Ezra did not enjoy hearing about a policeman barging into her life.

'Trust him not,' he said.

'He seemed OK, for a cop. He's got this massive honker. Hard to keep your eyes off it.'

They were seated in his little back room. He poured tea. She was appreciating these gentle tea ceremonies. The radio on quietly. Ezra seemed to have permanently tuned his ears to violins.

'Who is he? Does he have a name?'

'Cinq-Mars.'

'Sank-who?'

'Like the number five in French.'

'His badge number or his name?'

'Cinq then Mars, like the planet. Five Mars. Only you don't pronounce the "r" a hard way. It's French. Cinq-Mars.'

Ezra was staring at her rather oddly. Holding his teacup as high as his chin.

'What?' she asked him.

'He's Night Patrol,' he said.

'What's that?'

'A division of tough cops. Honest guys. Can't be bribed or intimidated. Sometimes they arrest a man. Other times they beat the crap out of a person they're after, warn him to find a new address in another city. I stay out of their way. Nobody wants to mess with them. Why are you talking to one of those, Quinn? Why are you important to them?'

'I dunno. Cinq-Mars seems to work in the daytime.'

Ezra sipped more tea then put his cup down. 'Could be there's two guys with that name. I'll check. From you, does he want something?'

'My eyes open and my ears on the ground. He wants me to keep my head up. How I keep my head up with my ears on the ground I haven't quite figured out.'

'Don't talk smart. This is serious. He has you for the robbery?'

'Yeah. I've been printed. Kinda cool. Being fingerprinted.'

'Not, as you say, cool. He has you for the robbery, yet he does not put you in youth protection. Serious, this. Did you forget? Your fingers were in the blood in the car.'

'Oh. Right.'

'He wants something from you. Think straight in a hurry, young Quinn. A cop like that, his hooks in you, that's front-of-the-line trouble. He's in control of you now, do you not know?'

'Ezra, it's not that bad. Nobody *controls* me.'

'Not that bad? So bad I don't want to know you.'

'What? You're kidding. Why not?'

'You'll sell me out.'

'I won't do that.'

'You will. Criminals sell out their best friends.'

'Not me.'

'They say that always. Not so many keep their word.'

'I will.'

'Your fingerprints are in the blood. Drink your tea,' he instructed her. 'Let me think.'

She did. They sat in silence in the dark little room, sipping.

Then Quinn asked, 'What should I do?'

'Be specific to me, what does he want from you?'

'Dietmar's old girlfriends. My old boyfriends. A list. In my case, it'll be short. He's looking for a jealous lover, maybe.'

Ezra considered that, nodding. 'Good. Not so bad. Give the list. Maybe he won't compare your prints to the ones in blood. Someday, he will ask how you sold your merchandise. What will your answer be not to sell me out?'

'You tell me.'

'Say nothing, when he asks. He'll push. Say nothing again. He'll push more. Show him you're afraid of the question. Make him push more. Then give him a name. Not mine. A thug on Notre-Dame West. Works out of a bar called Dino's. Tough crooks show up in the backlot. He comes out. They call him the Rabbit.'

'The Rabbit.'

'Guy Lappin. Like *lapin*, the French word for rabbit. An extra "p" in his name because he's Russian, his origin. He speaks French. English, too. Not Russian. Or speaks Russian in the privacy of his house. Except he's not the kind of man who has a house. Makes deals in the backlot in the moonlight. Tell your cop you were one of his crooks. He'll believe you. Know why?'

'Why?'

'Because it's credible. How would you know to tell that story or give up that name, if it is not true? Make sure you get your cop to promise he will never tell where he learned the information. He'll keep you out of it to keep you out of a body bag. He'll warn you to never go there again. So don't. Don't go back to this place where you have never been. Understand?'

'No problem. I won't go back to where I've never been.'

'Finish your tea, Quinn. Then go. You make me nervous. You with your cop from the Night Patrol.'

'You said you'd check him out.'

'I'll check. Now go.'

The hairs on her forearms crept up as she walked outside. She felt a tingling. Exactly as Ezra had forewarned. A big black Caddy was cruising down the block. The dunce-cap behind the wheel gave her the eye. One wolf whistle out of him and she'd throw a rock. If she could find a rock. Then she'd run. Head for the hills. Funny how his look could instantaneously give a girl the creeps.

He did a U-ey. This was not a street to do a U-turn on. She feared he might follow her. He still seemed to have his eye on her when she glanced back. She tried not to look again, but when he didn't pass her right away, she risked a quick scan. She saw him parking. She wanted an excuse to duck into a doorway. She didn't smoke but she could pretend to light up. Track him out the corner of her eye. Better than having his eye on her.

Oddly, he leaned against the rear fender of his car. The guy lit up a smoke for real. He seemed to be having a conversation with himself. Or talking to the car. This went on for a while, and because he was facing her Quinn stayed put. Then the man snuffed the smoke under the sole of his shoe and unlocked the trunk. He looked around before raising the lid and Quinn tucked her head out of sight. Then she poked her head out from behind the brick barrier to peek.

The hairs on her forearms were standing on end now.

A young man – not at all on the cute side as he closely resembled a sewer-dwelling waif crawling out of a nightmare – stuck a bell-bottomed pantleg out of the trunk. He then stood on the street facing the other man, as if squirming in place. They talked. No recriminations between them. No dispute, no violence, as though the young fellow had hitched a ride and was grateful for the accommodation while in transit. The two appeared to be in agreement. Then the waif walked on, in Quinn's direction, but crossed to the other side of the street. She was highly curious. Even more so when the driver came down the sidewalk and entered the Knightsbridge pawnshop.

She crossed the road and followed the boy.

She found the look of him amusing, the way he hitched his trousers above his skinny hips, jutting his shoulders as if squiggling through a narrow passage.

She never approached boys who held exactly zero interest for her in the way that boys interest girls. He was the sort she'd cross the street to avoid if she noticed him coming with intentions in his eye. And yet, if she was supposed to have her head up and her ears to the ground, this might be what that meant. A boy squirts out of the trunk of a car as if it was something he did every day. If nothing else, it was worth an expression of surprise.

'Hey,' she said. She was still behind him but catching up. 'Hold on.'

He turned. Noticing a girl with an interesting look, he stopped.

'English or French?' In Montreal, a necessary determination. '*Français ou—*'

'English,' he said. 'Or French. Or Swahili.'

'You don't speak Swahili.'

'I could learn. For you, I would. I'll enroll with Berlitz tomorrow.'

No dummy. Except that he carried himself with the indifference of a crash-test dummy. She could see him in the role.

'Not necessary. What are you doing right now?' She knew how that sounded.

'Talking to you. Before that, walking. Why? You got a better idea?'

'You weren't always walking,' she said.

He didn't respond. A bony shoulder shrugged. He hoisted his patched trousers with the wide flares at the shins. He could use a better belt. Either that or he could add some meat to his bones. He went to adjust his glasses but scrunched his nose instead to shift them higher.

'Why the trunk?' she asked.

The jig was up. He decided not to deny it. 'Don't you ride in trunks?'

'Neither do you. Why were you in *that* trunk?'

The young man pursed his lips, made a face, tried to configure an appropriate reply. 'Let's call it a business negotiation. The man driving the car expects me to modify my behavior. Just because. He thinks if I got bumped around for an hour or two, I'll be more inclined to see things his way.'

'Are you? More inclined?'

'Less so. Shook some dirt out of my clothes, though. Kind of like being in a washing machine. Less inclined to think like him, more inclined to do what he says. Which is probably the point. Look, we got to keep moving.'

'Why?'

'I need to piss. You would, too, if you'd been knocked around in the trunk of a car after a couple of beers. I can't hold it in.'

A short distance on, they entered a construction site and the young man relieved himself behind a stack of plywood. Quinn stood guard, to warn if anyone came by.

'What's your name?' he asked as he reemerged, zipping up.

'Quinn. Yours?'

'Leonard. If we become lovers and have six kids, still call me Leonard. Not Len. Or Lenny. I think Lenny is for accountants.'

'You're not an accountant and we're not going to be lovers.'

'All the girls say that before they change their minds.'

'I hope that happens for you once in your lifetime. What's the other guy's name?'

'Who?'

Quinn waited for him to figure it out. They were still standing on the construction site, the world of traffic and pedestrians visible through a gap in the fence.

'Arturo? Forget about him. You can't be attracted to Arturo. He's not worth your time.'

She stared at him, more dumbfounded now than when he crawled from the trunk. She turned and slipped through the gap onto the street. Her strides were long. He quickened his walk to catch up.

When he did, she asked, 'What's his last name?'

'Why?'

'Is it Maletti?'

This time, he was the one who slowed down. He had to bolt forward to be in step again.

'Why was he going into Ezra's place?'

'Why do you walk so fast?'

She stopped cold and he nearly bumped into her. 'I asked first,' she said.

'No idea. You know Ezra? Stupid question. If you know his name, you know Ezra. Are you a thief?'

Quinn was shocked. 'What? Why ask me that?'

He shrugged. 'You know Ezra. Ezra knows thieves. Doesn't it follow that you're a thief?'

She supposed it did. She also understood she had things to learn.

'Arturo interrupted my afternoon brew,' Leonard said. 'Want to join me?'

'You want to drink with a thief?'

'You want to drink with a drug dealer?'

'Is that you?'

'Who else gets to ride around in the trunk of a car? Drug dealers and kidnap victims. That's about it and I'm not a kidnap victim.'

'I'm underage.'

'Not at my place.'

He was decidedly the runt of the litter. If he believed he could take her on he'd be in for a comeuppance. In any case, he didn't seem bent that way. He seemed, under the mess of his outward appearance and insecurity, sincere.

'OK,' she said. Then added, 'Tell me about Maletti.'

'Is that how this goes down to the ground? We're about Maletti?'

'That's how it goes down,' she said.

She might not be a raving beauty, but she was closer to being one than any girl he'd ever invited home. As close to a raving beauty as he had allocated for himself in his wistful dreams. And yet, this could be dicey on any number of levels.

'Leonard, you said you'd learn Swahili for me. If that's true, you can sure tell me everything you know about Arturo Maletti.'

'Who are you? Where do you come from?' he asked as if she might mention another planet.

She stabbed a finger on his chest. 'Don't think that way, Leonard. Do what you're told. I'm telling you to talk to me about Maletti. Understand?'

'Yeah,' he agreed. Thinking otherwise had been lame. 'Sure thing.'

Mother-of-Pearl Inlay

(Condolences)

'Ezra, turn off the damn violins. We're not at the fucking opera.'

'A difference there is,' Knightsbridge informed his visitor, 'between an opera and the symphony. You, an Italian, should know this before you crawl out from your crib for a cannoli.'

'Right. I should be a flipping tenor.'

'Beats breaking legs.'

'I don't break legs. Punched a guy in the gut today. He went down like a—'

'Don't say this.'

'Like a ton of bricks.'

Ezra sighed and sat down. 'Clichés like that, I hate so much.'

'Sure you do. Keeps me awake at night, what you care about. Hey, that long-legged thing walking down the street just now. The blondie. Like she was carried on a breeze. Was she in here?'

Ezra Knightsbridge worked the edges of truth throughout his days. For him, lying was a practiced art that required both purpose and strategy. Life and death could be at stake. One should never lie out of fear, or from a posture of weakness. That was a game for the segment of society collectively identified as losers. He could lie to Arturo Maletti, claim that the young woman had not been in his shop. Except it broke a cardinal rule. He did not know what the other man knew. Had he seen her emerge from his shop? No one should lie when the quizzical party might know more than he let on. A lie should only fill a vacuum of ignorance and not be combative with the truth.

'She dropped by. Why ask?'

'Why did she drop by?'

'This is your business? How?'

'One of your thieves, Ezra? A girl like that, I could be interested.'

'You hop from the bed of the boss's daughter to raping a juvenile delinquent, this is your scheme?'

'Then she is one of yours.'

'She's not. She is a student of music. She came by to visit her accordion, play tunes. She misses her accordion. She works to raise the money back I lent her. The instrument here, her collateral.'

Arturo Maletti gazed at the accordion with the mother-of-pearl inlay. A prop gave a story its presence, its focal point. Always advantageous. That the instrument belonged to a 'crazy Hungarian' who played weddings, who was frustrated that people wanted only 'The rock and the roll, no more the polka,' he'd keep to himself.

'Let me buy it for her, Ezra. She'll date me then. She might adore me.'

'How do I sell what is not mine? Also, do I assist an idiot with his idiot plan to defile an angel underage? You are filth, Arturo. She is silk. Get her out of your head or I will be done with you. You know what means that.'

'No. I don't.'

'The father of the daughter of the boss has it confirmed who does the doggie style with his married little girl. The slow torture, Arturo. The miserable death. The body parts missing. Find them in the river.'

'You can shut up now.'

'Keep your filthy mind off my customers. Why are you here? Something wrong you did?'

'Always so suspicious. I need your help. I've done nothing to interest the cops. Still, a couple of detectives came after me.'

'Then what? After they came after?'

'I ran away. I gave them the slip.'

'You know why they came after?'

'Can you help me find out?'

'You don't know?'

'What I said. Do you?'

'Of course.'

'What do you mean "of course"?'

'You didn't talk to your girlfriend today?'

'Which one, hey?'

'You think this is funny? Your girlfriend's husband is shot dead in his own house, and who is the suspect? The one who is laughing.'

'Her husband's dead? Savina's! When did this happen?'

'When? Last night it happened. You weren't there?'

'Get off it. I wasn't there. If I was there, I'd know.'

'If you were there, you would say you were not. Same difference.'

'It's not the same difference. There's a big difference.'

'For you, maybe. For the police? Not so much.'

'What do you mean?'

'If Savina didn't do it, her lover did. You're the lover.'

'You're the only one who knows that, Ezra.'

'Maybe I was the only one, once. Me and Savina, we knew. That was before the fingerprints.'

'What fingerprints?'

'You left yours behind in the car of the dead boy. Remember telling me?'

'I smeared them.'

'Not so well, my connections say. Also, fingerprints are inside Savina's house. Yours. Why are you here when you should be running? You bring trouble on my house, on my business. Why?'

'Ezra—'

'Who has called me? Who wants to talk?'

'How should I know?'

'Figure it out.'

'Tell me who.'

'Tell me who you think.'

'Savina?'

'Not Savina. Are you an idiot, or only stupid?'

'The police?'

'The police don't tell me they're coming. What's the matter with you?'

'Then who?'

'Who do you think?'

'I don't know who!'

'That's the problem,' Ezra informed him. 'You do know who.'

'Who?'

'The husband is killed in the house of the daughter. Who is interested in the lover now?'

Very quietly, Maletti said, 'Not Joe Ciampini?'

'He's coming to see me.'

'Why you?'

'It's you he wants to see, but he can't find you today. Where have you been?'

'Driving around. An errand. Are you lying to me?'

'Lying is not something I do. I don't have the knack. Stick around, he'll be here soon.'

'Joe Ciampini?'

'Him.'

'Why . . .?'

'Stick around. Find out.'

'No, I'm going.'

'Where can you run to, Arturo? You killed the daughter's husband.'

'I never did.'

'Cops think so. Mr Ciampini agrees. Who told him that? Must be the daughter, and she was there.'

'This is crazy. Savina would never say that.'

'Sure she would, if maybe she killed him herself. You see? But I don't accuse her. Joe Ciampini is coming to talk about you. Stay. Talk with him yourself. Accuse his daughter to his face yourself.'

'What kind of advice is that? Ezra, that's insane.'

'I might be an old man, but I don't want to die this young. The truth I will say to Mr Ciampini. What else?'

'Ezra! This is nuts! What am I supposed to do?'

'Run,' Ezra told him.

'Run?'

'Fast. Best option, run far. The police have your fingerprints in dark blood. If you are innocent – how can you be? – it will come out. If you are guilty – how are you not? – you will be hunted down like a dog with rabies, foaming at the mouth. You decide.'

Maletti was standing, his head in disarray. 'I'm getting out of here,' he said. 'Can you help me?'

'I will try to smooth things with Mr Ciampini. Best I can do. But he's not an easy man to convince. It is the right choice, running. That's what I would do if I was you, except I would never be so stupid to be you – sleeping with the boss's daughter, then shooting her husband dead.'

'I didn't do that, the shooting.'

'That matters? No one will believe you. Run, Arturo. Where will you go?'

'I got a friend. He has a place in town. He's out of town.'
'You have the key?'
'He has mine, I have his. In case.'
'Hiding is the same as running when you do it right. That is true.'
Maletti beat it out of there, fast.

Satisfied that he had no customers, Ezra Knightsbridge consumed a butter biscuit. Then he got on the phone.
'Is he in?' he asked the man who answered. He told him who was calling.
He waited. A different voice said, 'Ezra, not a good time.'
'My condolences.'
'You heard?'
'Why we should talk. My place. At your convenience, Mr Ciampini.'
The pause was appreciably pregnant. 'Keep a light on,' the man said. 'I'll be down after dark. No sooner. Maybe later.'
'Thank you, old friend,' Ezra said, and they both hung up.
He wasn't sure how this next meeting would go, but he was sure that Arturo Maletti was a dead man. He was not the one to do the killing. That was something to arrange. The sooner the better. If Quinn was to live, Arturo Maletti had to be sacrificed. A good end to a bad life. Simple.
Ezra tidied up his space to prepare for his visitor.

Nun Stories

(A cluster of stones)

The boy who called himself Leonard cracked her heart open. He spoke of matters that confused her, enlightened her, inflamed her. A story he told reduced her to pulp. She shed her skin.
From Leonard, Quinn gleaned essential knowledge about Ezra Knightsbridge. He revealed that Ezra kept young thieves in tow. 'Hard to say how many.'

Being one of a crowd was off-putting. As if she'd been led into a cabal unwittingly, the doors locked behind her. Of course, she should have known. Ezra knew her parents. He knew thieves. He collected loot. The shock, then, was that he nurtured a youthful clientele; and as his crooks aged, he cast them adrift. She felt duped, but did it matter what designs he had on her, what plans he nurtured? Probably not. After Dietmar, she was probably done with stealing.

Leonard spoke of his own career as a small-time pusher. A separate education for Quinn. 'I'm called a pusher, but who do I push? People phone *me*. They want what I'm selling. My biggest problem is sorting through customers to finger the narc. Like tugging on Santa's beard to see if it's real.'

'That would be a problem.'

'Strange thing, every pusher in this city is known to the cops. They could round us up. Only they don't. Nobody cares. Soft dope is soft crime. Problem is, it's hardened up.'

'Meaning what?' Quinn asked.

Leonard explained, 'Used to be, we had our own sources. Grow-ops and import connections. The lines between suppliers and retail were wide open. Multiplied a thousand times over, small-time business is a big business waiting to happen. Who, do you think, could turn it into a big business?'

Not a difficult question. 'The mob?'

'The biker gangs, especially, once they took an interest. They've been coming after street dealers, forcing us to drop our old supply chains, adapt to the new. The "new" means the mob. Guys who resist enjoy three months in Montreal General to mend their broken bones. Their broken brains don't heal. Their spirits? Forget about it. Get caught a second time and it's six to nine months of hospital time and probably a lifetime of hobbling around. Some tough guys thought they could defend themselves. They bought guns. It got interesting. You think nobody is arrested for simple possession, but suddenly we have exceptions. Bikers advise the cops who to arrest. The guys who irritate the gangs are picked up off the streets, and when they're free they either come out in a box or run with a wolf pack themselves.'

'Not good,' Quinn concurred. He seemed plugged in. She saw the world as Leonard portrayed it, as a battle between the young, the free and the loving, against the dictates of an evil regime. The evil regime – part gang, part police – won every battle. The young and the free now served villainous masters. Dawning on her was the notion that she might not be immune to a similar trajectory.

'Used to be I bought and sold among friends,' said Leonard. 'All cool. Now I sell to friends and shit-bags, both. Nothing I can do about it. Instead of supporting an alternative sweet lifestyle – mine – I pay for mob bosses to sail the Caribbean. Thanks to my labor, nude girls bring them drinks and braid their short hairs.'

The sadness of his plight guided them into toking up. She thought he'd come on to her and plotted an escape that might not offend him. But if ardor moved through his bloodstream, perhaps the dope eased him off that thrum. They settled into talking.

Quinn, high, went first. Her life as a kid. Her daddy was a reformed crook, her mom passed away. 'I shouldn't say it like that. She *died*. She's dead. She lives in a box in the ground. Correct that. She doesn't *live* anywhere.' She dabbed a tear away. The dope eased her into a realm she rarely inhabited. What was usually a hollow of grief became a cavern of sadness.

Leonard started in on his own story. Overwhelmed by an emotional slurry, Quinn's defenses against an inner sorrow were annihilated. The beer, the dope and the story dismantled her dismay.

He had been raised by nuns, in an orphanage. Bad enough, it struck a chord because Quinn felt so attached to her own deceased mother that she could not imagine a childhood without that connection. Or, she imagined it too well and was mortified by the prospect.

The story grew more troubling.

'The nuns demanded that parents who gave up their kids at birth agree to baptize them into the Catholic Church. Most had no problem. Others who had a problem went along with it anyway. Some moms – or if the moms died in childbirth, the dads or another relative – said no. A small minority, but more than people realize.'

'You were one of those kids?'

'One of a number, so to speak.'

He appeared to be faltering. He was distant, carried away on the drift of marijuana, lured also to darker recesses of memory.

'Why "so to speak"?'

'If our birth mothers refused to let us be baptized, we weren't permitted to have names inside the orphanage.'

That edict hung in the air. Inexplicable, yet tempting her to comprehend it.

They smoked. They drank beer.

Leonard was sitting on the floor, his back supported by the low sofa behind him. He let his head loll onto a pillow. Quinn was on the floor also, cross-legged, yogi-style, slightly upraised upon a cushion. The music coming in through the window from a neighbor's transistor was obscured by a gently whirring fan.

Her voice quiet in the stillness of the room, Quinn finally asked, 'How could you not have a name?'

'The kids who weren't baptized were given numbers.'

And that was not all.

'Couples arrived looking to adopt. The kids with names were spruced up to look their best. The kids with numbers were purposefully left dirty and messy, so nobody would consider us. Sometimes, one of us got chosen despite that. I wish I could meet those parents today. I wouldn't shake their hands or hug them. I'd get down on the ground and kiss their feet. They gave hope to the ones always left behind.'

Quinn experienced a quaking inside her she did not comprehend. As if she was being shaken loose from a mooring, or from herself.

Leonard told her more.

The numbered children were permitted to watch the other children play with toys, but were not allowed to touch a toy themselves. The numbered kids didn't receive gifts at Christmas. The other kids did. They had to watch them open their presents and play with their new toys. For the Christmas meal, they were fed separately. They got a scrap of turkey, but none of the trimmings. During the year, they were never served dessert. No cake. No pudding. No pie. The other kids, with names, were served dessert. The shoes worn by the numbered children were the shoes discarded by the kids with names.

'Stop,' Quinn said, scarcely audible.

'Sometimes, the kids with names got chocolate bars. We didn't. That hurt. Really hurt.'

Children with names constantly instigated fights with the

numbered children, and when such a fight occurred the numbered children would be strapped across their palms until they bled.

Leonard was only a few years older than Quinn. This had all taken place while she lived in the comfort of her own home with a loving mother and an all-caring father, a man who had turned his life around to be a proper dad. Quinn's heart was breaking, not only for Leonard. His story of deprivation highlighted the loss of her mother in ways she never permitted herself to bear. She fell into a funk, missing her mom. She was calling out to her internally, in the way she could imagine Leonard as a child calling out to the night sky for reprieve, for help, for mercy, for love. His suffering was infinitely worse than her own, yet it drew hers to the surface from a deep and entrenched place. As if her mother was rising from the soil to smile upon her again, to hold her again, to say that everything was fine when nothing was.

'Puberty, what a horror—'

'Please, stop.'

'Children with names were taught dances in gym class.'

'You weren't?'

'We were. But with numbered kids, boys danced with boys, girls with girls. The girls didn't mind so much, except they saw girls with names dance with boys who maybe they were in love with. The girls with numbers cried at night afterward. We could hear them because we were stuffed in the same end of the orphanage. The boys cried, too, except we were quiet about it.'

Quinn's breathing grew troubled.

'Some days, priests visited. The numbered boys got it the worst.'

'Stop!' Quinn said sharply, and this time Leonard obeyed.

Later, he said, 'I never told nobody before. Not everything like that.'

They smoked.

Later, he said, 'When we see each other, us numbers, on the street – we're all doing shit – we don't talk. It hurts too much to see someone.'

Later, he said, 'When kids with a name see us, they want to spit on us. They don't, but they want to. They may not be doing so great themselves, but they were taught to despise us. Like it's in their DNA. I reckon they're really despising themselves. Their complicity. Although maybe I only want to think that way.'

'I feel complicit,' said Quinn. 'Having been happy as a child.'

'Why do you steal?'

She didn't answer.

Later, after they'd been quiet, she asked, 'Who named you Leonard?'

'I did. When you turn sixteen you get the name you were born with and they kick you out. I ran away when I was fourteen. They don't recognize my existence, so won't tell me my name. I took Leonard after the poet from here. The singer.'

She didn't know who he meant but nodded as if she did.

'I figured it might get me girls.'

'Did it?'

'Hard to say.'

'What's your last name?'

'I don't have one. Someday, I'll get a lawyer. Get a complete name. An official identity. Right now, I don't exist.'

'What's your number?'

'I won't tell you that. I won't say it out loud. Don't ask me to write it down.'

'Good. Never say it.'

'I won't,' he vowed.

'I have to go now,' Quinn said. She was falling apart. She felt spaces in her body, black holes in her head.

'OK,' Leonard said. He couldn't move he was so stoned.

'OK,' Quinn said. 'I'm going now.' About ten minutes later she struggled to her feet and left the apartment.

Quinn walked a short distance uphill onto Mount Royal, the city's largest parkland, with its prominent overlooks. Rolling grassland yielded to forest, hikers sojourned higher up. Quinn wandered serpentine trails. Other hikers were infrequent. Halfway through the maze, and off the trail, she sat upon an immense protrusion of tree root, sheltered by leaves and shrubs and rock. A chipmunk was annoyed and said so, chittering. She laughed. That emotional outburst broke a dam and she wept. She cried for the death of her mother. She had never fully submitted to tears before. Her chest cracked apart. She'd been too young to fully appreciate the grief that befell her at the time. She'd been confused and bucked against the reality. She felt bad for her father as much as for herself and resented the confluence of feelings. None of which she understood or could handle, though she didn't let them handle her, either. Leonard's story, the dope, the straits she was in, the beer . . . She was missing her mom and suddenly comprehended that her mother was no more, that she was dead. She'd said it at Leonard's house, said it that way for the first time. That her mom was *dead*. In a box. No more.

Quinn fell off the log of root and curled up and collapsed into a ball in a cavity and wretchedly wept. Her grief took over, she could scarcely breathe, scarcely cry, the whole of her torso aching until she grew worried for herself, fearing she would break. Any glimpse of sky or tree or leaf or soil or stone caused a convulsion, and she descended into fresh torment, gasping, coughing up spittle, breathing too rapidly.

She had no brown bag to assist her, no way to control her hyperventilating. Yet the pain of her body merely underscored the pain in her head, in her heart, in her being. She felt wrecked.

She believed she had wrecked herself. Her mind's eye veered to Dietmar and his death, and she believed she had wrecked him too. She was responsible. Who would do that? Stick a knife in his chest? Kill him. Oh, his last moments alive, how terrifying! Who would do that? But, also, who would think about taking a sweet boy in Social Studies and turning him into a getaway driver? Who would do that? *Who except me? Me. I did that. Deets's death was my fault.*

Thinking of him assisted her to resurface. In believing she had wrecked herself, in believing that she was responsible for Dietmar's death, she suddenly comprehended that she had both let herself and Dietmar down and let her father down, which had long been so important. A new dimension appeared as well – she had let her mother down, as if her mother remained a living being. Somehow. Somewhere. Out there. Or way inside herself.

She wanted to go back to Leonard and tell him how much she hated his bad nuns. The aching sweet solace of a mother's love, which she held night and day in her heart, had been denied him, and she hated that too.

She wanted to go back to Dietmar and say 'Sorry! I'm so sorry you're dead because of me! You were an incredibly sweet boy. You have no idea. I could've taken a deep dive for you in a major way.'

She felt so lost.

Then slowly she grasped that she was finding her way back

to herself. She tracked herself down. She was no longer crying, or shaking, or breathing too rapidly. She felt miserable, in pain and sore, but sensed that she could stand up if she really wanted to, that she could walk out of the woods if she found the path. She was not yet ready to do either, but when the time came she could. She'd haul herself up and go home. Live her life with a busted, blown-out heart. See what that did for her.

Quinn had to laugh at her own spark of sass. In a way, she felt sad to be returning to herself. Broken and annihilated, working through her pain had been real. Life never felt real enough. That's why she stole. She wanted to say that to Leonard, say it to him now if he was there. She stole in order to feel real. She stole to feel that life was real, that her mother had once been real for her. Only now her mother was dead and that was real, too. Her mother was gone, gone without her, and that would always be real.

She knew that now. Never again would she call anyone a moron for saying so.

Quinn remained in the woods, curled at the base of a broad tree between the huge root at her back and a cluster of stones. She gently clawed at the earth with one hand, tenderly scraped the soil. Then fell asleep in the warmth of the day. A tiny child in an immense wood with the thrum of the city coursing through the rock of the mountain and through the roots and trees surrounding her, and through her veins.

Plant 59

(Gin fizz for kids)

Cinq-Mars instigated the drive out to an industrial park near the airport. Giroux agreed to tag along if they stopped for burgers, and over lunch filled him in on his case regarding the theft of a painting. He pegged it as an insurance scam. 'When people don't piss and moan over what's missing and instead they brag about the value, it's a scam' went the gist of his conjecture.

'Yours isn't.' Cinq-Mars stabbed his fork into a French fry.

'Excuse me?'

'Isn't a scam.'

'What do you know about it?' Giroux scoffed.

'It's a Tom Thomson that was stolen, right?'

'Yeah, the painter was Thomson.'

'He's a big deal in English Canada.'

'Where does he live?'

They were occupying a pair of stools at a greasy spoon. Giroux ordered a strawberry milkshake, Cinq-Mars a Seven-Up.

'Yves, he's dead. One reason the painting is worth a lot.'

'Ah. He won't paint another one too soon.'

'Worth a mint if he does. Look, people often insure for less than the value.'

'Why do that?'

'To save on the premium. Or the market jumped ahead of them. Tom Thomson prices are exploding right now. Odds are the owner was caught underinsured. She could have sold it for a fortune – way more than the insurance pays – so your theory that she can hang the painting back up in a month doesn't wash.'

'Can't be hard. Stick a nail in the wall.'

'Yves, the painting is too famous for that.'

Giroux buried his face in the burger and thought things through. He resurfaced. 'Bona fide, the robbery?'

'A winner. Enjoy.'

They headed out. Soon after mounting the ramp onto an elevated expressway westbound, they were snarled in traffic.

'Beat the crowd? Go loud?' Cinq-Mars asked. He might be a stickler for the law, but mere rules were made to be circumvented. An illegal move, but who would arrest them?

Giroux grinned and stuck out his tongue. 'I got the siren. You do the lights.'

An overheated car had caused the snarl. Once past the bottleneck, they turned the sound-and-light show off and zipped along without traffic.

'Why are we out in the boonies?' Giroux wanted to know.

'Jim Tanner's an ex-con,' Cinq-Mars reminded him. 'He cracked safes. His daughter's a thief. Coincidence? It's not genetics. Did the father mentor his kid? Is he as clean as he looks? Also, did he have a grievance against the dead boy?'

'Woah! Heavy thinking there, Cinq-Mars.'

'Begs to be asked, no? Plus, my gut says the firebombing has nothing to do with Quinn. How does that fit with a kid? That leaves the dad. Who's he pissed off? What's he been up to in his day-to-day?'

'All right. We're dropping by his place of work, why?'

'I don't want the daughter to see me leaning on her dad. Besides, a man's home is his castle. At work, he's more vulnerable. He won't want to look like he's in trouble in front of his coworkers or his boss.'

Giroux agreed. 'We'll bust his balls.'

'Not what I had in mind.'

'Live and learn, Cinq-Mars.'

He wondered if he shouldn't have left Giroux behind, let him bully an old lady about her non-existent scam with a painting.

The area Giroux described as 'the boonies' was a mundane industrial park off the expressway. Jim Tanner's place of work, Plant 59 of the Continental Can Company, was noisy and hectic. The screeching of machinery, the shuffling of product and raw material – metals, fibers, glass – assaulted the senses.

Cops showing up didn't bother Tanner in the least, he welcomed the respite. He led the two men through a side door into the parking lot and sunlight.

'Suddenly, I like my job,' Giroux declared without explaining himself. Tanner took his meaning. He worked in a sweatshop, his days a grind.

'Honest work,' Cinq-Mars stated. The man went up a notch in his mind. Judging by the brief visit to the shop floor, it had not been easy to remake his life. Cinq-Mars was adjusting his line of inquiry when Giroux jumped in ahead of him.

'Have we met before, Mr Tanner? You have a record, but I doubt we go that far back. Have we had a run-in since your last arrest?'

'We met on a difficult day,' Tanner revealed.

'Then we've met. Did I chase you down a dark alley? What was difficult?'

Jim Tanner resisted combating the detective's tone.

'Wintertime,' he remarked. A man with a knack to draw a large picture with a few words. 'A mighty snowfall. I was on my way to work. Took the bus in those days. It was pulling into the curb when it shimmied on slick ice. As it braked, the tires locked. The bus skidded. I heard a scream I'll never forget.'

Giroux had never forgotten that day, either. Out of context, and without the hats and coats of winter, he'd failed to connect the man to the incident. The two men, in a twinkling, entered a private space, a quiet sphere of memory. Both gazed across the ugly lot, leaving Cinq-Mars on his own.

'What's going on?' the junior detective asked.

'A boy,' Giroux explained. 'About twelve.'

'Ten,' Tanner said. 'Tall for his age.'

'Ten. He was sliding behind the bus, hanging on to the bumper. The bus hit a dry patch and shunted him forward. A rear wheel caught his legs.'

'He was pulled up into the wheel well,' Tanner recalled. 'His legs went around and under. Lost them both, poor kid.'

The three men let that image settle.

'I happened to grab the call,' Giroux explained. 'First cop on the scene. This man,' he indicated Tanner, 'looked after the boy until the ambulance arrived.'

'Sounds terrible.' Cinq-Mars was a bit ashamed of the understatement.

'I couldn't deal with it,' Giroux admitted. 'This man—'

'I had no choice,' Tanner remarked, taking no credit but extending no blame. 'Covered him with my coat. Held him. I've seen him around the neighborhood in his wheelchair, so he made it. I went home. Skipped work. Told Quinn what happened. She was nearly off to school, but I had to talk to somebody and my wife had left for work. I think I hugged Quinn too hard. Scared her. I shouldn't have said anything. But I was in bad shape.'

Any plan formulated by Giroux to be tough in their discussion dissipated. He reverted to being as silent as on that tragic morning. Cinq-Mars, also deterred from his gambit, took a different tack, remembering something Quinn said.

'Who's your union, Mr Tanner?'

'United Steel Workers.'

'Is a strike looming?' Banners indicated as much.

'A vote next week. Do you think the Molotov is connected?'

'Do you?' He cocked his head. 'I can't link a firebomb to a teenager.'

'It's crossed my mind,' Tanner admitted. 'I talked to a few people. We're in a tough negotiation, but nothing nasty so far. No threats. Still, I can't rule it out.'

'Are you active?'

'Shop steward. Our nego-team is off-site, I'm point on the floor.'

'Sounds like a strong possibility of a maybe,' Giroux speculated. 'Your boss could have ordered it. Waited for you to be home so your house wouldn't burn down. Broad daylight so nobody gets hurt. Still, a message gets delivered.'

Neither Tanner nor Cinq-Mars would go that far, yet the possibility was viable.

'If that's what it was, it may be a one-and-done,' Cinq-Mars suggested.

'Us showing up doesn't hurt,' Giroux added. 'If the bosses wanted to scare you off, us being here may scare them off. Put an end to it, maybe.'

Jim Tanner was eyeing both men with intent.

'What's on your mind?' Cinq-Mars asked.

'My record. Banks, mostly. Private clubs. Back in the day, I could crack any safe. I had a knack.'

'You've gone straight since. You put in a hard day's work, look after your kid. We're not leaning on you.'

He believed that he could speak for Giroux on this one, as his senior partner's demeanor had conveyed respect.

The man remained remarkably still. When he broke off his self-induced trance, he took four steps toward the plant, then turned. 'Quinn, her stealing. I didn't know about it. I didn't put her up to it. It's tearing me apart, OK? I don't know what's going on with her. It's a kid thing. Just because I was in a ring . . .'

In stopping there, the man indicated that a doubt existed. He couldn't shake it loose. He wanted to say that he had done nothing to encourage her to steal, yet he couldn't rule out being a bad influence or a poor father. For him, Quinn's stealing and his career as a safecracker were difficult to separate. A mystery at its core. Had his parenting contributed to this debacle? He couldn't say.

Unable to conjure anything further that made sense to him, he returned to the bedlam indoors.

The two cops moved toward their car.

After they wedged themselves in and rolled the windows down,

Giroux had a suggestion. 'My oil-painting heist is a worn-out case, but I could get you up to speed pretty quick. Seems it's a genuine old-fashioned robbery, now.'

Cinq-Mars appreciated both the offer and the break in their mood. 'I could put in my two cents. My young thief will be taking up some time, though. I need to give her close attention.'

The senior detective indicated that he was willing to negotiate his schedule and duties, but had something else on his mind to run by Cinq-Mars first.

'I didn't talk it through with him or anything, but I figured something out.'

'Talked through what with whom?'

Giroux's response proved to be more complex than the question. 'Touton. Your old boss and mine. I couldn't figure out why he sent you to me. A sly codger, he doesn't do anything without a purpose. This isn't about you. He's not expecting me to train you. Also, it's not what you think – he didn't send you here to keep an eye on me. He sent you here for my protection.'

Which made absolutely no sense to Cinq-Mars. 'You've lost me in outer space, Yves.'

'Idiot!' he said, as if shouting but without raising his voice. 'I'm a dirty cop. I skim. Off the top. Touton knows it, and you've probably heard it.'

'Maybe,' Cinq-Mars concurred. Where was this frenzied confession leading?

The other man spoke in a hushed tone, but intensely. 'Grade-A bullshit, Cinq-Mars. The full load. Skimming gets me in. Cops think I'm dirty, and the bad guys presume I'm dirty. They figure they own me. They believe they can play me, but the whole deal's a play. Right down the wire. It's why I left the Night Patrol. Do you get it now?'

He looked at him through different eyes. If true, he was being initiated into a higher rung of trust and secrecy. Yet he remained skeptical. 'This is sanctioned?'

'In *this* department? I'd be whacked ten times over if people thought I was sanctioned to be a dirty cop. How would a play like that stay tight? Only one person knows. Just one. For my personal preservation. Check with him. You know who.'

'You're telling me, why?'

'Idiot!' he hissed between clenched teeth and slapped his own forehead with the stump of his palm. Cinq-Mars didn't know which of the two of them he was referring to. Giroux leaned in again. 'Touton's retiring. I need cover, in case my play goes south. He was my cover, now you are. He's set it up this way. What a bastard! I should have seen it coming. Plain as the nose on my face. Hell! Plain as the nose on *your* face. And that's saying something.'

They'd been partnered for a reason. Now Cinq-Mars knew why. He agreed that Armand Touton fit the general description of 'bastard'. Lovable, cranky, infuriating, and wise. And a bastard.

'How long have you been doing this?'

'Undercover, but not?' Giroux asked. 'Twenty years. Give or take.'

'That's hard time.'

'Tell me about it.'

Cinq-Mars put the car in gear.

'Three blocks straight on. East,' Giroux told him.

'What's there?'

'A bar. We got time owed.'

Cinq-Mars started out of the lot. 'You're such a bad cop,' he said.

'Don't worry about it,' Giroux counselled him. 'There's way worse than me.'

Giroux ordered a concoction called a gin fizz. Bars famously and illegally served the drink with minimal alcohol content to adolescents. The teens pretended to be barflies, downing their gin fizzes, and feeling giddy after four of them. Due to the warmth of the day, Cinq-Mars wanted something cool himself, and ordered a whisky sour. He was happy with his choice when it arrived, as was Giroux with a full jigger of gin in his and a silly paper umbrella.

'Cinq-Mars,' Giroux said, 'do both. Help me with the oil painting, put in time with the girl. I'm good with that. You blew off the insurance scam on a scrap of intel. I like that.'

'Knowing about Tom Thomson, that was just luck.'

'Maybe. But you heard it here first. You're good. Just don't let it go to your head.'

'I can blow off the firebombing too. It wasn't part of a union dispute.'

'You know that how?'

'I don't.' He touched the tip of his impressive beak.

'This is charades? You're a bloodhound? What?'

'What's the point of sending a message if the guy who gets firebombed doesn't know who did it or why? How is that a message? Plus, everybody in Plant 59 would be talking about it. Management, union, the receptionist. Guards would've been posted. Cops show up, a lot of people would be alert. Instead, nobody cared. I still say it involves the father, not the daughter. But it's not the strike. It's something else.'

'Like what?'

'Like I don't know what.'

'I'll drink to that.'

'Before you do. Tell me. What happens to the money you skim when you're dirty?'

'You're drinking it. This one's on me.'

'You could donate to charity.'

'To ease my worried mind? Like that would give me the image I'm looking for. If you gotta be you, I gotta be me. Truth is, I do give to charity.'

'Glad to hear it.'

'Maybe you heard of my charity. It's called the horses.'

'You gamble.'

'Don't sneer at me, you punk. I *live* at the racetrack.' He winked at him. 'Plenty of bad guys there. Talk gets told when people think they own you. I got ears.'

They stayed on for a second drink.

His old boss Touton wanted him to make connections. Cinq-Mars was learning why.

Sacrificial Zinc

(Prospective husbands)

That Giuseppe Ciampini visited Ezra Knightsbridge testified to his regard for the aging peddler. Normally, he took appointments only at his office. Scant few men were deemed worthy of a visit from Montreal's kingpin of crime.

Although he was always prudent, Ciampini did not travel

through town with trepidation. Neither did he flaunt his authority
or net worth. He had a driver and sat in the rear seat, yet his
vehicle remained a nondescript Chrysler. The driver didn't carry
a submachine gun in the trunk. At the pawnshop, Ciampini sent
his man inside to ascertain that the coast was clear, then stepped
from the car. He did not wait to have his door opened for him.
He had famously snarled that when he couldn't open his own
door he'd sign-up for beauty school.

He entered the premises under the jingling bell.

Among trusted cohorts, Giuseppe Ciampini was known
simply as 'Joe'. As a young hoodlum, he'd gone by the nick-
name 'the Whip'. An aunt had remarked that he was 'as quick
as a whip', and the name stuck until he scrubbed it from his
resumé. When a judge asked why he was called 'the Whip', he
replied that he was descended from lion tamers. The judge
pointed out that lions don't dwell in Sicily and threw the book
at him. Graduating from prison, Ciampini emerged as a leader
of men. Determined to eschew the customary trappings of the
gangster, he wouldn't drive Cadillacs or conduct business in
bars or visit his own strip clubs. He'd remain both tattoo-free
and bling-free. A businessman, he'd conduct himself accord-
ingly. He should be able to sit at a table with CEOs, as he did
for certain charities, without anyone being able to differentiate
the mob boss from legitimate businessmen. To those CEOs he
was Giuseppe or Mr Ciampini, while his close allies and enemies
in the business called him Joe.

During a brief stint in prison, Ciampini had forged a friendship with a man called Dezi, or Dez, whose full name was
Dezyderiusz Pilachowski. He might sometimes slip up and still
call him Dezi, or Dez, although he knew him now as Ezra
Knightsbridge. In prison, they had discussed opposing strategies
to guarantee they'd never return. One man desired to be the cog
in a machine no one noticed; the other plotted to insulate himself
within an impenetrable cocoon.

'A boat in the water,' Ciampini noted back then, 'needs sacrificial
zinc. You know this?'

'I was not informed.'

'Electrodes in water cause metal to disintegrate.'

'If you say so, Joe, then I believe with my whole heart.'

'The least noble metals go first. Zinc corrodes first. That way, the zinc spares the more noble metals, such as the bronze. When the zinc wears away, the other metals corrode, and fast. Replace the zinc, that's the solution. No corrosion.'

'I do not want to be the zinc.'

'Neither me,' Ciampini philosophized. 'I will circle zinc around me like a wall.'

'Makes sense. I will not live on water. I will be like dust.'

'Also makes sense. Underwater is where I breathe.'

'Should I call you the Dolphin?'

'You can call me Joe.'

'I don't know my name yet, Joe. Dezyderiusz has a record. A clean slate, I want. I will not be who I have been.'

'Good plan. Let me know your name when you are like dust,' Ciampini said. Decades later, as he stepped into the man's shop, he called out, 'Ezra, good to see you, old friend.'

'Good to see you, Joe. You look better every year. My eyes, hard to believe what they see.'

'What I love about you, Ezra. You talk like a nut.'

'From the heart. On a sad note, I am sorry for your loss, Joe.'

Ciampini gesticulated with a flex of his shoulders. 'I didn't lose my daughter. Only her husband.'

'Still, that's not right.'

'Our talk is connected?'

'Come into the back room. Let me lock up. Your wife is well, Joe?'

Ezra made tea. Ciampini sat expectantly, waiting for the kettle to signal the end of their introductory catch-up. A sortie into physical grudges – the liver, the lower bowel, the esophagus – came next.

'Gout in February. My God, Joe.'

'I heard it's bad.'

'A wickedness. The whole of your life lives in your big toe. Now, it's one more pill. Who can count? For the acid. Uric.'

'We're older, Ezra.'

'Are we wiser yet?'

The kettle whistled.

Ezra served the tea and added a butter biscuit on the saucer.

'How's business?' Ciampini asked. His tone shifted as nostalgia was put aside.

'I live free. No debt. No villa in France yet, either.'

'Before somebody shot my son-in-law, the surgeon, he was robbed.'

'A terrible thing. We live in a city of thieves.'

'You should know.'

'I will deny it to the police. To you, Joe, no.'

'Who else does not deny me?'

'Who would? No man.'

'The police. When I want to know what they know, I get answers.'

'Of course.'

'Her identity is known to me, Ezra.'

'Of course. You are speaking of the girl who robbed Savina. Foolish child. She had no idea who lived in the house.'

'Your friendship means a lot, Ezra.'

'Yours to me.'

'You know the girl. You don't hide this. I appreciate.'

'We cannot call her one of mine.'

'Is she not?'

'She does freelance. I am in a process, the beginning, to recruit.'

'I know where she lives. Do I have a good reason to send someone?'

'Why do I have a feeling?' Knightsbridge asked him. 'The hair on my arm rises. You look for someone who is not the girl. I sit in front of you. It cannot be me you are looking for.'

Ciampini rarely smiled, and only in response to humor. When he did so, his look was genuine. He was smiling now.

'A punk is missing. Gone to ground. The police hunt him, also. Remember Arturo Maletti? You trained him before he came to me. He's my sister's husband's aunt's long-lost cousin or something.'

'First, he went to jail,' Ezra reminded him. 'Not a kid anymore when he got out. A man, he went to you. He did not betray you then.'

'He did not betray you, either. He was too old for you when he got out.'

'I have no concern. I keep an age limit. The older ones grow less trustworthy when they learn too much. I do not have your resources for discipline.'

Ciampini nodded and sipped the tea. He bit off a portion of his biscuit and chewed with evident satisfaction. Tested a finger in the air briefly. 'I have concerns, Ezra. A surgeon with two bullets in his chest is no more a good surgeon.'

Knightsbridge was startled. 'He's alive yet?'

'Don't be ridiculous. He is totally dead. Did I not mention two bullets?'

'My heart goes out to Savina. The funeral, shall I attend?'

'Don't risk it. You don't like to be seen, and photographs will be taken by police. Not important. Savina will take a new husband. Do better next time maybe. An Italian man, maybe is next. What she cannot do next time is hook up with a man like Arturo Maletti.'

'Or exactly him, if I take your meaning.'

'Exactly my meaning. Her next man will not be him, a punk. A standard has been set. Maybe a lawyer will be good for a change of pace. An Italian would be nice, but not Maletti.'

Ezra nodded and caressed his left forearm. 'How do you prevent?'

'Find Arturo Maletti. The rest I take care of.'

'If I trip over Arturo, a stumble in the dark, I will call you.'

'I have no concerns. Even I will let the cops squeeze his balls. I hear they have a case. With me, I don't need a case. Either way, the lost must be found. The lost staying lost I do not accept.'

'I hope he trips over me, or me over him. Then I can help.'

'Good.' Ciampini cocked an ear toward the radio. 'Is that Andor Toth? I have the same record! But mine has scratches.'

'Exactly him.'

'A favorite.'

'I thought more of him when he was younger.'

'You're too critical. But when he played with Toscanini . . .'

'What the young can do. He was eighteen, then. I have a concern, Joe. Forgive my impertinence, please. No disrespect. But what if Maletti didn't do it?'

'Which murder we're talking about?'

'Either. Both. None.'

Joe Ciampini took a moment to think. Even after he made up his mind, he was willing to reconsider a position. 'Are you saying a terrible thing to me, Ezra?'

Knightsbridge put his cup down and spread his hands apart. A gesture of reconciliation. 'Only we think the best of our children. At times, disappointment knocks on the front door.'

'I'm aware,' Ciampini conceded, 'that Savina can be a bitch.

But even if Maletti is innocent of these two whacks, the both, does that make him an innocent man?'

Ezra was sifting for a nuance – he would not be given more – for verification. 'If it looks like Maletti did a terrible murder,' Ezra postulated, 'then to be accused is just. If he did not, he is a man who can stand being accused.'

'Always I enjoy talking to you, Dezi. In prison, nobody could understand us. Except us.'

'The girl? She will be a good recruit for me, I predict.'

'Send her to me, Ezra. We will talk. I can find her myself, but better if you send her.'

'What will you talk about?'

'I will ask her where is my baseball?'

Ezra expressed his curiosity the way many dogs and other creatures do, by tilting his head. 'Baseball?'

'It's my baseball. That stinking surgeon bag of shit was not supposed to lose it for me just because he got robbed. He stole it from me, the stinking hacksaw, the limp prick. The least he could do after that was keep it safe.'

'A baseball. Any old baseball?'

'Jackie Robinson signed. For Old Sal. Remember him?'

'A special baseball,' Ezra said. 'I will keep my eyes peeled.'

'Your eyes are important, Ezra. You know the thief who stole it. Get me the girl for talking to, and my ball back real quick.'

'For you, I will do my best. My utmost.'

'Track it down. Get me the girl so I don't need to trouble myself. Police are talking to her. They hang around. Why? That is a difficulty for me, that they hang around. A Night Patrol guy. If she comes to me on her own, not so difficult. You see? Be quick, too. That I will respect.'

'For me – forgive my request – you can do one thing. A small thing. For old times' sake, Joe. For all the good years.' Ciampini waited. 'Leave the girl alone.'

Joe Ciampini remained silent. Not a good sign. He asked, 'She's a good recruit?'

'Her father is Jim Tanner. Remember him?'

Ciampini nodded. 'The circle turns inside a wheel. The mother I remember, too.'

'Everyone remembers the mother.'

Ciampini gave it more thought, then said, 'Get me the baseball.

The girl, we'll see. If you spot that skunk Maletti slinking around, if you get word . . . If we find him and the ball, then the girl – so young, her mother's daughter – we can forget.'

After Joe Ciampini departed, Ezra Knightsbridge went behind the counter in his shop to process the talk. If he gave Joe the baseball outright, Joe would kill him. Possession of the baseball combined with knowledge of what it meant led to death, he knew that much. He was one of the few who had knowledge of what that baseball signified. Given the possible scenarios, Ezra did not believe he should be the one to die. A better outcome was warranted.

He could not allow the girl to fall into Ciampini's hands, either. If she did, she'd talk, reveal who possessed the baseball. He needed to keep the girl safe, if he could. Worst case, he'd adopt Ciampini's old strategy. The girl would be his zinc, to be sacrificed. He'd endeavor to avoid that, up to the point where he might be given no choice.

Raising Horses

(A snowflake in summer)

D usk sheltered the streets and tree-lined avenues of Park Extension as smaller children begrudged being called home. Older ones congregated on street corners or in parks or slouched off looking for trouble. Young adults also banded together.

The cusp between late adolescence and early adulthood was a precarious tightrope. Quinn Tanner divided her time between these two clans. Teens her own age looked up to her. Young men who were older thought of her as someone within their purview. Knowing the score, young women tolerated her status.

In Park Extension many streets bore bold French names. Champagneur. D'Anvers. L'Acadie. Querbes. Jean Talon. Saint Roch. These ran adjacent to streets reflecting a Scots and English heritage. Bloomfield. Ogilvy. Stuart. Hutchison. Ball. Wiseman. A mishmash of centuries-old allegiances. Those who gathered in Ball Park represented a broader world than that of the ancient battling nations of France and Great Britain. Kwang-Sun. Rahim. Padmini. Hideaki. Tomas. Dawida. Sanjay. Youthful men and women in a new world that proffered an open invitation to be explored. A world as baffling as it was inclined toward promise; a venture contradictory in its inducements and perils.

On that evening, Quinn separated from both those who were older and those younger, drawn toward a man who moved gently forward and back sitting on a swing. 'Need a push?'

'I've seen kids do this thing,' he replied. 'They stand on the swing. Get it going higher until they're parallel to the ground at both ends of the arc. Then they try a 360-degree spin, to go right over the top. It's impossible, except some do it. A few nearly kill themselves.'

'I've done it,' Quinn remarked. 'I was the only girl who could do it then, at that time. I was ten or so. Maybe all the kids go over now, once they're strong enough.'

'Doubt it. I agree with you, though – create a daring game, someone will take on the risk. I'm not surprised you did.'

'Ah, is that an insult?'

'A neutral observation, Quinn.'

'You bet. Are you hassling me, Mr Detective?'

Cinq-Mars liked the way she could suddenly turn direct and challenging.

'I'm sitting on a swing. Minding my own business. How is that hassling you?'

'You're here. You're a cop. You're keeping an eye on me. I call that hassling. My friends are wondering who's the guy in the suit.'

'You came over on your own.'

'Because I know who you are. Are you following me around?'

Rather than answer, Cinq-Mars began to swing a little. It felt pleasant. Quinn chose a swing two down from his and sat. She merely rocked and rotated on hers, at times imperceptibly.

He let his feet drag in the sand, slowing to a stop.

She made her case. 'How do I explain you to my friends? Oh, he's a guy who follows me around because he thinks I'm a thief or a murderer, probably both.'

'You *are* a thief.'

'They don't *all* know that. Although *apparently* a rumor is

flying around the block at the speed of light. The point is, they
don't know you're a cop. Yet. It'll break up the party when
they find out.'

'What's the rumor?'

'Why was Dietmar in his car in the Town of Mount Royal?
Why was he on the other side of the fence? Where was I? *The
Gazette* mentioned a robbery nearby. Some of my close friends
know I steal. They're asking stupid questions that maybe aren't
so dumb. Like did I kill Deets? I bet it's discussed behind my
back. God. Your being here does not help with that.'

'Relax, Quinn. Tell them I'm investigating the death of your
boyfriend. They might want to pitch in, help us out.'

An argument that made sense, although barely. She chose not
to concede the point.

'My fault,' she said. 'Deets getting killed.'

'Only true if you killed him. I only blame the killer.'

'You say. I say different.'

She looked straight up. Quinn gripped the swing's galvanized
chains and leaned back, looking at the sky. She let her head fall
further so that she was gazing at the street upside down through
the steel fence. As though her world had been turned upside
down and she was adjusting to it. Upright again, she stood on
the swing, bent her knees, flexed her thighs and drove her hips.
She reared back on the chains then released the tension, gaining
momentum, and swung back and forth. She went higher, leveling
off when she gained about sixty degrees beyond center. Her blond
hair flowed off her head when flying up, then over her face on
the descents. An anger, a resentment, a dismay returned, reminiscent of her time on the mountain when she wept and crawled
within herself in grief and loathing. This experience was not the
same; having been through it once, she'd been inoculated from
its repetition. Other latent emotional stimuli found traction,
though. Cinq-Mars could see in the force that she applied through
her arms, torso and legs, down into her feet, that this was not
merely a physical performance. An inner fury was expressed.
She was driving to go over the top, to do a 360.

The entire set of swings vibrated with the power of her fury.

'Quinn,' Cinq-Mars cautioned, quietly. He didn't want to pick
up the pieces.

She went beyond ninety degrees from nadir and fought for

greater velocity. She'd not been this tall or heavy when
performing the trick in the past. When she flung herself upward
to try to complete the circle, gravity yanked her back to earth.
The chain lost its centrifugal tension and she hurtled downward.
Not a full-on crash. She pulled out of her free fall, yanking
hard on the chains and twisting, her bottom thumping the seat.
Quinn reinvigorated the motion to try again, attempting to will
the full force of her propulsion to fly, fly, circle the moon, and
when she released herself again, she went higher, out to the
limits of her arc before she collapsed back, head first as she
hurtled down and past the swing's supporting bar, spinning in
the descent, crashing at the bottom, yet still holding onto the
swing before bouncing up erratically then falling off. She
grunted. Plopped on the ground, she fought off the wildly
gyrating swing seat. It smacked her once, hard. Finally, she
reached back, snagged it.

Half the people in the park were staring at her. Cinq-Mars
didn't stir. The girl might be bruised, but she was alive and OK.
He permitted her the dignity of recovering on her own.

Cross-legged, she took her time, then pulled herself up and
brushed off her jeans. She sat on the swing and offered her pals
a comforting wave.

'I missed,' she lamented.

'I know how it feels. Unable to do stuff you've done before.'

'Not the same,' she said. 'You're old. I'm young.'

'We're both younger than we will be. Older than we once
were.'

'Quite the philosopher,' she said.

'Point is I'm not old,' he corrected her.

That made her smile. 'You are to me.'

They sat on the swings in the deepening gloom of the
evening.

Street lights flickered on.

'I asked you to check on a few things, Quinn. Uncover
anything?'

She nodded. 'Arturo Maletti is one bad dude. A piece of royal
crap. I found that out firsthand.'

Not completely firsthand, he would learn, and only from a
distance. Still, she'd seen him in action. He was more than
surprised. He had expected she'd not come up with anything.

'He drove this guy around in his trunk to teach him a lesson.'
'Where'd you see him, Quinn?'
'Downtown.'
'Where downtown?'
'Let's leave it at that.'
'Who was the guy in the trunk?'
'A stranger.'
'Did you meet this stranger?'
'Doesn't concern you, really.'
'You met this person? You talked to him?'
'Yeah? So? It's nothing that concerns you.'

Like pulling teeth. 'What happened, if anything, that concerns me?'

A dribble of details. He got the impression that she'd had an adventure. She seemed affected and was quieter within herself. In her piecemeal retelling, her usual spiritedness was noticeably subdued.

'You religious?' she asked out of the blue.

Something had happened that day, Cinq-Mars was convinced.

'Treacherous question, Quinn.'

'How so?'

'No matter what anyone answers – yes, no, or only in a foxhole – the other person has no clue what that person really believes or feels. The short answer is yes. But you have no idea what I mean by that. You? Religious?'

'Not anymore. My mother was.' She shot a glance his way, indicating that she had something to confide. 'I'm Catholic. I've known nuns to be OK as people. Maybe a little weird. I've known them to be mean, too, but more like grouchy. In school, one of them enjoyed giving detentions. She set the record. Today I found out they can be evil.'

What had she learned?

'Priests, too,' Cinq-Mars concurred. 'Cops, as well. We're just people. Put a robe on a man, that doesn't make him a saint. Give a man a badge and call him a policeman, he's not necessarily a defender of justice. Ultimately, people are who they are because they are who they are.'

She was thinking, he could tell.

'That sounds like a rationalization,' she concluded.

'That's human, too,' Cinq-Mars said. Whatever was going on

with her, he understood that she was testing him. 'I'm sure you've rationalized being a thief.'

For a minute, she seemed to be mustering a response, then chose silence.

'What?' he asked.

'You're throwing my words back at me. I guess that's what you do, being a cop.'

Part child, part young woman. Unformed, but forming. Further dimensions resonated through her. Her responses indicated a range he couldn't fully grasp, more was going on with her than she revealed. Her friends took her to be a conundrum. Some knew she was thieving; among others, she kept that quiet. She knew that her friends were puzzled by her. A few condemned her.

She was right that he had thrown her own words back at her and done so as a policeman. No denying. Crooks frequently belittled arresting officers to demonstrate that the flaws in cops somehow excused their own, a continuous joust to show that no one should think themselves better than those destined for hard time.

Still, this wasn't a full-on interrogation. 'Asking questions is what I do as a detective. I'm not saying I have the answers. When people ask me if I'm religious or if I believe in God, I believe in the questions. The answers? Maybe that's why I'm a detective.'

She seemed less antagonistic with that notion.

'Speaking of questions, if you won't tell me where you saw Maletti and won't say who he dumped in his trunk and then released, what *can* you tell me?'

She preferred to ask questions of her own. 'Who raised you, Detective? Were your parents good, bad, or just boring?' Her spirit was returning, clawing back to the surface from a depth.

'Horses.' He had to keep her off-guard.

'Ah, you were raised by horses?'

'Pretty much. Like you, I lost my mom too early. I have a great dad. We lived on a horse farm. Horses, I think, taught me everything I know. I was going to be a priest. Then a vet. Now I'm a cop. Horses guided me every step of the way. Growing up, I was as close to them as to any person. Preferred their company. Still do, in a way. Not that I'm around horses much anymore.'

'Not if you live in Park Ex.'

'Exactly. What you brought up: I can be religious, but to be that way I have to accept the horrors of my religion. I can be a cop, but that means I contend with the evil that men do, including colleagues. There's a lot of criminals and other bad people in the world. Some are cops. Some are priests. You talk about nuns. In my view, even when the world is bright, the light still shines in darkness.'

Smiling again, amused. 'A philosopher, totally.'

She had started swinging once more, gently this time.

'And you, Quinn? What should you be?'

'To be determined, no?'

'I hope so,' Cinq-Mars told her.

He sensed that she was happy with his response.

'What's next?' she asked in reference, he understood, to their association.

'I ask tough questions. You return honest answers.'

She dug her heels into the ground to stop swinging.

'First,' he began, 'why won't you tell me where you were today? People your age are like that, but your circumstances are unique. Your boyfriend was killed. Why the big secret about where you were?'

Silence.

'Perhaps what you were doing pertains to secret things.'

'Like what?'

'Like what. I thought I was asking the questions. But since you ask . . . you're a thief, maybe you were out stealing the crown jewels. Or planning to knock over a bank. It's my business to find out stuff like that.'

'You don't take this seriously?'

'Of course I do. Here's something I was seriously wondering about. In the past, you stole items of value. You sold them. How did you off-load the merchandise, Quinn? Where did you get rid of your stuff?'

She'd had help. That had to be true. He anticipated her reluctance to share that level of information directly. To work around it, to work around her, he wanted to test the edges of what she kept hidden.

'Garage sales.' Ezra Knightsbridge had warned that the detective would be asking the question. Make him work for answers, then hand him a false one.

'Good reply,' he said. 'One thing wrong with it. You're not that stupid and neither am I.'

She stared at him a moment, then smiled. 'That's two things.'

'Shall we start over?' he suggested.

'There's this pawnshop on Jean Talon.'

'Nope,' Cinq-Mars told her.

'What do you mean, "nope"?'

'I know it well. They don't accept stolen property. Most pawn-shops don't, contrary to public perception. What else you got?'

She would have preferred drawing this out, as Ezra directed her to do – 'Say nothing, when he asks. He'll push. Say nothing again.' But this detective's tendency was to cut to the chase. What had sounded, on Ezra's lips, like a good plan wasn't working out so well.

'There's this guy down on Notre Dame.'

'East or West?'

'Ah, East. Yeah, East. No! West. I'm not sure. I get my directions mixed up.' Already her lie was crumbling, and she was only getting started.

'Let's say it's Notre Dame West for now. Who?'

'Do I have to say?'

'Yep.'

'You understand. It could be dangerous.'

'For who? Not for you.'

She delayed, then she said, 'What do you mean, not for me? Who else?'

'We'll get to that.'

'Get to what? Look, I'm answering your question, all right? I'm putting my life at risk here.'

'A tad overly dramatic, no?'

'You think so? When my boyfriend is dead?'

He conceded her point. 'Go on,' he said. 'I'm listening.'

'Look, you have to promise not to tell. Never tell. The guy I sell to scares the shit out of me. He works out of a bar called Dino's. Us thieves, we show up in the backlot behind it. He comes out.'

'Who?'

'The Rabbit. He's sort of Russian. But he speaks French.'

'Do you speak French, Quinn?'

'Enough.'

'Do you know what a snowflake is?' he asked her.

They were both rotating slightly on their swings.

'Excuse me? A snowflake's a flake of snow. No two are alike but I don't know who checks.'

'You're a snowflake, Quinn.'

'Excuse me? Because I'm blond? Up yours.'

'If you went to Dino's, if you met Guy Lappin . . .'

She shot a glance at him because he knew the man's name although she hadn't mentioned it.

'And if you tried to sell him stolen property, you would not have come through the experience unscathed.'

Lacking confidence in her reply, she tried it out anyway. 'Who says I didn't? Maybe I was molested a little.'

'With the people we're talking about, Quinn, there's no such thing.'

The lie wasn't her own, and she presumed that that's why she was failing at it so badly. 'If I'm not telling the truth, then how do I know about those people? Think about it. How do I know about Dino's, or the Rabbit?'

'Excellent question. It's not everyday knowledge. Only someone with deep experience would know the details. So, maybe someone gave you the story. That's what I'm thinking. Am I getting warmer?'

She declined to say.

'Did he invite you into his little back room?'

'Who?' she asked, but she knew who he meant. What she really wanted to ask him was 'How do you know?'

'Let me tell you about the man you know as Ezra Knightsbridge,' Cinq-Mars said, mentioning his name before she did. 'He's protective of young thieves, but only to a point. His people are loyal, but with him everybody has a shelf life. That's his pattern. How else can someone run a gang of juvenile thieves decade after decade and, except for Ezra himself, everybody stays young? My advice? Get out before you're twenty. On your own terms, not on his.'

Quinn was alternately studying the sand at her feet, drawing patterns with the toe of a shoe, and looking back toward her friends. She was listening, though. Cinq-Mars could tell that he had her attention.

'With Ezra – who has his virtues, cops leave him alone for a reason – with him, if you're on the inside, you'll never know if you're being protected or being set up to be sold out. If he feels the need to sell someone out, Ezra sticks a "For Sale" sign on the sidewalk. He'll hammer it home. Then wait for the highest bidder. Keep your eyes peeled. You'll see it for yourself someday.'

She finally had to ask, even though the question itself constituted an admission, 'How did you know?'

Cinq-Mars was glad she asked. He wanted to include her, to gain her trust through mutual knowledge. He was willing to give something back in the hope that she'd offer a nugget in return, now or another time. 'Everybody in the business – cops, crooks – they have their ways. Anyone who's been successful, and Ezra's been amazingly successful, has their signature ways. Ezra teaches his recruits how to explain things should someone ask. Trying to sic cops on the Rabbit is one he's pulled before. But it gives him away. If a thief blames the Rabbit, we can count on Ezra being behind that person. Anybody who worked for the Rabbit would never, ever, not for a second, give him up. Most people value their skin too much.'

'Their skin,' Quinn repeated under her breath.

'The Rabbit would peel yours off your bones for dickering on a sale. You, Quinn, would not last. Ten nasty men would do unimaginable things to you for free. They'd only promise to be violent. Then ten very gross men would pay to do the same. They'd want their money's worth. Then the Rabbit would hook you on heroin, what's left of you, and sit you down to map out your future. He'd set you up with clients around the clock—'

'Stop.'

'I'm not making this up. You have to know this.'

'I get it. Ezra said I should never go there.'

'I'm sure he did. That doesn't mean you never would. If you ever go down there, all I can do after that, all your dad can do, is pick up the pieces. Are you getting this?'

'I got it already. Will you stop?'

'First, what can you tell me? Where were you today? Who were you with?'

He waited.

'You think you shocked me, Detective. But I got shocked today, big time. Did you know that in Montreal nuns took in orphans, and if they weren't baptized they refused to call them by their names? Only by a number?'

Cinq-Mars knew the story and was familiar with the orphanage/

convent in question. Why was she relating the tale? What did it have to do with her?

'Quinn, did you meet someone who used to be a number?'

She nodded. 'He's given himself a name now. Calls himself Leonard. He ran away early, so he never learned what his real name is.'

'What's he like?'

'Skinny little runt. Nervous. He's all right, though.'

'Interesting. Do you know what his number was?'

'He won't say. I can't blame him for that.'

Cinq-Mars thought a few things through. 'We might be able to find it.'

'Find what? His number?'

'His name.'

'Really? He says you'd need a lawyer.'

'I might have the right connections without one.'

He had something to give to her now that surpassed anything she hoped for. Her chin lifted and dipped slightly, as if a nod was being vocalized, and somehow constituted a signed agreement.

Cinq-Mars stood. He dusted off the seat of his trousers. 'I'm off, Quinn,' he announced. 'Nice talking to you. We'll meet up again.'

'One thing.' Already she wanted to return the favor. 'You asked me to check out my old boyfriends and Dietmar's ex-girlfriends. I'll do that. But I was thinking, maybe you should check out the woman's boyfriends. We know about Arturo Maletti. Who says he's the only one? She had Maletti in the sack while her husband was off saving lives at the hospital. That tells me she's no saint. The husband, if he knew, might've been jealous, right? But what if she had more than the one lover? People think that boys are demons and girls are angels. But I'm a thief, right? Maybe this woman is more like me, wilder than anyone thinks.'

What counted was not to accommodate a new line of inquiry but to acknowledge her willingness to help. 'Worth looking into.'

'Can I ask a favor?' The girl, it would appear, grew increasingly demanding as their connection evolved. He liked that. 'Dietmar's funeral is tomorrow.' Quinn dipped her shoulder to indicate her friends on the other side of Ball Park. 'I heard through the grapevine that I'm not welcome. His family blames me. No surprise. Can you go instead? Tell me about it? This sounds crazy, but maybe you could . . . sort of go there in my place. You know? In a way.'

An emotion which went unexpressed underscored her plea.

'It's breaking my heart,' she admitted.

'I can do that,' he said. 'I read the obit. I know where it is.'

They shook hands. The girl was unaccustomed to the ritual. She never greeted her friends or parted with a handshake. This one felt weighted, significant. Separating for the night, Cinq-Mars believed he'd made progress. The time had come to talk with Ezra Knightsbridge. That old fossil would not be easily broken down. A reconnaissance mission had to be devised with care.

Missing Werewolves

(Mother Superior's numbers)

Half-asleep, Émile Cinq-Mars put the phone to his ear. A voice brayed at him with the persistence of an alarm clock. It took time to distinguish one word from another.

'Get down here, punk,' Captain Armand Touton commanded. He recited an address.

'Why are you calling me?'

'Aw, kid, am I waking you? Sorry. Let me put it to you a different way. Get your lazy butt the hell down here fast!'

Cinq-Mars struggled to read the hands on his bedside clock. 'This is when I sleep, Captain. I work days now.'

'Kid, if you work nights, you work nights. The bad guys are busy then. If you work days, you work day *and* night. Notice the difference. You want to be here.'

'Give me the address again.'

The North End. Traditional Mafia turf. He could be there in a jiff.

He showed up in his blue Volkswagen Bug wearing a T-shirt and jeans that looked as though he'd nipped them off a clothesline. He extended his badge to bully past an outer cordon. At the entrance to a lower duplex, Night Patrol detectives expressed surprise at seeing him again.

'Missing the werewolves, Cinq-Mars?'

'Break any big cases lately?' another cop asked. 'The Penny Candy Gang – work that one yet? Tough tit, I hear. A mean pack of eight-year-olds.'

He gingerly stepped around blood smears and a man's naked body before locating Captain Touton. 'Hope you got an alibi hanging off your ass, kid. People you talk to lately end up on the floor.'

'I never spoke to this guy. Who is he?'

'Arturo Maletti. Soon to be in a body bag.'

He looked back at the corpse in wonder. 'I've been looking for him, but never had the pleasure. He's been lying low.'

'Too low.'

Totally nude, the dead man lay across the floor on a shaggy cream carpet. A pair of bullet holes dotted his torso. Blood that had flowed freely stuck to the fibers.

'An arrest? Witnesses? Leads?'

'Who's that lucky? Dead of night. Not wearing pajamas. Not his house, and the tenant's away. You tell me who woke him.'

'Forced entry?'

'Best guess, he answered to a pal. Connected like he is, he let his own assassin through the door. Never figured he'd be the next tattoo on the man's dick.'

'Looks like a camera-free neighborhood.'

'That, and folks around here sleep soundly. Not a single insomniac on the block. Got to be a record.'

'Knowledgeable people,' Cinq-Mars surmised.

'Excuse me?'

'If nobody's talking, their mouths are staying shut for a reason. Not a good idea to talk.'

'You can shut yours, too. Some of us have a job to do.'

'Am I in your way? I'll move.' He took a step to his left. 'You brought me in, Armand,' he reminded his boss.

'Thank me later. Give the dead guy a once-over. Then we'll talk. I got something on my mind bigger than your fat head.'

That talk interested him more than the specter of Arturo Maletti prone on the floor. The man's demise was neither the stuff of nightmares nor a revelation. A simple, reasonably tidy, assassination. His secrets gone. Another minor victim in the simmering feud between rival gangs over the local and international drug trade. Montreal stood in a pivotal position on the map: the high point on a triangle, one side of which ran due south to New York, the other west through Toronto to Chicago. Gang operatives who preferred to work beyond the jurisdiction of the FBI found the city convenient for managing global transactions. Out of the country, out of mind. Intricately connected to the New York mobs, usually by birth, Montreal Mafiosi took advantage of their geography. Still, internecine battles waged. Arturo Maletti had been stung by gunfire. Another foot soldier. Another footnote.

Initially, Cinq-Mars had nothing to contribute to any discussion regarding Maletti's death. Until he broke off his examination, then he did. He waited for Touton to free himself up and come over.

'Whatcha got, kid?'

'Quick. Precise. Directed. Professional. One curious feature stands out.'

'Spill.'

'Two to the chest. One to the belly, off to the left, catching the liver. One to the heart. Almost the exact pattern to the inch that hit our surgeon, Dr Shapiro. Who might have been a moving target, as with him the shot to the heart missed slightly.'

'Why you're here, partly. Are you driving that shitty Beetle of yours tonight?'

'It's not shitty. I like my Bug.'

'Sorry. Meant to say shiny. Let's take it out of here.'

At a St-Hubert BBQ, part of a local chain, Touton ordered a whole chicken. He counted on the two of them demolishing it easily. Cinq-Mars raised the objection that he no longer took his meals in the middle of the night, which proved untrue. Over the course of their talk, he gnawed on a leg, ate a breast with his knife and fork, then picked away at a wing and the remains of the carcass. They ate and dissected the gangland slaying.

Eventually, Touton came clean. 'Didn't expect to be working with you again, Émile. This case comes with a bigger overlap than I thought. I won't be around to see it through. It'll be up to you.'

'Meaning?'

'Two bullet holes. Identical pattern. Easily a coincidence. A prosecutor might want five bullet holes just to hear you out. Even then, he or she might laugh. Less than three won't be considered a pattern if the defense attorney has a brain.'

'We both noticed. Identical.'

'Shut up and listen. Tonight's shooting was not the second time I've seen that pattern. It was the fourth.'

'Get out.'

'Going back in time. Memory can play tricks, but I believe I can still count. When the surgeon went down, my brain swung a bat. A foul tip. Nothing I paid attention to. When I saw Maletti tonight, I got hit by a pitch right between the eyeballs. I've seen that pattern before. Not only once. Twice. Four times in all. I know the killer. Of the surgeon, and of Maletti tonight.'

'If you say so. Who?'

'Giuseppe Ciampini, to some. Joe to the rest of us.'

'Hold on,' Cinq-Mars said.

'I won't. Catch up.'

'You mean Ciampini in person?'

'Exactly. Ciampini killed his son-in-law, and he killed Arturo Maletti tonight. He didn't *order* either hit. He came out of his man-cave and did the dirty deeds himself. Solve these two murders, Cinq-Mars, you put Ciampini away.'

'You know this how?'

'Because of two murders years ago. He wasn't always the kingpin. Was a time he was a lowlife punk on the make. He killed a mob boss back then. Getting away, he killed a cop. We couldn't prove it. But I know he did it. Tonight the same, and also with the surgeon. Identical bullet pattern for the same reason.'

'There's a reason?'

'The shot to the gut and liver inflicts the worst pain. He lets his victim roll around in misery for a minute or two. That's why we've got blood in the foyer. Maletti then walked, crawled, backwards until he fell. Agony, taking one in the gut. Then he kills him. Not so much to put him out of his misery, but there comes a time to get out. One bullet to inflict the worst punishment possible, the second to do what he came to do. Through the heart, to kill the guy dead.'

The slight smile on Touton's face was a giveaway. He had more to reveal.

'Go on.' Interested in what his former boss postulated, Cinq-Mars pushed him. 'What?'

Touton lowered his voice, as though to intensify the tale. 'The last two murders connect to the first two. Which is why Ciampini couldn't order them. He had to do the dirty work himself. To keep a secret under lock and key.'

What lock? What key? Cinq-Mars was wondering to himself. To Touton, he said, 'Tell me.'

'What connects all four? You came across it.'

'Not to my knowledge.'

'What pissed the surgeon off?'

Cinq-Mars had no clue.

'A goddamned missing baseball.'

The story went back to Touton's earliest days on the force. A mob boss was hit. Armand Touton was first to answer the call. The murder was meant to look like a robbery gone bad. Items were stolen. No cop believed that scenario, for no crook, not even an amateur thief, would break into the home of a mob boss. People in the rackets knew better. That same night, about a mile from the murder and before it was reported, a cop stopped a car for a traffic violation. That officer was gunned down, the pattern of wounds identical to the first shooting, but a different gun. 'If that cop had been in my place and I'd been in his, I'd be dead on the pavement. I took it personal. Never forgot that one. I'm not a crazy-assed Catholic like you, I don't forgive.'

Did the cop stop the original shooter? Investigators thought so, despite a second weapon being fired. Very possibly, that second gun was stolen from the gangster's home. Touton was handed the task of itemizing what the mob boss's widow claimed was taken, even if the robbery was a fake cover for the hit. The short list included a pistol, and also included a baseball with her husband's name on it signed by the legendary Jackie Robinson.

Cinq-Mars looked catatonic.

'I know you're a religious nut bar, Cinq-Mars. Every so often, break away from the code. You should express yourself. You want to. Now is a good time. I will forgive you, Émile. Say a Hail Mary later. Let it out now.'

Cinq-Mars thought about it. Then he said, 'Holy shit.'

'There. Don't you feel better?'

'*Holy shit!*' he said again.

'Don't get carried away. I don't want you sent to hell on my account.'

Both men were experiencing a rare euphoria.

'How come you didn't nail him way back then?'

'Nothing on him,' Touton admitted. 'Also, I was only a beat cop.'

'How do you know it was him?'

'It suited his purpose to let the street know he did it. Ciampini was the next tough guy on campus. He had to make sure that a few key people spread the rumor. He denied it in some quarters, let it fly in others. No trail to follow, though. What he was bragging about couldn't be called evidence. That a cop died, that's the only part that kept the case alive. Otherwise, one bad guy whacks another bad guy, who gives a shit as the years fade away? But a capital offence, that stays alive. A dead patrolman keeps it personal, not least because I was a patrolman on a different street that night and lived. The baseball would incriminate the killer if it ever showed up. Maybe it showed up in his daughter's house. Before you know it, her husband is dead, then her lover. Draw me a connection, Cinq-Mars. Visit me in my retirement home with the news that the king is dead.'

Cinq-Mars shook his head, reality sinking in. 'I can't convict on the old crimes.'

'Convict on the new ones. It helps – a ton – to know who you're looking for. And it helps to know who's in panic mode right now.'

Cinq-Mars concurred.

'Never forget, Ciampini is more likely to fear his friends in New York than his enemies in Montreal.'

Cinq-Mars raised an eyebrow, cottoning on.

'There's justice, then there's gang justice. Sometimes you gotta ask, "What's the difference?"'

Cinq-Mars continued to demolish the carcass before him. He ripped off a wing and circled it in the air with a different thought. 'Another shadowy figure from the old guard's involved, Armand. This involves the dead boy in his car, maybe, and the young female thief.'

'Who would that be?'

'Ezra Knightsbridge.'

Touton sat back. Cinq-Mars had the impression that he wanted to applaud. 'A case of that old saying. What goes around the mountain, comes around again.'

Cinq-Mars finished chewing. He couldn't believe how hungry

he was. 'Maybe I should return the favor. Wake you up in the daytime. Pay him a visit.'

Touton took it under advisement. 'I guess, when I retire, I'll switch over. Sleep at night. Prowl around in daylight. Maybe I'll take you up on that. Go for the practice.'

They clinked beer glasses.

'Boss,' Cinq-Mars said, 'you'll love it. Hunting, fishing, all daytime stuff.'

Touton clicked his fingers. A notion stirred. 'I'll need gear.'

The younger man caught on immediately. 'I bet Ezra sells fishing rods. Is he allowed to sell firearms? Either way, I bet he has rifles lying around.'

'Word of caution,' Touton said. 'I can't go with you. His old cell-mate might get wind. We have to be careful what we put out there.'

'Old cellmate? I didn't know he'd been inside. I thought Ezra was invincible.'

'It's not on his record. He changed his identity once he learned the hard way.'

'The cellmate?'

'Joe Ciampini.'

His projected chat with Knightsbridge had more potholes than a Montreal street after a frigid winter followed by a warm spring, which was saying something.

Touton was beaming. 'I got more. Hey, I don't get you out of bed for nothing.'

Sly bastard. 'Tell me.'

'Your first vic. The kid in the car?'

'Crooked?'

'Straight as an arrow. He took Social Studies, whatever that is.'

'This I know. So?'

'He applied for the Police Academy. He was accepted.'

'What?' He was stunned. 'No.'

'Wanted to be one of yours, Cinq-Mars.'

'Mine?'

'A bonehead cop with a university degree. A brainiac. The point is, he was one of ours. Could be he was going along with the girl to help put her away. Give himself a leg up, at least in his mind. Either that or he fell in love. Or lust. This isn't a cop killing, but the murder is starting to fit tighter to the bone.'

Cinq-Mars had much to chew on. He vented his energies on

the chicken. The news would shock Quinn. Her boyfriend had been a wannabe cop. She sure picked the wrong getaway driver for herself.

Or had he picked her?

Cinq-Mars drove Touton across the breadth of the island to HQ, then himself back to Park Ex. He caught a couple of winks before his alarm sounded, then called his new partner at home. 'I'm not going in.'

'You sick? Hungover again?'

'I'm on the job, Yves. I need to make a side trip, and I already worked half the night. Captain Touton will vouch for me.'

'I can go where you go. No law against it.'

'You won't fit in.'

'Anywhere you go, I can go too. A strip club in the morning? I'm there. Gambling den? I know a few. Stakeout? Give me a dog, a Coke, and a few French fries. I can hold my piss for hours with good food.'

'A convent.'

Silence at the other end. Then, 'OK. You can go on your own.'

'Catch you later,' Cinq-Mars said. 'Oh, did you hear? Arturo Maletti bought the farm.'

'No shit. Hey! Was that overnight? You know what it means.'

'Tell me.'

'A Night Patrol case. Frigault and Caron are out of the picture. Their one good suspect is no more.'

'Try not to celebrate too much.'

'Try and stop me. Get thee to a nunnery, Cinq-Mars. Don't wear out your knees.'

At the imposing front door to Our Lady of the Shores, Cinq-Mars was greeted with suspicion. His badge permitted him to posit a request, and he had reason to believe that Mother Superior Marie-France Dumont would admit him once she learned who was calling. Policemen in general might be kept at bay; he had personal history with her. Work they'd shared on a charity had been congenial.

As expected, he was admitted. She'd met his father, in different circumstances, and asked after him. 'He knows horses, Émile. As do you.'

'As do you, Mother Superior.' They hailed from the same rural region of Quebec.

'In another time. We have none of God's four-legged creatures within these walls, with the exception of vermin and the cats who cull their ranks.'

The walls of which she spoke were thick stone, in place for more than two centuries. They hoarded secrets through time. Cinq-Mars knew the mother superior to be contemporary, wise and formidable; she had addressed the culture and failures within the Order. No mean task. Cinq-Mars brought up past sorrows.

'You have neither his name nor his number?' Mother Superior Marie-France inquired.

'I hope to secure both.'

'Why both? Sad to say, he cannot have forgotten his number.'

'He knows it. I don't. If I can show him that I can accurately repeat his number, he'll be confident that the name I reveal is correct.'

'Yes. I understand the virtue of your proposal.'

'And I understand the times. This is a communication between the Order and an aggrieved young man. I see no value in the matter traveling any further.'

'Yet no guarantee,' the mother superior surmised.

'None,' Cinq-Mars admitted.

She nodded. 'Our past is not the secret many prefer.'

She gave him a prolonged gaze. Of regret, of sorrow. Also, of determination. Battling ghosts and history proved a difficult war.

Mother Superior Marie-France called in her secretary. They worked out the parameters for the date of the boy's abdication – their word – from the orphanage. Cinq-Mars described the boy's likely body type at the time, having garnered the information from Quinn, so that those too tall, too muscular or too heavy could be eliminated from the search. The secretary fled to undertake her study.

'This should take less than a fortnight,' the mother superior advised him. He trusted that she spoke with poetic license. 'Many abandoned children departed under unfortunate circumstances. Previous generations of our sisters declared that they were abandoning themselves. Ridiculous in the light of day. Since then, several have made formal requests to learn their identities. We no longer deny them outright. It's case by case. When we have the number, it's a quick notification.'

Without the number, his request was complicated. Cinq-Mars waited in an anteroom for half an hour. The stillness engendered by the stone walls compressed him. A resonance that echoed through time. Centuries of prayer, fasting, contemplation, ritual, lament and deprivation. Cinq-Mars had visited seminaries and monasteries – and once, a convent – when he'd contemplated the life. When the time came to decide, he rejected the calling.

A philosophical experience for him. In stepping away from one calling, he'd deeply felt the lure of another that was also invisible, and initially unknown. Whatever his work in life, he felt it had to be as vital, life-affirming and compelling as his expectations for the priesthood. He considered a life devoted to animals and believed it to be the answer. That calling, while attractive, never exerted sufficient heft.

Then he discovered work conjoined to a different animal: the human criminal. Justice and mercy, truth and lies, passion and compassion, to serve and protect . . . The calling was large enough, romantic enough, and challenging enough. Early on, Cinq-Mars accepted that he was born for the task. He demon-strated a talent for detection and seemed to possess an intuitive acumen.

Instead of wrestling with demons of the spirit world, he opted for battling their earthly counterparts. And yet, did he not still cling to the side of the angels? He hoped that that proved true, that his life might be well spent.

The secretary scurried past him. Sister Florence was not going to speak to him directly. She tapped timidly on the vestry door. She was quickly admitted, and without invitation Cinq-Mars followed her inside.

The mother superior, seated at her broad oak desk, studied the report before revealing its information. 'Please do not surrender the name until you and the young man confirm the number between yourselves. In case we miscalculated our assumptions.'

He accepted the proviso.

Away from the hallowed halls of contemplation and piety, he returned to work. Back on the streets of murder and deceit. Given that same decision to make again, he'd still stick his head and hands into human villainy.

PART THREE
THE PARK

Tombstone Ghost

(A rat's ass)

Along a ridge across the high ground of the cemetery, a figure moved with both impunity and purpose. Cinq-Mars detected a second form, this one below the ridge, less conspicuous amid the tombstones. A man of some years, it appeared, who differed from the granite by being mobile.

Following a shower, the day was muggy under threat of more rain. A scud of dark cloud pestered the mood of the funeral. Dietmar Ferstel had died under circumstances both baffling and frightening that left his family devastated, his friends sorrowful, and a killer on the loose who unnerved the community.

Émile Cinq-Mars discounted television funerals. In his city, people rarely made the trek to the gravesite. A service of remembrance in a sanctuary or at a funeral parlor might be well attended, but only immediate family and closest friends continued to the cemetery. Burials on the sprawl of Mount Royal presented logistical challenges for larger groups of mourners and were discouraged. He had no intention of witnessing the internment himself, and only at the last moment changed his mind. Mourners were embarking on the lengthy walk from the funeral home, possibly because so many were young. Uninitiated into the rituals of death, what they knew about the process was gleaned from movies. They were determined to see their friend into the soil.

The youths intrigued Cinq-Mars. Fault lines demarcated different groups. One derived from the young man's upbringing in Park Extension – their diverse ethnic mix one clue to their identity, their discomfiture with funeral haberdashery another.

A second conglomeration of young folk was composed of university students. They'd made no attempt to dress for the occasion. Not having anticipated the need, living far from home, they lacked the garb and came as they were, as if off to a summer class. They, too, were decidedly melancholy and bewildered.

The third group of young people were less easy to align. His interest in them spurred Cinq-Mars to drift along after the casket. They were quiet, somber, closely knit; fewer in number than the other representative groups. They made a point of sticking together and did not mingle with other mourners. Despite this apparent aloofness, or defensiveness or mere shyness, they obviously wanted to be there. Mostly male, this third group had shown up in black. Cinq-Mars hazarded a guess that a few had purchased suits especially for the occasion. They seemed emotionally stung by Dietmar's death and by the funeral itself. As if, Cinq-Mars speculated, they'd lost one of their own, a brother.

Across the plateau of gravestones, against the murky, gusty sky, one lone figure lurked on her own. Not permitted to attend by dint of a grieving father's decree, Quinn had asked Cinq-Mars to go in her stead. Then showed up anyway. She stood far off. When the final words were spoken – the reminder that dust and ashes await corporeal forms – Cinq-Mars wandered in her direction. He found her to be neither furtive nor embarrassed. Pale against the dark sky, Quinn stood still and waited for him to join her.

'I could have saved you the trouble,' she apologized. She was wearing a pale-yellow knee-length dress with a muted floral pattern, flats, and a small woven purse. With lengthy rope straps, the clutch hung over a shoulder and fell to her hip. 'A last-minute-type thing.'

'Not an issue. I might have come on my own.'

'Why?'

'To see who showed. When a crime boss or a high-ranking gang member is involved, cops attend. We photograph the mourners.'

'I hope you send them a copy of the album.'

'There's a thought.'

She lifted her purse and let it fall back again. Cinq-Mars took it as a sign of impatience. 'Deets wasn't in line for that kind of attention.'

'Maybe he should've been.'

Without either of them saying a word, they lit off in a generally downhill direction toward a gravel path. On the way, they tramped across wet grass in need of mowing.

'What did you mean by that?' Quinn asked along the way.

He'd wished he'd chosen a different route. Her feet and his

were getting soaked. 'Thieves might have been here. Do you know anything about them?'

'Dietmar didn't have thieves for friends. Neither do I.'

'You didn't know him that long.'

'Don't be crazy.'

He could inquire if she knew that Dietmar planned to join the police department but chose to save it. The third group might have been a band of cadets, future cops, not thieves. 'How are you getting on, Quinn?'

'I'm all right.'

'Need a lift home?'

'Mmm, sure. If it's not out of your way. Thanks.'

'I can drop you. I should make an appearance at my *poste*. By now, my fellow officers are wondering if I'm still on the payroll. Incidentally, did you see an old man walking around up there? He's slipped out of sight.'

'Up where?'

'Between where you were and Dietmar's grave. Off to your left.'

'I wasn't paying attention. Is it important?'

'Struck me as odd. Hey, let's pick up the pace. That cloud looks mean.'

The sky blackened as they hurried down the winding path and across the parking lot. They reached the Volkswagen Bug as the first giant drops smacked the windshield. Their arrival was followed by a cloudburst, a sufficient fury to keep them stationary and make them wait it out in the car.

Quinn removed her shoes so her feet could dry. Cinq-Mars endured in his sopping socks. He had a notion. 'Where am I on your trust meter these days?'

'Jury's out,' Quinn said.

'How about we pay a visit to your new friend from the trunk?'

'Leonard? I only just met him.' She shot a glance at Cinq-Mars, then qualified her remark. 'I guess he's a friend.'

'I found out his real name. We could let him know.'

Quinn stared hard at him. She would not relax her gaze. When she could not bore through his implacable exterior, she asked, 'How would he know – or how would I know – if you're telling the truth? Maybe you made up a name.'

'Do you know his number?'

'I told you. He won't say it.'

'I found it out. If I can verify it with him, then it follows that I also have his real name.'

He had her on that one.

'You could tell it to me,' she suggested. 'I'll tell him myself.'

He appreciated the wisdom of her proposal.

'That's where I am,' he noted, 'on your trust meter.'

'You're a cop. He sells weed for a living. You're not the best fit.'

'Oh, please. Do I give a damn who sells marijuana? What cop does?'

'It's still possible to put someone in jail for dealing. You'd have that over him. You might force him to tell you things. To become a snitch or a narc. Instead, trust *me*. Let *me* tell him his name.'

He continued to appreciate her point of view. She was right, too.

Quinn detected that she was gaining ground. 'What about it?'

In his official role, he ought to maintain position over the criminal element, never allow a person of interest any measure of control. This relationship differed from the normal cop–crook warp and woof. He could tell her the trunk boy's number and name and let her be the one to inform him. A gain to take away might be a measure of trust. A loss might be scored as well, for she'd believe that she could get one over on him. Not an ego issue – a time might arrive when she needed to believe that he could come through for her, when she might need to count on him. If she thought he was easily beat, it could work against each of them.

Cinq-Mars tried to strike a compromise. 'How about if we let your friend decide? Go to Leonard, ask if he wants to meet me. If he says no, I might still hand over the information, or not. At his end, it's a roll of the dice. If he agrees to see me, we don't have a problem.'

Quinn stared out the window despite having nothing to see beyond the smear of constant rain. They both reacted to a flash of lightning. When the rumble arrived it was distant, almost comforting in its steady, grumbling litany.

'Why meet him?' she asked. 'You want to, that's pretty clear.'

'I'm hoping to find out anything he can tell me about Arturo Maletti.'

'He's afraid of him. I doubt he'll talk about a man who controls his life.'

'Maletti no longer controls anyone's life. He was shot dead last night. We have a good lead on who did it, so don't worry. Leonard is not the object of my interest there.'

He had gained position again.

'Maletti's dead?'

'As a doornail.'

'I don't know . . .' she said, then stopped herself in mid-sentence.

'What don't you know?'

'Why so many people are ending up dead. Anyway, what's so dead about a doornail?'

'Good question.'

'Do you have an answer? I bet you do.'

He shrugged, somewhat shyly. As it happened, he did have an answer. 'It's an old expression. People once reused everything, including nails. When they built a door, they pounded big fat nails through the planks and the spike ends went right through to the other side, sticking out, so they'd pound them flat into the wood, bending the nails at right angles. It's called clenching. That "killed" the nail, so to speak. It couldn't be reused. *Voilà!* As dead as a doornail.'

She rarely received satisfactory answers to obscure questions. Quinn was enjoying this, as a slight smile demonstrated.

'Ohh-kay,' she said, in a singsong, teasing tone.

Lightening scorched the sky. Thunder shook the Beetle and the two people in it.

'Whoa! Close!'

'Holy . . .!' Quinn called out. Too jolted to finish her sentence.

They couldn't see or hear anything but rain. The sudden bursts were so violent they pictured trees toppling, or in flames. Often startled, they frequently grinned crazily at each other.

Cinq-Mars experienced a nudge. Readily identifiable. Quinn, in the car, was surprised by the flash of light and thunder's boom, her face animated. She was naturally expressive. They weren't so terribly far apart in their ages; she was nearly two-thirds his. Nothing he'd act on, and he was cross with himself that an inkling had surfaced. Nature didn't always ask permission. In acknowledging the nudge, the sexual zing through his bloodstream, he detected his own loneliness. He had hardly had time to mourn the demise of his recent romance, and in a way lamented its end now. More troubling to him: he was noticing her. Her own loneliness. Difficult to not respond. He turned away instead. He had to snap out of it.

The next flash was further afield, across the cemetery plateau.

'Deets is being watered in.' She didn't mean to be funny. She found it horrific.

Cinq-Mars had to straighten himself from his leanings. Internally, change the subject. He asked, 'Quinn, tell me, where's the baseball?'

She looked at him. Wondering how that had emerged, almost literally out of left field.

'That's important?'

'Might be.'

'I can't say.'

'Then neither can I, about its importance. Sometimes, Quinn, the time you buy for yourself is the time you waste.'

She gave him a different look. One he knew he deserved. 'What the hell does that even mean?'

He shook his head. 'Nothing. Something my ex-girlfriend said to me. I'm still trying to figure it out. Wrong context here. Sorry.'

That bolt of lightning had burned through his usual decisiveness.

Cinq-Mars tried again. 'What about Leonard? Should we help him?'

She nodded. Reluctant, but not intransigent. As if the lightning had charred her resistance, too. 'He lives in the Student Ghetto. If you park where you can't see me go in and stay in the car, I'll ask him. If he agrees, I'll take you to him. His place or elsewhere. But swear to me you won't hassle him. If you do, I won't cooperate for another second, even if you send me to juvie.'

'Oh, like you're cooperating now?' Cinq-Mars chided her. He grinned so broadly that he tugged a smile out of her too. Then he said, 'Done deal.'

The rain was beginning to let up. He started the car and they moved out of the parking lot, joining a string of cars doing the same.

The rain ceased as Quinn went off in search of Leonard. Sudden blue sky. Cinq-Mars lowered the car's visor.

He didn't take note of the young man approaching on the sidewalk. He had not expected him to arrive on his own, without

Quinn. Before Cinq-Mars could react, the boy opened the front
door of the Bug and slid in beside him.

The kid stuck out his palm. 'Leonard,' he said. 'I don't give
a rat's ass.'

'Excuse me?'

'I'm Leonard.'

'That part I got.'

'An expression – give a rat's ass. I don't, neither.'

'How do you do, Leonard. I'm—'

'I know who you are. A man with a big nose in a blue Bug,
Quinn said. I have a question.'

'The adjective I prefer is prominent. For my nose. Go ahead,
I'm listening.'

'What do you want with me?'

The young man had a look. Being wiry-thin and on the short
side, he pulled off to perfection the persona of the scavenging
intellectual on the run, as if to that mutinous manner born.
According to Quinn's story about him, that was the case.

'I have information you're interested in,' Cinq-Mars said.

'Not an answer to my question. What do you want with me?'

'What makes you think—'

'Your job.'

'That's cynical.' Cinq-Mars studied him.

The young man didn't back down. 'I'm out of here if you
won't answer.'

'My circumstances recently changed, Leonard. I was on the
Night Patrol. You've heard of them. Now I'm working out of a
suburban *poste*. I need connections. People on the street. You
could be part of that.'

'No fucking way. You're asking me to be your snitch? You
can forget that before you twiddle your next thumb.'

'That's not what I said.'

'It's what you meant.'

'Big difference between a connection and a snitch. A connection lets me know who's in trouble, who's been broken, who
needs help on an emergency basis, who's going to need long-term
rehab. A snitch betrays his friends, but a connection knows who
to call when things go south. Big difference.'

Leonard studied the man behind the wheel.

'Where's Quinn?' Cinq-Mars asked him.

'She's having the time of her life. I bought her a humongous ice-cream cone. Maple walnut. She'll show up when she's done. Why are you helping her?'

'Funny how you put that,' Cinq-Mars pointed out.

'How so?'

'About yourself, you asked what I want with you. About Quinn, you asked why I'm helping her. Interesting. I thought I was helping you discover your name.'

Leonard searched the policeman's eyes for some sign that he was being conned. If he was, he couldn't figure out the angle. 'Before we get into that—'

'Why before? I can tell you right now.'

'Do you know why I'm here at this moment? It's not for my name.'

Cinq-Mars was at a loss. 'Then what?'

'What you told Quinn. Maletti got whacked?'

'I don't ascribe to TV language, but yes, you can put it that way. Somebody shot him last night. Dead as a doornail.'

Leonard adjusted his glasses. First on his nose, then behind his ears and over his nose again. He looked back at Cinq-Mars. 'No shit.'

'None whatsoever.'

'This'll change things.'

'It'll make a difference in your life.'

'You gotta be careful what you wish for.'

'I understand. The devil you know.'

'Who'll show up to run this popcorn stand? There's a lot worse than Maletti. With my luck, somebody like that is on the way. I hope there's no damn turf war. Guess who'll be the first innocent victim, gunned down in the crossfire.'

'What's the likelihood of that, do you think?'

Leonard looked at him again, studied him, then shrugged. The shrug felt cooperative, rather than adversarial. 'No idea,' he said. 'Look, here comes Quinn.'

She hadn't quite finished her cone. The bottom tip was consumed as Leonard leaned his seat forward and she piled into the back seat behind him. As they settled again, Quinn chimed in, 'Cough it up! What's your name?'

A pause, then Cinq-Mars said, 'Leonard's been checking me out. We didn't get to his real name yet.'

'Oh, Leonard, come on!' A scolding.

'Well, what if I don't like it?'

'Oh, for Pete's sake.'

'I think it's a fine name,' Cinq-Mars revealed.

'There. See?'

Leonard took a deep breath. Before he asked for his name, he requested his number.

'One seventy-nine. It's written as zero-one-seven-nine. You'd be referred to as seventy-nine, though, for short. Or more commonly, as seven-nine.'

They were cocooned in the VW, sequestered by this covert knowledge. Quinn finally broke the ice.

'Is that it, Leonard? You were seven-nine?'

He nodded to affirm what he did not want repeated. 'Just hearing you say it gives me a migraine. And I don't get migraines.' Then he asked, at long last, 'So what's my name?'

A simple question, yet as composed as Leonard tried to be, Cinq-Mars felt the young man's defenses jump in. As though the query had a physical effect. He glanced back at Quinn. All eyes and ears on him. Leonard revealed his uneasiness by swallowing hard and inhaling another deep breath.

Then he said, 'Wait.'

'Leonard,' Quinn said. Not cross this time. Gently.

'I'm not ready,' he said.

'Take your time,' Cinq-Mars said. 'We've got all day.'

'You, maybe. I've got a business to run.'

The three new associates laughed. With the mood lightened, Leonard was prepared to learn his real name.

Mother Love

(The Spaniard in the dining room)

C inq-Mars left Quinn downtown to help Leonard adjust to his new name. Within two minutes of his return to his *poste de quartier*, he was wishing he'd stayed behind and hung out with him, too.

'Do you deserve your pay, Cinq-Mars?' Thin, of average height, Captain Pierre Delacroix combed his sparse hair straight back. His shoulders fell sharply away from the base of his neck, so that his head possessed a bobblehead quality, a feature that caused him to look perpetually slapped.

'Sir, I worked half the night,' Cinq-Mars explained, knowing it was futile.

'The man says he worked all night. On what?'

'A murder investigation, sir. Captain Touton brought me in.'

'Touton's a clown. What are you, his shill? Do you think I give a shit if some thug is gunned down overnight? Tell me, Cinq-Mars, were you drinking? Admit it.'

'No, sir. I mean, I was off duty. Maybe I had a beer. After the crime scene.'

'You admit to boozing it up and still expect a paycheck. If you spent the night in a whorehouse, would you want to be paid for that too? Paid to be inebriated. Paid to have a poke. Never mind that you don't work for Touton. That clown does not sign your sheet.'

'Sir, last night's murder relates to *our* murder.'

'*Our* murder? You're not working *any* murder. What precisely is the matter with you, Cinq-Mars? Are you a maladjusted fuck-up? Is that an accurate summation?'

'No, sir.'

'No? Was I asking for your opinion?'

'I thought you were, sir.'

'I'll let you know when I'm asking a question. Is that fucking clear?'

He wanted to ask, 'Is that a question?' Instead, he said, 'Yes, sir. Sir, it relates. The murder last night, the murder in the Town here. They both connect to the robbery I'm investigating with Sergeant-Detective Giroux.'

'You're not investigating that robbery.'

'I thought I was, sir.'

'I thought so, too. Instead you come in whenever you jolly well feel like it, stick your nose into other cops' beeswax. It's huge, your nose, but try keeping it out of the way. And stick this between your ears. You work with Giroux, you do not fly solo. Be his bosom buddy. Give him a hand job, if that's what it takes. Have babies together. Just don't leave his company. I want work product out of you two, and you will produce work product as I see fit. And stay dead sober. Understood?'

He was standing waiting to be formally dismissed, a command that did not appear imminent. Delacroix went on and on about cops. 'Do we recruit them out of drunk tanks or what?'

Sensing that he was already out of the room as far as his captain was concerned, Cinq-Mars took a speculative step backward. It went unnoticed. He took another. He said, 'Thank you, sir,' turned, and quietly departed the office. Safe, apparently, he rolled his eyes in Giroux's direction.

'Still carry a badge, your Glock?' his partner inquired.

'Seems so. I need to check if my testicles still function.'

'No suspension? A week? A day?'

'Go figure.'

'Drive with me, Detective.' Giroux pulled his sports jacket off the back of his chair. 'Work your way into his good books.'

'Will we produce work product?' They were already on the move, heading for the door. 'Delacroix said we're supposed to do that.'

'I don't know what that is.'

'Me, neither. What's the case?'

They were hurrying out the door. 'My oil painting. Dollarwise, the biggest heist out of this *poste* in years. Bust it, you can write your own ticket with the boss.'

'Fat chance. Practically a cold case by now.'

Giroux shrugged in agreement. 'It's your only hope. Your nuts are in a vise, Émile. Our captain's an elephant that never forgets. A way to ease the pressure. I don't know if it's "work product", but you got to find something.'

Sleepless and bedraggled, he had intended to request the afternoon off. Out of the question now. Perhaps talking to an octogenarian burglary victim might be the next best thing to taking a nap.

Quinn and the boy with a new name broke out his merchandise and toked up.

'I shouldn't do this here. But what the hell.'

'Why not?' Quinn wondered.

He tweaked his nose. 'A cop follows his sniffer. He not only nails a toker. With my quantity, I'm booked for dealing.'

'Paranoid much? Cops don't follow their noses. In the Student Ghetto, they'd be stoned if they did.'

The boy struck a match. 'You were right about your friend. His honker is huge. He calls it prominent.'

'He's not a friend,' she objected. Then asked, 'Did you like him?'

'What's to like? He's a cop.'

'Harsh.' Her comment felt harsh, as well, as the two of them were meant to be united in their disdain for authority. She attempted to moderate her reaction. 'How do you like it when people size you up? Oh, he's a petty drug dealer . . .'

'If it gets me girls, I'm fine with it. Who're you calling petty?'

'You two are alike. Neither of you is getting any.'

He bent forward with laughter, and that seemed to resolve the tension between them. They smoked in peace.

Then he said, 'Noel Graham. Who calls their kid Noel Graham?'

Quinn exhaled at length. 'Your mother did.'

'The Smith part I don't believe.'

'Some people *are* Smiths. The most common name for a reason.'

'Probably hiding her identity,' the young man speculated.

'She's like a spy now?'

'She's a single mom-to-be with a ton of baggage. She calls herself Smith to hide her identity from the nuns. Didn't want her bastard son looking her up someday.'

'Not buying it. If she was that way, she'd let you be baptized. "Feel free, girls. Sprinkle water on his head. Or drown the poor boy, whatever . . ." You'd have your real name from the get-go. Your mom had spirit. She was feisty. That's how I see her.'

'I dunno.'

'I do. She never imagined the consequences, you not being baptized. That part was never advertised, you know.'

She had a point.

'Her real name was Smith,' Quinn continued between tokes. 'To call you Noel Graham proves it. Names like that, they're part of her kin. Do you know why she called you Noel Graham?'

'You tell me.'

'Because she loved you. Accept it.'

'Get off the pot. So to speak.'

'She wanted you to grow up with dignity. Noel Graham. Strong name. She was trying to tell you how much she loved you. Yeah. That's what I think.'

'You're a snowflake.'

Her eyelids were reduced to thin slits. 'You're not the first to make that observation.'

The young man also was enjoying the dope's effects. 'I'll still be Leonard on the street,' he stated. 'If Cinq-Mars comes to arrest me, or whoever, I'll give my real name. Then stand before a judge and take my punishment like a man. Not like some throwaway alley cat.'

'I like you as a throwaway alley cat.'

'Yeah? You like me? Cool. The thing is, I can get papers now.'

'Like a driver's license?'

'A passport, even.'

'Shit, man, don't get carried away.' She started to giggle.

'Why can't I have a passport?'

'You off somewhere, big boy?'

'It's the principle of the thing.'

'Fine. Get a passport. Enjoy paying your taxes, too.'

'Why not? You think I won't declare my illicit earnings? If they let me be a real citizen, I will. Hey, Quinn, do you know why I want the name the most?'

'Girls. You want girls. Oh! You think that when you're doing it, they'll call out your real name. "Oh! Noel Graham! Don't stop! Oh please, Noel!" At least, now you'll know who they mean.'

She bent over double this time.

'Stop laughing. Not funny. When they say my name now – Leonard – which is not that often, I wonder who they have in mind.'

She recovered slowly. 'Tell me. What do you want the most?'

'Two things. Now it's two. One, a birth certificate to carry in my wallet.'

'We're in Quebec. You need a baptismal certificate, and you weren't baptized.'

'I believe that's changed. We've gone modern. And two, someday, my name on a tombstone. I want that the most. I'll have it chiseled in advance. To make sure it's done right.'

'You're thinking about your tombstone? This far ahead?' She gazed across the apartment's muddle. He had shelves stuffed with books. He lived within a university milieu, albeit as a soft-drug dealer. 'Know what? You can enroll as a mature student. Now that you have a real name.'

'Get off the pot,' he said, rather quietly she thought. 'Literally.'

'You could. You should.'

'Get the hell out of here.'

'You don't mean that, Leonard.'

He lifted his head. It seemed heavy to him.

'Noel,' he corrected her. 'In here, at home, my new name is Noel.'

'Sure thing,' she confirmed. 'Noel, dude, enroll!'

Émile Cinq-Mars assumed he'd be no help regarding the art heist. Someone stole a painting. Unless it showed up at auction in Singapore or Abu Dhabi there'd be no new news.

After being in the apartment for three minutes, he changed his mind.

He enjoyed meeting the grand lady of the house. The pleasure of her company prevented him from dragging Yves Giroux into the street and scolding him for being an idiot. The case was solved. All he had to do was put a few pieces together.

He engaged Mrs Amelia Reynolds in conversation, discussing plants, cats, the Queen, her grandson, her travels to the Far East and, of course, her art collection, which was impressive. She patted her coiffed and tinted gray hair to keep the edges at attention and showed how the thief broke in by jimmying the front-door lock. She gave him a summary of her nieces, nephews and grandchild, as she had outlived both her husband and her only son. When Giroux, bored out of his tree, insisted that they make a break for it, Cinq-Mars thanked Mrs Reynolds for her hospitality and assured her that she'd have her painting back soon.

'Cinq-Mars,' Giroux lectured him outside on the street, 'never say you'll return stolen property. Don't get their hopes up.'

'I solved your case,' the junior detective told him.

'A needle in a huge haystack gives us a better chance. If the needle's there, we'll find it. This case—'

'I was born on a farm.'

'What?'

'But not in a barn. My best friends were horses though.'

'Did you say something?'

'You didn't hear me?'

'Something about farming?'

'You're listening now? Good. I said, I solved your case.'

Giroux stood on the sidewalk as the brunt of his partner's declaration dawned on him.

'Sorry?' he asked.

'Solved,' Cinq-Mars said, and turned to face him. 'I know who committed the robbery.'

Now Giroux was looking at him as though he had a screw loose. 'I don't get it. Not an insurance scam, you said . . .'

'You can't pretend a well-known painting is stolen then stick it back on a wall. If you do, you can't let anyone inside the door ever again. Yves, she's a collector—'

'I noticed. So?'

'Imagine being a thief. You break into a house. The sole purpose is to steal a painting. You steal the Tom Thomson. But if you're a thief who knows enough about art to know the difference between a Tom Thomson, say, and some doodle that you could do yourself, and you aren't rushed for time, why would you pass up the Lawren Harris or the Jean-Paul Riopelle?'

'The who? The what?'

'They're painters, Yves. She's a collector. The A.Y. Jackson is small, but it's valuable. Those are only the Canadians. There's a Spanish name I don't know, but I liked his work. And, then, there's another Spaniard who you and I both know.'

'I don't know any Spaniards.'

'You've heard of Picasso.'

Giroux stood transfixed a moment. 'Which one?'

'In the dining room. On the right as you enter.'

'A fucking Picasso? The lady is loaded. She doesn't need insurance money.'

'That's not the point. The point is, no thief worth his salt would pass up the Picasso, or the others, and settle only for the Thomson. It's just not possible.'

'If you say so. Where does that leave us?'

'The lock wasn't jimmied. The door was opened with a key. On his way out, our crook scratched the wood to make it look otherwise.'

'He took a gouge of wood out, Cinq-Mars.'

'Exactly, and you fell for it. Relatively soon, her grandson will inherit everything. In the meantime, he wanted something on account. He took the Thomson. Probably, he had a sale lined up. He collects a bit of cash to see him through until grandma's demise, and when she does go he gets a share of the insurance payout as well. No point stealing the works. He can wait to inherit. He took what he needed to tide him over. Lean on the bastard, Yves. Incarcerate his skinny ass and get the painting back. Now, here's the deal.'

'Deal? What deal? We don't *know* that this case is solved.'

'It's annoying, but the case is solved. It's not rocket science. It's not even Art Theft 101. It's been done before, just not to Mrs Reynolds. Clean it up, Yves. Enjoy the glory and leave me alone. That's our deal. Cover for me when I'm AWOL. I've got stuff to look after.'

'How come,' Giroux asked, 'you know about these artists anyhow?'

Cinq-Mars didn't want to say. The poor guy needed an answer, though, if for no other reason than to make up for his own deficiencies. Cinq-Mars favored him with the truth. 'I had a girlfriend,' he admitted. 'She broke up with me. Recently. Life with a Night Patrol cop was too scary, too disruptive. The excuse she gave anyway. She used to drag me around museums, show me her art books. She studied art history. I just happened to get lucky that way.'

'That kind of lucky,' Giroux said.

'That kind, too. Do we have a deal?'

Giroux gazed at Cinq-Mars, looked back at the old lady's apartment. He shrugged. 'Sure,' he said. On the spot, their agreement was ironclad, as if chiseled in stone.

The Money Jar

(Bug speed)

Quinn took the Number 80 bus over the mountain and through the ethnically diverse neighborhoods bordering Park Avenue. Weariness perspired on the visage of every passenger. She offered her seat to an older woman with a babushka who wore a sweater despite the warm temperature. They exchanged a smile.

In a way she couldn't explain, the woman influenced her thinking. Quinn decided to spring cash from the food jar when she got home, head to the small grocer on Howard Avenue, then make something special for her dad. They'd been through a rough patch. Time to give him a break and a treat.

Cheer herself up, too. Dietmar's burial remained with her. Spending time with Noel helped, but an uneasy sorrow held sway. More than anything, she wanted her dad to complete his shift and come home. She'd cook up one of his favorites. Like scallops.

Yeah. If the fish market had sea scallops, she'd prepare a creamy linguine. He'd like that. He'd like it so much he'd have a bird!

Perhaps it was her weed buzz, or subliminal intuition. As she turned the key in the lock on the front door of her home something did not feel right. As if the door was already unlocked. She'd definitely secured it when she left. She never forgot, and after the firebombing had taken extra care. Entering, Quinn relaxed. Everything seemed normal. She made a beeline for the kitchen and the food-money jar.

A swift electric jolt shot through her.

A man standing there – cleaning his nails? – shocked her. She managed only a gasp before a hand covered her mouth. More hands on her. Her head forced back. She gasped again and half-hollered when the paw came off her mouth, instantly replaced by a gag. Someone – a man – knotted it tightly at the back of her neck. Her wrists were bound behind her. Her ankles. She was flung to the kitchen floor. Quinn flounced there, a fish out of water.

She squiggled around. Tried to look up. To see. To free herself. The man standing there had barely twitched a muscle.

He was cleaning his nails with the nails of his opposite fingers.

She squirmed around on the floor.

The man squatted down beside her.

He said, 'Shh. Shh. Relax.'

At first, she was seeing his hands. Deeply veined, alabaster skin. As though they rarely saw the sun. She twisted her neck to see his face better. A foliage of chest hair at his neckline. He was half-shaven. An eyebrow split by scar tissue. Buzz cut, salt and peppery.

He had a hard look.

'Shh. Shh.'

She tried to kick and flail.

He removed a penknife from his hip pocket. Nothing too large. Opened the modest blade slowly.

'Settle down yourself. Or bleed out. A choice for you.' His voice almost gentle.

She looked up at him sideways. He had this grin on his face. As though she should never believe he was not serious. Her rampant fear seized her in place.

'They call me the Rabbit,' he said. 'Never just "Rabbit". Don't call me that. Always "the". You're Quinn? That's you?'

Too afraid to deny it. She'd been warned about this man.

'Come with me. Better for you, go willing. Get me?'

She could not oppose the edict. Raised in Park Ex, she had no difficulty understanding his heavily accented English.

Other men in the room prepped her for transport. One went through her purse and found Leonard's parting gift. Passed the weed to the Rabbit. He tossed it into a corner on the kitchen floor.

The other man flung her purse across the floor. Items scattered loose.

The Rabbit grunted.

'Some fucking reason, a person don't want you dead, not yet. Later, maybe. Means I got to treat you nice somehow. Come peaceful, sweetie Quinn. Make no trouble. Get me?'

She nodded as though she did.

Jim Tanner took his usual lift home. He called out as he came through the door. No answer. For Quinn not to be home was common, but why was the door unlocked? He turned the corner into the kitchen, which included a small dining table. On it were three half-eaten meals. Fried chicken and French fries. Not his daughter's favorite, and why so much of it and only half-eaten? She may have had friends over, but usually they had voracious appetites. And Quinn never left a mess behind.

Her purse lay on the floor.

Panic overwhelmed him then. His brain fired up. His body jumped.

He noticed a marijuana baggie. He wasn't naive. Kids did stuff. Quinn was never careless about that sort of thing, and never left anything lying around. He turned. The screen in the back window was missing. The window open. He poked his head out. The screen lay flat on the ground.

His heart was roaring now. A terror lanced straight through him.

Jim Tanner went to the phone book. He wanted to reach the guy who'd been around lately. He got lucky. Quinn had left the card for the man's partner right on top. He dialed. A switchboard operator patched him through to Sergeant-Detective Giroux's phone, but no one answered. When the operator came back on, he requested Detective Cinq-Mars. She said he wasn't in. He clicked off, picked up the phone book again, found a number and called police headquarters. He asked for the head of the Night Patrol. A big department. And a fierce one. He was passed along and put on hold and then an intermediary answered.

'I need to speak to Captain Armand Touton.'

'Who is calling, please, and what is the nature of your call?' A pleasant, youthful, female voice. The sound of it redoubled his fear.

'My daughter's been taken.'

'"Taken", sir? How do you mean?'

'Abducted.'

She patched him through.

He was surprised when Touton answered. Growled at him, 'Touton. Yeah?'

'My name is Jim Tanner. My daughter's name is Quinn. She's been abducted. She's been in trouble lately. One of your guys – one of your former guys is what I heard – was looking into her situation.'

'You mean Cinq-Mars.'

'Him, yeah. I need him here at my place. Now.'

'Give me your address. If I can't find him, I'll be there myself.'

Jim Tanner recited the address, hung up, and waited. He sat in a kitchen chair. He got up and ditched the marijuana in a cupboard. If cops thought this was drug-related they might lose interest. He sat again and waited. He had learned to fear the police. Now he wanted them in his house, pronto.

When he answered the doorbell, only a few minutes had gone by. Almost five o'clock. Émile Cinq-Mars stood before him.

*   *   *

Men ripped her panties off and strapped her to a toilet. One arm was spread out, lashed to the base of the sink. The other was stretched opposite, tied to a radiator. A woman came in after she'd been alone for a while and had peed. Hearing the flow of urine, the woman came in to flush. Quinn thought she'd been abandoned. She had not been aware of anyone out in the hall.

'Why am I here?'

'Fucking shut it, bitch. Like yesterday. Like a week ago. Do I look like I want a fucking conversation with you?'

The woman delivered her declaration then vacated the room.

Abandoned. Although this time she knew that someone was nearby.

Her guard.

Who had carried no weapon. *Remember that. It might matter.*

Quinn tried to think what else she could say about her.

Tattooed. Druggie eyes. Attitude. Long dark hair, did nothing with it. A pained look to her. She'd been abused. *Don't tell her that.* She looked controlled. Probably as mean as shit and not the brightest bulb. *Don't say that.* Don't tell her she's a moron.

In Quinn's estimation, in any fight between the two of them, the matter would immediately escalate from hair pulling or cat scratching. Bad enough, as the woman had wicked nails. She might die in the battle, that level of carnage, that degree of weaponry. In a fair fight she could outlast her, being younger and healthier, physically and mentally. She could outwit her. Just because she could. *Remember that.* Endure. And think. *Keep thinking.* If it comes down to stamina, Quinn, you win. *You got her.* In mind over matter, you win.

You can throw things. Remember that. You've got an arm.

They might kill me. Don't let it happen. Don't let it. Stay alive, Quinn. *Oh shit, I can't let it happen!* Breathe. Come on. Panic won't help. *I'm breathing.* Stay alive. *Oh God, why am I on the toilet?* Breathe now. Breathe. That's it. Keep breathing. *Why did they put me on the toilet?* OK! Start over. Think. Breathe. Breathing. *OK.*

Instinct and training told Émile Cinq-Mars he had to act fast. An abduction required speed and luck if it was to be interrupted at the outset. Once the culprits sheltered in place, they gained control. A problem: he had no idea how long she'd been gone.

Cinq-Mars called back Touton to alert the Night Patrol. He

reached Giroux, who alerted Detective Caron and Sergeant-Detective Frigault. Every hand on deck.

They'd canvas the neighborhood for leads. If nothing else, they might establish a timeline. Jim Tanner returned home shortly before six. Quinn was last seen in the early afternoon, downtown, with the boy known as Leonard. How did Cinq-Mars know that? they asked. He was with her. What kind of time are you spending with this girl? They were detectives, they had a right to be suspicious. They were men, like him. 'Forget it,' Cinq-Mars warned them. 'I'm working her through this.'

'Until now,' Caron intimated.

'Yeah. Until now.'

Caron and Frigault agreed to find the boy. Cinq-Mars didn't have an address, but Leonard – Cinq-Mars gave them the only name useful to their cause – was an everyday peddler of soft dope. Somewhere in the system they'd know where to find a boy with a fixed address, though no identity.

'Student Ghetto,' Cinq-Mars decreed. Somewhere to start.

'On it,' Frigault vowed.

Giroux took charge of the house-to-house canvas, calling in foot soldiers. He coordinated with Captain Honoré of the night shift from his own station but made a point not to surrender authority. Cinq-Mars gave Jim Tanner his phone number and told him to man the fort. If he ever left the house, he was to leave a message giving details of his whereabouts.

'Sort of like Quinn's goodwill list.'

'Excuse me?'

Cinq-Mars had scrutinized Quinn's list. It indicated that she was going to the funeral. No update after her presumed arrival home. Her abductor had been lying in wait.

'Keep me informed as to your whereabouts, Mr Tanner. Like Quinn was doing for you. In case I need to get in touch.'

'I have a better idea,' Tanner said.

'What's that?'

'Let me come with you.'

'No can do, sir. Sorry.'

'Give me one good reason why not.'

'Because I plan to pull out all the stops on this. I can't have a civilian around. That would impede me. I also don't want a witness. You know, in case I dodge a few rules.'

Tanner appreciated Cinq-Mars's enthusiasm. Still, he wasn't going to be blown off easily, and what Cinq-Mars said next didn't help.

'Sergeant-Detective Giroux will stay here. We need you with him in case they call. We don't think there'll be a ransom, but you never know.'

'Giroux?' queried Tanner. Then explained. 'That day when the kid lost his legs. Giroux went behind a fence for half an hour. Vomiting. He was a total washout.'

Cinq-Mars eyed him closely. Took note of the ramifications. Tanner had been left on his own to look after the boy until an ambulance arrived. He could have used some help. 'Different circumstances, no?' Cinq-Mars pointed out. 'Look, he's on this – no stone unturned, that mode. Maybe he wants to make it up to you.'

Cinq-Mars could tell that in the upheaval of the moment more was coming. Would it be now or later?

Jim Tanner chose to make it now.

'Whenever I'm out at night, or at the bar or maybe at the bowling alley, Quinn always thinks I'm at a ball park, either the local kids or the Expos.'

'You go elsewhere,' Cinq-Mars concluded.

'The track.'

'You play the horses.'

'It's not like that. Two kinds of people are admitted to the paddocks. Horse people and wise guys, guys who are mobbed up.'

Where was this going? And why now? 'You've seen Giroux there?'

'A lot. He isn't tight with horse people. This is my daughter's life we're talking about here. I don't know whose side he's on.'

'That's fair. Look, I can vouch for him in this situation. He's on your side.'

Tanner kept staring back at him. His gaze as assertive as a blade.

'Maybe you've seen me in the paddocks, too,' Cinq-Mars said. He was catching on to where the man was coming from. 'Never with him, though. I never noticed him there myself. I just met the guy.'

'You're hard to miss.'

'I'm tall. All right, OK, my nose gives me away.'

'What were you doing there?' Tanner asked. 'Whose side are you on?'

'I'm whistle-clean. But why were you there?'

'I got friends inside. Still my friends, even though I'm on the outside now.'

'They're all right, for mob guys, you're saying?'

'My excuse. What's yours?'

'Same difference. Except I'm a horse guy. My dad raised horses. Still does. I'm in the paddocks on his behalf now and then, to buy and sell. Not drugs. Not contraband. Horses. If you think hard, you'll know that you never saw me with the wise guys, only the horse guys. I want your daughter back, Mr Tanner. I'm working for her, not against her.'

'In my life, it's hard to know. One reason I hang around with the old boys, I know who they are. Where they stand. Whose side they're on.'

'I hear what you're saying, Mr Tanner. I accept that. But in my experience they're not as faithful as you think.'

The conversation provoked a thought. He placed his left hand on Tanner's near shoulder and tugged him slightly closer to him. He spoke under his breath, confidentially. 'How are your old skills? You might want to brush up while you're waiting. Before this is over, I might need them.'

Though not comprehending what was in the air, Tanner nodded.

At that moment, word came in that Quinn had been seen entering the house around four. That meant her kidnappers did not have a massive head start.

'Rush hour. Hard to get around. If they travel a distance, she might still be on the move. It's possible—'

'*You* got here fast,' Tanner said.

'I live in the neighborhood.'

Then word came in from Giroux. Scouring the back yard, he found a muddiness from the earlier rain. Footprints. A slightly smaller, possibly lighter, foot was indicated amid larger ones. Two feet aligned together. As if tied together. Quinn had been taken out the back way. He sent cops to canvas the lane to find out what anyone saw.

Word returned.

'Three men with this blondie girl got into a blue van,' an older woman, stuck in her wheelchair on an upper balcony, revealed.

'Looked something queer to me, the way they rushing around.'
The girl's hands, the woman speculated, might've been tied.

'You didn't call the police?'

'Not my look-out, is it? Whoosh! Like that, they're gone. They
might've been the police for all I could tell. They backed up.
Most cars go straight. That one backed up.'

A blue van. Helpful. Barely.

'Put it out there,' Giroux ordered. 'Broadcast the info.'

Cinq-Mars headed out.

'Where to?' Giroux inquired.

'Don't ask.'

'Come on, work with me on this, Cinq-Mars.'

'Downtown, OK? But who wants to know? Keep it to yourself.'

'How do I reach you?'

'Night Patrol. Leave a message.'

Cinq-Mars told him the essentials. Where he was going and
whom he'd contact. Giroux chose not to stand on jurisdiction.
Possibly he approved. Night was falling fast. Bringing in the
Night Patrol was the right thing to do.

Cinq-Mars piled into his Volkswagen Bug and ripped
downtown at speed.

The Prodigal Mouse

(Blaze of glory)

At HQ, Cinq-Mars burst into Touton's office, finding it
vacant. Officers in the main room had no clue where he'd
gone. A miscreant brought in for throwing a punch at his
barber listened to the cops discussing the matter, then piped up,
'He went to the morgue.'

Not knowing the charge against this man, only that he was
cuffed and sporting a bizarre haircut, Cinq-Mars asked, 'Ours?
The basement morgue?'

The man shrugged. 'He told me he'd be in the morgue. Like
he wanted me to know. Weird. I don't think it was a suicide note,
but I'm not sure.'

'What happened to your hair?' Cinq-Mars asked him.

'Only my barber knows for sure. He might be conscious by now.'

Cinq-Mars tore off to the bowels of the building, praying to high heaven that if a newly arrived corpse had been dropped off it wasn't Quinn's.

The dead person turned out to be male, mid-fifties. A jumper. Lazy in his preparations for death, he'd botched the job. Instead of hitting the river off the Jacques Cartier Bridge, he'd done a belly-flop onto solid earth. The gruesome carcass was less the center of attention than an unrelated conversation, with raucous laughter, involving Touton, Huguette Foss and Dr Eudo Lachapelle.

They didn't notice Cinq-Mars enter and looked up only when he announced himself, loudly. 'Hey!'

'Look what the cat's dragged in!' Huguette exclaimed. 'The prodigal mouse. I mean, detective. The prodigal detective.'

The remark might have instigated a fresh round of repartee, except that Touton knew his former junior officer had a situation on his hands.

'What's the verdict?' Touton pumped him. His tone abrupt, intent.

'The girl's been abducted. Confirmed. An APP is out on a blue van. We got nothing else. Looks pro.'

'Ciampini, you think?'

'Over a baseball?'

'That ball could mean his life.'

'You two have been around the block.'

'All right,' Touton consented, 'I'll talk to him. Do you get what's going on? He's not worried about me or concerned about the law. His mob cousins in New York irritate him more. If they receive confirmation that in the old days he took out their favorite uncle, we'll be videotaping his funeral.'

Cinq-Mars agreed. 'That's why we need more than a chat with him.'

Nearby, Huguette was revisiting the jumper's corpse. He had to look away. One unholy horror.

'I can make our displeasure known,' Touton said. 'Twist the blade once it's in.'

'A reprimand won't make him give the girl back.'

'What's your thought?'

'Blaze of glory, Captain.'

Touton gazed back at him. He had an inkling of what was fermenting in Cinq-Mars's head.

Huguette ceased her ministrations.

'Some new trick?' Touton inquired.

'Armand, we've talked about it, but never gave it a name. Wouldn't it be great, we said, to go full throttle? Disrupt his night clubs. Shut down his bookies. Plow his drug pushers under the sidewalk. You know what I'm saying. Round up his addicts, bugger his clients, give his restaurant patrons indigestion.'

'Cinq-Mars—'

He wasn't finished. 'Disorient his hookers, scoop up their johns. Drive the pimps so deep manhole covers will be their rooftops. Maybe that time has come.'

'What is it with you and this girl?'

'I'm dead serious, Armand.'

'I see that.' Touton folded his arms across his chest, leaned back against a gurney. 'OK, we talked about it, or was that the whisky talking? The case against full throttle hasn't changed.'

'One thing has.'

'Explain.'

'Your retirement. Except for the back of your heel, you're already out the door. What does it matter if they give you the boot early? What's a few weeks?'

Touton understood the parameters. A blaze of glory. By the time department heads and political elites got wind of the operation, he and Cinq-Mars might have accomplished what they were setting out to do. They could put the business operations of Joe Ciampini through a meat grinder and inflict severe damage to his reputation in places where his reputation mattered.

'Doesn't mean we get to nail his tail to the wall,' Touton noted. 'He gets mad. Releases the girl to put an end to it. Maybe. Best case. We still don't come away with an arrest. Ciampini walks.'

'Let him walk. I promise to take up the cause after you stroll off into the sunset. He walks. So does the girl. Quinn deserves to live. We show Ciampini who's boss. We let him know that if she disappears, it's the end of him.'

'It won't be. The end of him. If she dies.'

Cinq-Mars twisted in the wind right where he stood, wrestling

with that reality. 'He doesn't need to hear it from me,' he determined. 'Convince him otherwise.'

Touton mulled things over. Cinq-Mars had learned that Touton
forged big decisions slowly. Patience was required to push him
in a new direction.

'If I'm the colossal idiot you think I am and buy shares in
your cockamamie blaze of glory,' the senior cop determined, 'it
still won't be enough. He'll knuckle down. He *needs* the baseball.
It follows that he needs the girl. If she has something to say,
she'll talk. Then what? *Poof!* We're fishing her out of the river.'

'I hate those,' Huguette Foss chimed in. No one was keen on
her dark tone or wanted her to explain.

'You understand my point,' Touton reiterated.

Cinq-Mars did. 'We need her to keep her mouth shut as long
as possible. Let's pray she buys us time. That's why I need the
Service de Police de la Ville de Montréal in its full glory, armed,
dangerous, and royally pissed off, to shake out the cobwebs and
hit the streets hard. I need Ciampini's head snapping back with
the sheer brute force against him. Shit hitting the fan non-stop
might keep Quinn alive for more than a few hours.'

'Émile—' Touton tried to sneak in a word of caution.

Cinq-Mars didn't let him. 'Keep Ciampini occupied. I've got
a plan. We'll put it into play and maybe get the baseball back.
Then we deal. When you're holding his balls – metaphorically
a pair, but specifically a baseball – in the palm of your hand,
then you talk to him.'

'You lost me at "metafork". Was that the word? So, how—'

'You don't want to know. Don't ask.'

'Really? This blaze of glory thing I'm supposed to pull off
– which, I don't mind telling you, has balls – it's your blaze,
too? You go out with a big bang too? Not just me? My retirement
is coming fast. You want to risk your career? I don't like that.'

'It'll be fine if it works. If not and the girl's dead, who cares
if my career's still alive? I'll sell horses with my dad.'

'You're more likely to check into a monastery. How's that
girlfriend of yours?'

'I lost her.'

'I knew that.'

'No, you didn't.'

'Really? You think I don't know why you left the Night Patrol?

You're a heartbroken sap. Rather than lose you altogether, I let you slide to the day shift. I didn't want you sabotaging what's left of your career over some girl you lost, and I don't want you to do it over a girl you might lose tonight. Follow me? You want a front-line assault on all things Ciampini? Promise me, here, right now, you won't toss your career off a bridge like this joker on the slab. I got more invested in you, Cinq-Mars, than that. Whatever you're planning – legal, illegal, that part I don't give a shit – make it work. Follow me on that, kid?'

'Yes, sir.'

Touton had still to give his approval. His mind was made up, but he needed to take his time, to consider the downside.

'Last chance,' Cinq-Mars urged him. 'One final fling. Like in the old days, with the old ways. Do we get our blaze of glory?'

Touton nodded. He spoke quietly. 'A fucking bonfire. He'll think his house is burning. He won't know what hit him. He won't know if it'll ever end. If I talk to him, it's because he's calling for the meet, not the other way around.'

They both straightened up, suddenly aware of what they'd agreed to do.

'Thanks, Captain.'

'You bag of yellow piss, don't thank me. You're always on my ass about the morals, the fucking ethics. "Don't bust his jaw, boss, how's he going to talk if it's wired shut?" I put up with your crap because you're smart, and maybe you're right – always, the times move on. Yet here we are – you messing with me, wanting to roll out the troops and damn the house rules.'

'Time and place, boss.'

'Your time, your place. Just tell me what you need with this scheme of yours. It damn well better work.'

Cinq-Mars hesitated only a beat. 'Eudo and Huguette.'

'What?' Touton demanded. 'Why? How?'

'Say that again,' Huguette asked. She already sounded thrilled. From the opposite side of the room Eudo Lachapelle boomed, 'What!'

Cinq-Mars spoke up for everyone to hear. 'I need a couple who won't look like two cops in disguise. The guy we're playing would sniff that out in the blink of an eye. I need two people who can pull off crazy as if it's their normal. I need two people who can pull off being in love as if that's their normal too. I need you,

Eudo, and you, Hu, to be your normal crazy selves. Can you be in love for a day?'

'Excellent!' Huguette exclaimed.

'Young man, I'm insulted!' decried Eudo.

The other three in the room laughed. Cinq-Mars drove home his offer. 'Your lives won't be in danger, but you'll be saving someone whose life is on the line.'

'We're both in,' Huguette said.

'Do you presume to speak for me now?' Eudo asked her.

'Of course!'

'Of course,' Eudo confirmed.

'I'll be in touch,' Cinq-Mars told them. 'Be home or be here. Agreed? This will be a daytime job. You might want to sleep tonight.'

Captain Armand Touton did something he'd not done before. He mimicked plowing his massive fist into the younger man's gut. Then let his hand fall.

'You realize,' he reiterated, 'this depends on the girl prolonging her silence. She won't hold out forever, if she holds out for even a minute. She can't.'

Cinq-Mars conceded the point. 'I'm aware. Everything depends on her.'

'Go,' Touton ordered. 'I need to put a war machine in motion.'

'Blaze of glory, Armand.'

'Depends on who lives. Who dies. Whose career gets washed away. We'll see.'

Dieppe Revisited

(A villa in Tuscany)

She caught herself on the verge of blubbering. An impulse that betrayed her. She needed to block it off. She could not permit herself to break down when they hadn't even started on her yet. Quinn clenched her facial muscles and pulled herself together.

Her guard opened the door. As if to check that she hadn't vanished as she'd been so quiet.

'What's going on?' Quinn's throat was scratchy, dry.

'Nothing. We're waiting.'

'For who? For what?'

'Don't rush it, sweetie.'

'Can you help me out? Please. Just loosen the straps a little.'

'Ask me that again, I'll cut your tongue out, make you eat it. You want mustard on that? Ketchup? Your own blood, that OK for the sauce?'

Quinn could tell when someone was trying to act super tough. Growing up in Park Ex, guys and girls often gave it a shot. They were all morons. This woman was a moron. She was not as tough as she talked. Maybe she was frightened by what might occur there. By what she might see. She'd made her point, though. Quinn would not ask a favor of her again.

Despair, like a drug, diffused through her veins.

Then, as though her despair really was a drug, she grew weary. Time ached by. With her arms spread wide and strapped in place, her head slumped forward. Then snapped up, waking her. It happened a second time. A lack of air, she thought. A lack of hope. She stayed awake for another hour, then bone-weary and mentally fatigued she allowed her head to slump again.

Waking up slowly – this time, not a violent, involuntary reflex – Quinn had no idea how much time had passed. She called out to her guard to tell her the time. She wouldn't. Had she slept for two minutes or forty? The dreams she'd had.

The spell satisfied her need for sleep. Alert again.

The guard poked her head in again, to make sure she wasn't up to no good.

'What if I scream?' Quinn asked her.

'Nobody will hear you.'

'You will.'

'See that roll of toilet paper? I'll stuff it down your yap.' The woman held up the roll. Half-used. 'Sounds good? The hole in the roll? Guys still come down your throat but you can't bite.'

Left alone again, she cried. Quinn couldn't help it. Embarrassed, ashamed, she wept. The woman had insinuated what might happen. She was terrified.

Her guard came back. She deliberately crossed her arms and stood over her. Without showing sympathy, she gave advice. 'Sweetie, tell them what they want to hear. Truth, lies, just tell them. Make it up if you gotta. You're better off saying what they want to hear.'

She believed her.

Alone again. Quinn tried to control her torment. It didn't help to think about her mother, but she did. That made her cry and perhaps it made her stronger, also, somehow. She felt less alone. She wished her dad could save her, but mostly she dreaded him finding out that she was dead. Or worse than dead. She feared the things that could be done to her and tried to halt the way her imagination was bending, but it wasn't easy. She needed to breathe. Breathe quietly. Easy. Easy, girl.

She held on.

Then, movement. Followed by footsteps. The door opened. A man stood there. She didn't know him. He stared at her. He wore a suit, like a banker. She felt her blood pool into her feet. Quinn glanced at him. She didn't want to provoke him and looked away quickly. He didn't look like anything, just a man in a suit. He was an older man. Maybe he wanted nothing from her except that damn baseball.

When barely removed from boyhood, Captain Armand Touton survived Dieppe. Wounded, exhausted from swimming out to a British destroyer only to see it blow up, he swam two miles back to the beach. Captured by the Germans, he was interned for the duration of the war. A French doctor operated on him for his three bullet wounds without anesthetic and declared him the bravest man he'd met. Near the end of the war, he was force-marched back to Germany from Poland in the dead of winter and was close to dying of dysentery when an American tank rumbled into view. He recovered in Montreal and became a cop after exposing a practice of doctors taking payoffs. Examining physicians declared perfectly healthy ex-servicemen who wanted to be policemen unfit, unless they received a contribution. Touton tore that system down by having military doctors attest to his good health and, further, they announced that any physician saying otherwise would be brought before a tribunal with his license in jeopardy. Armand Touton imposed himself upon a corrupt system and fixed it.

He'd spent two and a half years as a prisoner of war because the ship he was swimming to had exploded. Only after the war did he learn that the explosions were a pyrotechnical ruse to make the Germans think exactly what he believed: that the ship was finished. Nearly three years of fear and misery because someone pulled a fast one and he fell for it, hook, line and sinker. He nearly sank.

After that, having learned a hard lesson with horrific consequences, he kept his eyes peeled for smartass human shenanigans. No one put anything over on him again.

As a cop, his heroics, his bravery, his reformist agenda, his inherent attitude that if the Third Reich couldn't kill him neither could any crummy pack of hooligans, and the legendary power of his fists that could destroy a man's will to live with a single blow, made him both a national hero in line with hockey players or rock stars and a moral force within the police department.

The Night Patrol was being disbanded so that never again would an officer accrue his significance, fame, or power. Or, most importantly, his independence.

So. One last hurrah. Why not? He was all in.

Not easy, to organize a multitask strike force on the fly. He called in favors. Signaled friends. Arm-twisted the hesitant and fired up his loyalists. Rousted the day shift from their evening meals and TV sofas. Pulled patrolmen off their beats. Detectives quit their cases for a night. Any Captain or Loo or Sergeant-Detective with an idea – raid a whorehouse, disrupt legitimate strip clubs, barge into a numbers cellar, collar drug pushers on their rounds, end the festivities in Mafia bars and restaurants with a menacing police presence – was granted a green light to do so. He'd take the heat. Cops took the gloves off for a night, getting back at criminals who'd taunted them, provoking street fights without concern over warrants or arrests or convictions. One warden even issued a command to seize incarcerated henchmen from their bunks and drop them into solitary for the night.

Every cop made it known that Ciampini was to blame for the whole nine yards.

Within a seven-minute period, police hit twenty-three establishments – legit and illicit – then doubled that number over the next two hours.

Lawyers taking umbrage were ignored or asked to get in line behind the other lawyers taking umbrage. Or were arrested themselves on trumped-up charges later to be deemed accounting errors. Officers who signed the arrest warrants were found not to exist.

Arrested souls were lined up a block long and advised to hold their water. Processing them would take time. Roughly, the better part of the night.

Giuseppe Ciampini stood in the bathroom doorway, stared, assessed, and then departed. He returned ten minutes later with his jacket and tie removed. He sat on the edge of the bathtub and glared at Quinn Tanner as though that's all that was necessary to coerce her to collapse.

She stiffened. Became stronger.

'You sit on the can with your panties off. Why?' His voice remained calm, neutral. 'You know?'

'I think so,' she said.

'Explain to me why.'

'Because what you do will scare me. I'll go pee.'

'You go pee. What else?'

Her lower lip quivered.

'That's right,' he said. 'We'll scare the shit out of you, too. That's why.'

'OK,' she whispered. Quivering all over.

'Not only scare you.'

'I know,' Quinn said. Her voice weaker now.

'When you bleed, we don't mop up. Only flush. Easy.'

She peed then. The tinkling in the bowl not only embarrassed her, it made her angry. 'Oh Gawd!' she cried out. Then wished she hadn't. 'Please, don't,' she implored him, then wished she hadn't done that either. To be brave was too hard.

'We don't have to. We might enjoy, but we don't have to. I want to know what I want to know. If you don't tell me, the guys will hurt you. Maybe too much. I cannot control. You met the Rabbit. He wants first crack. Nobody says no if the Rabbit goes at you. You will scream everything to me if I put him on you tonight.'

She believed him. 'Don't. What do you want to know? I'll tell you.'

'I'll ask you when I ask you. When I ask, you will answer. First, I want you to understand our situation.'

'OK.'

'I can save you from the Rabbit. In Italy I have a villa. In Tuscany. You could go there, for instance. I also have one in Sicily. The one in Tuscany is a very nice villa. I could take you there, away from the Rabbit. Are you still virgin, you?'

Quinn didn't answer.

'I asked you serious question.'

She didn't know where her defiance came from, but it popped out. 'That's none of your business,' she said.

'I knew your mother,' Ciampini said. 'She taught your father everything.'

'What do you mean?'

He raised a hand and performed a dialing motion.

'What does that mean?'

'Your mother, I respect. She was a safecracker. The best. She taught your father. Then *he* became the safecracker. Not bad. Not as good as your mother. Later, she became everybody's mother when she got reformed. To go straight, I respect, but she wanted *everybody* to fucking go straight. Come on, I have a business. Whacko nut job, your mother. But I respect.'

'You're lying.'

'For sure I don't lie. Are you the one causing me my trouble tonight?'

'What trouble?'

'Mmm,' he said. He didn't want to say. He stood and moved close beside her. Then closer. He drew his thumb down one side of her jaw to her chin, then two fingers down the other side. He did the motion repeatedly. She tried not to turn her head away. She tried not to show how much she was repelled. She would not give him that. He got no reaction from her. She let him caress her jaw like it was nothing to her. Nothing.

'Answer me this time. Are you still virgin?'

She could not prevent the tears welling in her eyes.

'Of course not,' she whispered.

'So. You are a dirty little whore,' he accused. 'You admit.'

She hated how close he was. How his trousers brushed up against the side of her face. She broke. 'You're a gangster. A mobster. You're a fucking monster and you think calling me a whore makes me worse than you?'

'Nothing worse to me than dirty whores.'

'Yeah? I'll tell you who's a whore. Your own daughter. She's the whore.'

The slap was powerful and came as a shock. He was too close to her, the blow lost momentum when it struck high on her head, not on her cheek. A slap, not a punch. She understood the difference.

'I broke into her house,' Quinn railed at him. 'She was fucking another man. Not her husband.'

He took a step back to hit her a second time, and her head fell to one side as she suffered the clout.

Recovering slowly, she spoke quietly. 'Her husband's saving lives in a hospital while she's screwing around.'

He walloped her again. Open-handed, and she took that as a sign. Had he closed his fist she might not be alive.

He supported his hands on his knees and leaned down to speak at the level of her face, their mouths inches apart.

'Her husband,' Ciampini informed her, 'that fungus, that pile of mouse shit on top of dog puke, was outside his house sticking a knife in your boyfriend.'

Another shock. 'Why would he kill Deets? I don't believe you.'

'You want to know? You got a right. Savina found evidence. The doctor thought somebody in his bed who didn't belong. That fool got jealous. Like he had the right. Came home early. Saw the boy leave the house, the one who maybe helped you climb inside, eh? The doctor sees the handsome boy leave the house, go to the car. He pegged him to be Savina's lover. When my daughter and me found out this surgeon was playing like a gangster, killing her lovers, we had to discuss. Make a decision. The same way I need to make a decision with you.'

'I saw him come home, after Deets was already dead.'

'Don't be stupid in your face. He covered his tracks. Drove the knife away to ditch it. Maybe a knife from surgery. Except the stupid man left blood on his shirt – on the cuffs – for Savina to notice. You saw him come back the second time, after you robbed my daughter like you think you had a right. You never had that right.'

'I'm sorry, OK? I won't tell anybody anything. I promise.' She didn't like this. He had all but admitted to killing his son-in-law. How could he release her now?

'Oh sure, I am to believe you in my heart. I walk through my life with my belief in people. Now, I ask to you a question. You will give back to me the answer. We will hurt you if you don't. Me, the Rabbit, the Rabbit's men, maybe that whore outside. Then for sure you will tell us the right answer. But it's too late then, we go on hurting you more. Different ways. Because you did not tell to me what I want to know quick, fast, right now. Put me to the trouble, pay ten times over, then more. Tell to me. Right now. Where's my fucking baseball?' Then he said something that took Quinn by surprise. 'Ezra, him, does he have it?'

Rather than answer, Quinn said, 'I know why you want it.'

She was not denying anything. She was keeping him talking.

'You don't know the dick in your mouth from the one up your tight ass. Big, small, they're the same to a dirty whore like you.'

'It proves you killed your old boss,' she said. 'The baseball does that.'

That stopped him.

Then came a knock on the door.

Ciampini straightened up, not taking his eyes off her. She returned his gaze.

She didn't know if what she said would keep her alive or quicken her demise. Her pulse pounded so hard in her throat she worried she'd gag.

The knocking persisted, more urgent. Quinn glanced at the door, as though to suggest that Ciampini should, too.

'What?' Ciampini barked out.

The door opened a crack. Quinn waited for the woman guard to speak, but a man's voice parleyed a message. 'More trouble,' the intruder said.

'More?' Ciampini barked back again.

The voice sounded mildly fearful to be conveying the news. 'Hell, yeah. They're hitting restaurants.'

Ciampini turned, opened the bathroom door, and went out.

A few minutes later, the woman guard looked in.

'Still alive?' she asked.

'Still, yeah,' Quinn said. Clearly, she was breathing.

'Don't worry, babes, it's only temporary.'

Giuseppe Ciampini assessed the situation. His empire was under siege. New York called. News was traveling the pipeline.

Everybody around him was hot. He couldn't permit himself the luxury. He had to stay cool.

He was seeing for himself what the situation looked like when all hell busted loose.

'Every contact. Inside the police, outside, on the street, call it in. Tell me what they do next before they think it. When, where, who they hit, how. Smack me in the eyeball? I cut off their nuts. One ambush, we stop this in its tracks.'

'Kill cops?'

'Their funeral.'

'Everybody's already calling in,' the Rabbit told him. 'They scream it in.' He was better informed as to the scope of the operation against them. 'It's fast. We hear about a raid two minutes after they bust down the doors.'

'I'll make a call,' Giuseppe Ciampini said. 'Leave me alone. Let me stop this.'

He dialed Captain Armand Touton's number, and when Touton picked up, he said, 'Old friend, hello. We talk?'

As a reporter remarked, a crook could incriminate himself with a sigh. A deeper inhalation? Pull an overnight in the lockup. Blink? Be roughed up.

Typically, detectives and the serious bad guys were acquainted. On occasion, they'd have breakfast together. They talked baseball in summer, hockey once the snow flied. Inquired about each other's kids. That night, courtesies were set aside. Both camps knew that someday the status quo would be interrupted, but for that to happen right across the board created a shockwave. Cops knocked on the doors of criminals they monitored, said hi to their wives and kids, then hauled the hoods in.

'On what charge?'

'We'll make something up along the way.' Another shock.

'I'm calling my lawyer.'

'You can try. He's probably under arrest.' Alarm bells.

The news burned across mob networks like a pyromaniac's fantasy. Detectives pulled in anyone who was mobbed up, and Cinq-Mars set out to provoke an incursion of his own. Overdue. A chat with Ezra Knightsbridge. He intended to go soft, be physically benign yet tactfully and psychologically invasive. As he stepped inside the pawnshop, the jangle of the overhead bell announced his presence twice – once when struck by the door, and again when the tall man's head knocked it.

The old proprietor glanced up. Only a minute before closing, Cinq-Mars flipped the sign on the door to read FERMÉ. 'I decide if I'm open or closed,' Ezra Knightsbridge informed him. He chose to speak English as he was more adept in that tongue. His tone carried only faint authority, a surprise to both men.

Cinq-Mars stared down his impressive beak at the fellow. Hawk-like, this glare, as some were wont to say. Eagle-like, according to others. He could never parse the difference. He never told a soul that he had learned the gaze from a psychiatrist encountered on his travels. The physician believed that a severe look drew the bare truths from his patients that they were loath to impart. 'Another advantage,' the doctor quipped, disguising if he was serious, 'I can fade away yet look engaged.' Cinq-Mars, for his part, looked engaged. He introduced himself, omitting his rank and any reference to being police.

'Should I know you?' Knightsbridge answered back.

'Let me remind you of the times we're living in.'

A look of abject innocence.

'It's not possible that my name has not been mentioned to you recently. Yours has been mentioned to me by the same person.'

He stopped short of identifying Quinn by name. He wanted Knightsbridge to reach that conclusion on his own.

In his head, the pawnbroker ran down a shortlist of lies. None worked for him. 'Cinq-Mars. Formerly Night Patrol. Part of tonight's police rabble gone wild. Is that what you mean by the times we live?'

'That covers it, in part,' Cinq-Mars agreed.

'You're alone? No storm troopers?'

'On hold.'

'Beware the blessing in disguise,' the shopkeeper intoned. Then he had a thought. 'Maybe you should lock the door behind you.'

Cinq-Mars twisted a small nub. Serious deadbolts, requiring keys, were lower down.

'I'm glad you did that,' Knightsbridge stated.

'How so?'

'It suggests you're not here to haul me in on some ridiculous trumped-up charge.'

'That remains a possibility. We're trumping-up a lot of charges tonight. I thought we could have a quieter chat here than at the station. Utter chaos down there.'

Cinq-Mars crossed to the counter. He looked around as though something might be on view for him to evaluate. He processed details of the layout.

'How may I be of service, Detective?'

'Quinn's been abducted.'

Ezra Knightsbridge did not appear to know that.

'Your old cellmate is a suspect.'

The man was clearly taken aback that his life in prison was known to anyone. Let alone that anyone was aware he'd shared a cell with a criminal of consequence. He believed that era had been obliterated by the dust of time.

'Before we go one inch further, Detective, consider, please, the Cubans.'

Cinq-Mars stared down his beak at him again. The old man had more hair on his knuckles than on his head. Bushy white eyebrows, a gleam to his gaze. He knew him to be clever.

'You've lost me.'

'In part, you made your reputation thanks to the Cubans. The explosives.'

A secret story. In 1970, Cinq-Mars and Touton had been integral in disrupting the Front de libération du Québec, a terrorist cell devoted to the independence of Quebec. During that investigation, the Royal Canadian Mounted Police stumbled upon an arsenal of munitions protected by the Cuban embassy and meant to aid a clutch of terrorists. Enough explosive to level city blocks. The Cubans established the warehouse as embassy property, and therefore part of their sovereign territory under international law. Consequently, the cops were compelled to leave, and the Mounties were doing so when Touton arrived on a tip and refused to oblige. Cinq-Mars stood by his boss. Their puny pistols against a battery of high-powered weaponry. A stalemate ensued, one that was not resolved until the Prime Minister of Canada telephoned Fidel Castro. The Cubans stood down and surrendered the munitions, while the Canadians accepted a stipulation that they would keep the matter secret. The Prime Minister talked about an "apprehended insurrection" when speaking to the press and was mocked because he could explain himself no further, snared by an edict to never reveal what had happened. He never did.

Knightsbridge understood Cinq-Mars's reticence to discuss the episode.

'Ask yourself,' he suggested to the policeman, 'how the Mounties arrived on the scene in the first place. Ask yourself, who tipped them off. Then ask, who tipped you off.'

'I have no way of knowing.'

'And yet I know what happened. I'm not supposed to know.'

'What does that have to do with the price of milk?'

'Don't assume I'm not sympathetic. All I wish to convey, Sergeant-Detective.'

Cinq-Mars took a stroll amid the flotsam that had drifted into the store. More mental notes.

'How may I be of service?' Knightsbridge asked again.

'You attended Dietmar Ferstel's funeral. Wandering among the tombstones. I'm curious. Did you consider him one of yours? Did you set him up with Quinn? Hypothetical questions. No need to reply.'

'A man who answers his own questions is probably confused.'

'Ferstel was one of ours, too. Did you know he planned to be a policeman?'

Knightsbridge considered the news. 'Now I am the one confused. *Touché.* One wonders where his heart lay. With the police, or with a wilder society? Who was he preparing to betray? Tell me, Cinq-Mars, why are you here?'

'Without the storm troopers? They may yet make an appearance. Here it is. Quinn's been abducted. We don't want another funeral.'

Knightsbridge contemplated a reply. 'My scalp is in play,' he remarked.

'Be brave. One of those times. Look, you've lived a long life.'

'Well spoken. But I don't consider being foolish an adequate substitute for bravery.'

'I will keep your secrets.'

Knightsbridge remained still a moment. Then asked, 'You attack Ciampini on every front?'

'Every front we know.'

'And still you don't find her. Giuseppe Ciampini is weaker than in the past. His punks peter out. Old age. Death. Retirement. Key men incarcerated. Lesser powers establish satellite gangs. The young are impetuous.'

'You're saying he's weaker?'

'Yet powerful as ever. How can this be?'

The man was posing a riddle. 'I don't know.'

'Alliances, my young detective. Perhaps you and I can form such an alliance. Be beneficial one to the other one. In the future, the world will turn according to what alliances are formed. Ciampini is weaker now, yet equally strong. Where is his muscle? It's not in-house. It's no longer one hundred percent Italian.'

This seemed like a motherlode. 'Who then? What alliance?'

'The Rabbit.'

The policeman drilled him with the full force of his stare. Hawk-like, eagle-like, or just plain cop-like. The pawnbroker had a history of deflecting his own shenanigans onto the Rabbit, but this seemed different. Cinq-Mars could readily imagine a scenario where the Rabbit courted the favor of the Mafia and vice versa. They had much to offer each other: high-end organization and vicious street muscle conjoined.

'The Rabbit,' Cinq-Mars said at last.

'Hurry,' Ezra Knightsbridge implored him.

The man certainly had a knack for getting cops off his back. Cinq-Mars had to salute him for that. Still, this was a lead. He did as he was told. He hurried.

Touton expected the call.

'How's your health, Joe. Good?'

'Not so bad. Armand, I ask myself, how did things get this way? I ask, how do we make a truce to happen here tonight? I want your opinion. Your health, how does it go?'

'I'm fine. As for tonight, total capitulation will work,' Touton suggested.

'Don't be so ambitious in your old age, Armand. For argument, let us say it's not in the cards.'

'A truce won't work for me, Joe. It'll buy you time. You'll crank your lawyers up to speed, slide judges into place. Get your politicians and journalists on the warpath. What's the advantage for me?'

'I heard you retire. Pack it in soon. Congratulations.'

'Thought I'd go out with a bang. You're an old man, too. Why not pack it in?'

'You don't want me to retire, Armand. Like you, I might go out with a bang.'

'You could go fish, like me. Hunt and fish.'

'This could cost you your pension, Armand. Maybe I see to it.'

'Joe, that's only in the movies. Maybe other jurisdictions. Here, I'm in a union. My pension is rock solid. The Police Brotherhood took care of that before you. Now, I can shoot the Pope and still collect. What else you got?'

'Other ways exist to cut off a man's pension, Armand. You follow?'

'Try it. Maybe I'll enjoy shooting back. Like I said, I'll be hunting. I'll be armed.'

'What do you want from this, Armand. Just me?'

'I've wanted you my whole working life, Joe. You're my one big failure. Still, I can live without nailing you. But only if I get the girl. You know the one I mean. Harm the girl, this won't end. No further negotiation. The girl out, no harm done to her, *then* we can negotiate. Otherwise, this never ends.'

Touton hung up on him. The best way to deal with the man. An ultimatum backed up by refusing to share another word.

In the quiet of his office, he got to thinking and called Ciampini back for an encore. He phoned the Mafioso's office. Voices in the background sounded in full battle mode.

'I was just talking to him. We got cut off. Tell him to call me back.'

If nothing else, he might be able to trace where the call out of that office located their boss and go from there. Or trace the call coming in. Touton set all that in motion, then waited by his telephone. He waved off officers wanting to see him. For now, only this mattered. Two minutes later, Ciampini was back on the line.

'On me you hang up, why?'

'The phone slipped out of my hand. Look, I meant to offer you an incentive.'

'You put me in a shit mood, hanging up.'

'Calm down. Keep the girl safe and release her. That's number one. My part, if I can get you the baseball, I'll get you the bloody baseball. I know how much it means to you. You know how much it means to me. Remember, a cop died that night. I mention this to show how serious I am. I'll get you the baseball if the girl's released. Otherwise, it goes straight to New York City, to friends of yours. Relations. Cousins. Curious people like that.'

Captain Touton hung up on him again. He wasn't close to certain that he could deliver on a promise to return the baseball. At least, he had planted the thought that he was in possession of it, which might curtail any counteraction, stop Ciampini from hunting for it himself. Stop him from torturing Quinn to find out where it had gone. If he failed to deliver on the baseball, that might not be the end of the world – except that the girl, if freed, could be in jeopardy all over again.

In a curious way, this was like the exploding ship at Dieppe that never actually exploded. A bold gambit either works or it fails. In either scenario, if a few unfortunate people get held captive for the duration, so be it. Though he'd prefer that the girl not be held captive for the duration. For this ruse to pan out – for the girl to be safe after her release, if she was to be released – he had to place his trust in Cinq-Mars, in whatever scheme the kid had in mind. If he himself, and the department, the courts, and others, had to pay a price, so be it. He'd been down that road.

Not easy, to let go, to place one's trust in a protégé. Was Émile Cinq-Mars ready? Had he been properly prepared? Could he pull this off? Did he really have a clue? Or was he still a naïve wide-eyed choirboy, a failed priest with a degree in animal husbandry, of all things, with a wild idea?

Soon enough, they'd find out.

The whole city would find out.

The Rabbit slammed the door open so hard it smacked the side wall.

'Her white ass! Out! I mean like *now*!'

'What, are you talking to me?' Ciampini snarled. He was unaccustomed to anyone telling him what to do. Partnership required an adjustment. Especially when your new partner was a psychopath. 'Who you talking to?'

'Your fault, Joe. We're next.'

'For what are we next?'

'Dino's! My place. That pimp cop from Mount Royal, Giroux, called it in. We're next. I'm being fucking raided because of you, Joe. You make a fucking phone call to the police? What do you think? They don't trace the call? They don't look up the address? Fuck you!'

'Take it easy. I'm taking her out.'

'You take it fucking easy! This is my place. Get her ass out
of here! Like right now. Out. Go!'

The night was not progressing well for either man.

Ciampini made a call, then beat it out of there in a big Chrysler.

Quinn rode in the plush rear seat, behind the driver.

Her hands were tied in front of her. Otherwise, she sat unbound.

Ciampini rode in the back beside her.

He poked a pistol into her ribs.

'In case you get an idea. I like to put one in the gut first. Hit
the liver, too. Unbelievable, the hurt from that. I watch them roll
around in their pain. So much pain, so much blood. Then I finish
them off. You don't want that. It's not so quick.'

She had no argument.

Instead, she asked, 'Where are we going?'

As if they were out on a date.

'Don't play smart with me,' Ciampini warned her.

And yet she believed that that's what she had to do. Play smart.
Or die young.

The Airwaves

(Pure virgin white)

B y mid-morning, the corridors of the municipal courthouse
were a shamble. The press likened the situation to the aftermath of a riot. Many argued that the police were the rioters.

Mafia lawyers fulminated over the airwaves. Judges, some
rumored to be in their pockets, sympathized from lofty benches
but could make neither head nor tail of the night's events. Were
they experiencing an out-of-control police rampage? Or an
orchestrated scheme to take down organized crime? To compound
the confusion, dozens of crooks who'd been hauled in were
released without a preliminary hearing, the charges evaporating,
while line-ups for those waiting to be processed remained inter-
minable. The entire system was befuddled, and then a shift-change
complicated the chaos.

The Mayor of Montreal, commonly an ally of Armand Touton's and vice versa, turned on his office TV to listen to the pundits. His days were obsessed with preparing for the Olympic Games in a year's time and nothing was going well. Unions stymied him daily and the mob took a cut of every action, particularly in the construction industries. In Montreal, no crime had become more lucrative than pouring concrete. Commentators who praised the crackdown in the early going were equal in number and intensity to those who railed against it. Both viewpoints found impassioned audiences, and a theory coalesced that the mayor was eviscerating the unions and the mob to save the Olympics. The idea interested him. He called in advisors to discuss how to take advantage of this fortuitous development.

Emerging from his back-room lair, Ezra Knightsbridge responded to the bell above his pawnshop door as a tawdry youth who shouldered a backpack entered.

'Solace in a dire time of need. If you seek that,' Ezra told him, 'travel elsewhere. Common sense says be fleet afoot, dear Leonard. Go away.'

'Why?'

The pawnbroker sighed with genuine weariness. 'Am I too old for this?' he asked while rubbing his eyelids. 'Do I remain the only person in the trades who has not been vandalized by the authorities? One of their number did pay a visit. I was preyed upon. Others might soon ring my bell. Do you want to be here when they do? This is not a day for me to consort with persons such as yourself, or you with me. Today, you do not know me. I cannot know you.'

'Such as myself?' Leonard objected glumly.

'Petty criminals. No slight intended. Did I not include myself? I am wary of my own company, Leonard. What will happen this evening? The Night Patrol is on a rampage. Not my desire to give them an excuse to glance my way. My lights will be off. Go in peace. We'll talk when the mood becomes less ominous.'

'I'm here about Quinn,' Leonard stated. 'I know you know her.'

Ezra put a finger to his own lips, perhaps to silence him, perhaps to silence himself. He gestured for the young man to follow him through to the back room. There he switched the radio from the news to Brahms, only to decide that the music did not suit his mood. He turned it off and put his kettle on.

When Ezra sat down, the young man, who he thought of as being only a boy, was already seated. Waiting, his backpack on the floor. 'Of Quinn, what do you hear? Arrested, is she?' the old man inquired gravely.

'She's been taken,' Leonard said.

'Half the city they've rounded up. They set upon children now?'

'Not the police,' the boy explained. 'I wish. The Mafia took her.'

Ezra Knightsbridge was hoping for a better report. He ruminated on the news. Ciampini had intimated his intentions. The Rabbit was undoubtedly involved. How could that young detective, Cinq-Mars, counter such forces?

'For a fact, you know this?' asked Ezra. 'In times of war, rumors run wild.'

'I called her father. They snatched her right out of her house.'

'Oh my,' Ezra said. He preferred that Leonard not know he had already been briefed. 'Oh dear.'

How much of this explained the police action? Could everything really revolve around Quinn? Usually people reacted with such abandon only when at war or in love. Which was it?

'Curious, I am, Leonard. Why come here? Mafia, I have nothing to do with. What do you look for?'

'Your help, of course,' Leonard said. 'You're her friend.'

Ezra Knightsbridge felt inclined, in the spirit of the moment, to explain the facts of a criminal life to the orphan. Do so in a fatherly fashion. Leonard had acquired experience down wayward alleys, that was true, yet he was not well versed in how the larger universe operated. He might have impressed upon him that friendship had nothing to do with the criminal world, other than as a fast track to lengthy incarceration. The opportunity to do so passed as the tinkling of the bell above his front door signaled another interruption.

'Help yourself to a biscuit,' he said, and returned to the storefront.

Sergeant-Detective Yves Giroux moved through the overcrowded lockup slowly, scanning faces, until he noticed the man he was searching for. He then proceeded to ignore the figure and moved as though distracted until beckoned by a sound like hissing. He moved across to the man, who now leaned against the bars, his forearms hanging out.

'I gave you decent warning,' Giroux reminded him. He undertook the precaution to whisper. 'Not my fault.'

The Rabbit conceded the point. 'They know me. If they want me, they find me. Now, real quick, spring me out of this rat cage.'

'Spring you? I'm not a lawyer.'

'The law is all fart and no shit today. Some guys hear their names called out and get booted. Make me one of those guys, Giroux. For once, I'll take a kick in the ass if I land back on the sidewalk.'

Giroux understood. But he needed the Rabbit to fully grasp the challenge. 'Your record's as long as both my arms and both yours. Factor that in. It'll be a tough slog.'

'Not that tough,' the Rabbit predicted.

'Why? You have no idea—'

'I got you on my side, Giroux. You and your fat gut. I own you. Get me out.'

'I helped you. I warned you they were coming in.'

'What good does that do me now? Except I can trace the call – evidence about a copper who tipped me off.'

'Come on, no need for that talk. Anyhow, I called you from a booth. I was on the go. Not traceable. I took a risk.'

The Rabbit seized Giroux's belt buckle in his right hand and drew him tight to the bars. 'I been in here all night. Fun and games. Now I'm bored. Spring me out. That's a fucking order.'

Giroux nodded. He left the lockup immediately. If a man knew what was good for him, he did what the Rabbit requested. Outside the cell block, he exited down a corridor and turned right. The layout was familiar to him from his time in the Night Patrol, which felt like eons ago. He turned another corner and took the elevator up. He entered the corridor for the Night Patrol operations and hurried through a congested area of desks and busy cops, where he caught up with Émile Cinq-Mars.

'Well?' Cinq-Mars asked him.

'In the frying pan. Sizzling like bacon.'

'You and breakfast. OK, forty minutes to fry, then drain the grease.'

'That long?'

'He needs to believe it took time to shake things loose. Has to feel real.'

'I can stamp his release?'

'We can't hold him. If we didn't hijack his lawyer, he'd be out by now.'

'You arrested his lawyer?'

'Yeah, well, tomorrow we'll say we're sorry.'

'God, Émile, you're up to your eyeballs in this shit.'

'Something I don't know? Forty minutes, Giroux. No delay beyond that.'

Ezra Knightsbridge identified the customer before him as European. In a bilingual city where the predominant language was French, variations in dialect were quickly discerned by the citizenry. A Parisian's elocution was as obvious to a Quebecker as an Irishman's lilt to a New Yorker. Ezra was generally more comfortable with people from the old countries; he appreciated their shared experience. That the dapper gentleman was from Belgium took a modicum of probing to uncover. To his mind, it explained the handlebar mustache under the shock of alabaster hair, the huge eyeglasses that magnified his pupils, and the fellow's ebullient flair.

The man's younger female companion was a Quebecker. Timid alongside the gentleman's hubbub. While the man intoned that he was looking for a ring of antique distinction to place upon the finger of his betrothed, the woman's manner hinted at the frugality of their situation. He was looking for something old and distinguished, he said – by which he meant cheap. She was looking for anything that would do.

Ezra displayed three possibilities. One struck their fancy. Two hundred and fifty dollars would stretch their budget, but they'd consider it. Ezra was confident of a return visit unless they found an acceptable piece of junk elsewhere. Of modest value, the ring met their criteria, and according to Knightsbridge had once been worth more. The gentleman took him to be an honest broker.

On his return to the back room, Ezra stalled. Something nagged him. The hair on both his forearms rose. A sign of the tension of these days, he assumed. Leonard was not in the chair but roaming loose amid the merchandise – the last place he wanted a street urchin to be. He assured him, politely, that he would give every thought to Quinn and do his best for her. Now, under the circumstances, Leonard needed to depart.

'Noel,' Leonard said.

'Pardon me?'

'It's my real name, I found it out. I'm Noel now.'

'Interesting. You must tell me the story. Another time. Noel, I am thanking you to close the door gently as you go. No. Wait.'

Noel waited. Knightsbridge approached.

'Not to be offended. I trust a thief to be a thief, the ruffian from the streets to take what falls in his lap. Only is it natural.'

He rummaged through Leonard's backpack. Nothing but books and notebooks. The ragamuffin dope dealer was a wannabe student who hadn't stolen a thing.

'No offense taken,' the youth said as the backpack was returned to him. He left.

The pawnbroker turned on the radio news and obeyed his whistling kettle. While the tea steeped, he reflected upon poor Quinn. What could he do? He possessed dangerous knowledge. If he called Giuseppe Ciampini and offered him the baseball for her life, he might be shot for not giving it up sooner, or merely for knowing of its importance. If he tried to be an intermediary, a greater risk was apparent. Quinn might be shot the very moment she was no longer needed. Worse, someone might decide that secrets would remain secret if they both floated in the river. The two of them knew about the baseball. Where it had been. A knowledge that could be lethal. Either way, with the ball revealed or not revealed, Quinn was doomed. He failed to discern any significant benefit to dying alongside her.

Assuming that Ciampini had snatched Quinn to save himself, he was unlikely to let her go. If Quinn had a hope or a prayer, Ezra concluded, it did not rest with him.

He returned to the Brahms, although the music again failed to spark his spirit.

After forty minutes, Sergeant-Detective Yves Giroux went back to the lockup and isolated himself with the Rabbit.

'Still here,' the Rabbit pointed out. 'How come is that?'

'There's a thing,' Giroux explained. 'A ballbreaker.'

'Take care of it,' the Rabbit insisted.

'No can do. I can't work fucking miracles. It's what this is all about.' His eyes indicated the lockup, the men waiting to be processed. By extension, he meant the entire police action, the apparatus, and the night's wholesale operations. The Rabbit caught his gesture.

'Say.'

'A girl. Ciampini took her, the cops think. They raided his joints looking for her. Bars, clubs, restaurants, his establishments . . . You know what I mean. Not only his. Associates been hit, too. Still no girl. If we locate her, you're back out. If we don't, people need to wait their turn to be grilled by the Night Patrol.'

'Night Patrol,' the Rabbit repeated. His tone terse.

'For someone important like you, that means Touton himself.'

Almost twenty years earlier, Touton ruptured the Rabbit's spleen with a single punch. Over a notorious career, the Rabbit had been stabbed, slashed, beaten with knuckledusters and shot, all in a day's work, but he counted that episode with Touton as the greatest horror in his life. As he related to others, taking that punch was like giving birth to twins through his nostrils. He feared death less than he feared Touton's right hand. Never mind that the cop was getting on in years, as people said. He didn't buy into that tall tale.

'I don't sell out Ciampini,' the Rabbit whispered. 'How can I anyway? I don't know him.'

'Of course not. Of course, you hardly know him. But it's the girl, see. The girl. If she's not found, nobody leaves. This doesn't stop until the cops have her.'

'The shits,' the Rabbit summed up.

'OK, you don't know Ciampini, like you said. But if you can guess where the girl is—'

'Watch your mouth, Giroux. I don't sell out Ciampini. No price.'

'Not selling out. Not selling. Nothing to do with you, right? Just about the girl. That's all they need, these cops. This is strictly a rescue operation. Nobody's looking to put Ciampini away. He walks. You walk. Nobody gets hurt. Just a rescue.'

They hung on, looking around the overcrowded lockup. The body odor in the nearly airless room pungent. Soon, men would glow.

'Sounds like pure, virgin, white-ass bullshit to me.'

'Sure, it does. It's not legal what they do. Shit to pay for the cops. Touton doesn't give a crap because he's quitting. He only wants the girl.'

'Why the fuck care about some girl? There's lots of girls. New ones get born.'

'Nobody tells me why. The thing is . . .' Giroux allowed an implication to float in the air.

'Say.'

'Last night, I called you from a phone booth. Not a problem for me.'

The Rabbit waited.

'Earlier. What I hear. A call went from Ciampini's place to yours. This is not my operation. I'm speaking to you what I find out. Your name is all over this. Because of that call. They found out that Ciampini called your place. When Touton comes in tonight, you know what's next. No lawyers. No rules. He's in a real bad mood. Feeling righteous. That's when you don't want to know him. I prefer to get you out while we still have time.'

The Rabbit studied the detective closely. He considered what he knew about the man. Giroux had done all right, coming through the night before to alert him. Without that tip, he might have been nabbed with a kidnap victim on his premises. Never a good thing.

'Same minute?' the Rabbit asked.

'Not even,' Giroux assured him. 'Same goddamn second.'

'Get me a telephone.'

'Who're you gonna call? Ciampini won't tell you nothing. He knows you're locked up. Pass it on to me, your best guess where's the girl at.'

'I don't know Ciampini. Bumped into him once or twice. Who can avoid? Why he call my place I don't know. Wrong number? But maybe I know his driver. Maybe his driver knows who he drives around. Maybe he drops somebody someplace.'

Giroux arranged to take him to a room with a telephone.

The cops traced the call, as everybody knew they would. They'd pay the driver a friendly visit. The Rabbit was giving Joe Ciampini to the cops without mentioning anybody's name. He didn't have to utter a single incriminating vowel. He simply asked a guy over the phone where he'd been lately and accepted 'nowhere' for an answer. The cops knew then whose arm to twist. They possessed ways and means. The Rabbit stayed in the clear, soon to hop away.

Giroux was thrilled. Until the plan failed. His sure victory dashed.

The driver broke under pressure. With the sharp end of a fork pressed against a closed eyelid, he admitted to picking up a girl at the Rabbit's club. But later the drivers were switched. He took a cab home. He couldn't say where the girl went after that because he didn't know.

After more pressure on the fork, he could not reveal the identity of the second driver quickly enough.

The new guy was an assassin. Nobody's chauffeur.

He could not easily be tracked down.

They were out of moves.

Tumblers

(Halfway to Tuscany)

The young man who yapped about his name being Noel, or Leonard, or both, had successfully lured Ezra Knightsbridge into the back room. That cleared the way for Dr Eudo Lachapelle and Huguette Foss to enter the pawnshop, ringing the bell above the door. The pawnbroker heard them come in, but as he was occupied in the back room, he did not observe them enter. That allowed Jim Tanner to sneak in at that moment and hide. The plan worked like a charm. Tanner slipped behind the counter on the side of the room opposite the cash register while Eudo and Huguette attracted a world of attention to themselves. He slid under a counter and out of sight.

There he stayed. As still as dirt.

He waited for Knightsbridge to lock up.

Noel, he thought, to keep his mind alive while lying perfectly still. *Leonard*. He wondered if the young man realized Noel spelled backwards was Leon, the first four letters of Leonard. That would've been something had he chosen Leon as his invented moniker. Close enough to be spooky. He'd mention it if they got through this and freed Quinn.

He was in luck. Not wanting to be around when the Night Patrol returned to the streets for their last great expedition, the pawnbroker packed it in fifty minutes early and locked up. Knightsbridge never knew that his shop had been invaded.

With the proprietor gone, Jim Tanner emerged from his crawl space.

He suffered a rash of nerves.

He was relying on cops, which inverted his world. He was also relying on a skill set best judged as rusty, and with his daughter's life on the line. Failure was not an option, yet he could scarcely remember the last time he'd experienced success. Even his current union negotiations hinged on a difficult turn. He was bailing on his buddies right when they needed him the most. No explanation to anyone. How could he explain that he needed time away to crack a safe in a pawnshop to prevent his daughter from being slain by the mob?

Rampant, random thoughts needed to be cast aside. Such as the conviction that if the mob killed his daughter, he'd start shooting guys in the mob, the closer to the top the better. A vow. That it amounted to suicide was not relevant. Partly the point. He'd not be long for this world if Quinn died. He'd take others out with him – another thought to eject for now. Time to get to work.

Tanner evaluated the alarm system. Not the world's most sophisticated line of defense, as it protected the premises only from without. No impediment to his movements within the store existed. The shop depended on tried-and-true sliding metal grates, with locks, to seal off exterior windows and doors, as well as a rudimentary alarm. Break a window or bust a door lock and a loud signal would sound, alerting the street, but neither an alarm company nor the police would automatically be summoned. The primary intent of the installation was to protect the exterior, including the rear, where a steel door stood heavily bolted.

The system's sensors were not meant to be acutely sensitive – Knightsbridge could not have his alarm going off every time a garbage truck created an uproar in the lane, or a drunk beat his fist on the outside when berating the world. Any incursion or attempt to break in had to be blunt and heavy for it to be countered by an alarm's piercing battle cry. He assured himself again that no impediment challenged anyone who had already infiltrated the back room. If he failed to neutralize the alarm on his way out, he'd escape under that barrage of noise and be gone, home free.

His principal task, then, was to crack Ezra Knightsbridge's safe. He got to work. He had tools, which Leonard/Leon/Noel had stowed in his backpack and sequestered in the back room behind one of the countless boxes. Ezra had examined the backpack in case the boy was taking something *out*, but never thought that he might have smuggled something *in*. The plan was for Jim Tanner to start hunting behind boxes at eye level and work lower if necessary. He found his toolset almost immediately, then crossed to the far side of the room to investigate the safe.

Knowing Ezra from the old days, he counted on the safe being a relic. As tough as a tank, as heavy as lead. A correct guess. Fat and square, a black Diebold. In its time, the unit was overkill. Its mechanisms, as sophisticated as they were back in the day, had inherent flaws familiar to the former safecracker.

In its time, the Sargent & Greenleaf combination lock had been rated at twenty hours, meaning that an expert would likely require twenty hours to unravel its code. The dial was protected against the safecracker's technique of 'punching', and would reset whenever someone attempted the trick. That quick method, then, was out. On the plus side, he used to practice on S&Gs. Hours and hours of endless training. The safe itself bore a TL-60 label, meaning that an expert with the appropriate tools would require at least sixty minutes to physically break it open. When he first learned the trade, Jim Tanner found it convenient that safes indicated their level of defense and sophistication on an engraved label, as if to let him know what he was up against. The unit was also labeled x6, which meant that all six sides required the same length of time to cut or break through. Unfortunately, with his lighter-weight tools and no blowtorch, he had no ability to bust it apart.

Because of Quinn's predicament, whatever time he took might be too much. Yet he needed to be methodical. Mistakes could steal time and quickly compound. They could be fatal.

Confronted by a safe after years of abstinence, virtually against his will Tanner felt a surge of excitement, akin to sexual arousal, as he commenced his work. He was suddenly feeling buoyant and transported. He'd missed this.

A single dial on the outside of the safe. Internally, three dials revolved. He removed a stethoscope from his toolkit and placed it close to the exterior dial at ten o'clock. Very slowly, he spun the entire circle. He did so again with the stethoscope at two o'clock. Then at four o'clock, and again at eight. Those old wheels had served the unit well, yet time wears on everything. He would have a chance to flush out the combination, sparing him a forced entry.

An old technique taught to him by his wife jumped to mind. Worth a shot. She had learned the trick from her safecracking uncle, although never came across a situation to use the gimmick herself. Jim Tanner took out a small flashlight and put the dial under the beam. The theory went that a single owner typically spun the center of a large dial to select the first number in his sequence. He'd do it quickly. Then slow down to catch the next numbers, so as not to overshoot them. In doing so, the middle finger and the thumb ventured to the outer rim of the circle. Stopping there. Then the owner spun the center again but slowed down and located the next number the same way, with thumb and middle finger on the outer rim. After decades – in Ezra's case, thirty or forty years – the fingers imparted a stain upon the dial. Though imperceptible at a glance, if the light was right the marks could be detected by someone who knew what they were looking for. Close study could reveal them. Tanner needed only to imagine a horizontal line between two such opposite stains created by Ezra's thumb and middle digit. Then at ninety degrees above the center of that line, or very close to it, find a number in the combination. That digit, or its complete opposite at the bottom of the dial, depending on where the thumb had landed, would be either the second or third number in the combination's sequence.

He believed he could see the stains. Imprints left by finger oil having smudged dust through decades. He might crack this baby in record time. Through trial and error, he needed to discern the angle at which Ezra's fingertips typically rested.

He turned the dial again. Slowly, slowly. His stethoscope pressed to the metal.

When the first tumbler from one of the three internal wheels nudged into place, he knew that he could do this. Of course, it would take time. But damn it, he still had the touch.

Quinn! Quinn! Hang on! Everything, not only the tumblers, was falling into place.

* * *

A meeting was arranged, the security details agreed upon. Trust and its lack was a factor, as each side anticipated secret deadly force. A suspicion that would keep the peace.

Touton chose the location, a favorite restaurant in Old Montreal, and requested the *patron* to shutter the door. He proposed two dinners for the entire Night Patrol – half the gang one night, half the next. To take place on weekdays that were normally quiet, so that the *patron* would not be significantly out of pocket from this evening. They had done such business in the past.

Touton was granted the run of the place.

Subterranean, the bar resembled a cavern. Fake firelight from the lanterns caused sensual images on the walls to dance. Shadows played on the convex ceiling, as if macabre spirits were springing to life.

Something had to be done. The police had run amok the night before. No matter who controlled the streets and alleys by night – Touton or Ciampini, the Night Patrol or the Mafia – the two men had agreed that the battle was not civilized.

Having arrived first, Touton waited in his preferred corner, close to a red exit sign.

The Mafia boss walked in through the kitchen, via the back door.

Surprised at first that the man hadn't sent a goon ahead of him to scout the premises, Touton concluded that the unforeseen might be how this played out. Norms would be set aside. He wasn't going to pat him down for a weapon, either. What did he care if Ciampini pulled out a pistol? He'd smack his old man's jaw and the mob boss would wake up chained to a hospital bed, if he was lucky. In the morgue, if not. Ciampini was no dope. He'd not try anything that stupid.

'Armand,' Ciampini said. His tone of voice was pleasant. While his first language was Italian and his second English, and they would converse in English, his accent speaking the French name was pitch-perfect.

'Hey, Joe,' Touton said. 'You look good.'

'Red wine,' the mob boss stated to the *patron* behind him. 'Your best Italian.'

'Sir,' the *patron* said. He checked with Touton.

The policeman stipulated, 'My usual.'

'Bring the man his whisky,' Ciampini ordered, to indicate that he was picking up the tab.

The *patron* served the men himself. He did not send in a waiter. He gathered his staff in the kitchen and advised that anybody making a sound would be fired. Then moved back to the kitchen door to eavesdrop.

Ciampini settled into the booth. 'So,' he said. 'We talk.'

'Talk,' Touton instructed.

Ciampini did not do so. He sipped his wine. Shook his head. Sipped again.

Touton declared, 'So much to say. You should retire.'

Ciampini scrunched up his mouth, as if willing to consider it. 'Speak for yourself, old man. I have a villa in Tuscany. Very nice. One in Sicily, also. The one in Tuscany . . .' He contracted his mouth and kissed the tips of his fingers, then let them flay out.

'There. You see? You're already halfway retired.'

'Will you come visit, Armand? We could talk of old times. Drink fine wine.'

'That depends,' Touton sounded a note of caution, 'on what we say tonight.'

'Everything,' Ciampini agreed, 'depends.' He sipped his wine. 'Thank you for the truce.'

'Only temporary. Everything depends . . .'

'We put things right. Armand, let us make a permanent peace.'

Having his ear affixed to the safe through a stethoscope was like listening for his daughter's heartbeat. He had that thought. All Jim Tanner's senses were attuned to the present moment, then to the next. The safe sounded like a giant, still lung. That breathed.

In and out of traffic. Cinq-Mars pressed the accelerator toward the floor. He was glad he drove a nimble Beetle. Giroux was less enamored with the choice of transportation. Cop sedans provided more room for his legs and protuberant gut. Also, they had sirens. Given the rampage through traffic, he'd feel safer in a proper vehicle. But he did not suggest that the younger man slow down.

They sped on through the night.

Cinq-Mars had asked a question when they learned that the chauffeur couldn't help. 'The driver drove Quinn from the Rabbit's place. Correct?'

'Right,' Giroux confirmed.

'Who else was there? We raided, who else did we pick up?'

'The usual suspects. Bar staff. Working girls. A couple of customers were booked.'

'Who was upstairs?'

'What do you mean?' Giroux asked.

'Upstairs. Not in the bar. Anyone?'

'I can find out.'

'Find out.'

A process that led to a worn-out young tramp of a woman. A hooker off work while she recovered from a venereal disease. Cinq-Mars declared, 'Put her in a box. I'm interviewing.'

She was trembling when he entered the interrogation room. He showed her his card.

She reached for it. He pulled it back.

'Nobody can find this on you. Memorize my name. If you get jammed up, give me a call. If you want to be pulled out completely, same deal.'

She committed his name to memory. 'Got it.' Then she said, 'He can find out. He has ways.'

'He won't. You never talked to me.'

'What do you wanna know?'

'Where she is.'

Hard crust. And yet, she could relate. In her marrow she didn't want devastating harm to come to the girl. Cinq-Mars convinced her of that. It didn't take much. No need to twist her arm. 'She's a kid,' he said. 'Talk to me. No one will ever know.' The hooker doubted that. Still, she spoke.

When Ciampini was on the phone setting it up, she'd overheard where they planned to take Quinn. Her story was convincing because the destination for Quinn was logical. Brilliant, even. Cinq-Mars knew the place. He'd been there.

They ripped across the side of the mountain and sliced through the affluent streets of Outremont, where tall mansions loomed over the quiet sidewalks, then nipped across the overpass above the train tracks into the Town of Mount Royal. After that, Cinq-Mars slowed down, not wanting to attract attention. They meant to give the denizens of the sleepy suburb more excitement than they'd seen in a generation, but approached as invisibly as the wind.

Touton had suspended the random frenetic raiding. He wanted

Ciampini to relax. To let his guard down. He wanted him to feel confident that Quinn remained securely hidden.

A full-on raid might put her in deeper jeopardy. She could switch from being a kidnap victim to being a hostage exposed to a variety of lethal dangers. Cinq-Mars and Giroux needed to assess and devise the preferred course of action to extricate the girl without giving away their presence. To Cinq-Mars, that meant going in alone.

Thanks to the Rabbit's hooker, they knew where she was being held.

Right under their noses.

Quinn had been terrified all night and day.

Driven around the previous night, she behaved herself while looking and hoping for a way out. They knew that. They parked in an alley. She recognized the neighborhood. While scouting districts to plunder as an apprentice thief, she had passed through the area and been upset by the poverty. The alley was dark, empty. She feared her captors might shoot her on the spot and dump her body in somebody's messy scrap of a backyard amid rusting iron and cats in heat. They pulled her out of the car, and she wanted to pee again. But didn't. They turned her around. One man blindfolded and gagged her; she cooperated because she didn't want to be shot. She feared that that came next. They would force her to kneel and put a pistol to the back of her head and she'd cry out, through her gag, to her mom and to her dad. She felt so sorry for her dad. Her hands were already bound, and when they shoved her back into the car she didn't know what they planned to do. The car took on the aspect of a sanctuary. She doubted they'd risk staining the expensive leather upholstery with her blood and brains. The driver told her to stay down on the floor and another man pressed a pistol against her neck. The driver was not the same one as before. A different voice, a different attitude. She stayed down. The pistol on her neck. A different man, also. She didn't wiggle around. The driver told the other guy to shoot her if she budged. 'Don't hesitate.'

She didn't budge, fine upholstery or not.

They drove on. She listened when they stopped the car. A garage door opened, and the car went forward a short distance. The engine stopped, then the garage door closed.

She was indoors.

They got her out of the back seat. She hit her head hard on the doorframe and cried out, her voice muffled by the gag.

'For fuck's sake!' one guy said. The new driver's voice.

They marched her forward. Told her to step up when she had to step up. That was difficult, raising a foot blindly. But they never misled her. A stair was always a stair. She never tripped.

A door was shut behind her. She was inside a house, no?

Carpet underfoot.

Familiar.

She sniffed. The scent of the house was familiar. She'd been in this house!

She'd wanted to steal the wall-to-wall carpet, preposterous as that had been! Her nostrils quivered with the memory of stale smoke.

She totally recognized the smell of the place.

She'd been returned to the house she robbed.

Where Maletti had screwed the married lady upstairs and Deets was knifed outside. Where the surgeon was gunned down. Ciampini's daughter's house.

Their hiding place for her.

They lashed her to a chair in the basement and secured the chair to a pool table.

They took her blindfold off and the gag, too.

The two men who brought her there left her alone.

Then the house went quiet.

She thought she heard the garage door open. A car start up and leave. The garage door close again.

She was left alone.

Or almost alone.

A different set of footsteps came down the stairs.

Jim Tanner wiped the perspiration from his brow. He had to start over again.

This woman frightened her more than the last one. Hard to know why at first. The woman at Dino's had that tough, mean-chick look. Nasty tattoos. A cold attitude. A flinty disposition as though she was looking for any excuse to slap her. Quinn thought of her as half-demented.

The day had worn on. This woman frightened her, although she preferred to take her chances with her. Tall, skinny, made-up to the hilt, straight yet coiffed hair with bangs. Her house reeked of cigarettes. She reeked of money. She had a mean streak. Cruel. Quinn had not been convinced that the low-life woman at Dino's was inherently cruel herself, only that she was heartless and abided the viciousness of others. Although this other woman appeared to be cruel, Quinn suspected that she could talk to her, appeal to a sense of decency that resided somewhere in her bones. She'd just have to be smart about it.

'Sorry you got hit twice.'

'Excuse me?' The question back at her could not be construed as polite.

'First your husband. Then Arturo Maletti. You got hit twice.'

Quinn could not believe what the woman was doing. Rather than answer her, she picked up a magazine, readjusted a pillow on the sofa, took a cue stick off the pool table and returned it to the rack. Her notion of housework. Tidying up while one of her father's victims teetered on the brink of death.

Somehow, she had to force her to respond.

Quinn performed her best imitation of her from memory. 'Babes, we got another hour. Two, if you want. Don't go. I'm so damned crazy about you, babes.' She was willing to exaggerate. 'I'm so fucking crazy about you. Any way you want it. I love the hell out of you, sweet pea.'

The woman was staring at her with that cold, expressionless, seemingly vacant gaze. Like a dead person gazing at a corpse.

'I hope they cut your feet off before you drown,' she said. 'They can use my tub. I'll think of you when I take a bath. That'll put a smile on my face.'

'I know who your father is,' Quinn said back.

She smirked. 'An Italian businessman. So what?'

She had to break her down somehow. 'My father was a crook.'

'You want a medal? Violins? Or lunch?'

'I can eat. What was your mother like?'

'Quit the twenty questions!'

'Just asking. Did she know about your dad? How did that work?'

Savina Shapiro shrugged. 'My mom loved the yacht vacations

in the Caribbean. She had no problem with Tuscany in the spring, or any of that. Anyway, my mother was not my mother. She was my step.'

'Did your real mother die?' They might have that in common.

'I dumped her. Preferred to live with my dad, see.'

Quinn came at her differently. 'Tuscany. Right. Your father said I could be his whore in Tuscany.'

'I'm shocked. Really. Truly. Shocked.'

'You don't sound shocked.'

'He wasn't serious.'

'He sounded serious.'

'A gimmick. If it makes you afraid of him, good, he's got you. If you go along with the idea, good, he's got you. Either way you lose.'

'I didn't say yes. My mom would cry her eyes out.' An appeal to her sensitivity as a woman. Which went nowhere.

'She'll cry her eyes out anyhow.'

She realized the difference between the woman at the Rabbit's and this one. The tough chick imagined the worst and threatened her, but didn't know what might happen. This woman, from the nicer side of the fence, looked at her as if seeing her dead. In her eyes, Quinn was already a corpse. Still breathing, but only for now.

The woman said, 'Too bad for Arturo. But he had it coming. My husband? I had him taken out.'

Quinn didn't want to hear her confession. It sealed her own fate.

'Poor baby, you're shocked. You caused your boyfriend's death, so don't play Miss Goodie with me. You should be happy my husband's dead. I did you a favor.'

'Did *me* a favor?'

'He whacked your boyfriend. Your fault, but he did the dirty work.'

To keep her talking, she pretended not to know. 'Why?'

'Not sure. Mistaken identity, I think. Your boy came out of my yard. My husband must've thought he was screwing me. I found blood – your guy's blood, I presume – on my man's shirt. Not from performing surgery. He wouldn't have left the operating room bloody.'

The doorbell chimed.

Quinn's head jumped.

The woman was amused. 'Don't get your hopes up,' she cautioned her. 'Guards. Showing up for their shift. Hell, did you think I'd look after you all day?'

The Role

(Whisky warriors)

'So,' Ciampini summed up, 'you're looking for some girl. A man like you I don't insult, but isn't everybody?'

'So don't insult me, Joe. I praise you. You're an intelligent man. How else could you elude me all these years? I'm heading into my bloody retirement without my number one prize. And that, Joe, is you.'

'Can't help you put me away, Armand. Can't help with the girl neither. If I could, I would.'

'Let's say somebody else grabbed her. Could you help me then?'

The crime boss grimaced. In that situation, he could help.

'Then if you won't help me, what does that show?'

Ciampini mulled over the implication that all but proved his guilt. If he was unable to help the captain, then he must be holding the girl. 'You're a tricky fucker. That's not an insult. If I've been smart enough to escape you, is because I had to be. The man after me is one tricky cop. Tough, too. I hire mean guys. But tough guys? They're a different breed. I think of you first.'

'Listen to us, so kind to each other. I want you locked up, you want me in a box underground.'

'Visit me in Tuscany. I'll settle for that.'

'I'll settle for you living there. But, like you, I can't go just yet.'

'This girl. Why so important?'

Touton accepted that he owed Ciampini an explanation. Why freeing the girl mattered more than the man's head floating in a soup tureen.

'Look at life differently, Joe. You win this round. Hell, I'll give you the fight. Split decision. You win it.'

'How you figure?'

'Let's say I have the baseball in my possession. I could show it to you. The girl walks on the streets again, but I don't have your ass in the can. For her to be safe, I need to bargain with you. What's my bargaining chip? I give up your arrest, in exchange I get her release. An OK trade. Except, it defeats me. I fail in the main mission of my career to take down Giuseppe Ciampini.'

'You can't win them all. I did not win them all.'

Ciampini was easing into their talk and adopting a vaguely wistful manner. Two old guys, evoking the old days while ruminating on a current dispute. Despite their differences, comrades-in-arms. Old foes who could let bygones be bygones. Touton wanted to lull this man if not into trusting him – too much to ask – then into underestimating him.

'Joe, I lose twice. Imagine this girl walking the streets. A thief again, or she goes to school, marries, has kids. Whatever she does, she's vulnerable. She doesn't have the baseball because let's say I found it and gave it back to you, but she still has a story to tell connected to the baseball. A risky tale. Your rivals can extract that story if they want. If she is grabbed again, made to tell the tale of a baseball stolen from the home of your daughter, how safe is that for you? I wouldn't be using the word "vulnerable".'

'My rivals?' Almost a scoff.

'Your cousins, family. I don't want to say.'

'If they think a story exists,' Ciampini conceded, 'somebody might ask her to tell it. Verify old talk. Safe? Does not look like it to me.'

'My point. Who has heard this story? Savina's husband? Dead now. Arturo Maletti? Maybe yes, maybe no. But, he's dead too. And Quinn Tanner. Who is missing. Not yet presumed dead. At least, I have not dredged the river. She can say where a baseball with a certain signature and another name on it – Mr Sal – was hiding in recent times.'

Ciampini clicked his fingers. '*Patron!*'

The owner came through the swinging door.

Ciampini indicated the empty glasses. The restaurateur skipped back to the kitchen to fetch the bottles and returned to their table in a jiff. He poured and, upon receiving a nod from both men to indicate their thanks, departed.

'The cousins,' Ciampini confided, 'fingered me for the hit. They're not stupid. But I'm family, too.'

'Good point, Joe. Here's mine. They had suspicions. Only that. Suspicions forgive, suspicions forget. To do so is good for business, and you made sure that business was good. But proof? Proof changes everything. With proof, you must do something. You cannot lose face. The something they do will not be good for you.'

As Touton rendered his opinion, Ciampini reviewed the matter in his own way.

'You don't have the baseball,' he stated.

'True. The exercise last night, which I might start up again when we're done here, depends on how this goes. That exercise has two purposes. One, find and release the girl. Two, find the baseball to convince the New York families that you murdered their favorite uncle.'

'You're a cruel man, Captain.'

Touton laughed. 'I'm searching for a bargaining chip that works. The baseball could work. The ball for the girl. A trade. What do you think?'

'You, so optimistic in your nature. This is a dirty town. If this ball, like magic, shows up with Jackie's signature and the old godfather's name on it, I'm sorry to tell you it doesn't prove I whacked someone who is dead long ago. These days, I'm a peaceful man. I will be left alone.'

Touton deflected the man's opinion of himself with a dip of his chin. 'You weren't always peaceful. Like me. I used to beat the crap out of the bad guys. Sometimes your own boys. These days? I go through the courts.'

'You're like me. You miss the old ways. Which is why last night. Attacking, raiding my places, roughing up my waiters, my busboys, scaring my girls, arresting . . . These are innocent people. This might be a kick for you, Armand, but it's not civilized. It's beneath you, Armand.'

'Kidnapping an innocent girl, that's not beneath you, Joe?'

'It's a tough town. What is it we can do to improve the situation? Yours and mine. Explain it to me. Like I say, the ball proves nothing except to put a bad idea inside the wrong head. And still a girl walking on the sidewalk on a sunny day is not safe.'

'Let's say I have the baseball, find it before you do. Let's say you have the girl. You don't, you tell me. Fine. But let's say you find her first.'

'We'll say those two things.'

'Like in the old days, we make a deal. One you can live with when you wake up in the morning. One I can sleep with when I go to bed at night. A deal, Joe, that permits the girl to stay alive. Even when walking down the street anytime during the rest of her life. That's the bottom line. A deal, Joe – this is the hard part – that's never undone by nobody.'

The tumblers revealed the first number. Jim Tanner dialed through select choices for the second and third, based on finger-oil stains. Discouragement, running each digit twice, then the next one over, two back, then switching the numbers, then trying again, then their opposites, then the safe opened. Like that. A vault of heaven winding up its doors. On his knees, Quinn's father was too stunned to believe it. Then he experienced a release that felt heaven-sent. His life at that moment was scored as worthy.

Trepidation quickly returned.

He did not know what awaited him inside the safe.

No one did. The entire gamble nothing more than a fool cop's gambit.

Jim Tanner took a deep breath and pulled open the safe door.

At the front, in the center. Better than the Hope Diamond. A lonely old baseball.

He took it out. The august signature shone under the beam of his flashlight and shocked him with its veracity. The name Jackie Robinson trammeled through him with the bright joy of childhood. He went to games back then when the first black man was playing in the white man's leagues. So much hope, so much wonder, so much joy in childhood. Now life burned through him again, with the twin blessings of hope and wonder. Quinn might be freed by the ball's retrieval.

Another name on the ball. A blast from the past. Mr Sal. A mob boss.

Time to get a move on.

Jim Tanner scooped up his tools, repacked them, dropped the baseball in the bag and locked the safe. He was leaving bracelets and necklaces behind, rings and earrings, diamonds, gold and precious stones. In the old days, a killing. All that valuable junk was meaningless and worthless to him now. If he ever doubted it, he no longer did: He was a thief no more.

Set to leave, Jim Tanner slid open the heavy bolts on the rear door. Then returned to the alarm box to determine what might be accomplished. Alarms were never his specialty, and this one required cutting a wire. He flipped a coin in his head to choose which one. Snipped the blue. Wrong choice. The alarm was nasty. Loud and grating and pulsing. He skipped to the rear door, tried tugging it open. It wouldn't budge. The noise was bursting through his head now, wrecking his nervous system. He went over the door with his flashlight beam, hunting a hidden latch or a secret lock. Nothing. Then the alarm saved him. It infuriated him, a useful rage. Frustrated, desperate, he heaved on the latch and, stupidly, heaved again. Convinced now that he was trapped inside, that he'd be caught, that Quinn would die, that he'd not be free to exact revenge on the mob bosses, he hurled himself against the damn door.

Suddenly, it gave way. Merely stuck, having not been opened for millennia.

He shoved it further and stepped outside.

As he closed the door behind him, a car came speeding down the laneway.

It braked hard.

He tumbled into the back seat and pulled the car door shut.

As they tore off, he looked up. 'Who're you guys?' he asked, fearful again.

He was expecting Émile Cinq-Mars. Neither of these two were him. Then he recognized the Einstein haircut. Caron turned around in the passenger seat and said, 'Detective Cinq-Mars has a lead on your daughter, Mr Tanner. We got a real chance here. Did you get the ball?'

Jim Tanner clutched the man's shoulder and squeezed hard. Caron yelped, and flinched from the pain.

The restaurant owner ventured into the room. Sheepish, he was frightened to intrude. He addressed Captain Touton. 'Sir, the telephone. A message.'

'Go ahead.'

The man appeared embarrassed, as though his news was not sufficiently consequential for the proceedings.

'Jackie Robinson.'

He attempted to apologize. 'I'm sorry, sir, your man told me to say only that.'

'Appreciated.'

Giuseppe Ciampini raised his right hand. 'Bruschetta. Do you have? For two.'

Delighted, the *patron* leaped to do his bidding. He made the best bruschetta in the business.

Touton failed to contain his glee. 'I'll tell you what that message means.'

'Code,' Ciampini assumed.

'The baseball is mine. Got it first, before you. Now, we talk about releasing the girl. I can take that ball down to New York myself. Make sure the Italian families understand its significance. Or we can talk of how the girl will miraculously be found, by you or your people, and set free.'

Ciampini studied the cop's rugged visage. Touton was inscrutable, yet his conviction could not be doubted. Their negotiation was no longer hypothetical. The old cop had something tangible on offer.

Touton needed to keep the mob boss in the room. Whatever happened with the next play in their maneuver, Ciampini had to remain unaware.

Later, his awareness might be necessary, after it was too late for him to protect himself.

Cinq-Mars stopped one block from Savina Vaccaro Shapiro's house.

'Your trunk.' Giroux asked, 'Vests? Shotguns?'

'It's my personal car, Yves. Maybe next time.'

'No next time if we're dead this time. Tell me you're armed, at least.'

'Of course. You?'

'Rain or shine.' They were crawling out of the VW Bug. 'Something else. How come her name's Vaccaro? Why not Ciampini?'

'Ah,' Cinq-Mars said, and started in. 'His first wife was a Vaccaro. Their wedding annulled, the Catholic Church their friend. Savina didn't change her name after she switched families in her teens, moving in with her old man. Guess what? The first wife kicked it under mysterious circumstances.'

'Mysterious how?'

'Poison.'

'Nice. Daddy did it?'

'An accusation that didn't stick. I might know why.'

'Sure you do. Why?'

'The daughter.'

Giroux stopped walking and stared at Cinq-Mars. Then started walking again.

'Not just me. The detectives thought so, too. They couldn't make a case.'

'Fine folks. You looked this up, huh? You're one of those types. You look things up. How do we play this? Walk by? One at a time. Different directions. Call for a back-up that makes the most sense?'

Cinq-Mars was of a different mind. 'I say we go straight in.'

'Get serious.'

'We'll take your look around, then decide.'

'We're not going in through the front door. We don't know their firepower, their numbers. Forget it, Cinq-Mars.'

'No doors. There's another way in.'

Giroux took two seconds to catch up. 'Forget it.'

'We'll meet on the other side of the gate into Park Ex,' Cinq-Mars suggested.

'I'll take the shorter walk-by. Easier for you to drag your nose the long way around than me my belly.'

They completed a preliminary reconnaissance and passed through the gate, out of sight of the house. Traffic noise inhibited conversation. They spoke only when it let up, or when cars stopped on the red.

'Nothing new,' Giroux declared. 'No sign of them. In a shoot-out, the girl's their cover. Call it in. Surround, contain. Flush them with numbers.'

'That makes Quinn a hostage and puts us in a weak position.'

'Weak? Give us the girl or die. How is that weak?'

'Bring it on and the girl dies, they say back. Then what? What if one guy prefers death to prison?'

'We'll get him psychological counselling. What do you want from me?'

'I say we go in on our own recog.'

'And what? Ring the doorbell? "Excuse me, ma'am. Remember

us? Are you holding a young lady hostage? Could you check, please? Thanks.'"

'We know the way in, Yves. It's been done before.'

Giroux expected his partner to come back to that. If a seventeen-year-old girl could break into the premises aided by a boy, surely two grown men could do the same.

'Look,' Cinq-Mars pressed him, 'it's the timing. Her life or another minute of torture. Which do you want to risk?'

'I suppose *you* want to climb on *my* back.'

'Your belly fat. Too much for me.'

'Yeah, and you're the one with shit for brains.'

An impasse.

A cop car was coming toward them from Jarry, turning onto l'Acadie. Cinq-Mars flagged it down, identified himself, and ordered the driver to park the car up ahead and hustle back on foot.

'Ask,' Giroux shouted, 'for extra vests!'

They didn't normally carry them, an officer replied. They didn't have their own, either.

'Terrific,' Giroux said when he learned that.

Waiting for the uniforms to return, Cinq-Mars commented, 'I recognize that guy from somewhere.' Out of the car and on foot, the patrolman's identity became apparent. 'You were first on the scene,' he said when the young man returned. 'You found the dead boy in the car.'

'Brandon Wyatt, sir. What's going on?'

Cinq-Mars didn't reply. He looked in one direction, then the other, down the long stretches of chain-link fence and hedge. Something about that divide struck him. Poor on one side, *nouveau riche* on the other. Immigrants on one side, established generations on the other. High-density traffic and racket alongside peace and calm. One side denoted by struggle, the other by privilege. The divide spoke to him.

'What?' Giroux demanded, as though his partner had been thinking aloud.

'Why is Quinn in Savina's house?' Having asked the question, he answered it. 'Because it's the least likely place for her to be. Not in a back room in one of Ciampini's strip joints or bars, or in the meat locker of one of his restaurants. Not in the attic of some flophouse or junkie shooting gallery. She's in a nice house

in a quiet neighborhood, because nobody is looking for her here
and we've been blindly raiding his other spots.'

'Yeah. So?'

'Her house is not a fortress. They don't expect a raid. They don't
have ten guys inside with automatic weapons. Two guys, maybe,
to spell each other off. One might be sleeping, high odds on that.
We can go in, Sergeant-Detective. Don't turn this into a hostage
situation. Give the word. We take them out now. We got at least a
fifty-fifty chance that it'll be easy, especially with the element of
surprise and now we've got these two to shoot anybody who flees.'

The uniforms glanced at each other, intrigued.

Giroux gazed back at the house, largely hidden by the hedge.
In his life and career, he'd worked both sides of a different
fence. In deceiving people to believe that he worked both sides,
his life and his career had been adversely affected. A sacrifice,
and it wasn't as though he couldn't use a boost. Enjoy a victory.
Take a lap. This could be that moment.

'We go in,' he said.

'We seem to do better,' Touton paused to make sure he had the
right word, 'when we talk hypothetical.'

Ciampini was taken aback. 'Big fucker of a word.'

'How's the bruschetta?'

'Help yourself. The wine, too. You're a Frenchman, Armand.
You should drink wine, not whisky. Whisky's for the Irish, the
Scots. In our blood, the wine – for the French, the Italians.'

'Whisky's for warriors,' Touton rhapsodized. 'Wine, for lovers
and Italians.'

'Good. I'm glad that's cleared up. But what's going on? Do
you delay here? What you want for the baseball? How we do
this if I find the girl for you?'

Touton leaned in. He glanced back, in case someone was
listening at the kitchen door. He whispered, 'What do you think
about Cooperstown?'

'Never been. You're talking Hall of Fame?'

'Baseball Hall of Fame,' he repeated. 'Yeah, baseball . . .'

'You losing me.'

'I give Jackie's ball to the Hall of Fame. Along with part of
the story. You don't keep the ball, but neither do I. Neither do
your cousins. I don't put you behind bars, so that's fair, no?'

Ciampini glared back at him. 'Let's say,' he said, 'I send out my boys. Like you did. Turn this town upside down. Unlike you, I find the girl. I'm luckier. Do you think I go to so much trouble so you can send a baseball to fucking Cooperstown?'

'Hmm,' Touton murmured. 'If you couldn't find the baseball when it was in your own son-in-law's house, how will you find a girl on the run?'

'This helps? To insult me?'

'I apologize, Joe. You're obviously not too excited about the deal. Maybe if I add a sweetener.'

'Show me the sugar, Armand. The maple syrup.'

'Let me think.'

'Are you still stalling?'

'For what? I'm old and slow. Like you. Let me think.'

Shadows on the ceiling sashayed onto the walls.

Balancing on his partner's shoulders, Cinq-Mars found that the window screen had been replaced, but not repaired. While Giroux's knees buckled, he inserted his fingers between the twin incisions and pulled back the pair of triggers. He lifted the screen from its moorings and passed it down. He had guessed correctly that the window itself wasn't locked, as the homeowner didn't expect to be broken into twice. Cinq-Mars raised it, pulled himself up, and lurched inside. Looking out, he gave Giroux a circular OK signal. His partner pointed toward the front of the house, reminding Cinq-Mars that he wanted the door opened next.

Cinq-Mars obeyed orders, contrary to his partner's expectations.

Indoors a radio blared, from the kitchen, the volume cranked up. A blessing.

Having walked through the house previously, Cinq-Mars was familiar with the layout. The living room lay vacant. He sprung the lock on the front door and Giroux crept inside.

They unclipped their holsters, took their weapons in hand.

Time at a halt.

The moment's seriousness affected Cinq-Mars. As a calm, an inner quietude. He remained within that aura of calm, even as his pulse ticked up a notch.

He indicated the room that had been the husband's office. Giroux listened at the door. Opened it. Glanced in. Closed it carefully. All clear. They moved toward the kitchen, where over the radio *The Eagles* were urging them to take it to the limit.

Cinq-Mars peeked in and pulled his head back in an instant. Savina and a man were seated in the kitchen nook. She was pulling her hair back and stretching. A beer bottle in front of the man. A bowl of cherries, or maybe grapes, between them.

Cinq-Mars held up two fingers.

Giroux made an upright pole of his forearm and fist, then displayed two fingers. In return, Cinq-Mars held up a single digit. Giroux made a suggestive impression of cupping a female breast with his free hand. Cinq-Mars rolled his eyes and agreed. Yes. One man, one woman. He signaled with his chin for Giroux to slip around the other way. Two entrances into the kitchen. They'd pounce from both.

Flashing all the digits of his free hand four times, Giroux requested twenty seconds. They counted to three together, mouthing the words. Then mentally kept up the rhythm. At twenty, Cinq-Mars charged and dug his pistol into the back of the guard's head before Savina could react. When she did, she was confronted by Giroux's pistol in her grill.

Cinq-Mars whispered, 'Call out, make a sound, and you're the deadest man alive.'

The guard considered his options.

Giroux thwarted him from doing so. He took his pistol out of Savina's craw and shoved it against the man's cheek, bending it inward. He leaned down to offer his counsel. 'Screw this up, when it's over, I will personally pistol-whip your naked balls. *Capeesh?*'

The man indicated acquiescence.

Cinq-Mars shifted the trajectory of his pistol to Savina's right eye, then shook the gun to get her to stand.

On the radio, the Captain and Tennille were elaborating on what keeps them together. Cinq-Mars would've loved to turn them off but required their high decibel level.

Giroux provided cover while Cinq-Mars stripped the table of weapons – a handgun, a shotgun – and looked for someplace to ditch them. He decided on the fridge, to keep them cool. Then searched for a solution to his next problem.

He checked with Giroux. 'No cuffs, right?'

'I rely on my junior partner to carry steel.'

While they whispered, their captives scowled.

Cinq-Mars swiped two dish towels off a rack to gag Savina and her lackey. He hoped they didn't realize how tenuous the knots were. Then he lifted the curtain rod from above the kitchen window and slid off a pair of sheer curtains. He gave them a tug, to test them. Strong enough. Long enough. Flexible enough to be stretched tightly.

He wound the curtains around the thug's wrists and knotted them behind his back. He did the same with Savina's, and then used the excess tails to bind the two of them together. If they ran, they'd not get far.

Done, he asked Savina, 'Where?'

Fury and utter contempt blazed in her eyes. Sourly, she jutted her chin to indicate a kitchen door. Cinq-Mars opened it a crack. It led downstairs. That made sense. Lights were on. With his pistol, Giroux tapped the man's testicles to encourage proper behavior. They left their prisoners bound, gagged, and knotted to each other.

They listened at the top of the stairs. With the door open, the radio would sound louder down below. Undesirable – if the guard was alert, he now had a heads-up. They started down, Cinq-Mars in the lead. The stairs emptied into a broad recreation room. A pool table in sight. Cinq-Mars peeked. He saw Quinn. Quinn saw him. He looked back at her a second time. She jerked her head slightly to her left. Cinq-Mars held up one finger. She nodded in agreement.

Just then, upstairs, Savina threw herself onto the floor. A difficult feat when lashed to another person. She tripped the other guy and yanked him down on top of her, creating an unholy thud that shook the ceiling below.

The guard reacted to the crash in a split-second. He snapped his safety off and swung his pistol up. A shot was fired. Cinq-Mars leaped left. A second shot. He believed he had not discharged his own weapon. Giroux was at the bottom of the stairs, but he didn't have his bearings. Cinq-Mars aimed for the middle of the man's chest. The largest mass. In the heat of the moment, bullets never land where aimed. Hands are shaky, targets are moving. Adrenalin and training and instinct. Aim to hit your foe square in the chest, right through the heart, shoot to kill. He fired.

The gunman cried out and another report shook their senses. Giroux fired as well. Bullets hit walls.

The gunman collapsed to his knees.

He'd been struck.

Either Cinq-Mars's lone bullet or one of Giroux's had passed through his biceps, ripping his arm open. He was done. Incapacitated. He couldn't grip his weapon and fell back, his arm in agony. He looked at his own blood and sinew and, inexplicably, began to cough.

'Good shot,' Giroux murmured. Impressed. He didn't think it was his.

Then Quinn spoke up, with bountiful profanity, not always coherently, demanding to be untied.

'Fucking where've you been?' The girl was shaking, crying, kicking her feet. She was bursting apart. 'Where the fuck . . .?'

Laughing a little, tension ripping across his chest as if he'd been hit himself, Cinq-Mars holstered his weapon and worked on the knots binding her. They heard a commotion upstairs.

'Got it,' Giroux said, and started up.

The last knot slipped loose. Quinn jumped up from the chair and shocked Cinq-Mars, throwing her arms around his neck and squeezing him close.

Then they burst apart as a shotgun blast exploded in their ears, echoing like a raging trumpet. Giroux cried out and tumbled back down the stairs. Pellets had ripped across his legs, above and below the knees. Cinq-Mars spun, his pistol out again, and with his free arm pushed Quinn behind him.

He saw no one, only the effect on his partner. Giroux lay in anguish. His back on the floor, his legs pointing up the stairs. He swore in French, condemning the Mother Church and all her rituals. '*Hostie, tabernacle, calice!*' The host, tabernacle, chalice. Quebec's worst swear words, sexual profanity and body parts being left to other tongues.

'Police!' Cinq-Mars shouted to the shooter. 'Drop your weapon!'

'Save your breath, asshole. I don't need no fucking introduction.'

No mistaking Savina's voice. She and the guard had worked a butcher knife to slice the curtain sufficiently to free her. At her back, the guard remained entangled.

'Savina! This is the end of it. Put the gun down.'

'Just reloaded, fucker. How stupid you think I am? Better question, how stupid are you? I got the shotgun aimed at your partner's face. You want a Fifth of March massacre? *You* put your gun down or I shoot him again. Both shells, in the eyes. He'll bleed out through his eyeballs. After that, go ahead, arrest me. My dad will get me off. How about you drop your pistol on the pool table, Detective? Move over so I can see you. That way, nobody gets hurt too bad.'

'Savina, you don't want—'

She fired her weapon. Pellets scattered across Giroux's chest. The worst of the fire hit the floor. Giroux wailed and swore a streak now, tearing down cathedrals and humping the pope.

'The next one's in his face! Do what I fucking say when I say it, asshole! Now! Gun on the table!'

Cinq-Mars stepped over to the pool table. He put his weapon down. Savina descended the stairs cautiously with a gentle sashay of her hips, the shotgun aimed at Giroux's face. He was moaning and bleeding. Cinq-Mars looked. The wounds were worse than he first thought.

'Back away from the table,' she ordered Cinq-Mars. 'Slow, like I said, the way I like it.'

He obeyed. She bent to retrieve Giroux's weapon from the staircase, putting it down behind her. In a nick, she added another shell to her shotgun.

'Now we're in one big motherfucking pile of shit, aren't we?' Savina said.

'Your doing.'

Abruptly, she noticed the empty chair.

'Where's the girl?'

'Looking for me?'

Quinn cocked the hammer of the guard's pistol. Placed the barrel in Savina's right ear. Savina jerked a quarter-way around. No more than that. Her weapon aimed now at Cinq-Mars.

Under her breath, she advised Quinn, 'I'll shoot him. Blow him apart. Shoot me, the shotgun fires and kills him.'

'Really?' Quinn had learned from Savina's father. How to talk with utter calm yet be totally terrifying. She had also learned how to be convincing. 'You shot the other guy twice. He's still breathing. Anyhow, what do I care about a cop who took his own sweet time getting here?' She feigned enjoying this. Her voice was relaxed, in complete control. She tried not to look at Giroux. The sight of him might cause her whole act to crumble. 'Drop the shotgun, lady, or a bullet blasts through your ear and out the other side. Think about that mess for six seconds. That's how much time you got.'

'Who the fuck are you?' Savina wanted to know. 'Who the fuck do you think you are, robbing my house? You get off on that? Fuck you!'

'Quinn,' Cinq-Mars said. The stalemate was a bad one. The woman with the shotgun was in a bind. She was stalling for time. Looking to make a move. 'Don't shoot her.' He made eye contact with the young thief. She seemed to get what he was doing, just like that.

'Why not?' Quinn asked him, playing her part, the role of a girl with a gun and a streak of desperation. They both had to convince Savina that she'd pull the trigger even if unprovoked. 'Maybe it was her. Maybe she killed Deets. Eh? Lady? You kill my boyfriend, huh?' She shoved her a tad with the barrel of the gun.

'I told you already. My husband did it. He's fucking dead, so what're you going to do about it?'

'Let you join him.'

'This cop goes down, too.'

'Ask me how much I care.'

'Quinn,' Cinq-Mars said sharply. 'Don't do it. Savina, come on. You shot a policeman. That's bad. But you said it yourself, your old man can get you out of that. He's got judges in his pocket, prosecutors he walks over, folks he can intimidate. That won't happen if you kill my partner. A cop-shooting, he gets you off. Worst case, big reduction in sentence. Killing a cop is different. Your old man can't swing that. And Quinn, come on, don't shoot her.'

'Go ahead,' Savina proposed. 'I kill this cop. You kill me. No judges, no jail.'

'Put the gun down, Savina. End this.'

'Hey, little girl. Let's see what you're made of. Rice pudding, I bet.'

Quinn kept her pistol aimed at the woman's head. No one dared look to determine whether her knees were quaking. She heard in Savina's voice what she'd seen in her eyes. She had seen Quinn as dead meat and herself as dead, too. Now her voice betrayed that she expected, and perhaps desired, that exact outcome.

Cinq-Mars took a stride toward the two women.

'Nobody fucking moves!' Savina shouted. And then suddenly everybody did.

A shot fired. Quinn cried out, flinched away, as if a line drive had skimmed off her forehead. She'd been nicked by a bullet. Savina ducked and doubled over. Her shotgun went off in her hands. Cinq-Mars reacted, his body as slow as a tortoise, it seemed to him, yet his mind cottontail-quick as he surged toward Savina, seized her weapon, and sent her sprawling across the floor. Another shot fired. He went to shove Quinn aside, but she ducked ahead of his arm. As Cinq-Mars spun back to the pool table, he grabbed his pistol and aimed up the stairs, where the kitchen guard, sheer curtain still wrapped around one arm, was down on his belly, taking another shot at Quinn from the top of the stairs.

Cinq-Mars didn't fire back. The patrolman whose name he couldn't remember – Brandon or Brendan? Wyatt? – had disobeyed orders and come in the back way and pinioned the kitchen guard to the floor, yanking away his weapon in a quick struggle. Cinq-Mars was down in the basement but flying through the sky and zipping off a trapeze, and suddenly everything, almost, was under control.

'What did you shove me for?' Quinn griped. So she was all right, though her forehead was bleeding.

Savina Vaccaro Shapiro was no worse for wear. Except she could scarcely move from rage.

'Brandon! Wyatt!' Cinq-Mars called both names since he couldn't figure out which came first. 'Ambulance! Officer down!'

'Already called, sir. I can hear the sirens.'

The man had reacted to the first shots fired.

Savina found her voice, expressing her despair with a string of expletives.

'You're done,' Quinn told her. Taking the moment for herself. 'Your daddy won't save you now.'

A challenge that revived her foe. 'This ain't over. This ends when we blow your ass in two.'

Cinq-Mars demanded she turn around while remaining on her knees. He took rope previously used on Quinn to bind her wrists behind her back, and this time her ankles. He asked Quinn to watch her – a task she took to – and attended to his partner, who suddenly was quiet and still.

'Hang on, Yves,' he whispered. 'Hang on.' He silently prayed. Not every bullet was accounted for. He checked Giroux for more wounds.

The *patron* announced that Touton had to take a call himself. The captain stepped into the kitchen. Staff huddled close by. Touton said little. He returned to his guest, bringing wine and whisky bottles back with him. He poured. His demeanor grave.

'Our negotiation just changed.'

'How's that?'

'The baseball goes to Cooperstown. With it, a story. Of how Jackie Robinson signed it for a crime boss who was later slain. His killer stole the ball to make the murder look like a robbery. Running away, he killed a cop too. Find the baseball, identify the killer. Easy, except, the ball went missing. The killer kept it. He became a mob boss himself. Decades go by. The ball is stolen again. A son-in-law wants leverage over his father-in-law. I guess you two didn't get along. Trouble for you, you didn't know where it went. That must've worried you. Then the ball is stolen by a thief breaking into a house. The Hall of Fame will love the tale. They won't mind that it comes with another story. One that is to remain sealed pending the passage of time. Unless a certain girl is impeded, let's use that word, as she strolls down the side-walk. In which case, a truer, more exciting, tale will be revealed, with names spelled out with a signed affidavit. One signature on the affidavit will be mine. How do you like our deal so far?'

'Not that much,' Ciampini said. 'We been over this. What changed?'

'I have the girl.'

Ciampini went stone silent. As if he had stopped breathing.

Then he said, 'No, you don't.'

'Savina is safe. Under arrest. She shot a cop. Like father, like daughter. You must be proud. He may pull through, my cop, or not. Lucky if he does. For you, not only for him. If he dies, I can put both you and Savina away. I have the girl's testimony. I've got a cop shot up with a shotgun. Trouble is, we both know how this works. A hit-and-run. A drive-by shooting. Tragedy strikes. Suddenly, the girl is no more. Instead, I propose, that if the cop lives Savina does a little time. Nothing she can't handle, given her genes, not to mention your influence inside the pen. The ball goes to Cooperstown. You walk free. You leave the girl alone for the rest of your life and, as a favor to me, do nothing after your life to hurt her. As a favor to you, it all stops here. Savina gets a light sentence and she too strolls safely on the sidewalk. You walk, I stumble into my retirement. Pissed off you got away again, otherwise at peace.'

'You don't have the girl,' Ciampini said. Not a statement of disbelief, one of chagrin, defeat. Of course Touton had the girl if he knew she was at Savina's.

'Call. Find out.'

Ciampini rose from the table. He brushed a few bruschetta crumbs from his tie. 'Give me a sip of your warrior whisky.'

Touton stood, crossed to the bar, and returned with a snifter.

He poured. The two men clinked glasses. Together they said, '*Salut!*' Then looked off elsewhere, then drank and savored the whisky.

Giuseppe Ciampini held out his hand.

'One thing more,' Touton said.

'Don't bust my balls, Armand.'

'The Olympics are coming up. You control the unions and the contractors. You're getting super rich off both. Do what you do. In the end, don't stop the games.'

'Not my plan to prevent.'

'I believe you. But accidents happen.'

'No accidents, Armand. Deal?' His hand remained outstretched.

'If the cop dies, no deal. The girl goes into hiding. Her tough luck. My retirement? I suspend. You and me, we go to war. Two old foes. I'm told his chances are fifty-fifty. If he lives? We have a deal.'

'Done,' Ciampini said. 'May he live. Grace of God. If not, we fight.'

Captain Armand Touton shook the man's paw.

Otto's Pitch

(The swings)

T he summer evening fell sweetly. As sweetly as the water-
melons cracked open and sitting on a teeter-totter, one end
propped up to serve as a table. Time for the youngsters
to hurry home. After sinking their faces into the fruit, the kids
laughed and squealed, then dashed to their beds chased by the
sun's last glimmer.

Summer excitement sang through their limbs.

Quinn Tanner leaned against the tall steel fence that encom-
passed Ball Park. She didn't mean to present a look, a languid,
autonomous pose in the fading light. She remained aloof from
the bustle yet stood out. Set off that way, her presence amid the
shadows suggested a suppleness and sensuality evident to her
peers. A reaction she did not intend to provoke, though among
her friends she did.

They spoke to her infrequently. She possessed a reputation
for recklessness, and lately had overstepped even her bounds.
Others were increasingly cautious around her now, for her experiences eclipsed their own imagining. Rarely did anyone breach
Quinn's solitude. Whenever she moved, eyes followed her. Young
men and women pondered what they could not fully conjure.
Strangely, she was less an object of desire than the embodiment
of desire now. As though, for them, she nurtured life's mysteries
and shielded them within.

Quinn moved across Ball Park to the swings.

As he'd done before, Émile Cinq-Mars was seated there. He
swiveled slightly, ankles crossed, a heel anchored in sand. Quinn
sat in the swing alongside his, enfolding her fingers around the
chains. She noticed his sandals, his dusty bare ankles.

'What?' he asked, puzzled by her disposition.

She wasn't going to say. She asked, 'Did you hear what
happened with my dad?'

Work? The labor dispute?

'I didn't.'

'This boy I know. Otto Braup. He was into me once, but shot off his mouth when he should've been super discreet. I guess he should be happy we didn't stick it out. He might've been my getaway driver. That didn't turn out so well, right?'

'You're dangerous. Very true.'

She liked the tease.

'So, Otto came by. I figured – my dad did, too – that he was trying his luck again. I talked to him recently, when you asked me to check on my ex-boyfriends. Maybe that encouraged him.'

'My fault, then.'

'Totally. He thought my dad should hear what he had to say. Super weird, right? I think Otto was scared to be alone with me. He told me something he overheard.'

She'd been through a bad time. Talk was healthy for her now.

'Apparently, some morons were talking about me. Until I become yesterday's news, I'm like a celebrity for a week and a half around here.'

'What did they say?'

'A baseball coach was part of this group of guys. The rest were mostly his team, Otto an exception. The coach was drinking, the boys, too, and my name came up. The coach said he knew I keyed his car and stole his wallet.'

'A lie, I suppose.'

'Nope, I did all that. Fortunately, my dad already knew about it. He didn't have a bird.'

Quinn dipped her hips, just once, so that her swing moved. Then tucked her lower legs under her and let herself be rocked by the easy-going momentum.

'That's when the coach bragged that he got even.'

'How?'

'The man's a coward. He paid a couple of guys. That's how it is around here. Everybody knows a guy who knows a couple of guys in case the need comes up.'

'What did these guys do?'

'You know.'

He thought about it. 'The firebombing?'

'The fucking baseball coach firebombed my house. Then he's too much of a moron not to talk about it in public. Jeez. For him, moron is too nice a word.'

Cinq-Mars waited for her to continue. Her mind appeared to wander.

He asked, 'What about your dad?'

'Right. My dad. He's amazing, you know.'

'I know. He cracked that safe for you.'

'Really amazing! He says my mom helped him out. Of course, I didn't want him to get into trouble because of me, like beat up the coach or kill him. We talked about it. He pointed out that I keyed the coach's car, stole his wallet, turned his money into confetti, blah blah blah, and threw it on the expressway. So we're even-steven with the firebombing.'

Cinq-Mars nodded in the gloaming, not sure if the story had concluded.

'I'm conflicted,' Quinn continued. 'I don't want my dad to do anything rash, but I'm upset. I say, "Yeah, I guess." And we sit there. And then I say, "Except . . ."'

Cinq-Mars repeated her word. 'Except?'

'The coach tried to feel me up, didn't he? Top and bottom. That's why I did his car. We weren't anywhere close to being even. Me, I keyed his car. Him, he firebombed my house *and* messed with me sexually. He was the first to be in the wrong. I got back at him, then he got back at me. How's that even? Dad, then, says that he'll take care of it. Now I'm scared, right? I don't want him in trouble. Do you know what he did?'

'If it's illegal, don't tell me.'

She widened her eyes. 'He went to see the coach. *Dan-ger-ous!* I tagged along. Instead of punching him out – which I guess part of me looked forward to – he told the coach that he was accepting his resignation on behalf of Park Extension. Like he's the mayor or something. A bunch of people were listening. My dad told them the coach touched his daughter. He told everybody that the coach asked him – my dad – to be his third base coach, not because he needed a third base coach but because he wanted his daughter to come around more often. My dad told him that he – my dad – was the team's new field manager. That the old coach won't be permitted to watch a game, ever. Not if he wants to keep breathing. My dad is now the new field manager for the junior team. He said I can work out the pitchers when I want, but I said no.'

'How come?'

'Too much testosterone in one place. Keeping my distance.'

'Yeah. Not the same, but maybe it's similar. I love cops but sometimes I need to stay away from them.'

'You visit a thief, like me, instead?'

They both smiled. They let that hang in the air.

'How've you been, Quinn?'

'Not bad,' she said, not with any conviction.

'Have you seen Leonard?'

'We hang a bit. He's totally Noel now. He digs it.' They shared a laugh. 'I think he might contact you. If he does, don't complicate him,' she instructed.

'I won't,' Cinq-Mars agreed. Then asked, 'What about Ezra?'

She was silent then. She dipped her hips a few times, swinging, letting herself glide back and forth, then her momentum gently slowed.

Quinn said, 'I think he let me down.'

Cinq-Mars was thoughtful in his way, as if notions and conjecture needed a long time to work through his head, spilling detritus and picking up stray insights across a broad band of light and shade. He said, 'People have patterns. That's unavoidable. When they inhabit their patterns, rather than the other way around, people become fixed. Less fluid. That's when they can let us down. He helped you big time but, I agree, not right down the line.'

Quinn considered what he said, doing her best to unravel what it all meant. 'You think about things,' she said.

'People hate that about me.' He smiled.

'Mmm,' Quinn murmured. Then she said, 'Fuck 'em in left field. Up against a post.'

Cinq-Mars laughed. Then they began to swing. Quinn came to a stop first, then he did. 'You should get up, get out, find yourself a girlfriend,' she advised.

'I'm looking.'

'Good.'

'When do you turn eighteen?'

'Oh no. You'll still be way too old for me,' she told him.

'That's not remotely true. But you're way too young for me.'

'Not true either. Anyway, you'd still be a moron cop.'

'True. Hassling delinquents like you. Will you still be a thief?'

'I might be done. I'm not saying I'm a snowflake, but I met

a couple of ladies recently . . . When it comes to being a bad girl, I don't qualify.'

She easily made him laugh. 'Could have fooled me, holding a pistol in Savina's ear. Look, I had a reason to ask. Until you're eighteen, you're my case. Officially. I've decided, Quinn. I'm not turning you over to the juvenile division.'

'Damn! I was looking forward to some serious jail time in juvie.'

'Well, you won't get any. And forget about me and you.'

'You first.'

'Sure thing.'

'Done deal.'

She laughed. They began to swing again, going higher this time. When Quinn stood on the seat, Cinq-Mars warned her not to dare. She told him not to worry. Still, she swung higher in the dark of Ball Park, and he put his feet out and dipped his hips and swung higher himself. The swing set shook with their momentum.

'I never thought about it once!' Quinn called out to him in the dark.

He refused to answer back.

'Moron!' she shouted at him. 'What took you so long?'

'Traffic!' he yelled back.

They were laughing when they stopped. Then went quiet. Their heart rates settled. Quinn answered an earlier question. 'November.'

'That far off? Eighteen. You should throw a party.'

'Yeah, I should.' They sat quietly. Then she said, 'You should take me to a ball game sometime.'

'Your dad's team?'

'Cheapskate. No, he'd clobber you. Not to mention me. The big leagues.'

'Not a chance, Quinn.'

'The time you buy for yourself, Émile, can be the time you waste. Something I heard once.'

She dismounted the swing to join her friends heading out for the evening. She stopped once, turned, waved, and walked backwards for several steps. She turned again, and Émile Cinq-Mars stood for a moment, then exited the park on the opposite side, taking the long way around the block to head back to his place. Working the day shift, that is what he was supposed to do. Sleep at night. Quietly, peacefully. If he could, sleep at night.